HAPPINESS

The Devil that Danced on the Water
Ancestor Stones
The Memory of Love
The Hired Man

HAPPINESS

AMINATTA FORNA

Atlantic Monthly Press
New York

First published in Great Britain 2018 by Bloomsbury

Published simultaneously in Canada
Printed in the United States of America

First Grove Atlantic hardcover edition: March 2018

ISBN 978-0-8021-2755-6
eISBN 978-0-8021-6557-2

Atlantic Monthly Press
an imprint of Grove Atlantic
154 West 14th Street
New York, NY 10011

Distributed by Publishers Group West

groveatlantic.com

18 19 20 21   10 9 8 7 6 5 4 3 2 1

For Rosalind Hanson Alp

The Last Wolf

Spring snow, still, porcelain bowls in the hollows of the earth. Blue hour, the outlines of pine trees and houses stood against a deepening sky. The wolfer gazed upon the lights of the town. For days he had travelled, back to this place which he had once known but hadn't been near for half a life. From what he could see from the rise of the hill, he reckoned Greenhampton hadn't grown much in the years he had been gone, if anything the houses were fewer. Men had been upping sticks and leaving, he'd heard tell, men had left their homes and barns, abandoned their farms, farms worked three generations. Fathers and grandfathers had cleared the rocky soil of New England, had felled trees and then hitched mules to tree stumps and heaved each stump loose, had sunk wells and built walls around their farms, laid each stone by hand, had protected their livestock from predators. Now the sons of these men were handing the land back to nature and heading west to the plains, where a man could stand in one spot and turn around and see nothing but open space in every direction, and underfoot, when he kicked a boot heel into the ground: soil, black and rich.

The farmer who had written him was not somebody the wolfer knew, but he recognised the family name and that was what had made him answer, when he'd made up his mind to answer at all. They'd been looking for him, the letter writer said, some good time. They needed a wolfer as a matter of urgency, but wolfers no longer worked these parts. Supposedly there were no more wolves left, but now something out there was taking sheep and the last of the farmers had themselves convinced it was the work of a wolf.

Snow on the ground was good. A long winter made for hungry wolves, snow made them easier to track, meant they'd be furred out still and a winter pelt was a valuable thing. The wolfer did the figures in his head. Money for pelts came on top of his fee, plus the federal bounty of $15, but to claim that he'd have to haul back into town and deliver the scalp. A pelt in good condition could bring in maybe $25. His fee was $80. Winter the wolfer had spent camped out on the plains, in a small log cabin. Every day he set traps and every day his traps were full – he'd sold upwards of ten bales of wolfskins and covered the outlay on his gear in the first week. Everything from then on was money in his pocket. This job would be the closing number of a good season.

The wolfer climbed back up onto his wagon and urged his horse forward. Under the canvas in the back were half a dozen Newhouse toothed traps. Over his shoulder he carried a long gun, and slung low at his waist a skinning knife with a carved mesquite handle and a curved blade that was deep and short. He had half a pint of whiskey in the pocket of his buffalo calfskin overcoat. In one inside pocket of his wool jacket he had the letter that brought him here wrapped around three glass phials of white crystal powder.

The horse leaned its weight into the harness and dragged a hoof before finding purchase on the road. Leastways now was downhill.

At the general store, where the store owner's wife seemed to expect him, the wolfer checked his route and bought a bite of tobacco. To make town in daylight is what he would have liked, to drive his hunting gear through the centre, see the people turn to watch him pass, nod to those who waved and tip his hat at those who cheered. But so be it. The wolfer drew up in front of the lighted farmhouse. He wrapped a wolf fur around his shoulders and placed a fur hat on his head, the kind of attention to detail that persuaded folks they were getting what they'd paid for.

Morning found the wolfer in the woods a mile or more above the farm. He had scoured the way for the carcasses of fallen prey, tracks, droppings, any sign at all. He found nothing. A levelling in the hillside and a small clearing in a stand of hemlock provided him with a place to make camp. Afterwards he walked two miles in each of four directions. Once he came across the carcass of a steer, which might or might not have been wolf work, it was rotted too far down to tell.

At supper the night before the wolfer had entertained his patron with stories of wolves he'd trapped as far afield as Dakota and Nebraska. At first he pretended to wish not to be drawn, but after he had finished a plate of stewed oysters and cornbread he began to speak, slowly and with many pauses to allow his small audience the pleasure of urging him on. His reputation had flown ahead of him, he knew, and so he told selective stories of his battles with outlaw wolves, and some of those stories he embellished a little, and other stories he borrowed outright. The wolfer accepted a small glass of port (his hosts were not a rich family, but well-to-do enough having diversified early into tanning) and began on the story of the three-toed outlaw wolf of Harding County and the Queen Wolf of Colorado, who he had not himself trapped, but an account of whose execution he had on good authority. Roped and quartered by four horsemen riding in different directions, yes sir. Two hundred Christian folk had gathered to see the captured wolf brought in on the back of a cart.

The wolfer's father had been a wolfer in this part of the land; the wolfer had been born into the town. His father's work disappeared with the last of the wolves, but by then his father had been an old man. As a young man the wolfer headed west and in his time had done any and every kind of job there was: worked the railroads, ridden herd, fenced and mined ore — all for other men. Once he'd grubstaked his savings in a cinnabar claim, worked at it two years hard before he gave the whole thing up. The mercury, when it came to it, had been worth less than his time. Soon after he learned there was wolfing work around and learned too the kind of money a rancher was willing to pay a wolfer to keep his land clear. And so he bought himself a new skinning knife and took up his father's trade right where the old man had left off.

From the brow of the hill the wolfer surveyed the land on the opposite slope. What once was pasture and lush fields of wheat and corn now was weeds and white pine saplings. The farm owned by the wolfer's host had lost six sheep to the wolf, so they said. Another farmer had woken to find eight of his sheep dead, a ninth kicking in her death throes. This had been going on for a couple of years now. Though nobody had seen a wolf, nevertheless a wolf was said to be responsible. Wolves were coming back, folk believed and said so, had merely been waiting out the years for the opportunity, for men to lose their vigilance.

For his part the wolfer thought it likely a feral dog was at the root of it, but he kept his mouth shut.

Afternoon. The wolfer shot a buck, cut off and wrapped the haunches, dragged the remainder of the carcass behind his horse to a place about a mile from his camp. He took a phial from his inside pocket. He shook a few of the white crystals into an empty phial, added some snow, shook the solution until the snow melted and checked it against the sky. Then he slit and peeled back the skin on the underside of the deer and painted the flesh with the solution. He shot a second deer and repeated the ritual, this time a mile or so on the far side of his camp. Some people liked cyanide, he preferred strychnine, out of familiarity maybe, but he knew what worked for him.

On the way back to camp the wolfer spotted tracks and dismounted. Alike to those of a dog, the tell was in the size. The wolfer remounted. He scratched his chin and looked behind him and then to each side and then beyond the horizon. He reached into his pocket and took a swig of whiskey.

Morning. The wolfer set out to check the deer carcasses and found two dead foxes at one site and a dead bobcat at the other. The second morning, a racoon and another fox, a red-tailed hawk. This did not vex the wolfer. Most wolves could not resist a free meal, but there were some wolves who were naturally cautious. The wolfer climbed into the wagon and slung the traps out of the back. He tested them carefully one by one and chose the two whose springs were most sound. He adjusted and readjusted the pins until he was satisfied, then chose a couple of chains of fifteen foot each and to both he attached a large drag hook. He boiled the traps, dipped the soles of his boots in the boiling liquid and slipped a pair of gentlemen's dress gloves onto his hands. He washed the deer haunches in the stream and when he reached his chosen site he spread a large canvas on the ground and confined his work to the area covered by it. After he set the traps he dusted them over with loose soil and snow and then brushed his footsteps away.

At dawn he rode the mile to where he had laid the traps and found them empty.

The wolfer returned to the remains of the first deer, cut the glands from the dead fox and wrapped them in paper. He moved the traps each to a new location, again careful to make sure none of his scent clung to

4

them. He took the fox glands and squeezed drops of their liquid onto the ground by each of the traps.

Night and the wolfer slept. Morning of the fourth day he woke to a blind man's fog, when it cleared he returned to his traps to find them empty. In the snow a short distance from one of the traps: a dark, lozenge-shaped turd.

In the afternoon he trapped a snowshoe hare and put the animal in a cage while he worked. He set a nest of traps in a semicircle around a patch of brush, took the hare and tethered it to the ground by the hind leg. At first the animal crouched in still silence. As soon as he walked away it would begin to kick. When he heard it cry out he drew his breath and waited for the sound to stop, but the screaming went on into the night and he guessed it had broken its own leg in its struggles. That happened sometimes.

In the morning he found the hare untouched and frozen to death.

The wolfer spent the day scouring the hillsides on horseback, his sense now was that the animal was denned farther away.

Late in the afternoon he came across tracks, though they were some days old. The next morning, the sixth, he broke camp and journeyed back into town where he asked at the general store if there was anyone could give him the loan of a pair of dogs. That night he slept at the home of his hosts, where he ate a good meal but declined the port and went to bed early.

Dawn saw the wolfer high on the ridge with two dogs, foxhound/greyhound crosses, whose breeding gave them the advantage of both sight and smell. Handsome animals, thirty inches at the shoulder with brown and white markings and bright eyes, a brother and sister pair. He loosed them in the place he had found the tracks and watched them as they ran in circles, sniffing the ground and the brush. He ran them in the direction he thought them most likely to pick up a scent and was gratified when, no more than a half-hour or so later, the dogs' tails stiffened and they stretched their necks out nose to the ground and their pace became suddenly brisker.

They had been moving steadily along the ridge through stands of hemlock and white pine and crossing open ground, the sun rising ahead of them, when suddenly the dogs stopped and pranced lightly on their front paws, noses in the air. The bitch bristled and began to *growl, the dog lowered his head and raised his hackles. About three hundred yards away, there on a rock, stood a wolf. The dogs came alive and gave chase. The wolfer swung his rifle from his back and urged his horse forward.*

The wolfer expected the animal to head for some kind of coulee or cover, but the wolf had a good lead on the dogs and headed northwards across the flank of the hill. From time to time the wolfer dropped sight of the wolf among the trees, and would just begin to curse when he'd catch sight of it again. The dogs gave tireless pursuit and this pleased the wolfer who decided to hold off the final showdown.

Now the wolfer did not think wolves especially cunning or clever, he just liked to pander to other folks' fancies. But when he tried in the days that followed to piece together the events of the morning, it came to be his belief that the wolf had led the dogs into a trap of its own making. Here's how it happened. They had been on the chase for an hour and a half and had entered a large stand of hemlock when they came to a stream. The dogs followed the trail to the bank and then lost it. The wolfer, reckoning the wolf had crossed to the other side, urged the dogs into the water and they were halfway across when the wolf came at them out of nowhere and went straight for the dog where it stood mid-stream. The dog struck out for the opposite bank but was slowed by the steepness of the bank. The next moment the wolf was upon him and then they were running through the trees until the two were neck-a-neck. The dog twisted and snapped at the wolf and then, seeming to realise the true gravity of his situation, began to run for his life. All the advantage belonged to the wolf, who was faster and taller by more than a hand span; the animal was just waiting for the right moment, and then the dog was over and the wolf had him by the throat.

The bitch had given chase but all she could do now was go at the hindquarters of the wolf as he finished off her brother. The wolfer raised his rifle and looked for a clear shot. The chase had put a good distance between him and the animals. The moment the wolf raised its head the bitch would bolt and he would likely lose them both. He had no more than a few seconds. The wolf was still at the throat of the dog, which had squirmed and fought to free itself and now all but ceased to move. The wolfer lined his sight up on the wolf's hindquarters. An imperfect shot, he had no choice. But at the precise moment he pulled the trigger the dog on the ground gave a final kick and this sign of life in her brother seemed to spur the bitch, who leapt forward and straight into the line of fire. The wolf whirled around and with his second shot the wolfer took it down.

With the corpse of the male dog slung over the back of his horse, dragging that of the wolf along behind, the wolfer paraded the length of Greenhampton Main Street. He had thrown the carcass of the bitch into a low ravine. The mangled corpse of the dog testified to the brute strength of the wolf, would make it easier to face the owner who with luck would waive the cost of two dead dogs. People had begun to come out of their houses and the general store to see the wolf. A group of small boys ran behind and aimed kicks at the carcass. In the main square where the gibbet once stood they strung the wolf up by the neck until its eyes bulged and its tongue lolled, and they beat its body with poles.

Night and the wolfer thought about all that had happened.

In the morning he loaded his wagon and said goodbye to his hosts. He passed the body of the wolf where it twisted in the morning breeze. He set out at a good pace, but once he had rounded the hill, he eased off his horse. In a neighbouring town he found an inn and put up for the night. Next day he leased another pair of tracker dogs and headed back to the hills. There he mounted a rock close to where he first sighted the wolf and with a pair of field glasses carefully scanned the surrounds until he saw what he was looking for: between the trees, a slew of slabbed rocks which rested at angles one against the other. He struck out in their direction and, in a short while and as he had hoped, the dogs caught a scent.

The wolves had denned down in a low cave beneath one of the rock slabs. The wolfer called the dogs and rode back into the town where he returned them and paid their owner. Three more days, by his reckoning, was what it would take for the she-wolf to venture out in search of food. When the day came he was back in the hills settled within sight of the den. He'd decided against flushing her out, he was in no hurry. He checked the sky and slipped a chew of tobacco behind his lower lip. He was on his third chew when he caught a movement by the den. There she was, the she-wolf, come to search for her missing mate. He waited until she was clear of the den, out in the open, and when she raised her head, maybe to howl, he fired.

7

The wolfer approached the den with caution but nothing showed itself or came at him. He decided against finishing off the pups. If the truth be told it was a job no wolfer cared for: wolf pups were affectionate creatures, full of trust and play. These pups, fatherless and now motherless, would never make it through to spring.

One hour later the wolfer was on his way. He had his pelt. He would take the ears of both wolves and claim his bounties. Then he would head west and wait for summer, until it was time to begin again.

Chapter 1

At that time of day Waterloo Bridge is busy with shoppers and weekend workers who make their way on foot across the bridge to Waterloo Station. At that time of year too, dusk comes early, by four in the afternoon. By five it is dark. The fox wended its way through the pedestrians, who for the most part paid it no heed, for they would not so easily be distracted from their fixity of purpose. Through the slanting sleet many people didn't see the fox, those who did thought it was perhaps a loose dog.

A few people had observed the fox on its journey. Upon the terrace of the National Theatre, a pair of smokers had spotted the fox watching them from behind the corner of a raised concrete flower bed that was filled with dead lavender. The smokers and the fox looked at each other in stillness for several seconds. Then three things happened which caused the fox to bolt. A passing cruiser on the river gave a blast of its horn, which in turn caused one of the smokers to utter a high-pitched 'Ooh!' of surprise. This startled the fox which backed off and might have done little more than run down the stairs to the next level had not, third, a plastic bag, dislodged from a tree branch by a sudden gust of wind, borne suddenly down upon the terrace. Moments before all this happened another smoker had emerged from the theatre lobby and now stood with the heavy door propped open upon one shoulder for use as a wind shield while she lit a cigarette. The fox, escaping the threat of the carrier bag, dashed through the open door and into the lobby where it joined the lava flow of departing theatregoers. Down the stairs and through the crowd went the fox, and as it went it brushed against calves and knees, causing people to hop, exclaim and search the floor through the thicket of legs for the cause.

Down on the ground level the fox skittered across the hard floor. A young man selling programmes for the evening show pointed and cried, 'There!' in a kind of outrage to a pair of security guards, who, with a jangle of keys, lumbered into life. The fox headed for the glass doors leading to the outside. Onlookers stopped to watch, talk stalled to silence. Between the bank of glass doors and the concrete walls of the building the fox had nowhere to go.

On the other side of the glass a man painted top to toe in silver, carrying a silver cane and wearing a silver bowler hat, and who had spent eight hours standing motionless upon a box in the freezing temperatures of the day, approached the building with no idea of the commotion unfolding beyond. Just as the fox reached the last in the row of doors, the silver man pulled it open. The fox ran out. The security guards skidded to a stop, one nearly fell over, the other uttered an exclamation in Yoruba. Both laughed and adjusted their peaked caps, one clapped his companion upon the shoulder. Some people broke into a scattering of applause and the silver man took a bow.

Outside the smell in the air was of river water and traffic fumes. The fox ran up the stone steps to the bridge where it overtook a man carrying a bicycle. On the bridge the people walked unswerv-ingly, armed with bags, defended by earphones, looking neither right nor left and acknowledging nothing and nobody. Those who did not walk with purpose meandered in pairs, rocks around which the faster walkers flowed. Past a cameraman taking a time-lapse image of the river, the fox, moving at a metronomic trot, wove a line through them all.

A man so tall he appeared to be wading through the crowd was crossing the bridge in the opposite direction to the fox. The man's name, the name his mother had given him as though she knew to what size her only son would one day grow, was Attila. In his pocket Attila carried a theatre ticket. In addition he held a reservation for one at a restaurant in the Aldwych. He had chosen the restaurant after reading the menu displayed outside the entrance and now his reverie was of boiled beef *Tafelspitz* and chopped-chicken salad. Attila was newly arrived in the country by no more than a few hours and he relished, for the moment, the feel of wind and sleet on his face. He relished, too, the idea that soon he would sit alone in a dark place, surrounded by strangers, where nobody could find him. He moved slowly in the crowd, letting people pass. In the middle of the bridge, just beyond the cameraman standing with his camera on a tripod, Attila came to a stop and turned to admire the view of the Houses of Parliament.

Somebody ran into him.

The collision left Attila unhurt, a testament to his scale and size. By contrast, the woman who had run into him was thrown to the ground and Attila promptly bent to help her up. He apologised, in sympathy, for obviously this could not be his fault. The woman accepted his hand, stood up and brushed her backside. She wore jeans and a sweater and jacket, all in black. Attila retrieved a black day pack from the ground and held it out to her, but she left him holding on to it for some moments while she retied her hair into its ponytail. As he waited, Attila noticed two things about the woman, first that her hair was a rather remarkable pale silver and hung to the middle of her back, or would have done were she not already in the act of pushing it up inside a woollen hat, secondly that she was tall for a woman, she nearly reached his chin. The woman put her hand out so Attila might pass her bag, swung it onto her shoulder and said: 'I'm so sorry about that. Do excuse me,' in a way that suggested no particular sorrow at all. Attila nodded. A moment later he watched her walk away, her long strides. He could still feel the force of their collision, the imprint of her body on his.

Later in the theatre Attila drank a gin and tonic and forgot about the woman on the bridge. The show was a comedy and he laughed explosively at all the jokes until he had to wipe away the tears that rolled down his face. At the interval he bought himself a vanilla ice cream. He came to London infrequently but regularly enough to have formed certain habits. Late morning Attila had checked into his preferred hotel, the early part of the evening he had spent walking and buying theatre tickets. Now from the terrace he searched the skyline for changes and identified two new skyscrapers to the right of St Paul's Cathedral, one with a single sloped side, the other a concave structure – they had been built since the time of his last visit to the city two years ago. In the middle of Waterloo Bridge stood an engraved plaque of the skyline and Attila made a mental note to check it for the names of the new buildings. As he finished his ice cream the bell sounded and he turned with fresh anticipation to take his seat in the auditorium.

On his way back across the bridge Attila was driven by hunger and failed to check the plaque. A few minutes later he was being shown to his seat by the maître d' of his chosen restaurant. As he followed, Attila glanced covertly at the plates of the other diners. He liked and at times even asked to be seated near the kitchen door, a request so unusual it could always be accommodated. This way he had sight of the plates of food held aloft by the waiters as they emerged through the double doors. In places where he was known the waiters would sometimes pass by his table, dipping each dish to waft it in front of his nose. '*Tagliolini ai funghi porcini freschi, signor.*' 'Steamed whole tilapia, Dr Asare.' 'Today's prime aged porterhouse steak, sir.'

Despite the late hour the restaurant was full. Booths lined the walls and in the centre, like water lilies, an array of small and large round tables covered in white tablecloths. Attila was shown to a corner booth, the maître d' pulled the table out a good way to allow him to slide onto the banquette. He said good evening to the people at the next table and picked up the menu to remind himself of the good things on offer. He ordered calves' liver and bacon because both of these were hard to come by where he lived, and the potted brown shrimps because these too were a rare treat. A carafe of Rioja completed his choices, and as he waited for his meal to arrive he sipped wine and looked around at the other clientele. With the exception of a couple seated at one of the water lilies, everyone in the restaurant was white. Attila watched the single black couple for a while: they were young and close in conversation. The woman wore a fuchsia dress, the man was in a suit. An anniversary, thought Attila, and looked away. Some minutes later, as Attila was eating brown shrimp, the man walked past Attila's table and a few minutes later, on his way back from the Gents, he passed by again. This time Attila happened to look up and catch his eye. The man nodded, a single dip of the chin. Attila nodded back and returned to his shrimp. The nod was something that was exchanged only in certain places. Moscow, for example. Perth. Prague. São Paulo, no. Havana, no. Mumbai, yes. Rome, less and less often. All of Poland. Much of England beyond the M25. Belfast, yes. In London more rarely, although a nod might be exchanged in certain kinds of establishment. In this restaurant Attila drew no stares, but it was still a place the nod might occur.

Caramel and chocolate pudding, the chocolate sponge dusted with icing sugar. Attila struck the sponge casing with the back of his spoon and hot caramel poured from within.

He might have been tired but he was not. There was no question of jet lag for there was no time difference between Accra and London, but he had flown overnight. On the plane he had used the time to review the papers for the conference and details of his keynote speech, which though he had delivered it often in the past few years, nevertheless required updating. Attila worked while the other passengers slept or watched movies, the same one it seemed, for on multiple small screens Attila could see the same handsome actor grapple with the same armed men, race desperately through the same crowds and streets, to defuse the same terrorists' bomb. Tirelessly, over and over. Attila possessed the gift of being able to choose when and whether to sleep, one that had served him well on various tours of duty when sleep was impossible, when the environment was too hostile or the victims too many. Out in the field he would forfeit sleep to work long days, interviewing, assessing, collecting data, and then sleep for a fourteen-hour stretch back at the hotel. He never waited to return to base to draft his report but began it then and there, as soon as he woke and while the thoughts were fresh.

Following dinner, when it was by then after midnight, Attila walked briskly back in the direction of the bridge. Exercise and a little air were the things he needed now. Taxis passed him without slowing. The brutal concrete theatre buildings and galleries on the opposite bank were lit blue and red. The plaque was mounted on the balustrade at the apex of the bridge and faced east towards the river estuary, the engraving was worn, the lettering faded and it had been defaced by a scrawl of graffiti. But the moon was good that night and Attila bent and traced the skyline with his forefinger, the two new buildings though had not yet been added. He turned to walk back the way he had come. Tonight he would sleep well, in his mind he was already planning the breakfast he would order in the hotel dining room.

When he was away, in the places where he worked, places lost in the moral darkness, London seemed unreal and distant. Even street lighting struck him as an improbable luxury, lights left burning so the population of a city could walk home without fear of injury or crime. When he was in London, going to see plays and eating in fine restaurants, the city itself began to feel like a stage set, whose denizens enacted their lives against its magnificent backdrop. A theatre of delights, where nothing surely could go wrong, and if it did, all would be put right by the end of the third act. He stepped up his pace and clapped his hands as if in anticipation of what lay ahead, but in reality against the cold.

On the empty bridge an animal was trotting towards him, a shifting shape that slid in and out of the light and dark on the bridge. At first Attila thought it was a cat and then a dog, until finally the moving shape resolved into the form of a fox. The fox passed Attila by, carving a shallow arc around him, as if merely observing the rules of personal space. Attila walked on and then stopped and turned round. At the same time the fox, too, stopped and glanced back over its shoulder and seemed to regard him. Attila pushed his hands into the pockets of his coat. The fox held his gaze, unblinking, for a long moment, then turned and trotted on.

Morning. Attila faced the window of his hotel room, which offered a view of an office building, windows veiled in pale grey voile through which he glimpsed the occasional ghostly figure. In his hand he held the telephone receiver. Old friends had heard nothing from their daughter whose habit it was to call every Sunday upon their return from church. Attila, who had known the girl from babyhood and thought of her as a niece, had taken it upon himself to look her up. Now his attention was caught by a movement high above him. A falling feather swung slowly through the air, drifting past the floors of the office block and his hotel window. A bright green feather. Attila watched it, lost sight of it and found it again, followed it as it became caught up in the traffic below, buoyed upwards on the rush of air of a passing taxi to recommence its rocking descent until it was tossed again. Up, up, down, down. He became aware of the receiver in his hand ringing distantly and he replaced it on the cradle. When he looked back to see what had become of the green feather, he could no longer find it.

Twenty minutes later Attila stepped out of the hotel into the freezing day. The doorman, who knew him from previous trips, offered to call him a taxi. Attila asked where he might buy some gloves. The doorman gave him directions and Attila moved away, shoving his hands deep into his pockets. Already the tips of his ears sang. He was twenty yards away when the doorman called out his name and hastened after him, pulling off his gloves. He thrust them at Attila, who would have refused.

'They won't fit me,' he said.

'They will fit you,' said the doorman.

And they did. Just. Attila looked at the doorman and saw that most of his clothes seemed outsize: his greatcoat drifted past the back of his knees, his shoes were huge, his feet could not possibly have filled them. He looked like a child whose mother had been persuaded by an outfitter to buy his school uniform 'with room to grow'.

'What will you do?' asked Attila.

'I will stand inside,' replied the man, as if this were obvious.

Attila thanked the doorman but the man shook his head. 'After all,' he said. 'What is a pair of gloves between countrymen?'

Somewhere close to the Elephant and Castle, a stone's throw from the intersection known as the Bricklayers' Arms, at ten o'clock that same Monday morning, a young man pushed a very old man in a wheelchair across a rectangle of uneven tarmac. The chair rocked on the rutted surface; once a wheel caught where the tarmac was torn and briefly juddered to a halt. When they reached the far side of the space the young man performed a neat three-point turn with the chair and backed it up against the wall. Leaving the old man parked thus, he strode away. A few minutes later and the young man returned handling another wheelchair containing another elderly person, a woman, tiny, crabbed and swaddled in wool: cardigans, scarves, blankets. He performed the same sequence of manoeuvres with the chair and again walked away leaving the two old persons now parked side by side. Neither spoke, the old man lifted his face to the sun.

The young man departed and returned, departed and returned. Six times more.

By 10.30, eight old folk were parked against the brickwork. They sat with their backs to the sun-warmed wall, eyes closed as if with the reverence of prayer, faces turned to the sun, they might have been believers awaiting the appearance of their god. The young man stood to one side leaning with his palms against the wall. He felt the sun on his face, but he didn't close his eyes, instead he gazed at the red-and-yellow-brick building, the triple-glazed windows filmed with muck from the flyover less than two hundred feet away. A plane flew overhead and the sound of its engines carried through the air. Once the plane had passed other sounds rose up: cars on the flyover, the brief blast of a stereo, the pock pock pock of an unseen person bouncing a ball as they walked by, the claws of a squirrel struggling to maintain its grip on the trunk of a tree, the flap of a pigeon overhead. A dog barked thrice. The young man looked at the old folk who were oblivious to everything but the steel-sharp air and the rays of the sun.

A shriek, high-pitched and throaty, some combination of outrage and urgency. A green bird had come to sit on a branch just above the squirrel who climbed onwards and upwards. The bird tilted its head and called again, and with each cry the young man felt a tightening in his chest, as though he had just heard the sound of a familiar and much-loved voice speaking to him after a very long time. He watched the bird as it began to clean the underside of one iridescent wing with a bright red beak. The old people watched the bird too, with unblinking eyes, as though they had somehow been expecting this. The next moment the bird flew away. A few of those in the car park of the Three Valleys Rest Home watched it go, others closed their eyes and others still turned their faces back to the sun.

Half a mile south-east of the Bricklayers' Arms Jean, an American and resident of the city for a year, sat on the roof of her apartment and raised her binoculars to watch a fox as it danced along the boundary wall of the property where she lived. Light bright, she thought, how she would have described its coat, a true russet. The fox was small, a vixen of less than three years. This was the sixth, maybe seventh time Jean had seen her. Jean put down the binoculars and picked a camera up from the table and took a series of shots. The vixen stopped, raised her head and sniffed, as though she discerned some shift in the molecules of the air; the next moment she slipped sideways from the wall into the overgrown buddleia and was lost from view. At the edge of the viewfinder Jean's eye caught a movement. A green parakeet had come to rest on the branch of a dead tree and began to investigate the toes of one foot. Jean put the camera down, sipped her coffee and recorded the sighting of the fox in a spiral-bound notebook. She turned back the pages and totalled the number of sightings of the light bright vixen. Seven since Christmas. The first time Jean had seen the fox from the kitchen window had been one cold November morning. A skinny scrap of life, all legs with a coat that didn't look nearly thick enough to carry her through the winter.

Jean pulled her shawl around her shoulders, picked up a tin plate from the table and rose. The roof garden was the first thing Jean had set her mind to when she moved into this apartment. The apartment had seemed an improbable choice and the landlord, who owned the van rental business with offices on the ground floor, did not disguise his surprise at her interest. As soon as Jean realised the ladder and skylight led to a large flat roof, she'd made up her mind. The roof looked out onto the rows of white vans in the parking lot and, only a short distance away, the massive triple towers of a disused gasworks.

The garden had cost her three weeks' hard labour, long hours to get the plants bedded down in time for spring. She'd measured and partitioned off part of the roof with trellises, slotted together wooden planks to make raised beds into which she laid the pipes for a simple irrigation system before hoisting bags of top soil and compost one by one through the skylight and up onto the roof with a rope and pulley. In the place where the sun reached farthest into the day, she planted raspberry canes, blackcurrants and greengages. She trained vines along the trellises and runner beans up them. She hung bags of soil and seed potatoes from the walls. In the corners she placed pots for tomatoes. In the remainder of the raised beds she planted kale, onions, strawberries, carrots, broccoli, not in architectural rows, but intercropped without apparent pattern, in a way that could be mistaken for haphazard.

Beyond the enclosed area she laid a waterproof membrane and drainage mats, hoisted more sacks, this time of lightweight soil blend, which she spread over the whole area. There she scattered the seeds of wild flowers and grasses so that, when summer finally came and her vegetables swelled and ripened, beyond the boundaries of her walled garden a wild meadow sprang.

Now she walked, barefoot despite the weather, between the vegetable beds to where a bird table stood and tipped onto it the contents of the plate: pieces of apple, tomato, a few grapes, raw peanuts. Six months ago she had persuaded her landlord to allow her to put in a spiral staircase, it had taken up the rest of her savings, but had been worth it. As she reached the top of the staircase there came the flutter of wings. The parakeet flew from the tree to the table. A few seconds later another parakeet landed, and then another.

In the bedroom Jean changed into her running gear. She ran most days, even today after a late night and even if she didn't feel like it, she would run knowing that in the course of the run she would, through the ache of muscles, feel the oxygen enter the rivers of her blood, buoying her mood as it did so, until she arrived home at once tired and invigorated. Last night. The fox had passed her while she was having a coffee at a riverbank stand. A large dog fox, she thought she recognised the markings. And then, chasing the animal on to Waterloo Bridge, bumping into a man and being knocked to the floor. The man had been the first to apologise. 'Forgive me,' he'd said as he offered her his hand. Forgive me. As though he had done something more than stand on a bridge. By the time she had dusted herself off the fox had disappeared.

She had caught the 172 bus from the other side of the bridge and arrived home after midnight.

Jean ran whatever the weather, even rain was welcome. Rain washed the pedestrians from the sidewalks. Back home in Massachusetts, Jean enjoyed long riverside runs in the rain and even in the snow. When Jean was ten years old she had watched a woman called Katherine Switzer run the Boston Marathon chased at least part of the way around the course by furious male officials. Jean's mother tutted. Jean's father said, For Chrissake, let the woman run. Jean's mother tutted a second time at the profanity. Half an hour later Jean left the house and went for a run in her shorts and sneakers. She had run for the rest of her life, through the fashion for headbands and leg warmers, all the way to heart-rate monitors and energy drinks. She had run a dozen or more marathons, alongside men and women, alongside giant chickens and pantomime horses and once, a streaking man. The only time she had stopped running was before and after the birth of her son. She had run all the way through her marriage. Four years ago she ran out of her marriage.

Today Jean ran as she had always run, alone and in silence, in a minimum of gear. The only thing that had changed recently was that in London she wore earplugs to deaden the noise of the traffic, preferring to run to the sound of her own heartbeat and the rush of blood in her ears. Today was a good running day. Bright, but with a sting in the air. She headed for Burgess Park where she found dog walkers and mothers pushing strollers. At the top of tall trees a murder of crows faced into the wind and waited in patience. Jean looped Myatt's Fields and returned by way of Camberwell Green, through Calypso Crescent and Brunswick Park. Without giving it any conscious thought she chose routes that took her through whatever green spaces there might be. After Brunswick Park she joined the canal path and followed it down to Commercial Way where she turned left and the great gas towers hove into view.

The building was a tall, new block in the City Road, built on a corner and at an angle to the street. Windows placed on the diagonal added to an already vertiginous feel. Next to it another, equally high building was being erected, still half covered in protective sheeting. The woman was in her early forties, the nails of her pale hands were trimmed very short and her cuticles were pushed back to reveal a deep crescent of lunule. Repeatedly she dug her nails into her palms and into the pads of her fingers and three times in the course of the conversation she reached for a pair of nail clippers and dug at the red, ragged edges of her cuticles. Jean watched and winced. The woman reminded her of an anxious dog gnawing its paws.

'Once we have the structural work completed, if any is needed, I don't see the job taking more than a week, two weeks max. I'll use mature plants where I can, so you don't have to wait too long. You'll be enjoying it by the spring. Have you checked the lease?'

The woman nodded. She picked up one of the photographs Jean had spread on the table. The image showed a tall building, not unlike the one they were in. Out of one of the top corners of the building a small spray of green cascaded. The woman replaced the picture and picked up another. This one showed a row of rooftops, iron fire escapes and blackened brickwork, except on one of the roofs ferns, shrubs and a sapling grew. A third picture showed the balconied façade of a mansion block. Most balconies were empty, a few held bicycles or washing lines, one balcony was brilliant with flowers.

'The first one isn't too far from here. I could probably arrange with the owners to let you have a look.'

The woman shook her head, small violent twists, as though she was trying to dislodge something from her ear. Without looking at Jean she said: 'It's fine. We're decided.' Framed photographs of the woman and her husband stood clustered on a long credenza. The husband was open-faced with round blue eyes. The woman was smiling, tanned and freckled. Happier times.

'Good to hear. Let's take a look at the space.'

The woman rose and opened a sliding door leading to a wide terrace. Jean stepped out and saw the city laid out before her, cranes hovering over the skyline. They reminded her of the pump jacks back home, except that whereas pump jacks pecked furiously at the earth, the cranes swung and dipped in elegant slow motion. The terrace was entirely bare. Jean said: 'Do you want mostly grasses or mostly flowers or a mixture?'

'A mixture, I think. Or maybe flowers. Yes, flowers.'

'And what about biodiversity?'

'What?'

'Birds, insects.'

The woman shook her head jerkily, as before.

'No birds, then,' said Jean.

Inside Jean said goodbye and placed her business card on the glass table. 'Jean Turane. Wild Spaces'. Down on the street Jean realised she had not eaten all day. She found a sushi and salad bar, chose a tub of bulgar salad from the selection in the refrigerated cabinet and paid. Back outside she walked and ate using the plastic fork. At the end of the street she passed a trash can and threw the tub away. She thought about the meeting, the woman, her pale face at the barely open door, her scared, decisive head shakes, those raw cuticles. There had been a pile of plastic crates in the hallway, of the kind in which groceries were delivered.

She could run a few errands and be home by dusk. She was hoping for another sighting of Light Bright. If Jean was right the little vixen was out laying claim to a small territory she could call her own. And then in the next few weeks she'd begin the search for a mate.

Chapter 2

MONDAY

The first set of signs, painted on wooden posts, read: *Children's Centre. Outpatient Department. Social Services. Institute of Psychiatry. Cognitive Behaviour House. Centre for Neuroimaging Sciences. Clinical Treatment Centre.*

Attila entered the expansive brick building. He followed the signs to the Outpatient Department.

Centre for Anxiety and Trauma. ADHD Clinic. Alcohol Dependency Clinic. Brain Injury Clinic. Clozapine Clinic. Dietician Clinic. Adolescent Unit.

Below the clinics were listed the following services: *Affective Disorders Service. Anxiety Service. Chronic Fatigue Service. Challenging Behaviour Service. Conduct Problems Service. Eating Disorders Service. Depersonalisation Disorder Service. Female Hormone Clinic. Mood Disorder Service. Obsessive Compulsive Disorder Unit. Party Drugs Clinic. Psychosexual Service. Self Harm Service.* Attila let his eyes skim over the sign, which grew longer every year. He walked through corridors and across courtyards noting each new modification, contraction and expansion. He took the lift up three floors and made his way down a corridor with a new blue carpet past a row of identical doors. One door yawed open and Attila caught a glimpse of a semicircle of women, similarly dressed in baggy clothing, with universally prominent cheekbones and overlarge eyes. Since his last visit Eating Disorders had spread and now took over most of this new floor. Attila turned the corner into the wing of the old building and walked on. When he reached the last door he knocked with his customary vigour and the noise resounded down the silent corridor. A moment later the door was opened by a white woman with red lipstick and eyes that crinkled at the sides when she smiled. 'We're just finishing up,' she said softly, and with an Irish accent. 'Come in, why don't you? This will be quite a treat.'

Attila entered a room and found himself standing in the middle of a circle of chairs. The seated students gazed at him with an idle and polite curiosity. Kathleen Branagan said: 'This is Dr Attila Asare,' at which a murmur rolled around the room. A student rose and offered his chair and Attila dropped into it gratefully. The chair was low, with a sloping back and short legs, and once down Attila felt like a beetle on its back. He shifted to better position himself.

The student who had vacated the chair said: '"Post-Traumatic Stress Disorder in Non-Combatant Populations, 1979". You co-authored the paper with Rose Lennox. I read it while I was at university.' The young man, whose face looked Indian and whose accent sounded English, said: 'You were the first in the field, I am so honoured to meet you.' He bent and offered his hand to Attila who shook it.

'"Misdiagnosis of Schizophrenia in Refugee and Immigrant Populations",' said another student in a voice that declared he knew as much as the first speaker. 'You examined the tendency among clinicians in Western countries to over-diagnose schizophrenia in certain immigrant groups, you deduced they were misdiagnosing post-traumatic stress disorder.'

Attila nodded. 'Among other things.'

'Of course, disorders with overlapping symptoms.'

Attila nodded again.

A third student, a young woman, said: 'May I ask what you are working on now?'

Attila crossed his legs. 'Well,' he said, 'I'm retired from clinical work. These days I offer consultancies in related fields. The area has grown a great deal since I first published, as you know.'

'Maybe you have some interesting experiences you can share with us.' That was the first student.

Attila would have demurred but at that moment Kathleen Branagan interrupted gently: 'Maybe, Dr Asare,' she suggested, 'you could tell us a bit about your work in general. The doctor has consulted for the WHO and a host of other international organisations. He's being unduly modest.' She looked Attila flush in the eye and gave him an attractive and challenging smile. Attila surrendered with grace. For several minutes he described his work in Sri Lanka, Northern Ireland, Bosnia, Afghanistan, the Turkish/Syrian border and all the other places he had travelled in the last decade, where he stepped off planes to be driven through streets of shelled buildings, devoid of people and colour, it might be thirty degrees centigrade or minus fifteen, the air clouded with dust or with snow, the landscape flat or mountainous, from his perspective conflict looked very much the same in one place as in another. Refugee camps looked the same: UN standard-issue striped tents, white Land Cruisers barging through crowds of people who moved as slowly as a tide of mud. He at once wearied of his work and loved it. And at the end of the day a shower in a guest house or a hotel, if he was lucky, one of a chain if he was luckier still: Hilton, Marriott, All Seasons, Ibis, Radisson. There was comfort to be found in the identical layout of the rooms, the brand of toiletries, the mechanics of the shower, a degree of familiarity that held frustrations at bay. Though he had begun half-heartedly, he started to feel energised. A long time since he had spoken to students. When they asked for more he gave it to them. Twice he made them laugh.

After twenty minutes Kathleen Branagan said: 'I think probably we should stop there and thank Dr Asare for his time.' One by one the students stood up, collected their bags and briefcases. Attila accepted the hand of each of them from where he sat in the low chair.

'Sorry to hijack you like that,' said Kathleen.

'You're not in the least.' Attila levered himself up off the chair with effort.

In a coffee shop they sat before giant paper cups of scalding coffee and Kathleen thanked him for agreeing to address the conference.

'An excuse to visit the city. How many delegates do you have coming?'

'Eight hundred.'

'That's not a psychiatry conference, that's a football match.'

Kathleen laughed. 'We held a conference on the same subject six years ago and had a quarter the number of delegates. It's a hot topic and it's only getting hotter. The military take it a great deal more seriously these days. Then there's the insurance companies, certain employers. There's a lot of work for expert witnesses now.' She blew her coffee. 'Talking of which, there's something I said I'd mention, if you're interested—'

'No thanks,' said Attila, not waiting for her to finish.

Kathleen agreeably abandoned whatever she had been about to say. 'Tell me if you change your mind.' She sipped her coffee. 'I'm looking forward to your keynote.' The conference, which started in two days, lasted a week at the end of which Attila would give the final lecture.

'It's nothing you haven't heard before.'

'Don't be so modest.'

'I wish I were.'

She slid an envelope across the table to him. It contained an embossed invitation to an event by another professional body that night. 'I can't make it. Go along if you feel in the mood.'

'Thanks.' He slipped the envelope into his inside pocket.

A few moments of silence, then Kathleen asked: 'Have you seen Rose?'

'I only got in yesterday.'

'How is she?' said Kathleen, and then: 'What I mean is, how are things progressing?'

'She has bad days and sometimes less bad days. Every now and again there's something you could almost call a good day. We have tried all the drug regimes. She's more or less stable, but nothing is going to change the outcome.'

On the other side of the glass a bright-faced child threw back her head, stamped and screamed at the sky. A muted, time-lapsed version of the scream floated through the glass. The child's mother was on her knees apparently trying to reason with her daughter.

'Once upon a time,' said Kathleen watching the mother and child, 'that was what we called a tantrum and now it's—'

'Disruptive mood dysregulation disorder,' said Attila.

*

Back at the hotel Attila placed two telephone calls. The first was to his niece. He cradled the receiver between his shoulder and chin, and at the same time broke into a jar of Planters nuts from the minibar and threw them rhythmically into his mouth. When his call went unanswered he replaced the receiver and plundered the rest of the nuts. Then he telephoned the Three Valleys Rest Home and asked to speak to Emmanuel. In reply to the next question Attila said: 'Rose Lennox.' He was told Emmanuel wasn't available and offered a word with the duty manager instead. 'No thank you,' said Attila. He took an apple from the complimentary fruit basket and ate it while he looked up his niece's address. In the drawer of the bureau he found a map and marked the location. Having satisfied himself thus, he pulled off his shoes, loosened his belt and climbed on the bed.

Dusk plus one hour. Half a mile from home. Jean carried a map, the folds of the map were reinforced with tape and the map was marked with pencil lines in various colours, sometimes dashed or dotted lines. On the right side, a handwritten key. Names. Or what one would suppose to be names.

~~Babe~~
~~Black Aggie~~
Jumbo Riley
~~Jeremiah~~
Missy
Piper
Redbone
~~Finn~~.
Rocky
Light Bright

Next to each of the deleted names: 'Traffic accdnt. Traffic accdnt. Unknown. Fight?'

In addition to the map Jean carried a small backpack and a night-vision monocular. She leaned against a sign that read: *No Through Road* and raised the monocular to her eye. After a minute or so she switched hands and flexed her fingers, which had grown stiff with cold even inside her gloves. At the edge of her frame of vision she saw a greenish glint and shifted focus. There on the top of a high garden wall, a fox. Just twenty yards from the busy Old Kent Road here the streets were uniformly urban, but these rows of houses backed onto gardens: small squares of ground, paved or turfed or consisting of mud and weeds, they contained cookers and fridges, rusted cans of paint, children's plastic toys, bicycles, the occasional bird table, and in one a piano, its wood rippled and swollen, ivory keys scattered on the ground. At this time of year the gardens were rarely used by the householders, they belonged to the foxes.

A black man wearing a hat and carrying a briefcase heavy with papers turned into the street. Jean lowered the monocular and waited, but the man kept his gaze fixed straight ahead, at one moment passing within inches of the fox. At the door of a house he put down his briefcase, removed his hat and rubbed his head, then his eyes and felt in his pocket for his keys, all the time watched by both Jean and the fox. When the man had gone inside, the fox slid off the wall and trotted down the pavement away from Jean. At the corner it stopped and turned, in the way of foxes when they are checking to see if they are being followed. Jean spotted the dark smears running from each eye either side of the animal's face. Rocky. The fox slipped between parked cars and crossed the road, turned once to look at Jean again, lowered his haunches, sprang up onto the wall and dipped into the garden on the other side.

The foxes were the reason Jean was in London. Eighteen months ago Jean had been in a hurry in all kinds of ways, had hurried the proposal for an independent study of urban foxes and ended up miscalculating her overheads. Her reputation for this kind of work back home, as well no doubt as the low figure she named, landed her the contract with Southwark Council, which was funded in part by a grant from a European Commission urban development fund. It was to be a two-year programme and she had it up and running well within the timescale, but there wasn't enough money to meet her own living costs. So she had dreamed up Wild Spaces to cover the shortfall. She'd had no idea that living anywhere could be so expensive. Still, she was pleased with her work on the foxes so far. Hours of waiting is what it took, several nights a week. Jean had a few things figured out now. Whose territory was whose and whose was up for grabs. Jeremiah, Babe and Finn were all dead and their territories had been claimed anew. Jeremiah and Babe were both hit by cars, a street-sweeper had tipped Jean off, each time had shown her a stiffened corpse in a garbage bag. Jean had recognised Jeremiah, a large dog fox, by the white in the hairs on his muzzle. Finn's corpse Jean found herself, in Burgess Park, the crows had led her to him. He looked pretty cut up. As for Black Aggie, she'd just disappeared, Jean had had no sighting of her for months. Black Aggie was the first fox Jean had seen in London, named for her four black leggings and her seeming ability to appear and disappear like a ghost. In the time Jean had lived in the city the vixen had raised a litter of cubs in her den underneath a shipping container behind Jean's apartment building. Then one day, when the last of the litter was about ready to go, Black Aggie had disappeared. In her dreams Jean saw Black Aggie leaving London, following the railway lines or the canal paths to the countryside. In her professional opinion as a wildlife biologist, she knew the truth was likely to be different: most urban foxes were killed by vehicles, the rest by disease, a very few made it to old age.

Five o'clock Attila's alarm sounded. He roused himself, crossed the room to the portable music system he carried with him on his travels and put on some music. The piece was a tango by a young Portuguese composer Attila had recently discovered and much admired. He raised the volume. He flexed his leg and tested the strength of his calves and ankles and then he performed a dance step on the carpet beside the bed and then again, wearing his shoes this time, on the marble floor of the bathroom in front of the mirror. He flicked an experimental leg up behind him, but the bathroom was too narrow and so he went back into the bedroom, restarted the track and took up a position by the window. In his arms he held an imaginary partner. Together they slid across the floor, a mirror to each other's movements. When they reached the end of the room Attila swung the woman round and released her.

She turned towards him, shoulders back. Attila thrust out his chest. They circled each other slowly, pawing the ground, a pair of thoroughbreds. Attila flung the towel he was still holding down onto the bed, snapped his heels together and drew the imaginary woman towards him. They struck a pose. She raised a leg and wound it around his waist, touched the back of his thigh lightly with the heel of her foot and then twisted away. Attila caught her and pulled her towards him, she flicked her other leg in the air – again, snaked it fleetingly around him. In perfect unison they slid back across the floor. Attila snapped each foot behind him, once, twice, thrice. She came towards him, so close now her breasts touched his chest. Attila clasped her around the waist and threw her in the air.

He sat down upon the bed and listened to the remainder of the track while he recovered his breath. He reached for the telephone and dialled his niece one more time. No answer. He had a couple of hours. Why not, he thought, go to the reception for which Kathleen Branagan had given him an invitation? He showered and put on his dinner jacket, made for him by a tailor in Dakar, and which he carried with him for just this sort of occasion, his height and size rendering the hiring of such an outfit virtually impossible.

Downstairs in the hotel bar Attila ordered a gin and tonic and was rewarded with an accompanying bowl of Japanese crackers. The barman was a bronze-faced man who spoke English with the muted consonants of the Brazilian. It struck Attila that it might be a fine idea to ask him for a restaurant recommendation. The cuisine of Brazil was among the many Attila loved. He failed to understand how the Cubans, so close in heritage, could get their food so wrong with the same basic ingredients: chicken, pork, rice, beans, onions, tomatoes. Attila had visited Cuba a number of times for training and conferences, for their health service was second to none. On each of his trips Attila had enjoyed Cuba and the Cuban, whose stoic realism and ability to take pleasure where it might be found was in many ways similar to the West African's. Through the slaves they were all brothers. Which made the question of the food the more mysterious. He jotted the barman's recommendation down in his notebook: a place on the Old Kent Road, close to his niece's address.

The gathering was held in one of the City guildhalls. Attila walked up Fleet Street and when he reached St Paul's Cathedral he realised he had been there before for an event he could no longer remember. As he waited to check his coat the elderly man behind the counter said: 'Good evening, Dr Asare.'

'Good evening,' said Attila. 'You have a good memory.' Even though he was used to being remembered. He recalled only that the man was from Sierra Leone.

'Thank you, sir.'

'When was it we met?'

'Well now, sir, it would be perhaps six years ago or four years ago. The World Congress of Psychiatry. The dinner is held here every two years, but I have not seen you here since. Of course, I'm not always on duty. Madam was with you on that occasion, sir.'

'Then it would have been six years ago.' Maryse had been here then, yes, he remembered. They had spent the afternoon browsing bookshops. Maryse was an appreciative reader, who read as she pleased. She liked thrillers, for the reason that reading them relaxed her, she told him. Looking at the covers Attila could not see how this could be so, but Maryse insisted they took her mind off her work, plus there was the added bonus that the criminal was always caught. The same afternoon he had encouraged her to buy an evening bag embroidered with a hummingbird that she had seen in a shop in Covent Garden. She had it with her that night at the reception. He was grateful when an opportunity arose for her to accompany him on a trip and to accompany him to events such as this one. You would never have guessed by looking at Maryse that she was a very good mimic, and afterwards over dinner she had mimicked, though not unkindly, one or two of the guests. Her talent lay, not in her ability to fake accents or pull faces, but the way she had of conveying the particular trait she had identified in a person: the jaded, uxorious, ebullient, world-weary, gluttonous or irascible.

'Madam is not here with you tonight?'

Attila dipped his head. 'No,' he said. 'Not tonight.' And he turned away.

Attila walked along a wine-coloured carpet and up a broad staircase of dark oak. At the top of the stairs a short passage led to another set of descending stairs and the banqueting hall. Attila stood at the top of the stairs for a few moments. He liked to watch the English perform, enacting a conception of Englishness still held sacred in some quarters, among expatriates who went about their parties, bashes and games of golf with a kind of strained urgency, but also here on home turf, in this room, were gathered the guardians of the flame. Around Jermyn Street, where Attila sometimes went for shoes, there were shops, costumiers, that sold chequered trousers and mustard waistcoats, felt hats, boldly coloured socks, crested slippers and badger-hair shaving brushes, most of which in all likelihood went home as souvenirs to Tokyo or, nowadays, Shanghai. Were the French so self-consciously Gallic? The English behaved as though they were playing themselves in a farce. 'He sees himself,' Attila's mother used to say of people she thought guilty of posturing. And yet what was nostalgia if not loss dressed in finery? The English saw themselves and yet at the same time they did not see themselves at all. England was a nation of Miss Havishams.

Attila helped himself to a glass of champagne. He was the only person of colour in the room, with the exception of some of the waiting staff. He walked down the stairs where, within moments, he was accosted by a small man with tiny feet. 'So, where are you from?' the man commanded from below.

'From Accra,' said Attila.

'Ah, Africa! And do you go back often?'

'I live there,' replied Attila.

'Oh!' The man blinked as if this news was surprising. 'Never mind,' he said. He introduced himself.

'Attila,' said Attila. And waited for the inevitable.

'Good God,' said the man with all the impertinence of one whose confidence survives on the safety of the herd. 'Why on earth did your parents call you that?'

'I expect because they liked it,' replied Attila, with the tact of those who lack quorum.

'So what do people call you?' asked the small man. They were approached by a black man in a cropped jacket who was carrying a bottle, one of several waiters doing the rounds. The small man held out his empty glass. The waiter filled the man's glass to less than the halfway point and turned to Attila. 'Sir?' Attila nodded and the waiter stood by while he drained what remained of his drink. The waiter filled Attila's glass to the brim.

'They call me Attila,' said Attila. 'Please do excuse me.' He left the man frowning into the shallows of his glass and eased his way through the crowd until he reached a man with thick white hair, good teeth and eyebrows that soared like silver wings over the top of his glasses. He was standing next to a woman wearing a long mauve dress, they were just then being introduced to a young couple. As Attila approached he heard the man with white hair say to the young woman: 'Murder or suicide, my dear?'

She looked at him: 'I beg your pardon.'

'Murder or suicide? It's quite simple.'

'He's asking if you'd rather kill or be killed,' said the woman in the mauve dress.

'Kill your enemy or let them destroy you. Which one?' said the man with white hair.

The young woman hesitated. She looked appalled and glanced at her husband. 'I think I'd kill myself before I could kill anybody else.'

Her husband smiled with approval, the woman in mauve with pity. The man with white hair said: 'You or me. Me or you. It's partly disposition, partly the values you were raised with, by your parents, by society. Gender plays a role.' He looked up at Attila who had just joined the group, he said: 'Attila here is a murderer.'

'You know me too well,' said Attila. To the woman in the mauve dress Attila nodded and said: 'Lady Quell.' The young couple moved away.

'*Kiel vi fartas?*' said Quell.

'*Bone, bone. Dankon,*' replied Attila. It was a joke of Quell's to address Attila in Esperanto, a language they both spoke or rather had once learned, as the only chance either of them had to use it conversationally was with each other. Quell had spent his career as a crisis negotiator.

'How long has it been?'

'Since we spoke? Five years.' Attila turned to Lady Quell. 'I receive your Christmas cards. Thank you.'

Lady Quell smiled in acknowledgement.

'Ah yes, Iraq,' said Quell. 'What a business, what a business!' Quell shook his head.

Attila said: 'Still enjoying retirement?'

'As much as anyone can,' said Quell. 'One can only go on at these things so long, Attila, and then you start feeling it, you know. I did anyway, the impossibility. Now that I've left, I don't know why I didn't take my pension as soon as they offered it to me and leave by the front door.' He paused and took a sip of his drink and for a moment was silent. 'What is it they say about the difference between humans and apes?'

Attila smiled: 'Apes learn by experience.'

'Come and see us sometime, won't you? We're still in Sussex.'

'Haywards Heath?'

'That's the one.'

On Waterloo Bridge Attila turned up the collar of his coat and thought what a fool he'd been not to buy a hat. He looked over the balustrade in both directions and forgot the cold. This view: the Eye, the sinuous curve of the river, the Houses of Parliament lit with gold, and on the opposite side amid the dense constellation of lights, St Paul's and the behemoth towers of the City. He thought about Quell and the last time they had spoken. The case had concerned a hostage release. Quell had come out of retirement to advise on the negotiations. Attila had been part of the receiving team on the ground. That it had gone as well as it had was thanks to them both.

On the south side of the river Attila descended into the underpass where a white beggar with a stocky dog asked him for some change. Attila found his leather change purse and shook out a few coins. He remembered, as a schoolboy, a cousin recently back from studying in the United States who showed him a photograph of a beggar in California. The beggar had stumps where his legs had been and a sign around his neck: *Six Years in Vietnam*. The true purpose of showing the photograph was the fact the beggar was white. People marvelled. The beggar in the underpass was white but had no sign, just a phrase repeated so often he had worn smooth its edges: 'Spa'e s'm' change.' Attila dropped a coin into the upturned palm and received no thanks. Something about the dog brought Attila in mind of the dogs in the compound back home, who formed their own loose-knit pack and roamed from house to house in search of a spot to lie which offered shade or breeze, were fed by the stewards of each household who vied for their loyalty, so that they dined like kings. These days Attila was so often away from home he had lost sight of which dogs belonged to him. He liked it when they gathered on his verandah in the early evening as he listened to the World Service. Sometimes a dog would rise and move over to sit by his chair and rest its muzzle on his knee.

In the auditorium of the concert hall Attila sat back in his chair and prepared to enjoy the concert. The singer, an Ecuadorian woman past middle age, was possessed of a torso round and taut as a cricket ball, short straight legs and wrinkled knees. When she sang she threw her head from side to side to the beat of the music, hitched up her dress and banged a tambourine against her thigh. Her voice was rasping and lusty, her laugh raucous, she sweated visibly and flirted with the young men in her band. When the concert came to an end Attila sprang to his feet and applauded and in the foyer afterwards he bought a CD of her music.

He thought about his niece, diligently began the futile search for a public telephone and in the end was lent a house phone by the woman at the ticket desk. Once again he dialled his niece's number and once again he received no answer. He resolved to pass by after dinner. For Attila hunger and impatience were conjoined twins. 'Food!' he remarked aloud. Outside he hailed a cab and in less than ten minutes was seated in the Parrillada del Sur where he ordered *salchichas*, *hígado* and *falda* too, all in Cuban-accented but serviceable Spanish. When the waiter brought his food Attila drew the CD of the Ecuadorian singer from his pocket and asked if it might be played. Moments later the sound of the singer's voice filled the near empty restaurant.

This was Attila at his happiest.

Attila stood at the door to his niece's apartment. The hall smelled strongly of disinfectant, the base beat of someone's sound system resounded through the masonry. He bent and peered through the letterbox. Unopened mail on the hall floor, the rooms beyond lay in darkness lit only by the outside street lights. Attila straightened and stepped back; he thought for a moment. His niece had a ten-year-old son, it was unlikely she would go away without telling her parents. He crossed the hall, listened at the door. He could hear the sound of a television and the occasional clink of cutlery. He knocked. The clink of cutlery stopped. He knocked again. This time the television was turned down. Attila called through the door: 'I'm looking for Ama, the young lady who lives opposite. I'm a friend of her parents.' Attila heard the sound of bolts being slid, a key turning, a chain released. An elderly woman wearing a dressing gown, her hair in a head wrap, stood before him. It was close to eleven and Attila apologised for disturbing her.

Her eyes moved swiftly up and down, taking in his formal wear. 'You are from Ghana?'

'Yes.'

The woman sucked her teeth. Attila knew the sound from his earliest childhood: it could convey any of a thousand meanings from the deepest sympathy to the most hellish curse. All meaning lay in the accompanying gesture. The woman shook her head.

'Two days ago. Immigration.'

This was not at all what Attila had expected. 'Immigration? Are you sure?'

The woman nodded. 'I've seen them before. They carried her away.'

'What about the boy?'

'Him too. There was a social worker. I saw them but I stayed out of sight. I could do nothing. Next thing you know ...' She shook her head again.

On the way back to his hotel Attila considered the matter from the few angles that presented themselves. This was a problem and he must deal with it. To begin with he would almost certainly need to engage a lawyer. The freezing air and the lateness of the hour had driven people from the street. Attila walked on unheeded, measuring his thoughts alongside his footsteps. He dipped into the underpass leading to Waterloo Bridge and as he did so a sharp crack resounded. It came from the passage ahead which opened up into a kind of concrete atrium covered with a canopy of vines. It was the place he had seen the beggar earlier in the evening. And there he was, the same man, this time cowering on the ground, his dog pressed to his chest, screaming: 'Fuck off! Fuck off and leave me alone!'

A firecracker whizzed along the ground. The beggar scrambled away. The firecracker exploded. The dog writhed and bucked, somehow the beggar managed to keep his grip on the animal. A third firecracker came flying.

Attila stepped into the scene.

Two assailants. One boy of about fifteen bounced up and down on the balls of his feet, pointed his finger at the beggar and his dog and laughed idiotically. The other boy was lighting a firecracker with a lighter. Without breaking his stride Attila snatched the lighter out of his hand. The yelping laughter stopped. The boy with the firecracker, who had very pale skin and very pale blue eyes, said: 'That's my fucking lighter, you shithead, give it back!'

Attila held on to the lighter. 'It was your lighter, now it's a piece of evidence in a crime. And I am the witness to that crime.' He turned to the other boy who wore his hair in an uneven Afro. 'I can identify you both.'

'Give me my fucking lighter!'

But the boy with the Afro was no longer committed to the game. He turned and ran, the next moment the white boy changed his mind and ran too. 'Tosser!' he yelled as they disappeared into an exit tunnel. The beggar remained kneeling, crooning to his dog.

A woman stepped out of the half-light of another of the tunnels: 'Are you okay?' she asked the beggar.

'He's fucking freaked out!'

The woman bent and stroked the dog's head. 'Hey there,' she said to the dog. She spoke with an American accent and Attila recognised her as the woman with whom he had collided the evening before.

Sounds overhead. Up through the tangle of vines Attila glimpsed the night sky and, closer to hand, movement and shadows. He spread his arms and began to usher the other two towards the shelter of the tunnel. A stringed bundle hit the ground sending up sparks and then a series of small explosions as a dozen firecrackers went off at once, causing the dog finally to break free and bolt. When it was over all that was left on the ground was a string of tattered papers. Attila and the woman stood in shaken silence, the homeless man walked backwards in a tight circle, heel to toe, calling his dog's name: 'Digger! Digger!'

Foxes, thought Jean as she walked, foxes went for cover. Foxes operated alone in the world, beyond the safety of the pack. Foxes were fine-boned creatures and never took risks they could otherwise avoid. Dogs were pack animals who lived in the light. In evolutionary terms compared to foxes, dogs were toddlers. They had got where they were in the world by cosying up to man as wolves gathered around the settlements. In time man and the wolves learned to hunt together. The wolves found the quarry and brought it to bay, the humans killed it with their knives and spears. A pact was born which had lasted thousands of years. Those wolves who stayed out in the wild were excluded from the pact and man declared war on them. Now neither humans nor dogs were what they were once, but the pact held. You had to hand it to dogs. While the rest of the animal world was out there trying to survive, dogs had their place by the fire, their own branded food, beauty parlours and little tartan coats.

Jean stopped and looked around. Directly to her right, at three o'clock, was Stamford Street. At two o'clock, the ramp down to Upper Ground and the river. There was an overgrown and empty lot there, which is where a fox would have gone. She raised her eyes. Straight ahead of her, like a runway, lay the open reaches of the bridge. She imagined herself as the panicked dog, the sound of firecrackers ringing in its ears, heading for the open space.

Jean found Digger at the far end of the bridge, facing the way he had just come, hyperventilating and waiting patiently to be rescued. She fished half an energy bar from her pocket, crouched down and held it out, calling the dog's name, and when he came over eagerly, she petted him, unwound the scarf from her neck and slipped it through his collar. She led him back the way they had both come and met the big black man and the homeless man at the apex of the bridge. The homeless man made a fuss of his dog and then said he needed to get to the shelter in Vauxhall. The black man gave him a £5 note towards a taxi, and the homeless man replied that taxi drivers wouldn't take a dog, but pocketed the note anyway.

Together on the bridge Jean and the black man each waited for the other to speak. She had already recognised him from the previous evening. Tonight he wore a tuxedo which lent even more drama to his appearance. She said, apropos of nothing except the place they stood: 'The first time I ever visited London, the very first night, there was such a commotion here on this bridge, along the river. A whale had swum up the Thames, you see, all the way to Battersea Bridge.' She raised her hand and pointed. 'A *long* way off course. There was a rescue attempt, they were taking it back out to sea on a barge.'

The black man said nothing but turned to look at her, he was listening.

'We were staying nearby, we went for a walk.'

There had been camera flashes, helicopter searchlights, sirens and loudhailers. The assault on the senses had been tremendous. On Waterloo Bridge and on the river terrace people stood two and three deep, some held up banners. One man had climbed a tree and sat astride a branch. A person dressed as a porpoise wandered through the crowd and handed out leaflets. A cry set up as a flotilla of boats led by a police launch appeared. In the centre was the hulk of a barge. Helicopters dipped out of the sky, whipping the wind. A news cameraman and reporter pushed in front of Jean. The noise of the crowd grew louder as people shouted and cheered. The lights of the helicopters converged on the barge. A man in a bright orange jacket waved at them, a Lilliputian swatting hornets. In a few minutes the pod of boats was close enough for Jean to see: on the deck of the barge, held in place by yellow floats and swathed in wet blankets, a tapered shape, massive, solid and terribly still.

In the hotel bar she and Ray watched the progression of the cortège as it reached the river's giant flood barriers. Some minutes past seven the programme cut back to the studio. The presenter, caught unprepared, put his hand to his earpiece, his eyes darted to one side, he looked down at his desk and then straight to camera. The bar was noisy, Jean lip-read the words: 'The whale ...' The barman picked up the remote and raised the volume. The words blasted above the noise of the bar. 'Confirmed. The whale has died. The whale is dead.'

On the same bridge now, Jean realised the big man was watching her. 'They must have known ... I mean, the noise, the lights, the stress all that must have caused ... Why did they do it?'

To her surprise the big man laughed, a deep triple note. 'You know, a lot of people nowadays believe they're owed a happy ending.'

In the lobby bar of Attila's hotel Jean ordered a Jack Daniel's and Attila a Glenmorangie which led to an exchange on the qualities of sour mash versus single malt. Attila liked them both. Jean hated the peaty taste of malt. They had come inside to thaw out and the big man had made a point of telling the doorman that they would be requiring a taxi later. 'To ...?'

'SE1,' supplied Jean.

'SE1,' Attila relayed to the doorman.

'Let me know when you need it, sir.'

Jean took this as a declaration of the big man's intentions, he was putting Jean at her ease. She followed him to the hotel bar, noticing how nimbly he moved, he wore his height and weight with ease. Now Jean looked at him as he raised his glass. 'I'm Jean,' she said.

'My name is Attila.' Ah-til-ha.

'That's an unusual name,' Jean said.

'To whom?' replied Attila cheerfully.

'Well ... everyone,' said Jean.

'Not to the Hungarians or the Turks,' said Attila.

'Your parents named you after Attila the Hun?'

Attila smiled. 'Some people,' he said, 'name their baby girls Victoria.'

Jean smiled uncertainly, she did not know what he was talking about. He laughed, the same three-note chuckle, and said: 'You look hungry. I'm going to have a sandwich. Join me.' He called the waiter and ordered a steak sandwich and a bottle of claret. Jean chose a roasted-vegetable baguette and asked the waiter what it had in it.

'Courgette, aubergine, capsicum, and comes with a rocket garnish.'

'Zucchini, eggplant, bell pepper and arugula on the side,' supplied Attila.

'So that's how you knew how to handle yourself around those boys.' The waiter had gone and Attila had just told Jean he was in London to attend a psychiatry conference.

'Not at all. The truth is I worked as a doorman for a nightclub during my university years here. A place in Brighton. I'd work there Friday and Saturday nights and then go back to my digs at university on Sunday in time for classes on Monday. It worked very well and was most lucrative. In fact, I dressed then much as I am dressed now.'

'What in God's name would make those kids behave that way?' said Jean, still serious.

'Chances are they'll grow out of it. Let's hope so. Some children stop at pulling the wings off flies, others cut the wings off the family budgie. Some in my profession believe animal cruelty is an early indicator of worse to come. I'm told Jeffrey Dahmer decapitated dogs and impaled their heads on sticks. Ted Bundy mutilated pets and so did the Columbine kids, apparently. The boy who killed his schoolfriends in Pearl, Mississippi tortured his dog.' Attila stopped. 'Let's talk about something more pleasant. You are an American. I am a West African. The barman is South American. And here we are in the middle of London. Not one of us was born here, but we each have a reason to be here. He's learning the hotel business, I am on a junket. What's your reason?' His voice was deep, crumbly, the texture of rich earth.

'Work,' said Jean. She felt unnerved talking to a psychiatrist. She wondered if he would be able to tell if she lied. 'And life,' she added, in case he could.

'Of course,' he said. And waited for her to go on, his gaze kindly and acute.

'Nothing dramatic. I was divorced a while back. The work I was doing came to an end. I wanted a change. I don't have a full-time position, mostly I do contract work. Short- and medium-term stuff. Not much stability but I get to be my own boss. Something came up here. I grew up in the city, well the Boston suburbs, I lived all my adult life in the country, I wanted to try living in the city again, a real city, to see what it would be like.'

'And?'

'There are things I miss: clean air, silence, being able to see into the distance, real weather. People in the city can be pretty hard, but in other ways the city is easier. People care less, so they let you be.'

The waiter arrived and set Jean's baguette down in front of her. She opened it and checked the contents. She replaced the lid. She saw Attila watching her: 'Do you have everything you need?'

Jean nodded. Attila gave the large, starched napkin a vigorous flap then tucked one corner into his collar and picked up his sandwich. His hands were enormous, his fingers, Jean noticed, were long and tapered. She noticed too that he wore a wedding ring. Jean had not worn her wedding ring for years, even the pale circle around her finger where the skin never tanned had disappeared. Attila opened his mouth wide and took a bite out of his sandwich, tugging at the steak with his teeth. Meat juice ran down his chin and he lifted the napkin to wipe at it. Conscious she was staring, Jean looked away.

Chapter 3

*For the second morning now, tracks around the camp. A single trail
in the deep snow. Jean bent to inspect them. The distinct oval shape of
the front track, toes pointed slightly inwards. Coyote. The animal had
carved a wide, weaving path around the camp, avoiding the deeper
drifts, keeping a distance and yet clearly curious. The pattern of the
tracks meant the coyote had been moving at a slow lope and by Jean's
reckoning the prints were only a few hours old. She straightened up
and looked at the way the animal had come, traced the line of the trail,
leastways as far as she could see, over the shoulder of a nearby hill, down
across the fold, around the camp and then into a large stand of trees
about two hundred yards off. A single trail, she couldn't see a second or
third trail branch off at any point. But just because she could only see
one trail, one set of tracks, it didn't necessarily mean she was dealing
with a single animal. Jean crouched down for a closer look, gauging
the size of the track by using her thumb joint as a measure. She walked
a few paces and inspected another track. When a coyote pack moved
through a territory often they walked in single file, one coyote took the
lead, the second placed its paw print in exactly the same spot as the
leader, the coyote behind did the same and the coyote behind that one
and so on. The pack moved as a single entity with one pulse, following
their leader's tracks so precisely it looked to the inexperienced eye as
though only one coyote had passed. Jean was no novice but she always
checked and double-checked a set of prints. Coyotes had developed the
technique, some said, over the centuries to outwit hunters, had survived
by becoming masters in the art of disguise. You could sit and stare at a*

thicket of trees, or into the tall grass, without ever realising a coyote was standing there looking back at you, its coat merging into the sun and shadows, like there was nothing there at all. Folks called them tricksters, but to Jean they were no less than master illusionists.

Jean trudged through the snow following the neat tracks in the direction they were headed, her snow shoes leaving an untidy scar. Many years ago somebody had told Jean a story. A group of hunters out tracking coyote found and followed a line of prints all through the day and into the dusk, until it was too dark to see and so they rested and the next day resumed the hunt at first light. And so it went for three days, the men alternately tracked and rested. On the fourth day they came across a second, older set of tracks and a short time later discovered a set of human footprints which they soon recognised as their own. One by one each man came to the same realisation. They had been led in a circle over a wide terrain during which time the pack had gradually closed the distance between them. The coyote were now directly behind the men.

In the back of her vehicle Jean had a box trap and a cooler of bait: cheap meat cuts bought from the supermarket, a few cans of tuna. She scanned the area to see if there was anywhere likely the animal might be denned down. The temperature was dropping every day as winter took hold. The fact that the coyote had been around the camp on two mornings made it less likely to be a transient, more likely that this was its territory. She walked towards the trees and found a scat on the edge of the stand. She measured it carefully, noting the measurement in her journal. Seven eighths of an inch. Not a large animal, a female or smaller male. With a pair of forceps she picked up the scat and put it in a collecting bottle, which she held up to the light. Mainly hair, some fragments of bone, which might be deer. A lone coyote couldn't bring down a deer. And while a coyote would eat anything pretty much, from berries to birds, there wasn't too much around at this time of year. A deer that had slipped on the ice and broken its pelvis, which happened, or been hit by a car, would make a good meal, and that made it possible that the animal was hanging around to finish off the carcass and would then move on. The other possibility was that there was a pack somewhere nearby.

She followed the tracks into the trees. Beneath the tree canopy the snow was patchy on the ground and the trail less distinct. Out of the *wind chill the air was warmer and smelled of leaf mould and earth. A few yards in the acrid odour of coyote piss rose above the base note of decayed vegetation. Jean found the telltale scratchings of the scent post at the bottom of a white pine. A quarter-mile on and she came to a partly frozen stream, shallow but wide, and after failing to find a crossing point within easy distance, she stopped and pondered her options. In these temperatures she was loath to get her boots wet because that meant she'd have to build a fire to dry them out again, and that took time and energy. Besides, for now she had enough to go on. The scat, the scent post, she was pretty sure she was dealing with a single, possibly adolescent male who was travelling alone. He might be holed up in a temporary den, have finished with the deer carcass and lately been attracted to her camp and the possibility of food. The thing to do now was wait to see if he came back.*

For a third morning Jean awoke to a single set of tracks around the camp. The evening of the second day she had pre-baited the spot she thought to set the trap, had placed raw meat on the boulder and trailed blood around it, crimson drops that fell through the snow as if with the weight of mercury. This morning the meat was gone. And on the fourth morning too. Later the same day, when the sun was up and it felt less bitterly cold, she heaved the cage trap from the back of the truck and shovelled snow over the metal wires of the base. She wasn't too sure what to do about the rest of the cage, which remained perfectly visible; she went into the woods and found some large leaves and pieces of bark which she laid on top of the cage and covered with snow until the cage resembled a small igloo, then she baited the trap inside. In the after-noon she fetched her rifle from the vehicle, checked the sights and the trigger mechanism and laid it on the floor next to her cot. That night the bait in the cage went untouched, as it did the next.

The cold box was empty. Jean took a can of tuna and baited another rock, this time in a different location, further from the tent but still within range. She was new to this, the team was new to this, nobody had really figured out whether it would work, they only guessed it wouldn't be easy. She would wait it out. After she had eaten a supper of canned hot dogs, Jean stood outside her tent, wrapped her arms around her body and watched the rising of the moon. The sky was violet, the trees on the ridge ahead starkly black, the moon lit the snow-covered branches of trees, cast sharp shadows on the scorched snow and high-lighted the shape of the drifts and dunes. There was no sound, not even the call of a night bird. Jean stood unmoving and felt a deep sense of contentment, she did not wish to be anywhere else.

Saturdays Ray liked to cook curry. She thought about him thirty miles away in their Greenhampton kitchen, a ball game playing on the old portable TV in the kitchen while he grated ginger, ate poppadoms and rummaged through the cupboards looking for the containers of cumin and coriander and fenugreek among the ketchup, French's and Folgers. Where was Luke right now? In the den playing video games? Maybe he had a friend round. No. Luke liked to keep company with his father when Jean was gone, he was thoughtful that way. More and more, he was becoming his father's son. When Luke still slept in a crib, Jean had hung a bird feeder outside the window of his room. Mornings she would open the door to find him lying, watching unblinking the chickadees swooping in and out for seed. When the red cardinal appeared he would pull himself up on the sides of his crib, rock himself from side to side and coo. As he grew up Jean read him goodnight stories and wondered, for the first time, why children's books featured so few human characters and when they did, why the humans seemed so shadowy and remote, so that oftentimes all you saw of them was their feet and legs.

Those first ten years Luke had been Jean's son. At five he could name all the birds in the garden and around the fields. Jean bought him an illustrated guide and a pair of junior binoculars and he would sit at the window and watch the nuthatches on their topsy-turvy descent down the trunk of the maple tree in the yard, or wait for a glimpse of the groundhog that sometimes appeared in the early fall mornings to feed on windfall apples. At nine he accompanied her on long nature hikes along the Mohawk Trail. He begged for a dog and one day, driving along the highway from Greenhampton on their annual shopping trip to the Manchester outlet to fit Luke out with twelve months' worth of new clothes, they had seen a dog dumped on the roadside from a car in front. Jean had pulled over quickly, but it was Luke who leapt out and somehow cajoled the terrified animal onto the back seat. Bess, as she became, was a collie cross of about six months, and just as Luke was Jean's son, Bess became Luke's dog, had eyes only for the boy. When Jean and Ray refused to let Bess sleep the night on Luke's bed, Jean, coming down to the kitchen to make coffee in the early morning, more than once found Luke and Bess both curled up in the dog bed by the door to the back yard.

Jean didn't know when it started, the gradual transfer of affections. She was neither jealous nor alarmed, it seemed a natural boyhood transition. Though Luke still loved Bess, his interest in animals waned. When Luke started wanting to go karting at the speedway on weekends Ray was delighted. Jean and Bess went on hikes together. After a while Jean realised how much she'd missed the solitude.

No, she did not wish to be at home. She wished only to be here.

At that moment she heard a yip, then a yip, yip, followed by a long, high howl. It climbed and fell, wavering at the lowest and the highest notes. As it died away there came another yip, yip howl, this time from a mile or more away. And then a third voice joined in the call and response, each animal singing the same millennia-old song.

Some time before dawn Jean awoke. For a moment she stared into the darkness of the tent. Her arm was numb from lying awkwardly on the narrow cot and she turned to release it, feeling the blood pulse back into her fingers. The fall of snow from a branch was the only sound that came to her. She flexed her fingers and then reached for the flap of the tent and peered through the small slit. Nothing. She rolled over and poured a cup of coffee from the Thermos she'd made the night before and placed next to her bed. Lying on her belly she raised herself onto her elbows to drink. Again she opened the tent flap an inch or two. Outside the snow shone. She had sight of the bait rock and she scanned the surrounds carefully. There! A movement. Jean held her breath, realised she was doing so and exhaled slowly; she lay motionless. There! She narrowed her eyes and peered into the darkness, concentrated on the form she had seen, willing it to be more than a trick of the half-light. Across the silence drifted the sound of a far-off snow plough. Jean counted her breaths in and out, her eyes moved to the bait and back again to where she thought she'd seen the shadow move. There! It was him, she was sure. Jean took a long, deep breath. As she exhaled she reached for the rifle on the floor of the tent. She had left it loaded, with the safety catch off, in the way she had been taught never to do. She curled her fingers around the barrel and lifted it an inch or two off the floor. When the moving creature paused, so did Jean, her hand holding the gun a foot off the floor, until the muscles burned. She steered her concentration away from the ache in her arm towards her breathing and the shape in the distance and when the shape shifted again so did she, lifting the rifle to tuck the butt under her arm, carefully, slowly, she lowered her eye to the sight. Now she saw him. A young male, fully furred out, with a pale undercoat, the covering of black hair on his back blending into the darkness. He was close to the bait now, watchful, dipping and raising his head, hungry, tempted by the free meal, wary. Under that heavy coat he might be nothing but bones. He was taking his time, and so Jean took hers. She flexed her trigger finger, adjusted her eye to the sight. Once he raised his head and looked directly at the tent and it seemed to Jean their eyes met and he held her gaze, until the idea formed in Jean's head that this coyote had been watching her as she went about her days, standing outside her tent as she slept at night, all the time she had been here. Slowly the coyote lowered his head, sniffed at the bait and began to eat. Jean waited to take her shot: too soon and she risked missing, too long and he would be gone. The shot, when she took it, was a good one. The feathered dart struck the coyote in the shoulder. The animal twisted his head and sprang back, teeth snapped the air as he tried to bite the dart. Jean had placed it well, just in front of the shoulder blade and out of reach. His near foreleg buckled first, then the far foreleg. For some seconds he remained on his knees, dazed and swaying. In under two minutes he was down.

Jean sat up and swung her legs over the side of the cot, found her boots and her thick coat and pulled them on over her thermals. She slipped another dart into the rifle's chamber, grabbed the dart box and radio collar kit and left the tent. Fifteen yards from the fallen coyote she stamped the ground and called out, but the animal did not stir. She approached and knelt in the snow next to him. He had fallen onto the darted shoulder and she needed to turn him over to remove it. She put her arms under each of his front legs and, using most of her strength, hoisted him over. Working fast now, she pulled the empty dart from the animal's skin and replaced it in the box. Next she fitted the radio collar. She raced back to the tent for the receiving equipment and allowed herself two minutes to test it. Finally she prepared a syringe of the tranquilliser antidote. Six minutes had passed. Just before she administered *the antidote she paused for the first time in the whole process and looked at the coyote: on a whim she stretched out a hand and fondled his ears and stroked his muzzle. The coyote's coat felt smooth and soft, not greasy as she had been told. She stroked the fur of his underbelly. Finally she laid her cheek against his chest and felt the beating of his heart, turned to bury her face in his fur. The rankness had not been unpleasant; heavy with musk and the scent of sun-scorched earth. The coyote had been Jean's first. She had never forgotten.*

SOUTH-EAST LONDON, TEN YEARS LATER

Three miles into her run, Jean's feet were cold and wet. When it rained the lower path in Nunhead Cemetery flooded and turned into a pond, once Jean had even seen a drake and a hen mallard swimming on it. Jean splashed through. After another late night her thigh muscles ached. The years were at her heels. She laboured up the hill and stopped to catch her breath, jogging on the spot in front of the view of St Paul's, framed by the bare black branches of the trees. A small flock of parakeets fluttered overhead and Jean followed in half pursuit. She watched them land on the massive, dead sycamore tree which stood at the intersection of two of the grander avenues in the cemetery and where the flock nested in hollows carved into the soft wood. How had Argentinian parakeets come to live in this northern European city? And found a way to survive, to make it through the winters, just as the coyotes had when they'd moved from the western plains up north and east, from dry plains to snow-covered mountains, from creosote bush to hemlock forests, from one hundred plus degrees Fahrenheit to five?

On the downhill stretch of the path Jean picked up speed, she forced herself into a second half-lap of the cemetery. New England graveyards were uniformly understated, austere places, rows of grey headstones, trim lawns, barely a flower, people planted the Stars and Stripes above their loved ones, as though God was a patriot.

The first time Jean had visited Nunhead, soon after her arrival in London, she had been astonished. The innumerable hues of green: bright moss, candescent pale lichen on the gravestones, dark ivy which smothered every tree from the one-hundred-year-old chestnuts that lined the avenues to the thousands of saplings that had sprung up everywhere. She read names on graves, the kind of name people no longer seemed to possess: 'Oliphant', 'Cromblehome', 'Pfennig'. Four collared doves sat on a branch, each with its head turned to face the one behind, beak buried in the feathers of its back. Pigeons took off at her arrival, rising like grouse. For two hours she wandered. Children's names on graves. 'Our Beloved Dolly, 13 months'. 'Matilda, who fell asleep aged seven'. 'Jesus said suffer little children to come unto me, Dewey, 13'. On one tall stone, an infant's name, followed by the names of three adolescents, and of two men and then, at the end, a woman, the mother and wife who had survived them all, Anne, widow of William Luxton and John Elliott, both above. Buried with her first and second husband and three of her children. Another headstone bore the name of an entire family killed on 1 January 1900. How? Jean wondered. There was nobody to ask, if indeed the answer was there to be had. Late afternoon in mid-winter the cemetery was empty.

Later Jean looked up the graveyard's history. It was one of seven around London, built by the London Necropolis Company at a time when the English and their monarch were in the middle of a love affair with death. In those days they would photograph their dead as if they were briefly sleeping, sometimes surrounded by living relatives, coffins were transported in glass carriages pulled by horses the colour of mourning to graves around which weeping women clustered. Mausoleums. Monuments. Memorials. Then came the First World War. Death on an industrial scale. Dozens dumped in unmarked pits. Jean had seen graves bearing the names of one, two, three sons. And the names of places. Arras. Ypres. Gaza. A few decades later the cemetery was locked and later most of it was deconsecrated. Left to die, instead it thrived. Saplings sprang up, prising open graves, toppling obelisks and urns, knocking angels from their pedestals. Snowdrops burst from the soil in winter and in the spring bluebells, primroses and daffodils raised their heads. Moss greened the gravestones, ivy curled around pillars. Birds, bats, rats, foxes nested in the trees and between the graves. So much life, fed by the bones of the dead. Jean had seen a headstone caught and carried up a tree, an inch or two every year, to beyond the height of her head. Elsewhere a tree trunk had moulded itself into fluid folds around a gravestone. Of the Magnificent Seven, as they were known, Nunhead was the least famous and least favoured of them all, which suited Jean just fine.

On the run back an old Pete Seeger song looped through Jean's mind. Pete Seeger was, or rather had been, one of those old-time protest singers, the kind of person who had existed when believing was still possible. Jean's father sometimes hummed 'Where Have All The Flowers Gone'. The song going around Jean's head was a song about grass, not the kind you rolled, the kind that grew on lawns, and, as Seeger sang, just about anywhere it could find a spot. He'd sung about all the ways man had tried to smother nature with concrete, and somehow the grass always found a crevice or a corner to start to grow again. Maybe the song was about inevitability, or Mother Nature, or just grass, but Jean liked it and thanks to Nunhead Cemetery and Pete Seeger the idea for Wild Spaces had seeded. She thought about the city, the Old Kent Road where she lived, the sidewalks, flowered with discarded gum, in the warm weather they smelled like it had rained sour beer. The areas further south and north and east where clusters of mirrored monoliths had sprouted, full of expensive new apartments, and then those neighbourhoods Jean used to think of when she thought about London, of houses crammed together in a row, like a mouthful of broken teeth. Jean would bring back the wildness, create wild spaces in the air. And she had found a way she could afford to live in the city.

Heading north-west on the Old Kent Road she saw a street-sweeper's trolley parked up. The street-sweeper was sitting on a bench on the sidewalk, his arms stretched out along the back. He looked like he was chatting happily to himself until you noticed the headphones and cellphone. Jean slowed and waved. The sweeper halted his conversation and raised a finger at Jean. Jean pointed to the Payless Supermarket and indicated she was going inside and the man nodded and returned to his conversation. Sweating from her run, Jean bought a bottle of Lucozade, a drink she had never heard of before coming to England but for which she had somehow developed a taste. The owner of Payless, a dark-skinned man, from where Jean could not guess from either his appearance or accent, said as he took her money: 'Here last night, ripped my bin bags open.' He was talking about the foxes.

'I'm sorry,' said Jean, as though what foxes did was her fault.

The shopkeeper nodded, mollified. They all look the same to me, was what he had said when Jean sounded him out about taking part in her study, had enquired how many fox sightings he had a week and how many different foxes he guessed that might amount to. He had behaved as though her research was a waste of time and money, none of which stopped him from sharing his grievances. As he took her cash he said: 'They come here from the countryside because they hunt them there, see.'

'They banned fox hunting.'

'Yes, and so now they breed like crazy,' he continued, unhampered by logic.

Jean smiled and shook her head: 'Thing is,' she said, 'you need to put your trash in the dumpster.'

The shop-owner shrugged. 'Full up,' he said. 'The council don't bother to empty them as much any more, they fill up. So then what are we supposed to do? The foxes are animals, animals belong in the countryside, not in the city.'

Back outside Jean sat on the bench next to the street-sweeper and waited for him to finish his conversation, which he did promptly. 'You didn't have to rush,' said Jean, shaking his hand, as they always did when they met.

'No worries, Jean. How are you?' he said. Jean said she was fine and he took a small notebook from his breast pocket and read out to Jean a list of sightings and locations of foxes for the last week. When he'd finished he tore off the sheet of paper and handed it to her.

Upstairs in her apartment Jean removed her trainers and pulled off her sweat-soaked running kit, towelled off and wrapped herself in a dressing gown. She climbed the spiral staircase to the roof, found her binoculars where she'd left them and scanned the surrounds for the vixen. Since the foxes had moved into London their habits had changed. Once they were strictly nocturnal, now foxes could be seen walking down inner city streets in mid-afternoon. She paid a number of volunteers a small amount of money to collect data for her. All they had to do was use their eyes. Abdul, the street-sweeper, was one of them. Jean had recruited him on a whim, she'd seen him sweeping the early morning streets alone and so she'd approached him and asked if he'd care to help out with her study. In turn he'd recruited a number of his colleagues who seemed to enjoy the joint endeavour more than they cared about the money. So, in an outcome as accidental as it was effective, Jean had her research team in place within weeks of arriving in the city.

There, poised on top of the storage container, the figure of the vixen. 'And good morning to you, Light Bright, my missy,' whispered Jean.

Chapter 4

Three Valleys Rest Home, Bricklayers' Arms, some yards north-west of the Old Kent Road. Attila said: 'Rose Lennox, please.' He had placed his bulk in front of the light and now cast a shadow across the workstation of the receptionist who in his view had ignored him long enough. Presently a care worker arrived to take him to Rose and together they entered the static silence of the corridor. The woman wore soft shoes and moved soundlessly, save for the rustle of her lavender scrubs. Attila's leather lace-ups slapped resoundingly upon the black-and-white tiles. Strip lights burned overhead. The air smelled of boiled food, ammonia and talcum powder. Behind a closed door, the sound of weeping. Attila caught glimpses of the interiors of rooms: the same winged chair, flowered curtains, a figure in a raised bed, huddled under blankets, on the side table the flotsam of a life lived: photographs, a china cat.

The residents' day room faced the back of the building. A semi-circle of high-backed chairs arranged in front of a large window looked out onto a handkerchief of weed-pocked lawn. Each chair held a sleeping occupant, head lolled to one side or else folded chin to chest, skin pale and creased as origami paper, hands bent sharply at the wrist lay in laps like dying birds. The air fluttered with the sound of stuttered breaths. In here the curtains were drawn and the light of day cut through the still air and lit the dust motes. Attila advanced bearing in his hand a box of New Berry Fruits. He was aware of feeling powerfully alive, every beat of his heart, the rush of blood, vital organs throbbing with life, the snap of synapses, here in this roomful of fading souls.

Rose was sitting on a window seat in the lightest part of the room, wearing a blue cardigan. Her hair was more brown than grey, her cheeks tinged with colour. The woman care worker tapped Rose on the arm until Rose turned slowly away from the view of the window. 'Visitor for you, dearie,' said the woman in the kind of brusque baby talk favoured in such places. Attila stepped forward. He had expected Emmanuel there and would have liked him to be present in case Rose became agitated. But Rose looked at him so mildly, Attila relaxed and said: 'Hello, Rosie. How are you?'

And Rose replied: 'I'm very well, thank you,' with all the animation of a speaking clock.

Attila sat down heavily next to her. Rose turned back to the view.

'It's good to see you, Rosie. You look well.' When she didn't reply he reached out and took her hand gently in both of his. Reflexively she clutched at his thumb and held on to it. Her skin felt dry, almost scaly. Rose lowered her gaze and stared at their clasped hands as though at an object she didn't recognise, but she kept hold of his thumb. 'I brought a present for you.' At that Rose looked up at him, her face assumed an expression of – something. He removed his hands from hers and put the box of New Berry Fruits in her lap. In an instant the mood changed, Rose looked horrified. 'Take it away!' she said, aghast.

'They're your favourite,' said Attila. Where was Emmanuel?

'No they're not!' spat Rose.

'They've changed the box, that's all. The tree used to be bigger, I think. They're the ones with the soft centre.'

'I don't want them,' said Rose. Attila removed the box and put it on the table next to him. He wondered if he should go to find Emmanuel, but when he turned to look at Rose she seemed to have forgotten her upset and was staring intently out of the window. 'You see! You see!' She pointed. Attila leaned forward.

He saw nothing, a wooden bench on a gravel path, the sorry square of lawn bordered by chrysanthemums. He said: 'What?'

'On the bench!' A robin perched on the back of the bench. 'And there!' Rose pointed a wavering, accusing finger at the wall. Another bird, a second robin, stood on the brick wall.

Attila gamely played along. 'Ah yes,' he said. He wondered if Rose would object if he opened the New Berry Fruits.

'They say you can't have two robins in the same garden but you can!' Rose spoke so loudly that a nearby resident raised his head in confusion. Attila reached for the New Berry Fruits. Rose watched him. He offered her the opened box and she took a sweet and popped it in her mouth, chewed noisily. A moment later she helped herself to another. Attila ate steadily, jellied sweet after jellied sweet. He looked at Rose, who smiled back at him, and he had a glimpse of the spirit of the old Rose, reaching a hand up to him from the quicksand. He said nothing, preferring to sit in companionable silence, like the old days. Or rather, not like the old days. In the old days Rose and Attila argued and debated and sometimes fought, they drank whisky. Rose dressed in good sweaters and good shoes, stitched suede with tiny tassels, and she wore wide-leg tweed trousers. She mouthed words as she typed them, occasionally swore and ordered Attila to top up her whisky as they sat up late into the night, Rose typing the paper they were co-authoring on her Olivetti while Attila checked each new draft. They had met at the University of Sussex, Rose's family lived nearby in Haywards Heath and she had volunteered to meet and greet the foreign students at the start of the term. Attila was on a full scholarship and had arrived in Plymouth by boat. Rose teased him for his habit of wearing suits to lectures and told him he was the only African she had ever met who could pronounce 'Haywards Heath'. Attila delighted in enunciating the syllables, with long and breathy aitches. 'Hhhome to Hhhaywards Hhheath at ten to three. And is there hhhhoney still for tea?' Rose was the first woman Attila loved. Attila was the first man Rose loved. They spent their university years in love with psychiatry and each other. When Attila, after graduation, said he was going back to West Africa, Rose was hurt. They argued and fell out. Attila sailed in September. A decade later their careers threw them back together. By then Attila was married. Rose said: 'Why couldn't you have missed the boat?'

Then came a time when Attila found himself sending more and more pages back to Rose to retype, sometimes for mistakes so fundamental he called a halt to whisky during their late-night work sessions, but the errors continued. One day he pointed out a problem of syntax to Rose, and found she could not seem to understand why the sentence was wrong. Later he came to believe that the thought struck them at the same moment, from the way Rose looked from the paper up into his eyes and held his gaze, though neither of them said a word. A year later came the diagnosis: early onset Alzheimer's.

'I'm glad you came,' said Rose now.

'I wish I could come more often,' said Attila.

Rose twisted in her seat and seemed to regard him carefully. Attila looked back at her. It was so hard, so very hard to tell what she was thinking, if she was thinking. Eventually she said: 'I'm sorry, but you'll have to tell me your name. I don't think I know it.'

'Attila,' said Attila.

'Attila!' said Rose brightly. 'Attila! Do you know I have a friend called Attila. Now, isn't that something?'

'Yes it is. Something. It certainly is,' said Attila.

'I hope you'll get to meet him.'

'I hope so, too.'

She turned back to the window. 'Well, goodbye,' she said, even though Attila was not ready to go. Attila leaned over to take her hand again and stroked the dry skin. He stood up and searched the room until he found a pot of Atrixo by a sink in the corner. He rubbed some into Rose's hands and afterwards fitted a slipper back onto her foot. It was a mannish corduroy slipper, some trace of Rose's old taste had somehow survived. She seemed to accede to his ministrations and so he took a comb from his pocket and combed her hair, bent to kiss the top of her head and inhaled the faint, brackish odour of her hair. Then he turned and left the residents' day room.

At reception Attila asked for Emmanuel and was met a few minutes later by the Three Valleys centre director who told him Emmanuel had been let go.

'You mean sacked,' said Attila.

The woman, the only white person Attila had ever seen at Three Valleys besides the residents who were all white, pursed her lips. 'Actually strictly speaking no, because Emmanuel came to us through an agency, but in effect, yes.'

Attila asked: 'What was the offence, if I may ask?'

She gave him a careful look, measuring his trustworthiness, then said: 'This is confidential, you understand, and I am only telling you because of the particular relationship that exists between you and Miss Lennox, Emmanuel and Miss Lennox and therefore Emmanuel and you. The fact is, a few days ago Emmanuel took a number of the residents out of the building on nobody's authority but his own.'

'How can I reach him?' asked Attila.

Criminal, Family, Immigration. Behind the glass window of a shop front the lawyer recommended by Attila's compatriot the doorman worked in full view of the world. He was possessed of a peanut-shaped skull and the kind of pointed footwear Attila associated with dishonest pastors, but the lawyer listened intently without interrupting while Attila gave the best account of his niece's situation he could. When Attila had finished the lawyer said: 'Denunciation.'

'What?' said Attila.

'Once I spent my time dealing with work permits, now I spend my time attending to denunciations and deportations. These days landlords and employers must ask for all sorts of proof of the right to reside, the government wants to send as many people away as they can, because the whites don't want us.' The lawyer smiled as though this was a shared joke. 'So now anybody can call the immigration services and tell them, Oh this person, that person is here without papers. The scheme is contracted out to private companies, maybe they're on commission. The burden of proof is on you.' He pointed at Attila. 'You with the black skin.'

Attila was silent for a moment, then he said: 'Her name is Ama Fremah. The boy is Tano. Can you find her?'

'Yes,' said the lawyer.

'And the child?'

'Less easy because social services have their own rules, but I know people.'

Attila retraced his steps from the lawyer's office back up the Old Kent Road. In this part of the city his skin blended with the skin of many of those around him and he drew no glances. Once he felt as though someone had tapped him lightly on his shoulder and turned to see a splash of bird shit on his coat. A passing man carrying a stack of pizza boxes said: 'Good luck that, mate.'

Yet the day was turning into anything other than that which Attila had hoped. He bought a cheap mobile phone and SIM card and let the young man in the stall put it together for him. He handed the young man the slip of paper bearing Emmanuel's number and waited. 'Someone here wants to talk to you, yeah?' said the young man when Emmanuel answered. When they had finished speaking Attila fumbled over which button to press to end the call and thanked the young man when he leaned over to show him.

Ten minutes later Attila was sitting opposite Emmanuel in a Lebanese café. Balanced on a chair with spindly legs which in turn sat dangerously on a floor of polished tiles, he drank coffee out of a tiny cup with an inconsequential handle as he listened to Emmanuel. In his mind's eye he saw Emmanuel wheeling the seniors into the sunshine and cold, the busybodies at the windows watching before they telephoned the centre director whose day off it happened to be, not daring to intervene in case Emmanuel was deranged and therefore possibly dangerous. Emmanuel keeping guard over the residents, moving a hand under a blanket here, adjusting the position of a foot on a wheelchair rest there. The appearance of the centre director, called from home to deal with the emergency, a sensible woman who simply asked Emmanuel to please take the residents inside. Emmanuel wheeling them back into Three Valleys, as his co-workers strained to see at the window. One by one the old people turning back to look up at the sun, the sky, the single tree, before they were wheeled inside for ever.

Attila disliked Three Valleys, but a decision about Rose had needed to be made. She had never married, there were no children.

Attila was the person to whom Rose had given power of attorney, but he had been away in a place where he could not be easily reached. Now he said: 'The only problem is Rose.'

Emmanuel stared at his hands on the table. He was a good-looking young man, with a small goatee beard and hair about an inch or so high, parted on one side, in a style Attila hadn't seen for decades but noticed had become recently fashionable again in London. Attila had worn his own hair that way when he was a university student in his twenties. If Emmanuel wore glasses he would look like Patrice Lumumba. In Attila's day they had all seen themselves as freedom fighters. Now Attila was several stone heavier, and the last time he had attempted a beard it had grown mostly silver, as was the hair on his head. Attila patted Emmanuel on the shoulder, and invited him to eat, but Emmanuel said he needed to go into the agency to see if he was still on their books. When they left the café Attila went in search of a restaurant, it was mid-afternoon but already darkness was falling. As he walked he turned matters around in his head. In the past twenty-four hours he had acquired two new problems, but such was the nature of life, worse things happened to better people. In regard to his niece there was little more he could do but wait for the lawyer's call. Rose was all right for the time being. He felt sorry for Emmanuel, he sensed the boy's melancholy, knew it had fostered this small act of rebellion. Attila ruminated and every now and again spoke a word aloud, as was his habit. 'Patience!' he remarked to the members of a bus queue. 'Money!' he declared to a street vendor counting the notes in his cashbox. It began to rain: luscious drops that struck the back of his neck and rolled down inside his collar. The rain forced him into some kind of action, he decided he would take a taxi back to the Aldwych and there he would eat in the brasserie he had found on his first night. But this was south London at four on a weekday afternoon, the capital's taxis had all been drawn to the waterhole of Zone One. He tried to think where the nearest tube might be, but he had lost his bearings.

Somebody spoke his name. He turned to see Jean. She said: 'What a surprise! What are you doing here?'

'Trying to leave,' said Attila.

'Good luck getting a taxi.'

'In that case might you direct me to the tube station?'

'Elephant and Castle, about fifteen minutes' walk. But you'll get soaked. Come to my place, we'll call you a cab from there.'

She turned and Attila followed her because it seemed the sensible thing to do. She walked fast and swerved only when a collision looked otherwise unavoidable. Attila stretched his legs. As Jean walked, she talked. 'In a city of eight million,' she said. 'What a coincidence. Really something.'

Once in Washington, DC, Attila had hailed a cab to find himself addressed by name and found the driver was a man he'd employed as a security guard years before. In New York he entered a shoe shop to find one of the only people he knew in the entire city buying a pair of loafers. In Rome he had been sitting drinking beer alone in a square watching the people as they passed and had a strong presentiment he was about to see somebody he knew and sure enough, there was a good friend walking towards him. In Colombo he had dined three nights with a former schoolmate who was in the city selling gemstones. They had both been pleased to see each other, neither man had acted in the least bit surprised. He smiled and said: 'Yes, isn't it?'

In the apartment Jean fetched a towel and threw it at Attila who rubbed the great dome of his head dry. Jean disappeared and Attila heard the whine of a hairdryer. When she reappeared her hair around her shoulders shone so luminously it caused him to blink. She set a bowl of pistachios and half a bottle of white wine with two glasses on the table, lifted the bottle and poured them each a glass. Without waiting to be invited Attila fell upon the nuts, opening the shells and popping them into his mouth. Jean watched the nuts disappear and said: 'Shall I make us something to eat?'

'Yes,' said Attila without hesitation. 'That would be very welcome.'

'Let me see what I've got,' said Jean.

Alone, Attila sipped his wine and looked around the room, which was sparsely furnished by any standards: a few CDs, a small number of paperbacks, a stack of scientific papers sat by a laptop on a table. The furniture looked like a mixture of second-hand and flatpack. Attila picked up a framed photograph that stood on a chest of drawers. Jean, perhaps fifteen years younger, cheek to cheek with a boy of thirteen or so. They were wearing woollen hats and had reddened cheeks, both were sticking their tongues out at the camera. He examined the CDs and found no common musical theme: an album of songs by a vast South Islander, Neil Diamond and two Linda Ronstadt albums. There was a CD-R with the words 'Night Calls' written by hand on the plastic case in black marker, which Attila took to be a CD Jean had mixed herself. He eased it from its case and put it on the player. For a moment there was nothing, then a hissing which could have been static or might have been the wind; Attila wasn't sure so he cranked the volume. A scream tore through the room, delivered at such a pitch it caused Attila's scalp to shrink, the follicles of each hair to tighten in alarm. He fumbled for the volume knob and turned the sound down. Jean entered the room carrying a tray. 'Listening to coyote calls?'

'They sound like the devil.'

Jean smiled. 'I made that when I was working on a project with coyotes. Somehow it found its way into my bags when I was pack-ing up to leave. We made a lot of recordings of coyotes. You go out at dusk or at dawn, the times when coyotes are most active, and you play the tape. If they're around, with luck they'll answer you.'

'And then what?'

Jean shrugged. 'Well, then you know you've got some.' She set the tray down on the table, pushed her laptop and papers aside and began to lay out various bowls. 'Come on,' she said and waved Attila into one of the two chairs. Jean had produced the meal in what seemed to Attila a remarkably short time and when he sat down he saw why. Whilst there were a large number of dishes, the amounts on each seemed to Attila to be quite modest. Hummus, olives, a quartered lemon, bulgar wheat which he recognised from the refugee camps. There was a bowl of shredded cabbage, there were carrots, a dish of spinach. 'Eggplant.' Jean pointed at a bowl of grey mush. Attila, driven by hunger, covered his disappointment, sat down and helped himself to several slices of pitta bread of which at least there was plenty.

'So,' said Attila reprising his thoughts of a few minutes earlier, 'you say it's a coincidence we have met three times. What if I tell you I don't believe in coincidences? By which I mean the idea that coincidences are out of the ordinary, coincidences happen far too often to be considered extraordinary. People are always saying it. My, what a coincidence!'

Jean thought about that. She nodded: 'True.'

Attila munched on some of the cabbage tossed with fennel seeds, which he found quite flavoursome. The eggplant tasted of nothing and he was experiencing an aversion to eating the bulgar for all that it represented. 'A statistician will tell you that you are as likely to get a row of zeros on a winning lottery ticket as a row of different numbers. We should be less surprised when life takes an unexpected turn. Life is disorderly. In certain parts of the world, in the absence of plagues and floods it's easy to mistake mundanity for normality and therefore to react to what seems extraordinary. But what we call coincidences are merely normal events of low probability. There is another possibility, of course.' He popped a piece of hummus-smothered pitta in his mouth.

'What's that?'

'That you have been stalking me.'

Jean laughed with her mouth full of food and raised her hand to cover it.

'Well,' said Attila. 'You are out late at night, alone, dressed' – he waved his hands over her as might a conjuring magician about to change a dove into a rabbit – 'dare I say, as an assassin.'

Jean smiled and told him about her work with foxes that had brought her here and kept her out late at night.

'And I was at the theatre and then a concert. So you see,' said Attila, 'we could never have run into each other if you were in a more conventional line of work. It was not a true coincidence, closer really to a statistical likelihood.'

'Of course you're right. I'm a scientist, I should never have used the word coincidence. There's less synchronicity and more causality than we often think. Things happen. Sometimes in ways we couldn't even start to imagine. Let me ask you a question?'

'Go ahead.'

'Do you like fried chicken?'

Attila confessed that he did and hoped this meant Jean was about to serve some.

'A man called Harland Sanders opens a restaurant in Kentucky sometime before the Second World War and his fried chicken is such a hit that he opens another restaurant and then another, this time serving nothing but fried chicken. Around the same time on the other side of the Atlantic, just about where we are right now, the government has ordered the slums to be cleared. The poor families are moved out into public housing, new residents are taking their place in nice houses with what we in the US call yards and the British call gardens and actually gardens are different from yards, back home ours are mostly just grass, a place for the kids to play, but here in Britain they do it differently, they grow stuff, vegetables, borders with roses. The area does well. Then along comes Adolf Hitler.'

'Hitler,' repeated Attila, not knowing in the least where this was going but enjoying the ride. 'Did he like fried chicken?'

'He bombs the hell out of London. The east gets the worst of it, the south-east suffers too. After the war the bombed-out buildings and streets get ripped down, a lot of the former residents move out to Kent, same as the last lot did. More nice houses with gardens get built to replace the bombed streets. All of that time the rail network is growing and it takes the work from the docks, which is where most of the men in this neighbourhood worked, so Southwark more or less empties out. The docks close down in 1970. Guess what they build there instead.'

'Tell me.' Attila removed an olive stone from his mouth. All that remained on the table was the olives, so he was tackling the last of these.

'A theatre.'

'Ah ha!' Attila poured more wine.

'The area slides backwards again, the gardens grow neglected. Foxes find a use for them, they build their dens and raise their cubs. Once they used to come into the city from the surrounds to scavenge, now they stay. There have been foxes in London for decades, it's just that their numbers stayed low. I'm guessing people hardly ever saw them.'

'So what happened?'

'Colonel Sanders.'

'Dem chickens?'

Jean laughed: 'Fast food. Fried chicken, burgers, kebabs – the sidewalks have turned into an "all you can eat" buffet for foxes. The same is true in cities the world over. Heaven for rats, pigeons, you name it. In Britain nearly ten years ago the government banned fox hunting, so some people imagine that's what has caused the number of foxes in the city to grow, because somehow it stands to reason the two must be connected, right?' She smiled as she said: 'It can't be a *coincidence*. Wrong. It was fast food and the change in the urban landscape. I'm here for the foxes, you're here for the plays. Really, it's all thanks to Harland and Hitler.'

Some time past midnight Attila drove up the Old Kent Road in the back of a minicab. He was floating on his first sense of well-being all day, pushed along on a light alcoholic breeze. The Old Kent Road was busy, shops were still open, bars, people waited at bus stops. The taxi turned off the main road to circumvent some road-works and proceeded on a route Attila knew less well. Down a narrow road a police car and a white van in front of them came to a halt. The width of the van blocked the road, the driver held a hand out of his window to signal patience. The side door of the van slid open and two uniformed and helmeted men stepped out onto the pavement and walked towards a shuttered recess in the building. Attila saw the light of a torch. The driver of the van shifted his vehicle out of the way. The taxi squeezed past. On the side of the van the words: 'Immigration Enforcement'.

The taxi drove on and twice Attila saw a movement, a shadow in the crease of building and pavement, and once the driver braked causing Attila to lurch forward in his seat. In the road, the opalescent eye shine of an animal.

As often as he could when he was away on assignment Attila would call Maryse. Then came a time when the obstacles to calling from remote villages without working telephones, or because the town exchange had been bombed or he was somewhere beyond the reach of satellite communications, became such that Attila began to write instead, and over time he grew into the habit. He would write knowing he would not post his letters but would give them to Maryse when they were together. In his presence she would put them away without opening them. He thought she read them, he had no idea when.

My darling Maryse ...

So far today Attila had waited half an hour for the commander of the militia to arrive. This was his third attempt at a meeting. On three consecutive days Attila had been shown to a different room. The aide detailed to mind him made and received many telephone calls in his presence; to Attila he would nod and relay the message: 'Coming soon.' But the commander never came. Attila missed the services of the translator detailed to the fact-finding mission, who was presently travelling with the rest of the team as they continued their work, while Attila waited in this unheated room. The commander was reputed to speak French, having spent some years as a career criminal in several cities, in Toulouse where he conducted a series of armed robberies, later he had been arrested and imprisoned twice in Brussels and in Basel, escaping on both occasions. He had returned home some years ago to Belgrade, where he had become the leader of a football fan club. This information had formed part of the briefing Attila had been given by telephone. 'It's not strictly our problem,' Maurice Quell had said over the satellite phone. 'But since you're in the region. And it all helps, it all helps with things around here.' He'd meant inter-departmental politics at the UN headquarters. His instructions to Attila were: 'He'll be wrong-footed when he sees you. Tell him there is no way we can accede to a request of this nature. It's completely out of order.'

Attila stared out of the window at the mud. To Maryse he had written about the mud, how it stained the hem of your trousers like no other mud, refusing to wash out. There were no tarmac roads around the town, heavy military vehicles churned up more mud. Mornings the mud was frozen, dusted with snow, like icing on a turd. Leaving and entering any building was to navigate mud. Attila slipped often and thought he might fall. He was wearing the wrong kind of shoes, had flown straight from New York. The hotel was not the kind where you could leave your shoes outside the door and have them returned in the morning. Breakfast every day was the same: boiled eggs, bread, a jam of a composite fruit flavour. Dinner was pork, always. Even the act of eating had been turned into an insult to be performed by the victors upon the vanquished.

The evening before Attila had met with the captain of the UN peace-keeping force. He found him sitting alone in the lobby of the hotel, hands folded over a slim folio of papers on the glass table in front of him. He wore battledress and a blue beret. The Kenyan was almost as tall as Attila, though easily two thirds of the weight. When Attila offered him a drink he ordered tea and it came in a tall glass with a Lipton's tag swinging from the rim. The man held the string of the tea bag in between his long forefinger and thumb and drew a circular motion.

'What do you think?' said Attila.

'My men have no wish to be here. They would accept it.'

'It would be wrong.'

'Tell me one thing here that is right.'

They were silent. The Kenyan twirled the tea bag: 'The first day here we went out on patrol through the villages to the east. Most people had gone and the houses were empty, our orders were to enter and make checks. We were afraid of mines.' He shook his head, picked up a long-handled spoon and squeezed the tea bag against the side of the glass. 'There were no mines, at least we had God to thank for that. Outside a house I found the body of a woman. I went through the back door into the kitchen. I searched upstairs and came down, I found nothing. Only there was a bad smell. When I passed back through the kitchen I noticed something I had not seen on my way in, a large pot on the stove. There was a baby's body sticking out of it. Someone had taken this woman's baby and pushed it head down into the meal she had been cooking there. The skull had burst, the brains ...' He shook his head and placed the long-handled spoon on the saucer. He did not drink his tea.

Attila listened. Before he had been detailed to meet the commander, Attila had spent his days in and around the camps, now deserted, which had been set up in warehouses in the town's industrial zone, in a technical school, in a remote farm estate. He had listened to the testimonies of the survivors. Militia men and their captors, both men and women, were housed side by side. He knew what the commander allowed his men to do for sport during the long nights. The work of excavating the mass graves from the mud would go on for years.

My darling Maryse. *Attila had written to Maryse about the Kenyan captain.*

Years before, arriving home after a mission, he had gone to the bedroom to wash his hands before dinner. Maryse had the cook prepare chicken yassa *for him, the dishes were being laid out on the table in the dining room below. Crossing the bedroom he felt the sense of stillness one gets from entering a room which has lain undisturbed for some time in an abandoned house. There were his evening shoes on the floor beneath the stand which held the jacket he had worn the day before his departure. The wooden dish of cufflinks and the assorted coins of several nations sat on the shelf below the mirror. His wife's gown hung on the chair in front of her dressing table. It was all exactly as it had been the moment when he had turned at the door, suitcase in hand, to check whether he'd forgotten anything. Now he moved around the room making an inspection. A pair of earrings lay on Maryse's dressing table – she had worn them to the Alliance Française, where they had both been to see a film the Friday night before his Sunday evening flight. She had come home and taken off the earrings, he remembered watching her do it, they had been talking. What had they been discussing? Not the film. He weighed the earrings in his hand and then replaced them on the dressing table. Black crystal teardrops. He had bought them for her and then forgotten them in his briefcase. They had flown with him in and out of five different countries on three continents. Attila realised that Maryse had not slept in their bedroom those days he had been away.*

She slept at the hospital where there was a day bed in her office. After he was gone she packed her own small valise and left the house too. Sometimes, when it proved impractical to stay at the hospital, she slept on the settee with a bedspread and a pillow. She could not bear, she told him, to reach across and feel an empty space, a cold sheet beneath her palm.

'Do you want me to travel less?' he had asked.

And she had replied: 'That's not necessary.'

Day three. On this day the commander entered the room and sat in the chair behind the desk where he made several phone calls and reviewed a number of papers before he acknowledged Attila. Attila allowed him this display of power and waited in silence, for he had nothing else to do that day and nowhere else to be. His colleagues had departed the hotel before dawn. Now they were out collecting evidence of the methods used by the man sitting in front of him to terrify a civilian population into abandoning their homes. Not just abandoning them, but willingly signing their houses over to this man and his cohorts to reassign to his followers. Afterwards some of the dispossessed were boarded onto buses and driven away. Most were left to make their way on foot across the freezing, mud-encrusted land. Many were slaughtered. Others were kept alive for sport and sex.

Attila relayed Quell's message while the commander listened without looking at him. When Attila had stopped speaking the commander placed his hands on the table and spread his fingers. The reason they were in the same room, Attila and the commander, was because Attila was working to have him placed behind bars for as many years as possible. They both knew this. Now the only stratagem at the commander's disposal was courtesy or the lack thereof. This is what it had come to. An end game. He said to Attila in French: 'It is impossible. My men do not accept it.'

'And you?' Attila answered in the same language.

'I do not accept it either.'

'What is the nature of your objection, if I may ask?'

A short, incredulous laugh. 'To take orders from dirty, uncivilised savages.' Only now did the militia commander look Attila in the eye. Attila met his gaze without blinking and then switched to the view of empty fields and a line of trees out of the window just to the left of the commander's right shoulder. In layman's terms the commander was what was called a psychopath. There was a popular but misguided supposition that psychopaths were clever, but this was not true. The IQ of psychopaths mirrored that of the average population, which meant, of course, that there were some very bright psychopaths, but there were also plenty of average intelligence and a fair few stupid ones. The truth was that men like the commander were more typically easily frustrated and highly volatile.

Attila was shown out by the aide, this time by a different exit, one that took him down a corridor and past a room thick with cigarette smoke and the sounds of a televised football match. Inside the commander's men jeered the opposing team.

There was no big secret to war, Attila thought. There would always be people who relished violence, all they ever needed was a leader and an opportunity. If someone could unite the gang members of New York or Chicago or London, they could take over their respective cities, if that person was the president they could take over the country. A lot could be achieved by offering young men power and sex. In the filthy work of clearing up after other people's wars, listening to the survivors' accounts of what had been done to their sisters, mothers, brothers, fathers, themselves, sometimes, like in this place, on his way to and from the camps, he passed the perpetrators at roadblocks. He wanted to stop and ask them questions. What did they dream about? What had war brought them? Nobody funded those kinds of conversations, public sympathy was what defined who would be treated as the victims. Those who were done to, those who saw what was done, never the doers. That was the way the outside world assuaged the guilt for whatever failings had been laid at its door.

Light was leaving the sky as Attila waited for the Land Cruiser to be brought round. Beyond the lake of mud, among the tattered bushes at the perimeter fence not more than thirty yards away, Attila saw a movement. A moment later there came the crack of gunfire, a shout and a laugh. An animal of some kind sprang forward and bolted the line of the fence until it disappeared through a hole in the wire. 'What was that?' Attila asked the aide.

'Fox. Somebody used to give food before. Now comes here looking. First one shoots it wins.'

'Wins what?'

The aide shrugged. 'Wins bet.'

The next day Attila was called to the satellite phone at Command HQ. It was Quell. 'Forget it,' he told Attila. 'It's over. They've decided to meet the commander's terms.'

'That's it?' said Attila.

'That's it,' replied Quell. 'Sorry to waste your time.'

In the evening Attila met the Kenyan who listened in silence with his elbows on the table and his chin resting on his steepled fingers. When Attila had finished he merely nodded. 'My men don't want to be here. They are cold, they can't eat the food. I'll tell you the truth, I don't want to be here either. If this is what it has come to, we will not make an argument of it. We will return home.'

Attila leaned back in his chair. Neither man spoke until the Kenyan said: 'You see how the people here do not look at us, they will not meet your eye.' He leaned forward and looked directly at Attila. 'But it is not because we are black. No. It is because they are ashamed that now we have seen what they are.'

Chapter 5

In the dying hours of their marriage, Ray issued this ultimatum: 'All or nothing', in a note on the kitchen counter. By the time Jean found the note it was mid-morning, she'd worked late and over-slept, Ray was downtown in Ray's Classic Cars showing a 1971 Dodge Charger to a customer. To Jean the statement seemed ridiculous, but it turned out Ray wasn't joking. He wanted to matter more, he wanted to be loved more (than Jean could love him, although she did, she did love him). He did not want to share her, not with another man (there was no other man), not with the members of her wildlife team, not with a pack of coyotes. Ray loved the classic cars in his showroom in Greenhampton. He loved the Dodges, the Chevys, the Plymouths, Pontiacs, Cadillacs, Chryslers and Corvettes. He passed hours burnishing their hoods, their hub caps, tracking down spares. At six o'clock it was over. Every day Ray pulled down the shutters, locked the showroom door, and came home without regrets. He loved the cars and his job restoring and selling them. He did not love them more than his home. He did not love them more than his family. He did not believe the same could be said of Jean. Jean listened to Ray in silence.

Jean wondered if this was a difference between men and women. Women. Raised to believe love was something to be earned, by being pretty and good and not too clever and not too slutty. Taught to hold on to their husbands by staying pretty and good and not too clever and never slutty. Add keep your figure and a decent home.

Men. Raised to expect unconditional love, first from their mothers (and mothers did love their sons more than their daughters, whatever anyone said), and then from every woman afterwards. So much love, thought Jean. Ray felt he deserved more love than Jean could give him and maybe that wasn't his fault.

There seemed to be no expectation other than that Ray would remain in the house, a side-gabled bungalow with a covered verandah, a cedar shake roof, paintwork that in the last five years had begun to peel. Ray had a business in South Street. The year before he had attended the forty-year reunion at his high school. His best clients were people he'd known all his life. Jean had lived in Greenhampton a mere thirty years. She had restored a house, not only restored a house, for four years had put her everything into restoring that house, from the basement heating system to the running trim that decorated the verandah. She had designed and planted the garden, a task which had consumed and delighted her, and for which she discovered for the first time she possessed a talent. While her neighbours' houses were surrounded by uniformly mown and empty lawns, Ray and Jean's house was fronted by inkberry and sumac and silverberry trees, covered in vines and adorned with wisteria, surrounded at different times of year by asters, sedum, Carolina rose, peonies and azalea. Out back she raised every kind of vegetable from peas to pumpkin.

Their son's gradual home-leaving and the end of the marriage ran along roughly parallel lines. Luke left for college, a first-generation student, neither Jean nor Ray had been away to college, Jean's degree had taken six years of community college classes. Ray had been proud of her. It would be too easy to make out he was equal parts blue collar and redneck. In the world they grew up in people dated and then married, most of Jean's friends went straight to work. Those were the years of the Massachusetts miracle, the economy was on a vertiginous upswing, the early, early days when the big tech companies were opening up, you didn't need a college degree to hold down a decent paying job. Jean had financed her education doing a few of those, that's how she knew she'd go crazy doing that kind of work. Ray had been great about it, they held off having Luke. So no, it wasn't the fact of Jean working that was the problem, it was that Ray felt he could not compete with her work. If she had run her own nail salon probably they would still be together.

Jean filled the space left where her marriage had been with more work. She did not work frenetically and in order to forget, she immersed herself in work, gradually and pleasurably, as though she were walking into a warm lake. She worked without guilt, freed from the negotiations over time, the couples' curfew, the roll call of meals, she worked the way she had always wanted. If she needed to stay out all night, she did so. She began to draw up proposals and to carry out her own studies. She cooked less and ran more. Her body became tauter, more elongated, as though Jean were returning to her pre-marriage self.

'Jean Turane?'

'Yes.'

'We're ready for you.'

Jean stood up and followed the researcher. The young woman waved her pass at the security guard. They entered the revolving glass doors where they stood squeezed uncomfortably together while the doors inched around. In the studio Jean was ushered into the seat opposite the host whose name was Eddie Hopper. Eddie Hopper was reading a link, leaning into the microphone and waving his arms around. When he had finished he took his earphones off and extended a hand across the hexagonal desk to Jean.

'The fox lady, am I right?'

'I guess so,' said Jean.

'Or the fox-y lady!'

Jean said nothing. The host put his earphones back on, shuffled scripts and conducted a conversation with his producer of which Jean could only hear his side. After a few minutes he looked up at her: 'Thirty seconds,' he said and began his introduction. 'Are there too many foxes in the city?' Before Jean knew it, he had come to her. 'I'm joined in the studio by Ms Jean Turane, a ... Well, why don't you explain to our listeners what it is you do?'

'I'm a wildlife biologist,' said Jean. 'Specifically I am an urban wildlife biologist. I study animals in the city and human–animal coexistence.'

'And you're here to study our foxes.' He flicked his eyebrows up and down at her in a way that seemed vaguely improper. 'Can I ask who is paying for this?'

'The study is being conducted on behalf of Southwark Council in conjunction with the European Commission. There are animal populations in the urban settings of most Western countries including the United States, there's a lot of information we can share. In the US we have considerations about deer, racoon, skunk; there's, even been the occasional moose in a shopping mall.'

He interrupted her: 'So this is what the European Commission is spending our money on? Why am I not surprised? And what is it we need to know about foxes that we don't already?'

'We need to know how to manage them and in order to do that we need certain data, where they are concentrated, what their habits are.'

'How many foxes there are, for instance? What's the answer?'

Always one of the first questions. Jean began to explain how hard it was to get a fix on the number of foxes there were in any area, these were wild animals, not even herd animals who could be rounded up and counted but solitary, nocturnal creatures, you couldn't just call a census. But he had lost interest. 'So the answer is, you don't know. But we're talking thousands, right? Maybe even tens of thousands? Too many.'

'That depends on how many people can tolerate. If you leave foxes alone they'll pretty much leave you alone.'

'Foxes leave their crap on my lawn.'

'There are controls you can use, repellents.'

He looked at her as though she were demented. 'So you're telling me it's my problem?'

'You could try putting up a sign,' said Jean. 'But they're animals and animals don't follow rules.'

'Absolutely right, my friend! They raid dustbins and scatter litter all over the streets, they defecate wherever they please and carry disease. And let's not talk about that late-night screaming because this is a family show.'

'It's all a matter of correctly managing them,' said Jean. 'Don't leave your' – she remembered to say 'rubbish' instead of 'garbage' –

'rubbish bags out on the street and that won't happen. As for disease, the most common disease foxes carry is mange and the greatest victim of demodectic mange is the fox population itself.'

'What about household pets?' he interrupted.

'Excuse me?' said Jean.

'Dogs, cats – they can contract mange.'

'Yes, but—' Jean said.

'Next you're going to tell me that if my dog gets mange it's my fault.'

'A healthy pet dog is not at any serious risk.'

'But what you would call serious' – he spoke the last word with invisible inverted commas around it – 'might not be the same as our pet owners out there. After all, you're on the side of the foxes.'

'I'm a scientist,' said Jean. 'I don't take sides. We need to take a realistic view of the situation. Everyone wants an easy answer, but maybe, just maybe there isn't one.' Jean was handling the interview badly, she knew. The more she talked about foxes, the harder it seemed to become. To her it was all so obvious. Only one party in the fox versus human battle was capable of changing its behaviour. You could wish for Christmas to come in May all you liked. She was reminded suddenly of Attila, on the bridge. The whale. People wanted what they wanted. They wanted a whale set free regardless of the cost. Now they wanted London cleared of foxes. For the next ten minutes Jean sat in the radio studio and took calls from the public, people accusing foxes of stealing children's Wellington boots from outside the back door, digging up plants, one caller claimed a fox had attacked his Staffie. The first two were likely, the last extremely unlikely, a fox wouldn't get into a fight with a larger animal unless it was cornered. The caller seemed to want the fox arrested. 'Somebody should do something,' he said, before hanging up. Then there were the callers who fed foxes, putting food out for them at night. They thought Jean should laud their efforts and were annoyed when she didn't. One caller was convinced a fox had mated with his Labrador.

'I doubt that very much,' said Jean.

'What makes you say so?' asked Eddie Hopper.

'Yeah, how would *you* know?' said the caller.

'There has been no verified case of cross-species mating between foxes and domestic dogs.'

'But wolves and dogs mate,' said Eddie Hopper.

'Yes, but ...' Jean exhaled. 'I'm afraid you can't use one example of cross-species mating as proof of another. What we're talking about here is evidence. As for dogs and wolves, humans and chimpanzees don't mate, even though they are our closest genetic cousin.'

'That's disgusting,' said the caller.

'If your Labrador whelps be sure to call the zoo, they'll be very interested,' Jean told him. The host threw her a look but Jean ignored him.

In the closing minutes of the segment came the inevitable: 'What about our children?'

'What about them?' asked Jean.

'What happens when a fox attacks a child? Are you going to be responsible?'

Jean began to rehearse the mantra of wild-animal attacks on children, the figures for which were extremely low. Your neighbour, your car, your own pet dog and its shit, these risks were all a thousand times higher.

Eddie Hopper interrupted. 'Can I ask,' he said. 'Are you a mother?'

She should refuse to answer the question. Instead she replied wearily: 'Yes.'

'Well then you should know better,' spat the caller. The only people who heard this were Jean and Eddie Hopper because the producer on the other side of the glass was already fading out the call. Jean didn't listen to Eddie Hopper round off the show, she was already removing her headphones.

The lawyer's choice of footwear belied his true self as a diligent and energetic worker and not a thieving clergyman, for he telephoned Attila early in the morning with the news that Attila's niece was no longer in police custody, indeed the lawyer's intervention had not been required. A mistake had been made, so the authorities maintained. As far as they were concerned, the matter was closed, unless

Attila wished to make more of it. Attila did not think he did, at least not at this point.

'Where is she now?' asked Attila.

'In hospital,' said the lawyer. 'Apparently she was taken ill. That would explain why you have been unable to locate her.'

Attila said: 'She is Type 1 diabetic.'

The lawyer tutted in sympathy. He gave Attila the ward name and the address of the hospital. Attila thanked him and the lawyer said: 'The boy.'

'Yes?' said Attila. Somebody would have to arrange for him to be returned to his mother. Social services, Attila assumed.

'I told you I had some contacts in social services. The boy was put into temporary foster care, this is typical in such situations. It would seem he disappeared from there yesterday evening.'

'Are you serious?' asked Attila. 'They've lost him?'

'Unfortunately so.'

A few minutes later Attila replaced the receiver. The lawyer had refused his offer of a fee, saying the whole matter had taken no time at all. 'Your niece was able to prove her right to be here, in her case it was simple enough.' He told Attila to call if he required anything further.

Within half an hour Attila was standing at the foot of his niece's hospital bed. He had arrived in haste and unannounced. He found Ama sitting up, her mobile phone on her lap, her thumb on the buttons as if she had just ended or was about to make a call. The skin beneath her eyes was dark and oily, a deep crease lay between her eyebrows. At the sight of him she said: 'Oh, Uncle! Thank God! Thank you!' They embraced and she put her arms around his neck and held him tightly for a moment.

Attila had wanted to break the news about her son to Ama himself, but as he suspected social services had already sent someone. It seemed another boy in the home where Tano had been staying had confirmed that Tano had run away. Several local authorities and the police were involved. There was no evidence of a crime or the involvement of a third party and for that reason no child rescue alert had been issued. What they had wanted to know, she told him, the policeman and social worker who visited, was whether Tano had ever run away before. No, Ama had told them, never. Was he happy at home, at school? Yes. She was frustrated. 'He wanted to go home. They took him away, they put him with strangers. He wanted to go home. It's obvious.'

She had been on the telephone much of the night and morning calling neighbours and friends, and though she was anxious, she was outwardly calm, except for the fingers of her left hand which opened and closed around her phone continually. The nurses were being kind to her, she told Attila, several of them were from home. They let her use her phone, even though you weren't really supposed to. She needed to get home. She stopped, raised her fingers to her closed mouth and turned her head to the window, the light and tears brightening her eyes. Attila sat on the bed and put his arm around her, and Ama pressed her forehead in his shoulder.

'Tano has his own keys, correct?' asked Attila.

Ama lifted her head, breathed deeply and nodded.

'I'll go,' Attila said.

The boy had been a pensive six-year-old when last Attila had seen him. Self-possessed, Attila thought. His mother had been the same, more so, she had been the only child Attila had ever met who did not believe in magic: Santa Claus and the tooth fairy she viewed with suspicion, she had been born with an innate capacity for critical thinking, or so it seemed. Years ago on a visit to her family home in Accra he had watched her, at the same age he had last seen her son, check each window of the house for entry points before returning to interrogate her mother about the size and aeronautic abilities of the tooth fairy. Achieving no success with her mother, she had turned on Attila: 'Uncle, do you believe in the tooth fairy?' And Attila had replied simply: 'I don't know. I only know that when I lost a tooth as a child and put it under my pillow, in the morning I found a coin.' Ama narrowed her eyes as she looked at him, scenting the play but not old enough quite yet to challenge it.

In that respect Tano was different from Ama, Tano believed in magic. Attila knew how to make a coin disappear and reappear, to appear to remove a thumb and replace it. The same tricks which had failed to impress his mother delighted Tano. Ama smiled at Attila whenever he performed for Tano. When the boy turned to his mother,

78

Ama would shake her head in mock amazement. Attila remembered, too, how from time to time the boy would break from play to run across the room and embrace his mother, before he returned to his game, as though the physical reminder of her was all he needed.

The radio in the taxi was tuned to a talk station and Attila gazed out of the window as the taxi wound its way through the narrow streets that enclosed the hospital building. In his hand he held the keys to his niece's apartment. Jean was on the radio, she was talking about foxes. Attila listened. It cheered him to hear her and he chuckled at her answers. Something in Jean reminded him of someone. Who was it? He thought about Maryse. Maryse, like all people who worked with sick children, had a voice that was measured, clear and patient – calming or infuriating if, say, you were trying to argue with her. Not that Attila had done that very often. Nothing on earth would tempt Maryse to pick a fight with a talk show host, as Jean was doing now. Maryse moved fluidly and, though she was not a small woman, had a certain daintiness, in the bend of her wrist and the way she held herself, the straightness of her back and the tilt of her chin. Maryse wore a white coat at work and a kaftan at home. Maryse loved both music and food.

'Pull over, please,' said Attila to the taxi driver. He stepped down from the cab and made his way through to the back of the building. There were two keys on the ring, one for the top and one for the bottom lock. He put the key in the top lock but it refused to turn. The same was true of the bottom lock. He bent to peer through the letterbox and as he did so the woman on the opposite side of the hall opened her door. She pointed with her chin: 'They changed the locks.'

'The landlord?'

She nodded once.

'Have you seen the boy?'

She shook her head.

'If you do.' Attila tore a piece of paper from his pocket book, wrote down his mobile phone number and handed it to her. The woman held it to her breast as she watched him walk away.

*

'Thank you.' Attila ordered a coffee and cake in the Lebanese café on the Old Kent Road where he had been with Emmanuel and sat down on one of the delicate chairs to speak to Ama who listened and after a short silence said: 'The landlord wanted to raise the rent, but I have a fixed tenancy. He can't unless I agree, which of course I didn't. He was talking about a thirty per cent hike.'

'So he accused you of being here illegally.'

At the other end of the phone Ama sighed. 'Landlords are supposed to ask for proof of right to reside. He probably just called whoever and said I had refused or failed to provide it.'

'Give me his name,' said Attila.

Next he called the lawyer, who listened and said: 'Let me be the one to deal with this.' He could feel the little man's energy crackle down the line. For a few minutes he sat and sipped his coffee, which was sweet and strong. He took a fork to the cake. He called Southwark social services. He called all the numbers on the list of names Ama had given him. She had called many of the people herself and the remaining numbers yielded no new information. Her son had not gone to stay with any of their friends. Attila finished the rest of his cake, paid, and left.

Bricklayers' Arms. He found Rosie in the residents' day room, sitting in the same chair and looking out of the window. As she turned to him she smiled slightly and Attila thought he saw the light in her eyes change. Maybe she recognised him. And because he had dared to hope he said nothing for fear of bringing disappointment down upon himself. He gazed out of the window at the lawn and the glossy, poisonous laurel. 'The robin was here this morning,' said Rosie.

'Shall we go out into the garden?' he asked suddenly. 'Go for a walk.' It occurred to Attila to wonder if Rosie had been outside at all since she had become a resident of Three Valleys. She hadn't been included in Emmanuel's escapade. Only those in wheelchairs. Attila stood up in front of Rosie and extended his hand, as though he were asking for a dance. Rosie looked up at him, raised her own hand and accepted. With a hand at her elbow he guided her as though onto a distant dance floor. None of the residents of the day room raised a head or watched them as they passed. Rosie and

Attila walked through the doors of frosted glass and onward down the corridor of hushed sounds. Rosie watched her feet in their corduroy slippers upon the tiles. At reception when Attila asked how to access the garden, the receptionist said: 'You want to go outside? Into the garden?'

'Yes,' replied Attila.

'You want me to call somebody to fetch her back to her room?'

'We'd like to go into the garden together – to take a walk.'

'I'll have to get permission.' The woman picked up the telephone and dialled, her eyes remained fixed on Attila.

'Oh, it's you,' said the centre director when she saw Attila. She looked at him levelly, she regarded him as a fellow professional. 'You want to go into the garden, is that right? I don't see why not.'

Rosie took the stairs slowly, placing one foot and then the other on each step, before reaching for the next. She held on to the banister and on to Attila. At the bottom of the flight she waited while Attila opened the door and then she stepped outside where she stopped while the door closed behind her, she lifted her face and turned it, first to the right and then to the left. She seemed to be adjusting to the sense of space. After a few moments she looked around, appearing to take in the garden, the hedge and lawn, the bench in the middle. She nodded slowly. Attila took his coat off and would have placed it around Rosie's shoulders, except that she began to feel for the sleeves and so he helped her into it.

'Where are the flowers?'

'It's winter. Can't you feel it?' They had almost completed a tour of the garden. He remembered a poem he had once known off by heart. '"All the names I know from nurse,"' he began out loud. '"Gardener's garter, shepherd's purse, bachelor's buttons, lady's smock ..."' He faltered and then found the final words: '"And the lady hollyhock."' He didn't know what came after that, so he repeated the verse. They completed one turn of the garden. Attila stopped and Rosie came to an obedient halt. She began to speak ever so softly. Attila bent his head: '"Fairy places, fairy things, fairy woods where the wild bee wings ..."' Attila listened and realised he had indeed once known more of the poem. He joined his voice to hers: '"Tiny trees for tiny dames – these must all be fairy names!"'

Attila looked up at the building's façade: in several of the windows an elderly person sat, caged behind glass. Attila had thought to go back inside, but Rosie turned to him. 'Shall we go again?' It was what she had often said, at the fairground on the carousel, at a dance in their student days, boating on the lake. Shall we go again? Attila did not know whether she meant the poem or the walk around the garden, so he embarked upon both.

Midday.

'I heard you on the radio,' Attila said to Jean.

'And what? You thought you'd call to remind me about it?'

Attila laughed: 'Where are you?'

'At home.'

'I'm on the Old Kent Road, come and have lunch with me.'

'I've just come back from a run. I need twenty minutes. Do you want me to throw something together here?'

'No,' said Attila, more quickly than he intended. 'Let me bring some food.' The turns of the morning weighed on him. As he headed south down the Old Kent Road he stopped in several shops and purchased persimmons, grapes, sugared almonds, stuffed vine leaves, baklava and two takeaway cartons of couscous with chicken and vegetables. In a supermarket he found a Lebanese wine, Chateau Kefraya, and bought that too. He arrived with his arms full.

'Lordy,' said Jean.

They ate and Jean talked about her trip to the radio station. 'The only reason I do it is because so-called outreach is part of my job description. I am supposed to be sensitising people to how we might manage urban foxes.'

Attila laughed. 'Do you know what a diplomat I once worked with told me? That in government they are taught to treat the electorate like six-year-olds. If you ask a member of the voting public a question on any subject most of us can only come up with three words we identify with that thing. The words depend on what our concerns are or what the papers tell us our concerns are, so if you asked what people associated with foxes, oh say, forty years ago, they might have said fur stoles, craftiness, *The Belstone Fox*.'

'The Belstone fox?'

'A children's book, very popular in the '70s around the time I was a student here for the reason that it had been turned into a film. The story was about an orphan fox cub raised with foxhounds that forms a particular bond with one of them. It was about fox hunting and friendship and ...' He hesitated.

'Inter-species relationships.'

'Thank you. It made a lot of people angry about fox hunting. The film's sympathies lay with the fox and therefore so did those of the audience. Now let's say you asked people which words they associated with foxes today, what would they answer?'

'Urban, disease, destruction.'

'True?'

'Not in my view.'

'But most people believe it because they read it in the papers and whatnot. The trick of politicians is to know what those three words are and appear to be addressing the concerns they raise, if only by making sure they repeat them often enough. The public likes to be indulged, and there are those happy to do so in the interest of their careers or ambitions,' said Attila. 'But you would not indulge the listeners of the radio show. You spoke plainly, it is your job as a scientist to deal with facts and it is also your nature. You treated the listeners like adults. It's hard not to feel frustrated when they don't respond in kind. The problem isn't with you. That's the good news. The bad news is you'll never get elected.' Attila smiled.

Jean began to tidy a few of the dishes on the table and he took those moments to study her, her bare feet and her hair caught in a ponytail. Her forthright manner in the interview and now, he liked it. He was used to the English, he understood their language of elision, you could say he was a native speaker, had been schooled in Ghana in a British-built establishment, where he had been taught by teachers from this country. Ghana had its own codes and customs. Attila understood more codes than most people. He had been trained for it. All those places where he had worked, full of secrets. Yet Attila had a reputation as a plain speaker and a fondness for the trait in others. He was struck in that moment by exactly who it was that Jean reminded him of. It was Rosie. Young Rosie with her tweed trousers and tasselled shoes and good whisky. Rosie who swore and smoked. Jean was speaking to him, he realised, asking him what he had been doing at Elephant and Castle. He told her about Ama and Tano.

'So the son still hasn't been found?'

'I'm told the authorities are handling it,' said Attila. 'I don't doubt that's true. But his mother is very anxious. I've been to the apartment to check, he's not there.'

'Where is it? The apartment?'

Attila told her.

Jean crossed the room and returned with the map she carried for work, reinforced with tape and marked with coloured pencils. She pushed the remainder of the dishes to one side and spread it across the table. 'Her apartment is here, yes?'

Attila leaned in and peered at the street name. 'Correct.'

'The boy, how old?'

'Ten.'

'Now hear me out, okay? Look at it as a place to start.'

'I'm listening,' said Attila.

'Once he had run away he'd head home obviously, all animals do, he'd head back to the den. But he can't get home because the locks to the apartment have been changed. He doesn't know his mother's in hospital, he thinks she's in some sort of trouble and so therefore is he, to his mind, so he's going to stay out of sight. That's what you've just told me.'

Attila nodded again.

'But he's going to stay close by and not just because of his mother. These' – and she indicated the markings on the map – 'are all fox territories. Foxes stake out an area and then they stay in it. Why? Because that's how they sustain themselves, they know where to hunt, where to find food, water, shelter, where they feel safe from predators. The boy is no different, he's going to stay where he feels most secure. I'm guessing an area roughly this size,' and she drew a loose circle around the X where she had marked the position of the flat, overlapping several fox territories and where the streets were so tightly drawn many of the street names were abbreviated. 'This is where we start.'

Chapter 6

High above the townhouses and the cathedral of Southwark, the buildings of Guy's and St Thomas's Hospital, high above London Bridge Station where the railway lines converge like electricity wires through a junction box, a peregrine falcon rode the air. On the thirty-second floor of the building known as the Shard, business-men, tourists and visitors from the provinces were enjoying early evening cocktails. Most of the clientele ignored the view across the city, having admired it quite sufficiently in the progression from lift doors to bar stool. Instead they watched the activities of the barman, the flick of his wrist as he held the cocktail shaker, the slow pouring of the liquid into glasses that were frosted, rimmed with salt, sugar or lime and once, thrillingly, dipped into a mixture of chocolate and chilli powder. From time to time the plop of an olive produced a pleasing end note. The drinkers watched the barman while they talked and reached for bar snacks, as though he were a television in the corner of the room.

At a table by a window a husband and wife sat in silence around the ruins of afternoon tea. They were white people who wore out-of-season tans. The husband sat with his eyes averted from the view for the reason that he had in recent years developed a touch of vertigo, of which he was only ever reminded in places such as this, also the Burj Khalifa in Dubai, the city in which they lived. Opposite him, his wife checked a list of items she wished to buy. London had once been home to them both, but had not been home for fifteen years. Every time they came back for a visit, they found the city had changed and changed again. They did not recognise it, they told their friends. The husband was born within the sound of Bow bells and therefore counted as a true Londoner, as he liked to tell people, as he had told the barman when they first came in and he had ordered a Johnny Walker Blue Label (for which he had developed a familiarity if not fondness in Dubai). The barman had been born in São Paulo, he worked five shifts a week here and two at a hotel in the Aldwych. He smiled at the Englishman and said: 'Welcome home, sir.'

To the young girl standing with her back to them and her nose pressed against the glass everything about the city was new. Right now she was watching a bird. To the child the bird looked like a sky diver, falling through the air with outstretched arms: wings spread, beak down, feet angled backwards, its feathered body shivered and shook against the wind, flight feathers rippled. Once or twice a wing dipped as if the bird was a tightrope walker who had momentarily lost and regained balance, now the bird was lifted on a thermal and set back again seconds later. The child blinked and watched. She did not try to tell her parents. She stood as still as the hovering bird.

Then the bird was gone. The girl started. She looked this way and that and then up and down. Gone.

'All right, darling?' asked her mother.

'Yes,' replied the child. 'Can I have a falcon when we get home?'

'We'll see,' replied her mother.

Six hundred feet below a pigeon departed the world. The pigeon, which had been pecking at the discarded crust of a pasty from the West Cornwall Pasty Company booth by platform six in the station, was flying away with a piece of pastry in its beak when it was hit at two hundred miles an hour by the falcon and promptly fell to earth to be snatched back up in the raptor's claws a split second later.

The falcon carried the pigeon eastwards, parallel to the riverbank, over the city's municipal buildings in the direction of Tower Bridge, where it turned south. Somewhere in this first twenty seconds of flight the heart of the pigeon stopped beating. A drop of dark blood fell to earth from the pigeon's breast, down it went, the drop of liquid pushed into new shapes by the rush of air. The falcon flew until it arrived at the abandoned gasworks on the Old Kent Road where it perched on a metal strut and with its beak tore open the pigeon's heart.

Attila looked down. A drop hit the pavement. He tilted his face to the sky but he felt nothing, no heaviness in the air or sudden darkening or other presentiment of a shower on its way.

'We've covered that section.' Jean had divided the map into workable areas, areas they could cover on foot, she had numbered them, like postcodes, in a radial pattern from the centre. They had started at the outside and worked their way inwards, had now walked four in total, putting leaflets (drafted and printed in haste at Jean's flat) with the boy's face on them through letterboxes and tacking the same leaflets onto trees and telegraph poles. They had entered a dozen or more shops and spoken to the shopkeepers. So far nobody had seen the boy. Though one or two claimed to recognise him from the locality, they said they had not seen him recently. The photograph had been sent by Ama to Jean's phone and from there Jean had texted it directly to her network of street-sweepers. Attila appreciated her willingness to help him, was impressed by her mastery of her phone. He tried hard to imagine or perhaps to remember himself at the age of ten. What might he do? Where might he go? Would he be frightened? He seemed to remember a sense of fearlessness as a child, for lacking the knowledge of death, he supposed, for still believing bad things happened only to other people. How long you held on to that particular belief depended on where you were born.

Now as they walked together down a darkening street Jean asked: 'Did you ever run away from home?'

'No,' said Attila.

'You were that happy?'

'Yes, but anyway the market women would have reported me to my mother and she would have beaten me. What about you?'

'Sure. I used to want to run away and live among the bears. I thought I was born into the wrong family. My mother didn't read books, she read shopping catalogues.' When Attila didn't answer she continued: 'We lived like we were in front of an audience.

Whenever we sat down to eat there'd be all this talk about what we were eating. My that *is* good? Did you really make this with Jell-O? Is that sherry I taste?' Jean remembered how mealtimes were filled with the talk of food such that there was no time for any other discussion, and had concluded some years after leaving home that it had been a deliberate, if unconscious, effort to avoid ever having to talk about anything in their lives.

Maybe it was the time, thought Jean. Her mother and father were richer than their parents: happiness had been achieved. Did people really feel that? Maybe it was the post-war euphoria of victory. She remembered how as a family they used to visit neighbours to see their latest purchase and they, likewise, would invite people around to view what they had bought. Lincoln Continental. Twin-tub washing machine. Kelvinator ice box. A sideboard-sized record player. Colour TV. She related this to Attila. How each purchase was treated like the arrival of a new baby and was christened accordingly: a ride in the car, a spin of a record, cold drinks from the new fridge, one with a clever dispenser, or they might be allowed to watch an episode of *Dragnet* or *Car 54* on the new TV.

Lately when she thought about it, she had come to see her father's quietude less as collusion than a kind of silent protest. He retreated into the den with his Pete Seeger albums and encouraged Jean to run. It was he, not her mother, who fetched her a glass of iced tea from the pitcher in the fridge when she came back sweaty from team practice, who pretended not to notice her mother's little disappointed smiles, allowing Jean to do the same. Her father, Jean saw later, had been a gentle nonconformist. He didn't rock the boat, he lay on the deck and dreamed at the stars. He found his escape inwards, she had found hers in the outdoors. As a child she was drawn to the wooded places around their suburban home, the small regional park with the creek that ran through it. The outdoors for Jean began as a refuge from the boredom of home and transformed into a passion.

'In Accra,' Attila was saying, 'there are photographic studios where you can have your picture taken against any backdrop you like, for example at the airport with a plane behind you, or in a new kitchen, or a car, or in some big man's office with a large desk and swivel leather chair. These are painted canvas backdrops, you understand, like theatre sets. Other photographers keep boxes of props, hats and clothes, wigs, briefcases, handbags and suchlike, so people can enact their dreams. Such places are extremely popular.'

'My mother would have loved that,' said Jean.

The walls of the alley were low enough to allow Attila a view into the backs of the houses. A woman with her hair in a turban sat on a black leather sofa cutting her toenails. A line of underwear dried on a radiator. In a kitchen a man lay on his back in a single bed. A radio played filling the silence with the hectoring rant of a preacher. A woman's voice cried: 'Amen!'

'My grandfather was Turkish,' said Jean. 'He went to America from Turkey when he was a young man and got a job in the tanneries and then the railroad. He went alone, most of them did. They lived together in dormitories and never learned English. When Atatürk took over he wanted all the men to come back and work for the new republic so he sent ships to get them. That was some time in the 1920s or 1930s. Most of the Turks went home. My grandfather didn't go with them, he'd met my grandmother and he stayed to marry her, changed his name from Turan to Turane.' Jean had inherited her father and grandfather's looks, the aquiline nose and dark eyes and eyebrows, and had her hair not turned to silver when she was in her twenties, the same dark hair.

Jean stopped and tacked a picture of the boy to the smooth bark of a tree. Tano. He had long eyebrows that sloped down towards his cheekbones and which lent a touch of sadness to his smile, he was dressed – for church or a wedding – in a white collared shirt and a clip-on bow tie. The boy had never been apart from his mother or known any other home. All children wanted was certainty, not just children – Attila had seen people stay on in their homes, refuse to leave even when shellfire fell more regularly than rain. While some people easily sought new destinies in distant lands, Attila had met people who walked hundreds of miles to return to the place where their hut had once stood. For him it was not the same. Homesickness was an adjustment disorder, that was the long and short of it. Attila lived half the year on aeroplanes and in hotels.

When he was at home he enjoyed the routines of domestic life, the comfort of the familiar and the absence of the requirement to think. After a while he grew restless. When he was not at home he did not seem to miss it. He had analysed this in himself, the absence of longing for place, and come to no real conclusion. He missed Maryse. At times the thought of her, alighting upon him suddenly when he was busy with something else, left him as winded as a punch to the stomach.

They walked an hour more and covered each of the sections Jean had outlined on the map. Then they carried on walking, in the way that people do when each person is being guided by the steps of the other. They did not discuss which direction to take, they walked until they reached Southwark Cathedral and the banks of the Thames and there began to follow the river upstream towards Waterloo Bridge. The steps leading down to the river disappeared into the dark waters of the high tide. Barges were moored in mid-stream. A tour boat drifted by, the passengers ate an early dinner and gazed implacably at the riverbank. Commuter hour, the foot traffic grew dense. People overtook them and shouldered past them. There were joggers with backpacks, running as though fleeing the scene of a disaster. From time to time somebody would walk between them.

Jean had spent the remainder of the morning after her radio interview sitting with her sketchpad and coloured pencils spread out on the table, designing the terrace garden of the woman in the apartment in City Road. Of the whole process there were certain moments she loved more than others. The imagining was one; she sketched four planting plans in the colours she foresaw for each of the seasons. She'd had to learn new plants here, adjust for the overlapping seasons and an uncertain summer. Afterwards, running in Nunhead Cemetery, she had seen the first snowdrops, had left the main path to run the narrower trails through the woods where she found graves adorned with thousands of the small white buds, heads bowed in constant sorrow.

They stopped for Attila to tie a shoelace. On a carved wooden bench by the river path were written the words: 'The Thames will carry her sons for ever. Bruno. Conrad. Max. 1991–2011.' Jean stared out over the river. Working outdoors in winter she had learned an early respect for the dangers of water. In the river a child would survive less than a few minutes, dragged down by underwater currents in the freezing water. The body might never be found or not found for weeks.

On a stretch of wasteland between the theatre and the bridge, Jean caught the movement of a fox, the same large male fox she had seen on Sunday evening when she had run onto the bridge and collided with Attila. The fox moved unhurriedly towards the far edge of the patch of scrub where it leapt over a pile of builders' scrap and headed towards the bridge. Now it picked up speed as it ran up the stairs. Jean followed at a trot. As before the fox headed north. It weaved unhesitatingly through the throng of people, even timed its crossing from one side of the bridge to the other for when the changing traffic lights caused a pause in the traffic. Jean ran behind. Attila followed at the best pace he could.

The fox reached the far side of the bridge and turned left into the bright lights of the Strand and then left again down a narrow side street. It was quieter here and Jean saw a row of iron railings behind which there was a small churchyard, gravestones, and what appeared to be an old stone chapel. The fox disappeared around the next bend. Ahead of Jean framed by pairs of double yellow lines the road led under a bridge that joined two buildings. Lights. Distant sounds. The stench of garbage. A wire trolley stood parked outside a service exit. Wheeled bins and laundry carts. Two men stood smoking. They appeared identically dressed in tight black pants and striped jackets. The props and actors of the service industry, this must be the back of a hotel. She was walking now, searching for the fox which had vanished. Down the next turning she saw it and followed. Here there were cobblestones and on one side the stone wall of the chapel building, on the other a red-brick building with a pair of arched doorways above one of which hung a light shaped like an old-fashioned carriage lamp. On the edge of the circle of light the fox sat down.

On a step a man sat. He wore splash-stained rubber clogs and the checked pants of a kitchen worker, he was smoking a cigarette.

After a moment he crushed the stub beneath the sole of a rubber clog, reached into a plastic bag by his side and threw something to the fox, which crept forward, belly to the ground. As it entered the bright ring of light Jean realised she did not recognise it as one of hers. She had thought it might be Rocky but now she saw that though this fox displayed similar markings it was much younger. The fox retreated with a scrap of food in its mouth.

Jean found Attila waiting at the end of the street. Together they walked into the underpass. A black man wearing long rubber gloves and pushing a bin of slops stopped and watched them in silence as they approached. Attila nodded at the man and the man gave a slow nod back and after they had passed Jean heard the sound of metal wheels on asphalt once again. Partway into the underpass they turned into a dimly lit passage (Attila seemed to know where he was going), climbed a short flight of stairs that led into a side street crowded with ventilation shafts and fire escapes. A moment later they were back on the Strand.

'I thought it was one of the foxes in my study and I wondered what it was doing so far from its territory. Usually they only cross territories if they have been ousted or are looking for a new mate. But that wasn't it at all. This fox is being fed by ...' She looked past Attila at the horseshoe driveway, the doormen in their yellow and black livery. 'What is this place?'

'The Savoy Hotel,' replied Attila.

The American Bar, the Savoy Hotel. Attila was telling Jean about the refurbishment of the building which had taken months and cost millions. In her leggings and boots Jean felt underdressed.

'Don't worry,' said Attila as if he had read her thoughts.

Jean, who had never been inside a place like this before, found it remarkable that this man, a black man no less, seemed so at ease in the world.

'I thought you might like it here, that you might feel at home.' Attila smiled. He was making a joke, Jean realised. 'But if you're uncomfortable we can go.'

'I'm fine.'

'Have a whisky sour.'

'Okay,' said Jean with minimal grace.

'I wanted to say thank you for your help today.'

Jean eased up on him, she smiled: 'We will find him.' They raised their glasses as one, but for some reason neither spoke the boy's name. 'Do you have children?'

'No,' said Attila.

'I'm sorry,' said Jean automatically and wondered why she had done that, why people offered condolences to people without children. The spectre of barrenness? Or mortality?

'We were happy.' Attila spoke in the past tense, Jean noticed. She waited for him to say more, but he said nothing and instead took a second sip of his drink. Then: 'Do you like this music?'

Jean tilted her head and listened to the piece the pianist was playing. She could identify it only as jazz. Attila tapped his finger on the bar. His expression was reflective, eyelids half lowered.

Jean might have stopped herself but she failed, she was curious about this man: 'Is your wife in Accra?'

Attila opened his eyes. He looked at Jean. 'My wife is dead,' he said.

And for the second time Jean said: 'I'm sorry.'

When Attila arrived back in his hotel room he found a light flashing on the telephone. A message was waiting for him from the centre director of Three Valleys. Attila called her back.

'It's Rosie,' said the centre director. 'She became very distressed earlier on this evening. She kept asking for you, but we couldn't reach you.'

'How is she now?'

'One of the staff had the presence of mind to call Emmanuel and he was able to come. They checked with me first. I said it was fine. She calmed down almost immediately. Thank goodness. They had even considered sedating her.' She paused. 'It was good of him,' she said. 'Very good of him indeed. He's gone home now. We'll cover his time and expenses, naturally.'

'Thank you,' said Attila. 'Do you want me to come over?'

'She's sleeping. You know,' and here the centre director paused. 'Rosie isn't really the same demographic as the majority of our residents. Most of them require relatively little in terms of mental stimulation. Perhaps we should talk about whether this is the best place for her.'

Downstairs in the lobby Attila asked the receptionist to help him add credit to his phone and then called Emmanuel. In search of an improved signal he went to stand outside on the pavement. When he had finished the call he put the telephone in his pocket and stood in thought.

'You okay, boss?' It was the doorman, he stood with his peaked hat pulled down low and his chin tucked into the collar of his greatcoat.

'I'm okay,' said Attila. 'It has been a long day. How are you?'

'If you're okay, I'm okay,' replied the doorman.

Since it was this man who had put him in touch with the lawyer and the lawyer was proving useful, Attila told him about the boy. He mentioned Jean's notion of texting a picture of the boy around the street-sweepers of Southwark.

'Let me do the same for you,' said the doorman. 'The doormen and security people, they are my friends. Most of those boys who work in security are Nigerian. We Ghanaians, we prefer the hospitality industry. Many of the doormen at these hotels you see around here are our countrymen. The street-sweepers, the traffic wardens are mainly boys from Sierra Leone, they came here after their war so for them the work is okay. Some Nigerians do warden work when they first get here, before their friends in the security business find them something with greater job satisfaction and a seat inside.' The man chuckled and tucked his chin back inside his coat. Attila laughed too. He found the picture of the boy on his phone and the doorman did the rest. Attila thanked him. The doorman nodded by tilting his head to one side as if to say think nothing of it. What he actually said was: 'He could be my son.'

Jean walked home through the streets they had searched just hours before, passing the flyers of the boy's face as she went. One already fluttered loose. Jean stopped and pressed a pin in a corner. She returned home after two more hours and a mostly luckless night. Of her study group she had only spotted Redbone. She couldn't stop thinking about the boy, had found it impossible to wait for the appearance of a fox for imagining that he might be somewhere nearby. Now she passed men pissing in the side streets, the rising steam lit by the headlights of passing cars, dark tracks running across the sidewalks, the men did not bother to zip themselves as she passed. On a sidewalk five hundred yards from a pub with a George Cross over the door a man stood talking on his cellphone, his legs either side of another man convulsing on the ground. When she reached home she headed for the kitchen and boiled the kettle for a cup of herbal tea and while it brewed she flipped open her computer and checked for messages. No email from Luke. She counted the weeks since she had spoken to her son and realised it had been two months. There had been messages and mail containing jokes, the last of which had been two crows perched on the back of a park bench, the strapline: 'Attempted murder'. That had amused Jean a lot. Yet, somehow they had both avoided the exposure of a telephone call, the lagged pauses and occasional echoes, the sounds of satellites realigning, as Jean thought of it, serving to underscore the hesitations. The hissed rebuke of static on the line whenever words failed.

Up on the roof she warmed her hands on the sides of her mug. To her right the vast black pit of the empty gasworks, to her left the City sculpted in lights. Above her the lights of not one but three planes traversed the sky. In the distance the sound of a circling helicopter ebbed and rose. Out there, Jean thought, a child is trying to find his mother.

She thought about Tano and she thought about her client up in the sky-rise apartment she never left, yearning no doubt to be free of its walls, to dare to be outside in the city in the damp and the darkness.

There came the sound, like a baby's cry, only this was the cry of no ordinary baby, but the soul-curdling shriek of a devil child. Less than a minute later the cry came again, and again, each time with mounting intensity. But there was no banging of windows, no shouts, or sirens, the sound was of no interest to the city dwellers. It was the mating call of a vixen. Light Bright had begun the search for her mate.

*

Three miles distant a dog fox crossed Waterloo Bridge. In its jaws it carried the bone of a Berkshire pork chop, the remainder of which rested, along with a side order of sautéed mushrooms, the Dorset crab starter and a quantity of decent claret, in the belly of a fund manager now headed due west in the back of a cab. The fox climbed the stairs to the open terraces of the National Theatre until it reached the third level where it jumped onto one of the raised flower beds, sniffed at the earth and dug a shallow hole into which it dropped the bone. Afterwards the fox trotted down the stairs back to the ground level and skirted the side of the building. Briefly it stopped in the shadows to watch a pair of security guards pass and then ran onto the ramp down to the basement car park. Some years before workmen had removed the front panel of an access shaft and never replaced it. The dog fox lowered its head and slunk inside, turned around in the space several times before coiling its body and dropping down to the floor. For a few moments it stayed watchful, ears pricked and eyes open, and then, reassured that all was well, the fox went to sleep.

Chapter 7

To be alone, if she were honest, was Jean's preferred state, to be alone in emptiness. Out in the field she liked to wake up in the night to the black hush. In the white noise of the city she missed that silence. But the city was an easy place to be alone, easier than a small town with the constant sociability. Jean liked her own company. Sometimes Jean even thought that she would have been happy to remain a spinster her entire life, but for the sex. It was sex that had propelled Jean into a marriage and motherhood. Nature's way and nothing to be done about it. She envied a creature like Light Bright, who carved out her own territory and built herself a den and only then searched for a mate. There were those pairs (domestic dogs, for example) where the male abandoned the female as soon as the act of coitus was over, but most other canids behaved differently. Male wolves, coyotes, foxes all stayed to a greater or lesser degree to raise their pups. Coyotes most of all. In between litters of pups the mating couple made other arrangements. Sometimes they stayed together and hunted side by side, other times they returned to their own territories and paired up again the next year. Sometimes one or both were killed.

Jean wondered how it might be to go out into the night and howl for sex. The clarity of purpose was appealing. No games. The vixen said: 'I want it. Who's got it?' The male foxes put themselves forward. The vixen chose.

Jean's first relationship in London had been with a fellow American she had been put in touch with by a friend back home.

97

There had been some obfuscation about the nature of the first meeting and Jean wasn't sure if it was meant to be a date. She had arrived at the restaurant early and casually dressed. Jean possessed a kind of reflexive habit begun in high school and never quite lost of playing a game that in more modest times had been called 'kiss or die', but now was called something else. This was not a habit Jean much admired in herself. Alone in a crowd, she would look at the men around her: 'Die, die, die.' She condemned three men at a table nearby as she waited to be seated. 'Die.' A man reading texts at the bar went down. The maître d' survived as did the waiter who showed her to the table. As did her date. A Romanian, who had emigrated to the US at the age of twenty, a former truck driver who now owned a haulage company. He had a bad back which was the reason he had given up driving and the reason, too, that he eased himself into a standing position every so often during dinner and addressed Jean from a height. Jean wondered if she should stand up as well, but the two of them standing by their table brought the waiter hurrying over. So Jean sat and the Romanian stood and thus they conducted their date. He made her laugh. A few days later she went to bed with him and had gentle, tentative (the back) sex. When he moaned Jean could not tell at first whether it was in pleasure or pain. The sex was good. Jean had wondered if it would be difficult to be with another man after all her years with Ray, but it was not. His body, though, was not how she imagined it: beyond Ray she had no experience of the bodies of men in late middle age. The hair. The heft. He wanted her to spend the night, she needed to get to work. His palpable disappointment fed into the rest of the relationship, which ended after three more afternoons of slow sex.

Jean's second relationship was with a client. It began on the finished roof garden. They met regularly and infrequently, had lunch or dinner followed by sex. Sex with Hans felt like a performance, Jean the unsuspecting audience member hauled onto the stage. Sometimes she imagined Hans might have hidden cameras in his bedroom. Hans was younger, a cyclist. Sex with him left Jean sated. Hans was like a book you enjoy, put down partway through and never feel compelled to finish. She was fond of Hans the times he was there. In his absence she missed him not at all. She was both sorry and glad when he mailed to tell her he had fallen for a triathlete.

Attila she had bumped into on a bridge and knew next to nothing about. She admired his air of assurance and his unexpected laugh. She had imagined him a married man and had forced herself to check her own imaginings. Did his being a widower make it any easier? He seemed shadowed by an invisible presence, it was in the way he moved through the city, imbibing its pleasures as though he were on a trip with a loved one rather than a man alone. But in the end we are mere mammals, thought Jean. A coyote or a fox died or was killed, the mate waited. After a time the waiting came to an end.

A skin of ice covered the puddles in Nunhead Cemetery, the wind whipped up whorls of damp leaves. The cold had emptied the graveyard of people. A rat hopped across the path in front of Jean and leapt into a hole beneath the ledger stone of a grave. A scattering of crows eddied in the air above the ruined chapel. At the midway point in her run, at the brow of the hill, Jean jogged on the spot before the view of St Paul's. The sky above the city was streaked a sulphurous yellow. Nine o'clock in the morning and it felt as though the light would never break through. Jean turned and began down the hill.

At the intersection of the main avenues, just beyond one of two areas in the graveyard where the ground remained consecrated and burials still took place, a small crowd of people had gathered. They stood with their heads turned upwards, not to the sky, but to the upper branches of the parakeets' tree where a man stood at the top of a tall ladder. Above a murmur of disapproval there were occasional yells and accompanying gestures, on the outskirts of the group a young man spoke angrily into his cellphone. Two of the keepers watched with the detached air of off-duty policemen. Jean recognised a few people she saw regularly in the cemetery: a woman who wore an Australian cattleman's hat and who stood holding the leads of six dogs of different breeds and sizes, and the man with the bad limp who walked in the company of a small collarless mongrel. There was a man with long brown hair Jean had often seen walking quickly through the cemetery as though on his way somewhere else. She recognised another runner, a tall, lean man who ran with a jerky, upright stride.

The man at the top of the ladder wore a hard hat and an industrial dust mask. He had his arm up to the elbow in one of the hollows of the tree. Jean knew what he was doing. He was addling the eggs, removing newly laid eggs from the birds' nests, rubbing them with corn oil and replacing them. The birds would sit on them through the spring but the eggs would never hatch. Jean had addled eggs in the past as part of her job, in places where populations of Canada geese had got out of control. Their droppings contaminated water and the birds could be aggressive. But why oil the eggs of the parakeets?

'They've had complaints, so they say,' said a woman in a green oilskin. 'Noise. Damage.'

'Damage to what?' Jean asked.

'I don't know.' The woman shrugged.

'Who sent you?' somebody shouted from the crowd. The addler didn't answer, he replaced an oiled egg in its nest.

'The council?' shouted somebody else. 'I'm on the phone to them right now.'

'DEFRA,' said a third person, with an air of knowledge. The Department for Environment, Food and Rural Affairs, which oversaw many wildlife matters.

A number of adult birds perched on the branches of a nearby tree and watched the desecration of their nests. One or two wheeled and fluttered around the egg addler who continued his work slowly and methodically, as if nobody else was there, the only tell being that he never looked in the direction of the crowd or wiped his nose or scratched or took a call on his cell, or any of the things people naturally did. After a few minutes more protesters showed up. They formed a circle around the tree and the egg addler and began to chant: 'Hey ho! Away you go!'

Jean waited and watched. On the East Coast the birds nested at the top of telegraph poles and the authorities were forever sending men to climb the poles and clear the nests. There were protests there, too. The birds divided people. To some they were destructive invaders, to others they were exotic beauties. Jean thought they were an example of nature's immeasurable adaptability. Animals adjusted to survive, some were especially successful, despite the efforts of man. Around the London parakeets myths swirled, the first of which went like this: in 1978 during the filming of the James Bond movie *Moonraker*, Pinewood Studios was transformed into an aviary built to accommodate thousands of birds, the plan being to create a rainforest for the film's jungle scenes. The aviary was planted with trees and vegetation, water sprinklers fitted to the ceiling kept the plants moist and could create the effect of a rainstorm in seconds. Toucans, parrots, macaws, hookbills, egrets and flamingos were shipped by the boxload from nearby zoos. And of course, green Argentinian parakeets. One day a workman accidentally failed to secure the massive studio doors. Thousands of birds flew away into the London skies. The paradise birds perished with the onset of cold weather, but the green parakeets, for whatever reason, made it through that winter, and the next and the next.

Jean might have given the story some credence but for the fact that exactly the same story was told about the parakeets in different parts of the States, the difference being that the parakeets there all made their escape from Petco.

The second story had it that the parakeets were escaped pets. Having flown their cages they banded together in the green spaces of the city to form colonies of the free. Every month or so they were joined by new arrivals. There could be truth in this story. Once Jean had come across a young woman talking to the man with the limp and the little bitch at the cemetery gate. The young woman had been told of a tree where the parakeets nested, and was looking for it. Jean offered to lead her there. On their way the young woman explained that her elderly father's pet parakeet had flown away that day. The bird was often let out of its cage to fly about the room, her father would sit in his chair and hold a mirror, the bird responded to the mirror's light and would come and settle on his person, regard its own reflection in the glass. That week the father was in hospital and the woman and her mother were left to look after the parakeet. Her mother had opened the cage to let the bird fly around the room but failed to spot an open window. For several minutes the bird sat on the sill and stared into the open, seemingly deciding the course of its life, ignored their efforts to draw it back inside and eventually took to the air. Somebody had told her about the free parakeets, she had come to see if her father's bird was among them. She showed Jean a mirror she had brought with her in the hopes of luring back the absconding pet.

The young man who had been on the phone now walked through the crowd gathering names, email addresses, telephone numbers. 'In case we need to call on you.' Jean gave him hers, she watched for a little time longer and then she moved on. Behind her the protesters chanted: 'What do we want? Justice! When do we want it? Now!'

Attila had asked Emmanuel to meet him at the hotel, he had a proposal for the young man. He found Emmanuel outside talking to the doorman. Attila ushered him in with a hand on his shoulder. In the lobby he ordered coffees and after they had arrived and when the performance of milk and sugar was done (Emmanuel took plenty of both) Attila said: 'The centre director has agreed to let you visit Rosie, as a friend.'

Emmanuel smiled and bowed his head. 'Here.' Attila handed the young man a paper bag inside which was *A Child's Garden of Verses* by Robert Louis Stevenson. He had searched high and low for a bookshop to buy it. 'Try reading her those, I think she'll like it.' He leaned forward. 'What are your plans, Emmanuel?'

Emmanuel shook his head. 'I have work. The agency has found me some jobs. Nothing permanent.' Emmanuel had been assigned to care teams who went into private homes twice a day. 'You don't know them, they don't know you. You take them to the toilet. You wipe them. You take off their clothes and wash their bodies.' Emmanuel shook his head again. 'It's shameful.'

Attila said: 'I have an idea and I want to talk to you about it. What if you lived with Rosie? I take her out of Three Valleys, find you both a suitable apartment. You can have your own room and look after Rosie. How would that work for you?'

Emmanuel nodded, as if to say go on.

'We'll get some support services in place, respite care, say, for the afternoons and some of the evenings, so you have some time to yourself.'

'Maybe I can help with that,' said Emmanuel. 'My colleagues at the agency ... I know some would be very grateful to have something regular.'

'Good. You look into it. I need to work a few things out at my end, the practicalities, what benefits Rosie's eligible for and so on. But if we can make it happen what would you say to the idea in principle?'

Back in his room Attila made a series of calls. No news of the boy. The name of Ama's landlord he passed to the lawyer, who called back later to tell him the property had been sold six months previously. The lawyer located the new owners through a records search. He'd send them a wrongful-eviction notice and have an injunction before the court in the next seven days. Attila asked if anything could be done to speed the process. 'I'm a lawyer, not a miracle worker.' The lawyer gave a muffled laugh.

When he had finished making calls Attila sat on the edge of the bed. He pinched the bridge of his nose between his thumb and forefinger. He reached over for the MP3 player on the nightstand and chose a track. He lay back on the bed and put his arms behind his head. A Congolese rumba. Attila smelled rain and wet earth, smoke, sweat, bougainvillea and beer. He saw lights revolving on a wooden dance floor, women in long, tight print dresses, their hair piled on top of their heads. Men in high-waisted flared trousers. He saw men dance with women and men dance with men, women dance with women. He heaved himself up from the bed and began to shuffle his feet, swaying his hips and moving his shoulders, clicking his fingers. He danced with his eyes closed and his head back.

When the tune was over he remained standing at the window. He thought about the boy and what should be done next. In his work the world over he had witnessed the search for missing persons. Sometimes, when the search teams knew they were looking for a body, they travelled with forensics experts to sites where the discovery of a corpse had been reported. In places such as those people tended to disappear one at a time. At times of fighting, when people were separated from their families and their homes by the tens of thousands, teams from the Red Cross set up tents, interviewed people, asking them the same carefully formulated questions, prised creased photographs of loved ones from their fingers. The information was entered into a computer and matched against the answers of other people across the country, across several different countries sometimes. Attila looked out of the window and considered what he had. He had a city of eight million people, he had a lost boy and he had a team of doormen and dustmen.

'Can you see me?'

'Not yet,' Luke said leaning forward and looking into the camera eye so that his face loomed large on Jean's monitor.

'Never mind,' she said. 'Let's just talk.'

'There should be an icon with a video camera, look for it.'

Jean looked and found it.

'Okay, click on it.' They both waited. Presto! Jean's face appeared in miniature on a screen in the bottom right-hand corner of her monitor.

'Hi,' she said. A second later the little screen went black.

'Looks like your camera crashed.'

On the larger screen she could still see him, her heavily pixelated son. He was wearing a bathrobe, his unmade bed behind him. Jean felt as if she were looking through a one-way mirror. She realised she really knew very little about his life. There could have been a lover who until very recently had lain in that bed and had now gone to shower or to make coffee while Luke talked to his mother. 'Try again,' Luke said.

Jean obliged, double clicking on the video icon. 'There we go! How are you?'

'I'm good. I can hardly hear you. Let me try the volume.'

Holy smoke, thought Jean, and all this was supposed to make life easier. 'One, two, three, four, five … Can you hear me now?'

'Much better.'

'So how are you?' she began again.

'I'm good. You sound different. Are you talking with an English accent now?'

'I don't think so.'

'How's it going?'

She began to tell him about the progress of the fox project. After a while she saw he was no longer looking at the screen, but at something in his hand. He was texting. She stopped talking. 'Awesome,' he said. He looked up and smiled briefly. 'Go on. I'm listening.'

'You're doing something else.'

'Texting the office. I can listen and text.'

Jean pressed on. She felt the way she did talking to the radio host who had shuffled scripts on his desk while she spoke. When she finished there was a pause and Luke said: 'That's cool, Jean.' And Jean remembered how, when Luke was a child, he would tell her a story, share some detail of his school day, and if Jean failed to answer or answered distractedly, she would turn in the silence that followed to find tears on his lashes. 'You're not listening!' A voice full of hurt and accusation. She would urge him to begin his story again, so she could pay proper attention. And, with the unselfconsciousness of children, Luke would begin at the beginning, as excitedly as he had the first time. Three months ago Jean had invited Luke to London for Thanksgiving, a month later for Christmas. 'I'm going to Pops',' he'd said at Thanksgiving. Jean hadn't minded, Thanksgiving meant nothing in Britain anyway. When Luke declined her invitation to Christmas she minded more. And how come Ray was still Pops, but she had become Jean? Her son treated her like an equal, or perhaps the kind of old schoolfriend you have outgrown, but to whom you remain bound by a shared history and a sense of loyalty. Since the divorce the landscape of their relationship had changed, so slowly she had not even been aware of it, like a tide coming in, so that when finally she looked up she saw Ray and Luke were on one part of the beach and she was on another, and in between, a stretch of water she couldn't quite work out how to cross. Now Ray was the one to whom Luke told his stories. As for Jean and Luke, what had seemed to come easily now required work: they no longer knew how to behave around each other.

Luke was speaking, this time it was Jean caught not listening.

'Can you say that again? The sound dropped out,' she lied.

'Forget it. It's not important. I have to go. I'll catch you later.'

They said their goodbyes. A few seconds later came the signifier of the finished call, a sound like the air being sucked out of a small space.

Jean sat at the table for a minute then started to call Ray. She tapped his number, her old number, out on the computer. Partway through she forgot what came next. She recited the number from the start, it sounded strange to her ear, the way a familiar word upon too close examination can suddenly appear misspelt. Jean couldn't check the number because she had no note of what she had held in her head for three decades. She began again and tried not to think about it and this time her fingers automatically completed what her brain could not.

'Hey you,' she said when Ray picked up.

'He-ey,' he said softly. 'How are you? What's up?'

'Nothing, I just called to say hi.'

'Well, hi.' There was a moment's silence. Then Ray said: 'You sure everything's okay?'

'I'm sure. I just . . .' She wanted to talk about Luke, but she wasn't sure exactly what it was she wanted to say, the thoughts were too fluid. She wanted to ask Ray if he remembered the time Luke had climbed onto the roof of the sun room, somehow reached by way of the branch of a tree he'd been climbing. He'd called down to her where she stood in the garden. Look at me! Look at me! Jean had urged him to stay still, terrified into absolute calm, her voice low, while Ray went to fetch a ladder. She had watched as Ray crawled over the tiles towards Luke, positioning herself where, if the worst happened, she imagined she might at least break Luke's fall. Or the awful time they discovered Luke was allergic to wasp stings, the rush to the hospital. Ray's patient and persistent removal of the wasps that tried to build their nest in the attic space every year. The steady bump of childhood mishaps.

'Jeannie?' What only he ever called her.

'It's all good,' she said finally. 'How are things going with you?' Ray talked about the business, which was doing okay given the economic climate. He had finished restoring a 1950 Chrysler Town

& Country and a Chevy Bel Air. He was taking them to a show in North Adams at the weekend.

'You want to guess what I saw on South Street the other day?'

Jean waited. A typical way for Ray to make conversation was to recite news items he had heard, regardless of whether Jean said she had heard it too. He liked to ask her questions about her day and what she had done. He liked facts, he did not like opinions and did not venture them himself, he preferred to talk about places rather than people, objects rather than ideas. Where and what and not why. He spoke about what he had seen or done, not what he had thought or felt. It was part of his nature. Opinions, people, ideas: these harboured the potential for conflict. Ray's great gift was conflict avoidance and that was what gave him his reputation as a good-natured guy. The people who thought this about him weren't wrong, he was a great guy, it was simply that the foundations of his personality were built not so much upon cheerfulness, as upon an entrenched unease around disagreement. He was a peacemaker. Ray had been the filament that bound Jean and Luke together.

'A coyote,' said Ray. That surprised Jean who had been expecting him to say: 'A 1957 Ford Thunderbird, right there on South Street, what d'ya know.' 'As I was locking up. Not in the least bothered by me, no sir! Heading toward Main Street. He slipped away before I could get close enough to see ... you know ... if ... He had a very thick coat, it could have been there underneath all that fur.'

Ray meant he couldn't see if the coyote was wearing a radio collar, which would have made it one of the Greenhampton study coyotes, the final project in which Jean had taken part and the first she had led. This was a peace offering, Jean knew. Ray was trying to make amends for that final piece of their history together. To say see, no hard feelings, we can talk about this. She said: 'I don't think it could have been. But thanks.'

'I keep a lookout, you know.'

'I know.'

'And it means ...' Ray paused. 'It means they're still here.'

'Yes, it does.'

Jean closed the computer, made coffee and carried the pot up to the roof garden. In London she had been introduced to the French press, cafetière as they called it here, and preferred the coffee it made to the filter machines back home. She thought about what Ray had said and what it might mean. The study had begun six years ago and lasted two years, before it was terminated. The age of the eldest of the coyotes had been gauged to be around seven, the youngest at two. They had all been caught and collared in a six-month period. If, and it was a big if, the coyote Ray had seen had indeed been one of the Greenhampton coyotes, it would be maybe nine years old at least. In the wild the animals could live up to fourteen or fifteen, but that was rare. Most died before their third birthday and in areas where coyotes and humans lived in close proximity, the easiest way for a coyote to die was under the wheels of a car.

Jean picked up the binoculars on the bench and scanned the yard for Light Bright. The vixen was probably sleeping off last night. Jean's cellphone rang in her back pocket. She was tempted to ignore it, but then took it out and saw on the screen it was Abdul, the street-sweeper.

'Good morning, Jean.'

'Good morning, Abdul.'

'How are you, Jean?'

'I am fine, thank you, Abdul. How are you?'

'I'm doing fine too.' Conversations with Abdul began this way, Abdul was a man who liked to observe formalities.

'What can I do for you?' Jean had learned this gentle way of moving him on before he could begin to ask after her family.

'I'm calling about the boy.'

Attila met Jean in the underpass below the IMAX by Waterloo Bridge. There was no sign of the homeless man or his dog. Jean arrived accompanied by Abdul and Attila came with the hotel doorman who, having been on duty since dawn, had been about to take his break and offered to come along. Attila realised he did not know the man's name. 'James,' said the doorman, as they introduced themselves.

The person who claimed to have had sight of the child was a traffic warden whose beat covered the encircling streets. The man arrived, recognisable by his uniform. As the hotel doorman had rightly predicted, he came from Sierra Leone. He spoke with a stammer and whenever he stumbled over a word he blinked and thrust out his lower jaw, out and then down and to one side and then the other, like an opera singer doing warm-up exercises. His name was Komba. He had seen the boy near Stamford Street. A lot of people overstay the meters on the slip roads down to Lower Ground, he explained. He had been checking the tickets in the car windscreens. He saw the boy watching him and wondered if the boy was acting as lookout for somebody. People did that, left their children with the car in case the traffic warden came by. Komba checked the tickets, some were just about to run out of time, he decided to take a look at the cars on the slip road on the other side of the bridge and come back in a few minutes. By the time he did the boy had gone.

'So he was with one of the drivers, you are saying?' asked James the doorman.

The traffic warden shook his head. 'A short time later I saw the same boy again.' That time Komba was walking with another warden. The boy was standing by the river, watching one of the performers. 'One of those ones who make money by standing in the same position all day.' The boy was gazing at the living statue of a man in a silver suit and a silver bowler hat, carrying a silver cane. Komba saw a child run forward with a coin given her by her parents. The child dropped the coin in the hat at the feet of the statue who began to move.

'What about the boy?' This was Attila.

Komba blinked. 'That was the only other time. As I say, I noticed him because I had seen him before, that was the reason. Nothing more. I had no purpose to talk to him. Then your man Abdul sent us his picture.' He pulled out his phone and brought up Tano's picture. Attila showed him another photograph of the boy, taken from a different angle. 'Yes,' nodded Komba.

'Is there anything else you can tell us?'

Komba shook his head. 'Except that there are always boys like him around here. Sometimes they are looking for something to do. Maybe they have no homes or maybe they don't want to go home. The skateboard park is one place they like to go to.'

'How did he seem to you?' Jean asked.

Komba regarded Jean. 'I see a lot of people without homes to go to, ma. All over this city. They are dirty, it's not easy. But also they have a look in their faces or else they look at nothing but the ground all the time. This boy was not the same. He was watchful, he was alone, he kept himself to himself. He was not okay but also okay. You understand?'

Abdul thanked him and Komba headed back to work. 'Let's have a look at the skate park,' said Jean. They passed behind the theatre and James stopped and introduced them to two of the security guards, both Yorubas, who stood up from where they were sitting and removed their caps to be formally introduced. 'These are some of my boys,' said James, with a proprietorial air. Then the four, Attila, Jean, Abdul and James, walked down the side of the building towards the riverfront.

'Look,' said Jean. She pointed at a silver man in a silver suit and bowler standing on a metal bucket. They gathered around him. Attila, at his great height, was practically level with the performer's nose. 'Excuse me. We need to talk to you,' he said into the man's face. The silver man did not reply, nor did he move. He was steeled against people who tried to interrupt his act. He had performed in Graz and Munich, Prague and Bruges, nowhere as bad as this. In those places kids pulled faces in front of him, or posed for selfies next to him without dropping so much as a euro in his hat. Here he had stood immobile before a drunk's mooning buttocks, endured the coarse laughter of women on a hen night who flashed their breasts to see if they could 'make something else move'. Day after day tourists asked him directions, holding their maps up to his face as though he had been placed there by the Mayor's office. The silver man fixed his gaze on a far-off point on the bridge, allowed his expression to glaze over and, with an effort of will he had trained himself into, he faded out all nearby sounds.

Jean frowned. 'Let's just go check out the skate park.'

'No, hold on.' Attila pressed buttons on his phone until he found the picture of Tano and held it in the silver man's face. 'Have you seen this boy?' Without visibly adjusting a muscle in his face, the silver man redirected his gaze by an infinitesimal fraction.

'What is this man's problem? Doesn't he know how to talk?' asked Abdul, outraged.

'If you would allow me, sir.' James took a coin from his pocket, reached past Attila and dropped the coin into the hat on the ground in front of the bucket. The silver man came to life, a rigid hand shot forward and snatched Attila's telephone out of his hand, so fast Attila had no time to react. The silver man's hand swung like a marionette's, his head bobbed as if it was balanced on top of a spring. He cocked his head right and then he cocked it left.

Attila, who tended to save his patience for when he needed it, said: 'Stop that!'

The silver man's shoulders slumped, he switched his gaze onto Attila, his big mouth pulled down on either side in an elaborate expression of sadness, a poor man's Pierrot. He raised his other hand, which held his cane, and threw the cane into the hand holding the phone and back again. The action seemed designed to provoke.

'I think perhaps I should slap him,' said Abdul in a vexed tone.

'Have patience, everybody, please,' said James. He nodded to the statue.

With a series of robotic movements the silver man raised the camera up to his face, rolled his eyes like a doll and switched his gaze upon the image. Seconds passed. The silver man blinked, slowly, once, twice. His whole body seemed to melt and his limbs reconstitute themselves from tin to flesh as he climbed down from his bucket. He handed the phone back to Attila and asked: 'Who is he?'

'My nephew.'

'Earlier today. Here. Not look like runaway.'

'How do you mean?' asked Attila.

'Clothes were neat. Face, washed. You understand?' The silver man nodded. 'How long?'

'Two days now,' said Attila.

The skateboard park was in the graffiti-covered undercroft of a building. There were a handful of skateboarders and even fewer spectators. The kids there were all boys or young men (too old in Attila's view to spend their time in this way) and all white. He showed them Tano's picture and they looked at it with serious expressions and passed the phone around, but they all shook their heads until finally one of them handed it back. Sorry, mate. Not here, mate. Sorry, mate. Their interest ended abruptly when one of their number, who had been standing immobile at the top of a short ramp for some time, issued an invisible sign he was about to perform and the young man next to Attila whispered in a tone of awe: 'Frontside axel stall.'

Chapter 8

THURSDAY

James had returned to work and Abdul had gone to East Street Market to buy vegetables. Jean and Attila were seated in a café that Jean had come to several times before. It was a vegan café – coming here made Jean feel she was doing the right thing. Now she was on her own she had practically given up eating meat. 'Soy latte, please.'

'I'll have a coffee,' said Attila.

'Soya milk?'

'No milk. Black. What cake do you have?'

'We have a raspberry oat slice, non-dairy carrot cake, gluten-free lemon biscuits, also vegan chocolate and cherry, vegan banana loaf and a vegan date loaf too.'

Attila frowned. 'Raspberry slice, please.'

'Ice cream with that?'

Attila nodded.

'Our dairy-free is also vegan.'

'Just ice cream,' said Attila, who didn't understand.

'We don't serve dairy ice cream,' said the waitress.

Attila felt weary and bemused. 'Okay,' he replied, unsure if this meant he would get ice cream or not.

After the waitress had gone Jean said: 'Dairy-free is for people who are lactose intolerant.'

'I see,' said Attila, who didn't. 'So what is vegetarian ice cream? Surely ice cream doesn't contain meat.'

'Vegan ice cream,' corrected Jean. 'Vegetarians don't eat meat. Vegans don't eat any animal products and that includes eggs and milk. This is a vegan café.'

'I see,' said Attila again.

Jean switched the subject to the boy: 'The positive thing is that he's in good health or so it seems. Two different people have said as much. He's found some kind of shelter, a place to stay maybe.'

'I tried every telephone number his mother gave me.'

'He's a bit further from home territory than I thought. I wonder what the draw is?'

The waitress returned with the order and Attila watched her lay the things out on the table. Jean watched Attila. 'You look tired,' she said.

'I have a lot on my mind. The boy. And then I have a friend I need to help find a place to stay.'

'An apartment?'

Attila nodded.

'Good luck with that.'

'What do you mean?'

'All I mean is that London is an expensive place to look for a rental.'

Attila knew the city as a visitor and for visitors all cities were expensive, though in London you could still go to the theatre for less than £20. In Vienna you could attend the opera for a reasonable sum, if you booked well in advance. Theatre in New York was unaffordable. Once in Colombo, seeking release from his work in the killing fields, Attila had seen a performance of classical dance for no more than five hundred rupees. He asked Jean what she paid for her place and she told him. When he'd spoken to Emmanuel, Attila had thought he was solving two problems, that of Rosie's accommodation and Emmanuel's employment. Now his solution, seemingly so elegant, was suddenly out of reach. Rosie's money would not be enough. Attila tapped his fingers across his bottom lip while he recalibrated his options. He listened as Jean gave him an account of her own arrival in London, how she had wound up living where she did. By the time he had finished his coffee Attila had come to a decision. He excused himself from the table and stepped outside where he telephoned Kathleen Branagan in her office at the hospital. 'The expert witness position. Are they still looking for someone?'

'You've had a change of heart?'

'Something has come up.' The money would be enough to bring his plan to move Rosie back within reach.

'I don't know. Let me find out. I'll call you back.'

While she waited for Attila Jean picked up the newspaper lying on the next table and began to turn over the pages. On the bottom of the third page she read the headline: 'Fox enters house. Attacks cat'. The story was just a few hundred words long, below the headline bullet points of presumably vital information:

Brazen creature seen prowling through a garden just yards from where cat was attacked.
- Pet euthanised after vets fail to save it
- Neighbours say foxes have been a 'menace' in the area
- Experts warn humans have created problem of foxes coming into homes

The fox had entered the property through the cat flap, the article said. The couple had been woken by the cat hissing and growling. At first they had thought a couple of the local toms were having a spat, but realised the noises were coming from inside the home. The wife had been first downstairs and beaten the fox back with a vacuum cleaner hose.

> Mrs Entwistle said there was a problem with foxes in Bromley, south-east London, where the family lives, adding: 'They're here during the day and they are not bothered by humans.'
>
> Neighbour Adam Taylor said: 'There are two large foxes who prowl around here. We won't let our children play outside because we're worried. Mayor of London Don Cob said: 'We must do more to tackle the growing problem of urban foxes.'

The accompanying photograph of a fox running across a lawn was clearly taken on a sunny summer's day and although the country was now steeped in winter the caption underneath asked: 'Is this the killer fox?'

Jean looked out of the window to where Attila stood speaking on his cell. He couldn't see her, and so she watched him for a while longer. When she saw him finish the call, pocket the phone and turn towards the café door she bowed her head back to the newspaper.

They walked along the riverfront, both thinking about the boy. Jean's eyes roved over the faces of children in the crowds, visiting London with their families. The river smelled of dead trees and diesel. They passed a row of food stands and the smell of sausages and caramel peanuts mingled with the dark scent of the river. A vendor stood in front of a charcoal-filled brazier. 'Ah,' said Attila clapping his hands. He brought a small change purse from his pocket and paid the vendor for two bags. He handed a brown paper bag to Jean: 'Careful, they're hot.'

Jean peered inside. 'What's this?'

'Roast chestnuts. Have you never had them?'

'No,' said Jean.

'You don't have them in the United States?'

'No,' said Jean. 'The chestnut trees were wiped out by a blight a century ago. Eventually they restocked with European trees, but in the time I was growing up there was no such thing as roasted chestnuts.'

Attila showed Jean how to peel off the outer shell and the papery skin. Jean burned the tip of her tongue and then tasted a buttery sweetness. They sat on a bench facing the river. Seagulls wheeled over the water. The wind scattered Jean's hair around her shoulders and a sudden gust coming off the river tossed it high above her head. Jean reached up with one hand and then the other, trying to retrieve her hair from the rough and tumble; she took a band from around her wrist and held it in her teeth while she captured flying strands, the task made all the more awkward by the need to balance the bag of chestnuts on her knees. 'Here,' said Attila.

'May I?' She thought he would take the chestnuts, but instead he took the band from her mouth. She turned her back towards him, feeling the electricity of his hands moving across her scalp, smoothing her hair over the crown of her head. His movements were deft and brisk as he slipped the band around the ponytail and laid it against her back.

'Thank you,' said Jean. They both turned around to the view of the river, chestnuts cooling in their paper bags. Jean felt self-conscious and intensely aware of Attila's being, though when she looked at Attila he seemed entirely relaxed. A squirrel waddled into view. A few yards from Attila and Jean it stood up on its hind legs. Its paws, tiny, thick-fingered hands, dangled in front of its chest. It gazed at them with the orbs of a space alien. Attila and Jean stared back.

'Is this about who blinks first?' whispered Attila.

'I don't think so.'

'Then what does it want?' Attila maintained eye contact with the squirrel.

'It wants your roast chestnuts, I think,' said Jean.

'If I give it one, will it go away?'

'I doubt it.'

Attila threw a chestnut towards the squirrel, which hopped over to collect it and sat holding the nut in its paws and nibbled. It cast the husk derisively away and fixed its gaze upon them once more, seeming to focus on Attila.

'Now you've done it,' said Jean.

Attila laughed. 'Shoo!' He stood up and advanced upon the squirrel, which held its ground longer than either of them had anticipated, before finally waddling off.

They sat in silence. Jean said: 'I feel like you know a great deal about me and I don't know much about you. I know you're in London to deliver a speech at a conference. When does that happen?'

'Wednesday next,' said Attila.

'Tell me about your work.'

'Oh.' Attila did not turn to look at her, but kept his eyes upon the water. 'There's not a lot to tell.'

She persisted: 'You're a psychiatrist, you work in war zones. What do you do there?'

'I specialise in trauma, among civilian populations principally,' said Attila. 'Much of my work is as you would imagine. Teams of us go in, some to count the dead, others to trace the living and return them to where they should be or send them somewhere else. I work with the survivors. My job is less to fix the damage than to catalogue the extent of it.'

'What happens then?'

'After us? More reconstruction. The aid agencies, the people who have won the contracts to fix the roads, mend the dams, repair the bridges.'

'I meant to the victims.'

'We file our reports, they can run to thousands of pages. Sometimes a perpetrator or two is imprisoned in The Hague. A few of the survivors will be called as witnesses and have their moment in court. They get to see some general or president or warlord whose name they have heard but who they've never laid eyes on put behind bars. They go there wanting to face the person who tortured them, but that never happens, the system doesn't work like that. The lawyers argue about chains of command, utmost responsibility. Those words don't mean anything to the woman whose daughter was taken away or whose son's bones turned up in a ditch he had to dig himself.' Attila shrugged. 'While all that's happening, somewhere in the world somebody else gets ready to go to war.'

'Wow!' Jean exhaled, not knowing what to say next.

Attila gave a small wry smile. 'I'm not being cynical, just realistic. War is in the blood of humans. The kind of people who torture and rape during war, they're always among us, every time you walk down a busy street you're passing killers waiting to kill. War gives them licence. We tell ourselves people are ordinarily good, but where's the proof of that? There are no ordinarily good people, just a lot of people who've never been offered the opportunity to be anything else. As for the rest, the followers and foot soldiers – well, you can't imprison half a nation. For them and for everyone else life carries on, only not quite as before.'

In the short time they had been talking the clouds had darkened, the wind had turned from lively to irate, it shook the branches of the plane trees and tossed the litter out of a nearby rubbish bin. Jean and Attila sat watching the elements come together, a storm was on its way. On the other side of the river Jean could see the day was still clear, people walking about with only the usual briskness, whereas here they were beginning to dip their heads into the wind and run. It began to hail, pebbles of ice. Attila sprang up, removed his overcoat, swung it around Jean's head and shoulders and propelled her towards the doors of the theatre before Jean, who had never been on the receiving end of quite this kind of treatment, could raise any sort of protest. Around them the hail bounced off concrete, iron and glass, coming at such a rate and force it was as though Attila and Jean were being stoned by a crowd.

Inside the theatre atrium and oblivious to the gunfire of hail outside, a band played and couples danced a slow tango. The dancers moved under bright lights, with movements that were curiously mechanical, faces stiffly averted, all except one woman who danced slumped against her partner's chest, her arms around his neck as if to stop herself sliding to the floor. Jean returned Attila's coat to him. Crystals of ice lay on his shoulders and in his hair and she would have brushed them away, but she hesitated and the moment for it passed. They could find nowhere to sit and so they stood shoulder to shoulder facing the dance floor. The music ended and the dancers swept away to a cordoned area. They seemed to be mostly middle-aged, the women's lips were painted red, some wore seamed stockings, others had combs in their hair, several carried fans. The men were dressed in black shirts, waistcoats, Oxford bags. The clothes looked like they had been borrowed from an outfitter's and Jean decided they must be members of an amateur dance group, an impression lent weight by one man who alone of the group seemed possessed of a dancer's bearing, and to whom the group seemed to defer. When the music started he rose and Jean saw how each woman cast her gaze towards or ostentatiously away from him, hoping to be chosen. He extended his hand to a woman dressed in a black leotard with a shawl around her waist and the couple walked onto the floor, followed by the rest of the group who began to tango in the same slow, stilted style.

'Do you dance?' asked Attila.

'No,' said Jean.

'No? Just like that?' Attila grinned at her. 'Some kind of aversion?'

'I like it, I think. I can't remember the last time, to tell you the truth,' said Jean.

'Would you like to try?'

Jean shook her head and thought Attila might persist and persuade her onto the floor. The relief came edged with disappointment when he did not try. Fleetingly she had imagined the feeling of their bodies pressed together, of his arm around her waist.

Within minutes the hailstorm was over and they stepped out to a clear sky. Jean decided she needed to visit her client and show her the plans for the roof garden. Attila said goodbye to Jean at the top of the steps leading up to Waterloo Bridge and watched her as she walked away, then he turned round and headed into the underpass. The homeless man was there and Attila showed him the picture of Tano, but the homeless man shook his head. On the other side of the underpass his phone began to ring. It was Kathleen Branagan, she said: 'Sorry it's taken a while to get back to you. It seems they had already found someone, but they reckon you carry more weight, it was just a matter of deciding to make a switch at this stage of the game. This is the final appeal. Anyway, it's done now. You're on.'

'Thank you,' said Attila. He asked her what she could tell him about the case.

'Well,' she said, 'not a huge amount, but it's as you would expect. The defendant is a woman. The charge is arson with intent. That carries a stiff sentence. The defence are claiming PTSD, which is where you come in. Good?'

'Yes,' said Attila. He had lost count of the number of expert witness briefs he had turned down, with them the opportunity to earn tens of thousands of pounds. The work had proved lucrative for many of Attila's colleagues as the number of defendants claiming trauma as a whole or partial defence had escalated over the years.

A good deal of the work was in the criminal courts, involving men who had served in the armed forces and had failed to adjust to life back home, whose rage and fear rippled beneath the skin and when it erupted they attacked a stranger in a car park who just happened to be reaching for the keys in his inside pocket, or stove in the head of their best friend after too many beers. On behalf of these men the defence teams constructed a claim of diminished responsibility. They told juries how the men were suffering flashbacks at the time of the offence, believed themselves the subject of imminent attack due to their hyper-vigilant state, or else were in a state of dissociation, simply did not know where or who they were. Over time the cases stretched out to include battered wives and abused children who killed the people who had hurt them, or sometimes, many years later, an innocent person who reminded them of their abusers. At first Attila watched all this with clinical detachment and a certain intellectual interest. This was what he had worked for, recognition of the damage that violence does. Claims for bullying, harassment or discrimination began to include a psychological injury component. Then and somehow, it seemed, inevitably, the no win/no fee lawyers smelled the scent of easy money, the number of civil claims multiplied, fed by the numerous minor workplace accidents, the rear end shunt in the car park, the trip down the marble stairs of a shopping mall, the slip on a restaurant floor, the hours spent trapped in a malfunctioning lift. Suddenly everyone was a trauma victim.

Attila continued to turn down offers. He earned more than anybody in his family ever had, plus his travel schedule made these kinds of obligations complicated. But that was only part of the reason. Attila had once accepted a case. It was the first time he had done so and it became the last for the reason that it involved one of his rare errors of judgement.

Alan Julan, a civilian with an enthusiasm for guns and other weaponry, a physical fitness buff and a member of the Territorial Army's 21st SAS, shot and killed his girlfriend. Julan's claim was that he had shot his girlfriend accidentally while cleaning his rifle and then, in a state of dissociation caused by the shock of seeing her wounded, had shot her again. According to the pathologist's report the second had been the lethal shot. Julan had never seen action during his time in the Territorial Army, which had been served in the years between the wars of the Falklands and Iraq. Julan had joined too late for one and quit too soon for the other. Attila agreed to examine Julan and found his story entirely consistent and utterly lacking in detail. Julan himself was extremely conversant with the symptoms of PTSD which Attila felt certain was due to his contact with the armed forces. He was controlling and cocky, with bright blue eyes and a pinched, handsome face, the kind of liar who delights in telling transparent untruths, ones which yet cannot be disproven. That he'd been assured by his counsel Attila would do what was needed was evident. Attila declared him fit to stand trial and was unsurprised to find his services terminated. But for all that Alan Julan had failed to convince Attila, he succeeded in convincing a jury and was acquitted. Attila's error of judgement, for which he chided himself, had been in not offering his services to the prosecution.

For the second time in the day Attila walked in upon a dance in progress. On arrival at Three Valleys Rest Home he had gone to the residents' day room bearing a box of New Berry Fruits to find Rosie was not there, had returned to reception to be redirected to the dining room where a tea dance was taking place. A space had been cleared of tables and a number of residents in wheelchairs were arranged in a circle like wagons around a campfire. Piano music played quietly, a waltz. In the centre four or five couples, each consisting of a carer and an elderly person, turned so very slowly some hardly seemed to be moving at all. Attila spotted Rosie and Emmanuel immediately. He unwound his scarf, removed his gloves and unbuttoned his coat. One or two of the seated residents nodded, although whether inspired by the music, from essential tremors, or through the effects of the heat and lunch, it was hard to tell.

Attila had a friend, a Senegalese, retired by some fifteen years, who lived on Gorée Island in a modest villa surrounded by books and bougainvillea. He loved to remind Attila of the disparity in their ages, to treat the great psychiatrist like a small boy, a game Attila was happy to indulge – the man had been his teacher a long time ago. The old man also loved to joke about his impending death, which he regarded with something bordering on cheerfulness. He regularly began a sentence with the words: 'For those of us in the departure lounge', would pause and wait with a small smile for Attila to appreciate his joke, before continuing to his observation. Fluorescent lights that shone all night, TVs playing constantly, piped music and the impersonal cheer of its staff, Three Valleys was Heathrow Terminal Three. Attila felt grateful to whoever had organised the tea dance for Rosie looked entirely content as she turned around the floor in Emmanuel's arms. She held herself upright, her head on his shoulder. She looked like a young woman in love.

The music stopped. Attila waited, New Berry Fruits in hand. Couples shuffled off the floor. The carers settled one set of elders back into their chairs and turned to encourage new partners up, easing them to their feet. Rosie and Emmanuel did not move. Somebody said 'Excuse me' and Attila turned round to find a woman carer leading an elderly man in a checked dressing gown by the hand. He moved himself out of the way and as he did so heard Rosie say his name. He put up his hand to wave to her, 'Here I am,' but she did not turn his way. As the music lifted, he saw Rosie look up to Emmanuel and heard her say the words: 'Shall we go again, Attila? Shall we go again?'

Attila sat down, he placed the box of New Berry Fruits on his lap and he waited.

Emmanuel and Rosie danced two more dances before Emmanuel led Rosie over to where Attila was sitting. She looked at him without recognition, but with a faint, dazed smile. Her cheeks were coloured by the exertion and she was beautiful. When she sat down he handed her the box of New Berry Fruits which she received graciously and when he opened the box helped herself to two of the sweets and stuffed them into one cheek.

The next dance was a foxtrot, played at a tempo too fast to ignore, and as a result the floor cleared. Thoughts pressed in upon Attila. Was it a surprise? He supposed not. With his goatee and neatly trimmed hair, Emmanuel looked more like the young Attila than Attila. In the time Attila and Rosie were together Attila wore suits, narrow ties and dealer boots in preference to bell-bottoms and Paisley shirts. Now half the young black men in London dressed the same way he had once. He nearly chuckled aloud but then anguish bit his heart.

To distract himself he turned to Emmanuel: 'Do you know this dance?' Emmanuel shook his head. 'It's called a foxtrot. It's easy to learn. Come on, I'll show you.' He stood and walked into the middle of the floor. Emmanuel gave a quick look around the room, but followed Attila. As the introduction to the song came to an end, Attila said: 'It goes slow, slow, quick, quick. Just follow me. You'll pick it up.' He took one of Emmanuel's hands in his, Emmanuel's other hand he placed upon his own right shoulder, he put his right arm around Emmanuel's waist and set off around the circle, counting out loud as he went. Emmanuel followed, frowning with concentration. Once or twice he put in an extra step. When he trod on Attila's toe he said: 'Sorry, sorry!' and hopped as though his foot were on fire.

'Keep going!' said Attila with military authority. A couple more circuits of the small dance floor and Emmanuel had acquired sufficient mastery for Attila to speed things up. 'Follow me!' he called above the music and broke through the barricade of wheelchairs, dancing with Emmanuel off across the floor of the dining room. Around and around they whirled to the sound of Frank Sinatra singing 'Too Marvelous for Words'. Once a chair toppled over in their wake. They returned to the dance floor for the finale where, with a flourish, Attila spun Emmanuel and, one arm firmly around his waist, dipped him elegantly backwards before flipping him back onto his feet again. The music stopped.

'You did very well,' Attila said.

'I have watched this kind of dancing on television,' answered Emmanuel. 'It's very popular here.'

'Ah, and I thought it was your natural sense of rhythm,' said Attila.

Then came the sound of clapping, from Rosie first, who laughed aloud. She was joined soon by the carers and several of the residents who raised their trembling hands and with great concentration put them slowly, soundlessly together.

Chapter 9

> Alas! For the rarity
> Of Christian charity
> Under the sun!
> Oh! It was Pitiful!
> Near a whole city full,
> Home she had none!

In Thomas Hood's 1844 poem a fallen woman throws herself from Waterloo Bridge. After the poem became popular the bridge became known as the Bridge of Sighs. It was a second-rate, even a third-rate, poem, but there was nothing second-rate about the bridge. The first Waterloo Bridge was an architectural beauty composed of Doric arches carved from Cornish granite, whose grand opening in 1817 (two years after victory in battle) was attended by the Duke of Wellington himself. Soon enough the deserted, the disgraced and the destitute began to throw themselves over the balustrades. Some took their lives intentionally, others in error. The American former seaman, high diver and daredevil, Samuel Gilbert Scott, who liked to perform acrobatics suspended by a rope around his feet and his neck, accidentally hanged himself from the bridge before a great crowd in 1841 when the noose slipped and tightened. When the structures of Waterloo Bridge began to fail, London City Council had it demolished and replaced with a new bridge built by a task force of twenty-five thousand women who were paid less than their male counterparts and written out of the opening ceremony of

1945. All the same, somehow, and for a while thereafter, the bridge became known as Ladies' Bridge. The old bridge was painted first by Constable, under a turbulent sky, riverbanks dense with cascades of greenery and royal barges of gold and scarlet bobbing upon the water – and the new bridge by Monet from his bedroom at the Savoy eighty years later, many times and in all the colours of the imagination, from glowing gold to deepest violet: the colour of water lilies or the noxious fumes and wastes of the towering chimneys of the new revolution rising on the South Bank. In 1978 (by which time Waterloo Bridge was simply Waterloo Bridge) Georgi Markov, a Bulgarian dissident waiting for a bus to take him home from his job at the BBC World Service at Bush House on the Aldwych, was assassinated by a Bulgarian secret police agent who poisoned him with a ricin-coated pellet administered by a jab from an umbrella to the back of the dissident's thigh.

Dusk. Forty-eight hours missing.

Outside the café of the British Film Institute, where the second-hand booksellers do business underneath the south side of the bridge, a small crowd had gathered: Attila surrounded by those volunteers he had been able to muster. There was James the doorman, still wearing his green greatcoat and cap. Abdul was there. Komba the traffic warden, who brought three of his colleagues, two of whom were women. Like James the four still wore the uniform of their trade, as did several of the street-sweepers, of whom there were five, all men. At the last minute they were joined by the Yoruba security guards from the theatre, who said they needed to be back before their shift began. Their names were Olu and Ayo. Finally came the silver man, who had watched the gathering from his post and run to join them carrying his silver cane. He had, he said, several hours before he needed to be at the restaurant where he loaded and emptied industrial dishwashers until 5 a.m. Fifteen volunteers, then. Jean passed around copies of her map, she pointed out key locations, the boy's home and the two recent sightings. Her plan was to begin with a search of the locality and then a sweep of the area in pairs, each taking a different route headed towards the same destination, covering as many roads as possible.

The final rendezvous was the corner of Trafalgar Avenue and the Old Kent Road. She distributed flyers and encouraged everyone to talk to as many people as possible. She began to point out streets with restaurants and food shops, churchyards and hidden squares, until one of the women parking attendants stopped her and said in a gentle voice: 'These are our streets, we know them.' The group split up. The two security guards went together. Komba's group divided neatly in two. After a little shuffling and reshuffling, it was decided that Jean would walk with their new silver friend, while Attila paired up with Komba. The silver man shook hands with each person solemnly, as though on the eve of a great battle. And so the troops headed out towards Borough and Bermondsey.

Earlier in the day, after he had visited Rosie and danced with Emmanuel, Attila stopped by his niece in the hospital. The doctors still refused to discharge her and the anxiety was doing her no good. Attila telephoned Jean who said: 'If I was in her position I'd want to know that everything that could be done was being done too.' She had wound up her meeting with her client and hurried to meet him.

Attila walked with Komba to the big roundabout. A blind man tapped his way along the pavement. A church door stood open showing rows of empty pews, a soup kitchen in the church court-yard advertised today's minestrone. Outside the bars hundreds congregated despite the cold, holding on to pints of beer as though they were the anchors that prevented them being swept away by the passing throng. Komba said: 'What' – he stretched his neck and jutted his lower jaw so far forward it looked as though he had dislocated it, then moved it slowly from one side and then the other as if releasing air from his inner ear – 'kind of boy is this we are looking for?'

'Quiet from what I remember.'

'He is not a troublemaker. He is a serious boy?'

'Yes,' said Attila.

'Why then did he run? Does his mother drink? Does she beat him?'

Attila shook his head, he explained something of the situation.

'So he is not a street boy?'

'Not at all,' said Attila.

'Then I think we should search the station.' Komba stopped and joined a crowd waiting to cross the street at a set of lights. As he walked he talked, twisting his head and neck to free the words. 'The boys who are troublemakers,' he said to Attila. 'Those ones stay together. They like each other's company and they carry on thieving from shops together, one will watch out while the others steal. A boy like yours will want to stay away from those boys or they will cause trouble for him. What else does he have to fear?'

'What do you mean?'

'Police?'

'He saw his mother taken away, but he's bright enough to know she is unlikely to have done anything really wrong and nor has he,' said Attila. 'He wants to go home, but he can't. He has nowhere else to go. He's probably trying to figure out his next move.'

The concourse was a well of sound and light. *La salle des pas perdus*, the French called it. The hall of lost footsteps. To Attila the name evoked perfectly the way sounds ricocheted upwards off the walls and were lost in the air. He followed Komba, noticing how Komba disappeared in the crowd, all but invisible to passers-by in his traffic warden's uniform. 'A boy like yours' – Komba looked over his shoulder to address Attila – 'would come somewhere like this, where he can be warm and where there are other people. He would hide ...' Komba grimaced so that all the tendons in his neck stood out. 'How do you say?'

'In plain sight.'

'Thank you!' said Komba.

But if Tano was at the station they did not find him. Attila, following Komba back into the cold, said: 'It was a good thought.' He looked at Komba for a moment. 'Does this knowledge come from your job or elsewhere?'

Komba smiled. 'I used to be one of those boys, not like yours, like the others. When I was young I was a troublemaker. In the end it took me into some very serious trouble when war came to Sierra Leone. It's by God's grace I am here today. Now I'm a changed man.' He patted the front of his jacket. 'Ah, that war! First the Nigerians came, they stopped it but not for ever. Then the United Nations came and tried and then the British came back. We thought okay, these people from overseas are going to keep coming. Then we were demobilised. Some stayed and joined the government army but not me, I was too young and too short.' He laughed. 'So then I was sent to school to study, I was lucky. Before that I could not even read and write. My family was dead but I had an aunt here. When I was a fighter I didn't even have a uniform. I had a gun but I went barefoot. My nickname was AK.'

'AK?'

'47.' He laughed. 'It was very popular as a *nom de guerre*. But look at me now.' He patted the front of his uniform. Komba shook his head, still smiling tenderly as if at a memory, though whatever it was he did not share it with Attila. They began to walk south.

'If we keep walking,' said Komba presently, 'will we reach the sea?'

The name of the silver man was Osman. Jean and Osman walked the riverbank from Waterloo Bridge to Blackfriars Bridge. At Blackfriars Road they turned south and headed past the office blocks towards Southwark, handing out leaflets to office workers. Here and there a head swivelled as Osman passed, a child tugged her mother's hand, a group of men drinking outside a pub jeered and yelled at Jean: 'Is he silver all over, love?'

'You are American?' said Osman. He brought out a packet of cigarettes and offered Jean one. When she declined he shook one out and lit it, apparently oblivious to the attention.

Jean affirmed this. She very much hoped they weren't going to have one of those conversations about how much he wanted to go to America, or movies – everyone thought they knew America from the movies – or 9/11 or gun control. But Osman only nodded. 'And you?' Jean said.

'Rotterdam,' said Osman. 'We moved there from Bosnia when I was twelve.'

'Give him one of the leaflets, would you?' Jean pointed at a *Big Issue* vendor standing outside Southwark Tube Station. They walked on, skirting the people waiting at bus stops. Osman smoked and hummed. His dark eyes were quick and liquid, rimmed with silver.

Jean wanted to ask him about his colour, how he applied it and how he removed it. Suddenly Osman said: 'How do you know all those Africans?'

Jean told him about her study.

'So how soon do you think for animals to take over the city, if the humans disappeared?'

'Well …' Jean had actually thought about this before. 'Foxes are here *because* humans are here, so too are rats and mice and pigeons, most probably there'd be way fewer of those. For other animals the city is good, without humans even better. Bats would move into the buildings, birds of prey love the heights for their nests.' Jean told Osman to go and look at Nunhead Cemetery, if he wanted to see what could happen, from lawns to meadow to woodland in under thirty years. 'Once the decay sets in, well then you'd see things really begin to change.'

'Like in the Will Smith movie.'

'*I Am Legend*,' said Jean. She'd watched it with Luke and he'd asked her the same thing. Jean argued the city in the film was way too tidy: a few birds, some loose deer, a scattering of weeds the only evidence of three years of abandonment. In an early scene in which Will Smith as Robert Neville spun through the city in a red racer, the highway central islands were less overgrown than their neighbours' back yard. Where were the coyotes? She'd argued they would have taken over the city, but later she rejected that theory. With humans gone the deer and the coyotes would probably return to the habitat beyond the suburbs from which they'd been ousted. Some time later Luke had been interested enough to make it the subject of a second-year dissertation. 'Rewilding New York City: Fiction and Fact in *I Am Legend*'. Ray had come in and sat on the back of the couch and listened to their conversation. When Jean finished talking Ray leaned over and said: 'And now, if you're such a know-it-all, tell us what the car is?' He'd thrown a wink at Luke.

'A Ford Mustang, obviously,' said Jean as she went to fetch herself a soda from the mini fridge they kept in the den. She held up a can and when Luke nodded she threw him one and another to Ray and as he caught it she had added: 'GT500.'

Jean stopped walking and scanned the street this way and that. Osman said: 'I look left side, you look right side.' They carried on, looking into the face of every dark-skinned child they passed.

'*I Am Legend*, yes,' said Osman presently. 'The zombies can see in the dark. And the dog gets bitten.'

'They're mutants,' said Jean, remembering.

She loved this stuff, imagining the world being given back to nature. She liked to watch those movies. *The Day After Tomorrow*. Less so *Mad Max* and *Waterworld*. *The Road*. *Planet of the Apes*. Especially *Planet of the Apes*. The films were a form of penance for what humans had done, had you cheering for the apes and against the humans, not so much failing the Darwin test as screwing up the paper and lobbing it into the trash can. She said to Osman: 'For starters cities like New York and London are built at sea level, for the reason that lots of major cities start out as ports. First thing – the water level would begin to rise. The drains would get all blocked up, nobody to work the pumps that stop the sewers and subway from filling up with water, nobody to man those huge flood barriers. One big surge would likely breach the riverbanks. The city would flood.' They passed under a railway bridge. Jean pointed to the moss growing on the underside of the arch: 'It would start with moss and grass in the cracks and go on from there. Buddleia' – she pointed to the guttering above a shop sign – 'the damage that stuff can do to a building. You'd be amazed!'

'I had a job clearing it from the sides of the railways one year,' said Osman.

'Then no need to tell you.'

She was silent for a moment, following the progress of a child on a bicycle, but he was too old to be Tano. She tried to hand a leaflet to a man passing but he shook his head as he walked away. He probably imagined she was some sort of evangelist. Osman handed a leaflet each to a line of people standing at a bus stop. 'Please,' he said to each one, before pressing the paper upon them. 'Please. Take. Look.'

They walked on. 'Go on,' said Osman.

'So yes, the city would flood. Fire too. Gas leaks, lightning strikes and no fire engines to call. The cement and asphalt would start to break up. Without anyone to clear all those leaves from all these trees … and London has a lot of trees, soon there would be a layer of rotted leaves covering the roads and the sidewalks. You know like when you don't sweep the garden deck in the fall, by the time you go back out there in the spring there's moss and tiny plants and stuff growing all over it? Like that. The whole city.' They passed a tall tree and Jean slapped at the bark. 'Do you know what this tree is called?'

Osman shook his head.

'It's a tree of heaven, Chinese ailanthus, they're everywhere on the East Coast.' Jean had been interested to see them growing in London alongside the ubiquitous plane trees. 'Imported. Big, big mistake! They're an invasive species, basically giant weeds. A tree like this will produce several hundred thousand seeds a year, and they'll root in any crack they can find. Sycamores are the same. It costs city councils a fortune to control them.' In theory removing humans from the playing field should even things out and give biodiversity a chance, after all humans were the ones who had culled and controlled so obsessively for centuries. But maybe that wouldn't happen. Maybe England would become a mass of Japanese knotweed and giant hogweed, with tree of heaven forests. Aloud she said to Osman: 'You know, when Trafalgar Square was excavated one hundred and fifty years ago they found an ancient riverbed and it had hippo bones in it. There was evidence of elephants and lions. Hyenas. Hippos once wallowed in Trafalgar Square.'

'Awesome,' said Osman. 'Is it true?'

'Yes,' said Jean. 'Then came a mini ice age and when that was over what hadn't frozen to death was hunted into extinction by humans. Bears were wiped out a thousand years ago and wolves five hundred years ago.'

'We have wolves still in Bosnia. I never saw one though. I had a fox for a pet once. Well, kind of like a pet. A tame fox. When I was a child, it came round to the place where I was with my father and some other men. I used to feed it. It was very young. I would throw food to it. The fox came almost every night.'

'You shouldn't really feed them,' said Jean automatically.

Osman shrugged. 'I like animals. That fox stopped me from going crazy, it was like having a friend. There's one that comes to the place where I work now.'

'Really?' said Jean, interested. She stepped away from him to let a kid on a scooter by. 'Where's that?'

'In the evenings I work at a big hotel. Do you know this one? Famous all over the world. The name of the hotel is the Savoy.' He turned his face like a luminous moon towards Jean who had begun to laugh. 'This is funny why?'

The teams moved at a steady pace through the streets, converging within less than fifteen minutes of each other at the rendezvous. Three hours had passed and it was now something past nine o'clock. The temperature had dropped and the people most effectively dressed for the weather were the traffic wardens in their all-weather outfits. The women wardens threw furtive, amused glances at Osman and giggled behind their hands. The other members of the team stood huffing white puffs of breath, stamping their feet and clapping their hands. Each new arrival was greeted with a slap on the back, a squeeze of the arm, like an old friend after a lengthy interval. There was a great racket from the road, the passing lorries, the buses. James stepped away to inspect some coco yams displayed outside a nearby shop and returned a few minutes later with a bag full of groceries.

When all were gathered Attila swept them off to debrief at a nearby bar called Pardis. At Pardis he was delighted to find Guinness Export on sale and ordered a round for everybody, except Olu and Ayo who could not drink before work and Abdul who was a Muslim. Osman said he was Muslim too, but not *that* much Muslim. Jean said she'd give it a try. More hops, Attila explained, hops act as preservatives, enable the stout to travel longer distances, more hops, more alcohol. The important thing, said Attila, was to serve it ice cold. In England you had to come to an establishment such as this to be sure, otherwise it would not be cold enough. With the first sip Attila was returned briefly not to Accra, but to his time in Freetown, a place he had known there called the Ocean Club, where in the first years he and Maryse would go on Sundays to eat curry and Attila to drink a pint of cold Guinness. The restaurant was outdoors, facing the beach, and with the taste of the beer came the smell of the surf and of the tiny, local roasted peanuts with papery skins that the hawkers measured out in cut-down tomato-purée tins, a quarter, a half, or a full tin, to be wrapped in old newspaper.

It would be wrong to say anyone had expected to find the boy that night. What was true was that an air of expectation had accompanied the night's search which owed itself to the belief that they would turn up something, a hard lead, some new information, a person who might prove to be useful. As each team gave an account of their part of the search, it became apparent little was forthcoming. Jean tried to keep the mood positive, saying that no news was not necessarily bad news, when Osman stood up suddenly, raised a fist and said to noisy assent: 'We go again tomorrow night! We keep going. Tomorrow night, next night, night after!'

Attila rose and went to the bar where he spoke to the barman, and when Jean next glanced in his direction, he was exiting the building. Outside a keening wind blew, the window of the bar shuddered and flexed. Attila returned shaking raindrops from his head, he was carrying a bundle wrapped in a plastic bag. 'Rations for the troops.' From the bag he took a large package wrapped in paper and opened it, spreading the contents on the table. Some of the group gathered round and began to help themselves. Osman picked up a wooden barbecue skewer of meat: 'What's this?'

'*Suya*,' said one of the Nigerian guards. He spoke the word with a mix of reverence and delight, plonked himself down and gathered up several skewers.

'Like kebab,' said one of the parking attendant women, who had taken off her cap to reveal a red weave. She leaned over Osman's shoulder and helped herself from the diminishing pile.

'Ah, kebab.' Osman tugged a piece of meat from the stick with his teeth.

Attila picked up the end of a skewer and passed it to Jean who hesitated.

'You don't eat meat, Jean?' said James the doorman.

'I do, just not a lot,' said Jean and slid a chunk of the meat from the skewer with her fingers.

'What kind of person doesn't eat meat?' said Olu. 'Meat is the food of life.' He stamped a foot.

'Lots of people don't eat meat,' replied Osman.

'Not in Nigeria!'

'Not in Nigeria,' concurred James. 'But here, yes. At the hotel we have many people who don't eat this thing or that thing.'

'Like Jews and Muslims,' said Osman. The Nigerian looked at him, mollified, for that much he understood. 'Some Hindus don't eat meat.'

'So you are a Hindu, Jean?'

Jean shook her head.

'Yes, yes.' James was still talking. 'They want to have food delivered, made with only certain ingredients. Some won't eat animals. Others they want different things. Some will not eat vegetables, some will only eat vegetables. Some want all their food raw, some—'

Here he was interrupted by Komba who said: 'They eat their meat raw?'

'Hmm!' said James. 'Let me see. There are those who will not eat vegetables and those who will not eat meat, and those who only eat uncooked food, but I cannot remember if those ones eat meat. No, I think they do not. Others will eat no solid food and want special juices – well those we can offer through the hotel kitchen, there we have a very big juicing machine and we can make any kind our customers want, with kale and carrot and wheatgerm, celery, special ingredients say ...' He hesitated briefly, then said: 'Spirulina, seaweed! Whatever, whatever.' He raised both his hands and shook them like a minstrel. 'That's for them that is "detoxing". We also can provide all the gluten and lactose things.'

'Gluten- and lactose-free,' corrected Jean.

'That too,' said James. 'It's my job to know about all these things and offer assistance to our guests. I know the chefs at the restaurants, I can call them up and ask if they can make such and such, whatever. Like, let me say cabbage soup, some people will only eat cabbage soup or watermelon.'

'I no dae believe you,' challenged the fiery-haired traffic warden. She folded her arms, drew in her chin and sucked her teeth.

'What do *you* know?' replied James. 'Let me tell you. One night I was sent out in the middle of the night to search for watermelon. I'm the one who is sent, yes. Let's say if the weather is very bad. It was two, maybe three in the morning, the guest wanted to eat but would only eat watermelon. The concierge asked for my help. What did I do? I called one of my countrymen who drives a taxi, I told him to come here to the Old Kent Road and buy a watermelon at one of the late-night shops and bring it right back. I sent it straight down to the kitchens.' His gaze travelled their faces as he winked. 'When the time came for that guest to leave, I reminded him, I said, I hope you enjoyed your watermelon, sir. Then he gave me a good tip. £5.'

'What does he eat watermelon for? Is it his religion?'

'For weight loss, I believe,' said James. He frowned: 'Or maybe detoxing.'

'Maybe I will try it,' said the woman parking attendant and patted her hips as she leaned over the back of the chair and reached for another skewer of *suya*.

'Weight loss, detox, health, long life,' said James. 'Others have "intolerances".'

Attila unwrapped another of the packages he had brought. The group leaned in to watch.

'Ah, plantain!' exclaimed several people. Attila served Jean first, using a piece of paper as a plate and handing her the plastic fork. Jean ate. It tasted good, not much like the banana it resembled, but like a distant, denser cousin from the vegetable rather than the fruit side of the family.

'So what does this watermelon man eat when there is no watermelon?' said Komba. 'This is what I ask myself.'

Everyone turned to look at James who replied with comic timing: 'Honeydew.' And then he said: 'But most of them take it very seriously. They will only eat what they will eat. So now those of us in the hospitality business must find a way to meet their needs.'

There was a brief silence and then Komba asked: 'So let us say they are in the middle of the sea or the middle of the desert. What then? They still go looking for watermelon?'

Minutes past midnight the group left Pardis to be mugged by the wind, which came at them down the street like a gang of thieves.

Heads down, they battled their way up the Old Kent Road, trying to cluster together but scattered by the gale, except for the women traffic wardens who linked arms like marching suffragettes. As they passed Burgess Park there was a discussion about bus routes in which almost every word had to be yelled, relayed or repeated. With the exception of James, Attila, the two security guards Olu and Ayo and Jean, everyone was headed south. Jean wondered whether to invite Attila back to her apartment, and whether she could do so in front of everyone else. Above the wind she caught briefly the sound of dogs barking. She stopped and listened. Between gusts she heard it again. This was not the barking of city dogs, who barked when they were alone, simply to remind themselves they were alive, but rather the baying of hounds in mid-chase. That moment a fox barrelled out of the park gates and straight into the road where it only narrowly avoided being hit by a car. On the other side it slid between railings and disappeared. 'What in the hell?' Jean whispered to nobody but herself. She turned and entered the park gates.

The creak of trees and the hiss of the wind replaced the sounds from the road. Flashlights switched through the darkness, people were spotlighting in the park. Hunting with spotlights was illegal in a good many places in the US. Here they called it lamping, and men had been at it for centuries, poachers oftentimes who lamped for rabbits and hares. Now lamping had come to the city. In the country they used lurchers, for their speed and gentle mouths. The dogs could take a dazzled rabbit before the animal even knew it, and bring it back to their master to wring its neck. In the city they hunted foxes for sport and in the city they used not lurchers but Staffordshire bull terriers, whose powerful jaws were capable of locking on to their prey, of tearing a small animal in two.

Jean was familiar with the park, but darkness altered its dimensions. Where now was the path? Ahead of her a trash can metamorphosed into the shape of a crouching man and back again. Jean felt in her coat pocket for her own flashlight and switched it on. The further behind she left the street the denser grew the dark. The wind whipped her hair across her face. Somewhere in the distance a siren sounded. Grass gave way to gravel. Ahead she saw two men coming towards her. Jean stopped. When they reached her the men stopped too. They wore dark jackets and woollen beanies and that these men were two of the lampers was beyond doubt. Now they stood before her in silent confrontation. A knowledge hung in the air and nobody seemed about to pretend otherwise. Jean, who had no cover story she could think of, made to move past them but the men blocked her path.

'Who's this?'

Jean's voice was steady as she said: 'Excuse me, please.'

'Why? What have you done?' said one of the men. The other one laughed mirthlessly.

'You don't want to go there.'

'I don't know where you think I'm going. But if you'll excuse me.'

'Yeah but, you don't want to go there,' said the same voice. 'I'm just telling you.'

'I heard sounds.'

'Oh that's just the foxes – they're all at it this time of year. Sex mad.'

She moved and the men moved with her.

The second man spoke: 'Listen, love, you're not in Kansas any more. So why don't you fuck off home? Go on, get your ruby slippers and piss off.'

Behind the two men lights flashed. Momentarily the wind died and at the same time the dogs started up again. Jean dived past and started to run, she sprinted, fuelled by adrenalin and cold, heavily because she couldn't see where she was placing her feet. The wind seemed to be coming from everywhere. Shadows crossed in and out of the beams of the flashlight. The dogs had been loosed. She could almost feel the vibration of the ground caused by their galloping feet. Furiously she urged herself on. One of the men behind her shouted. His voice coming from a distance. Ahead of her the flashlights disappeared and all was blackness. Then came a scrambling and a snarling, the thud and roll of bodies. An animal screamed. Jean stopped. For a few seconds she stood breathing hard. She could hear nothing from the two men. She turned off her flashlight but held on to it tightly in her right hand. She began to walk towards the gates of the park, now some distance away. A hundred yards from the gate and she ran into the two men again.

'Well, well, well,' said the first. 'Anybody would think you was following us.'

'She likes us,' said the other.

'Do you like us? Is that it?' said his partner. Light fell on the face of the man who spoke. His expression was impudent and unpleasant. Something new was in play, a score to be settled. Jean felt prickles of sweat under her arms and at the back of her knees and the queasy, involuntary knotting of the muscles of her belly and between her legs. Her mouth tasted of tin.

Jean said: 'Okay, I get it. I'm leaving.'

'Oh, now the lady wants to go.'

'She loves me, she loves me not.'

'You wanted me to go, I'm going,' said Jean.

'You know what ah think we have heah?' said the second man. His voice was altered: now he spoke with a wheezy Texan accent. 'What we have heah is a fayl – ure to com-mun-icate.' The captain from *Cool Hand Luke*.

Jean said nothing. Behind the men she saw movement, people heading their way. She made out Attila by his height and one of the security guards by his cap. Someone had spotted her leave. They must have waited and then decided to come looking for her. She forced herself to stand still until they were within distance, then she walked quickly towards them. The men started to move in on her, but spotted the group, the array of uniforms, and fell away, disappearing into the darkness.

'Are you okay?' said Attila as Jean reached him. Someone patted her arm. The feeling of danger receded.

Another person said: 'Look at Osman!' and there was gentle laughter at the sight of Osman, who glowed nacre in the moonlight. Jean asked Olu to lend her his flashlight which was more powerful than hers and, accompanied by Olu and Osman, she headed into the darkness, to the place she thought the fox had been taken down. Let it not be Light Bright, she thought, for the park was close to the young vixen's territory. The fox that had escaped was a male fox, judging by the size of him. That meant, and Jean was as sure as she could be of this, that the dead fox would be a vixen. A hundred yards on she found the carcass.

'Shame on them,' said Olu and took off his hat.

The fox lay on its side, a tangle of steaming entrails beside it. It was a vixen, but it was not Light Bright.

In an Ethiopian restaurant, close to two o'clock in the morning, just Jean and Attila. Attila ordered knowledgeably from the menu and the dishes arrived steadily one after the other in small bowls. Jean was hungry and ate. The food was good. Jean tore a piece of the spongy bread on her plate and dipped it into a bowl of beans. The phone in Attila's pocket rang. He stood up and moved away from the table, one hand clamped over his free ear, the phone held to the other. When the call finished he walked to the waitress, handed her a £20 note waving her to keep the change. Back at the table he removed Jean's jacket from the back of her chair. 'Come on!' he said. 'Our good Yoruba friends think they have found Tano.'

'How many exits?'

'Four including the one that leads up to the theatre. I have put a man on each of them. If he comes we will catch him,' said Olu.

'Okay, but take it easy. We're trying to persuade him to come with us. The sight of the uniforms might alarm him. Can I reach your men on that?' Attila indicated the walkie-talkie at Olu's waist. Olu unhooked it and handed it over.

'You just depress this button here,' said Olu. 'And say whatever you want. They will all hear you.'

Attila cleared his throat: 'The boy's name is Tano, he is from Ghana although he has lived much of his life in London. His mother's name is Ama. Use his name and mention her by name, it will reassure him. Tell him someone is here to take him to see his mother. Everyone stay in position. Olu and I are going down to the car park.'

'What do you want me to do?' said Jean.

'Come with Olu and me,' replied Attila. 'You make us look less imposing.'

They followed the main ramp down to the car park below the theatre. Low ceilings. Square pillars. Freezing air. Puddles of water on the concrete floor. Odour of exhaust fumes and oil. A huge graffiti on one wall, part of a person, a hand perhaps, green and violet diamonds. The deafening hum of the building – they had to raise their voices to be heard. Strip lights deepened the shadows between the cars and in the far recesses of the space.

'Do these gates get closed every night?'

'Yes, sir,' said Olu.

'What time?'

'The theatre itself finishes say ten o'clock, so then maybe people go to the restaurant to eat. It can be midnight.'

'So he's got plenty of time to get in here.'

'Exactly so.'

'Tell me what happened when you saw him.'

'Well,' replied Olu. 'We received a report about an animal down here so we came to investigate. The complaint was made to the front desk early in the evening and it arrived with us when we came on duty. We looked. We didn't find any animal. But one of our men saw this boy, standing ver-y still. At first we thought he was here to steal from the cars, but then we saw that this was the boy you were looking for. Because you sent us his picture. We called to him, but he ran.'

'And you lost him?'

'He was quick. We were slow.'

'And you think he's still down here?'

'If he had gone up the ramp we would have seen him. If he had tried to get into the theatre we would have heard him. It's possible he could have escaped up the stairs, yes. But I had my men on those exits very fast. It's my belief he is down here. We did not want to alarm him further. We called you.'

A few paces behind Jean was thinking, If I was a child, where would I hide? The basement car park was several degrees colder than outside. She imagined she would think about climbing into a car. A car would be warmest, but probably feel too risky.

'What in God's name is that noise?' she asked Olu.

'The ventilation exhaust for the building is located down here, ma.'

Jean took the lead and walked towards the sound. Soon enough they turned a corner and came upon the ventilation exhaust, two powerful fans behind a grid. To the right was a single door. To the left a double door. 'Are those doors locked?' asked Jean.

'I believe so,' said Olu. 'I am not the one who holds the keys.'

Jean tried the handle of the double doors. Locked. Then she walked to the single door, did the same and found it open. It led into the room which held the fans, two squat aluminium beasts. On the floor were cigarette butts, a ticket for the car park, a discarded cable spool, a couple of wooden planks. Tucked behind the planks she found a Fruit Shoot bottle and a scarf and wrapped inside the scarf, a Nintendo console. She handed them to Attila. 'It doesn't look like he's sleeping there though.'

'Tano!' Attila called.

Silence.

'Tano!'

'Tano!' Jean called and then so did Olu. 'Tano!' The boy's name echoed around the underground chamber and vanished. They waited in silence. Neither Attila nor Jean were aware of the boy's approach, only of a faint shift in the atmosphere and then the realisation that a boy was standing between a pillar and the rear of a utility vehicle less than twenty yards away.

'Tano,' said Attila gently. 'I'm your uncle. I'm here because your mother is looking for you. Do you remember me?'

The boy nodded.

'Come!' said Attila. The boy moved out from behind the car, he hesitated. Attila dropped down to a squat, so that they were now the same height. The boy stepped towards him.

Filigrees of frost formed on the windscreens of cars, on dark tarmac, creeping outwards on pale concrete, crystallising on the underside of the leaves of the trees along the river. On Waterloo Bridge a fox trotted at an easy pace in the shadow of the balustrade on the western side. The fox was headed south in the direction of its den, but the fox would not return to its den this night, or the night after, or the night after that. The human shouts and cries in the early evening had disturbed a fragile sense of safety, triggering a survival impulse in the animal's amygdala deep in the recesses of the temporal lobe. In two days he would make a new den in a new place. From there he would continue his search for a mate.

Nobody knew if the war had ended or would ever end. The railway hotel had been closed these thirty years since the death of the railway. Now a renovation had begun and abruptly ended. Tall weeds had been slashed down, a pile of building detritus heaped and half burned in the old driveway, bamboo scaffolding erected, the façade partly painted white in overlapping brushstrokes. Then the enterprise suddenly abandoned.

Instead a smaller guest house had been built adjacent to the grand hotel. The guest house had a well and its own generator which ran until ten in the evening and was where Attila stayed on those occasions he had reason to journey to the north. On this day he had arrived to collect a patient. The patient had a diagnosis of schizophrenia, had been an in-patient at the mental hospital more than once: the family felt at ease calling upon Attila. At their home Attila had been greeted by his patient from the balcony of the house where he stood like a lookout on a ship. He was dressed in baggy white trousers tucked into oversize Wellington boots, wore a blue tailcoat, hand-stitched and made from rough indigo-dyed cloth, and a tall black hat. He told Attila his name was John Bull.

Five to six that same evening, Attila waited for the Kenyan in the ground-floor room of the guest house which served as a bar and restaurant. A football game played on the television in one corner. Attila sat with a Star beer, his back to the screen, and looked out on the red dust road and the mosque opposite. At six o'clock a Land Cruiser bearing the insignia of the UN drew up and the Kenyan stepped out. Attila clapped both his hands on each of the Kenyan's slender shoulders, the two men embraced, stood back and regarded each other, and then embraced again. They had not met since the tumult of Bosnia. The Kenyan's tea came in a tall glass with the label of a Lipton's tea bag and the sight of the Kenyan's long fingers holding the tea bag by the string and twirling it around in the hot water brought back to Attila a memory of mud and cold, of abandoned houses and men who shot at foxes.

'How is the family?' he asked.

'They are well. The youngest starts teacher training college in Tambach. How is your wife?' asked the Kenyan.

'She's well.' A year after the war came to the capital city Maryse had returned to Ghana. Attila saw her less frequently than he would like. She wished he would relinquish his post and come home.

'And will you?'

Attila smiled. 'What would I do?'

'There are many opportunities for somebody like you.' The Kenyan smiled and then grew serious, he said: 'I'm happy to see you but whatever brings you here, don't stay too long in this town.' His soldiers were outnumbered. The rebel army was armed to the teeth. There were reports, rumours. He had orders not to engage in combat. 'Same in Rwanda, same in Congo. Don't stay in this place longer than you must.'

'I leave in the morning.'

Attila called the manager and arranged for a meal to be sent out to his driver and then he himself stepped out to check on the young man. Ibrahim was sitting in the driver's seat listening to the radio. At the sight of Attila he snapped it off, pulled his seat upright and would have jumped down but Attila held up a hand. Ibrahim was the nephew of Attila's last driver who had been obliged to retire due to the onset of night blindness. Ibrahim was shaping up. The 4Runner was so well polished it hurt to look at it.

Nine o'clock. They were eating chicken and fried rice when the Kenyan's two-way radio buzzed and he left the restaurant to speak. At that moment there came a spit and crackle in the air, like the sound of dry lightning. Then came the crash and quiet of an explosion. The crickets fell silent. There was only the sound of the television and the generator. The guest-house manager stepped from behind the counter, disappeared out of a back door, the generator went silent, the lights went out and the cheering football crowds quieted. The Kenyan came back inside only to shake Attila's hand: 'My friend,' he said, and was gone.

Next morning Attila came out of a fractured sleep to the sound of a cockerel's cry and the call of the muezzin. Outside a woman sprinkled water on the dry dust of the compound floor as if she were sowing wheat. In the compound below Ibrahim stood barefoot on his prayer mat, passed his hands over his face and knelt.

They drove to collect John Bull. The madman sat in the back seat of the vehicle and looked out the window like a visiting dignitary. From time to time he chuckled, once he wound the window down and stuck *his head out. Ibrahim drove in watchful silence. They passed a land-scape over which the sun burned and in which little moved. A woman carrying firewood stepped off the road at their approach and disap-peared entirely, to be enfolded by the trees. The road ahead shimmered, shrinking blue-black shadows. A vulture hopped thrice and took off, leaving the corpse of a snake.*

Past a hut outside which a lone family sat selling palm oil, a man in military uniform stepped from the trees into the road. The Kenyan. Ibrahim stopped, Attila climbed down. The UN troops had been surrounded in their quarters and were held hostage. The Kenyan who had been returning from dining with Attila had evaded capture, he was on foot, forced to abandon his vehicle. Attila said: 'There are two checkpoints, one at Massiaka and one at Waterloo. We'll tell them you are one of my patients.' He looked the Kenyan up and down. 'You'll need to take off your clothes.'

When the Kenyan was naked, Attila picked up a handful of dirt and rubbed it into the Kenyan's hair and onto his chest. He searched the ground, found some excrement and smeared that over the Kenyan's torso. The Kenyan grimaced and raised his chin to avoid the smell. Attila gave the man's uniform to the family sitting outside their hut and told them to hide it. They walked back to the vehicle. John Bull looked at the Kenyan and laughed gravely.

At the Massiaka checkpoint a man was sitting on a huge boul-der at the side of the road. He was dressed in combat trousers, boots and a black T-shirt, an automatic weapon lay across his knee, he was surrounded by henchmen.

'Stay here!' Attila stepped out of the vehicle and approached the group of men. Step after step he recalled the man on the boulder's story. He had once been Attila's patient. Psychosis. Drug-induced. They filled the beds in the wards of the hospital, an unending flow, all young men, jobless in the city, smokers of cannabis. On the eve of war the family had come to retrieve their son and return with him to the provinces. And now here he was. He remembered Attila and smiled. 'Ah the great doctor.' They shook hands. 'You don cam find me?' Have you come here to find me? He laughed and the young men around him laughed too.

Attila humoured him: 'This is a welcome meeting, in fact I am on the road.'

'Where have you been? Visiting family?' Another bark of laughter, followed by its echo. He leaned back and, resting both hands on the weapon which lay across his lap, grinned at Attila. Attila knew his first task was to offer him applause and so he smiled and shook his head as though he was happy to be teased. In war the checkpoint was a door between worlds, where a great many people disappeared. All eyes were on him. Attila kept his own eyes fixed on the commander. The commander climbed down off the rock and pushing through his men he slipped his arm through Attila's, said: 'Come with me,' in a way that offered Attila no choice. They walked into a nearby house and the commander sat down in a large armchair and invited Attila to take a seat on a huge velvet sofa. The room was stiflingly hot.

'I need you to help me.'

Attila waited.

'This war,' said the commander. He picked up a packet of 555 cigarettes and shook one out, lit it and sucked the smoke into his chest. He did this three or four times and then he ground the cigarette out under the heel of his boot. With the nail of his forefinger he gouged dirt from beneath the nails of the other hand and flicked it onto the floor. He looked up at Attila, narrowed his eyes and tapped his skull. 'I cannot sleep.'

'None of us can sleep these days.'

'Remember at the hospital, how I was then?'

He had been paranoid, delusional and violent. 'Those problems are continuing?'

'Yes. And sometimes I lose myself, I wake up and I don't know where I am. I dream bad dreams.'

'You smoke cannabis still?'

'What else is there?'

'If you stop it will help,' said Attila. 'You'll do a lot better without it.' He spoke like a doctor, knowing it was pointless.

'I want you to give me something for it.'

Attila took out his notebook and pencil, he wrote a prescription for an antipsychotic drug. How the commander would get hold of the drugs wasn't Attila's problem. The commander looked at the piece of paper. Thought Attila, he cannot read, so Attila repeated the words he had written aloud and the commander folded the paper and put it in his pocket. He stood up and together they walked outside. The 4Runner was surrounded by fighters, staring through the window at John Bull and the naked Kenyan. One of them was tapping on the window with a stick. Ibrahim was sitting with his hands on the wheel, staring through the windscreen. The commander shouted, the boys backed off. With each step Attila could feel the sweat drops rise between his shoulder blades, trickle from his scalp onto his forehead. He looked for a way to stop, shake the man's hand and say goodbye, knowing there was none. He felt the commander's rising curiosity: it was there in the angle of his neck, in his narrowed eyes, his murmured replies to Attila's talk. When they reached the 4Runner the commander placed an arm on the roof and leaned over to peer into the vehicle. To Ibrahim he said: 'Who are these men?'

'They are patients, sir. Dr Asare is taking them to hospital.' Ibrahim kept his eyes lowered.

The commander looked at John Bull. 'What's your name?'

'They call me John Bull,' said John Bull looking at the commander with a raised chin.

The commander looked him over, then broke into loud guffaws: 'Yes, yes! John Bull. The great white trader. I see it.' He stopped laughing and turned to the Kenyan. 'And you?'

The Kenyan was silent.

'You! What is your name?'

To Attila the Kenyan looked every bit like a foreigner, his high cheekbones and slender physique, he was at least circumcised. The commander repeated his question. He knocked on the window, a frown forming on his face. Attila slipped into the front seat: 'Can you believe,' he said to the commander, 'this one thinks he only speaks Portuguese?'

At that moment John Bull belched, a huge sound that seemed to rise from the depths of his soul. The commander broke out laughing. He stepped back from the vehicle and banged the roof with his fist. Inside the car the noise resounded like a gunshot.

Ibrahim started the engine and they moved forward towards the checkpoint: a cantilevered pole across the road, the end of which was *attached to a piece of string held by a young boy. Attila watched the boy perform the motions of checking the vehicle. When he came round to Attila's side of the vehicle, Attila wound down the window and told him they were on their way to the capital. The boy opened his mouth but no sound came, he twisted his neck one way and the other, a knotted vein rose, he thrust out his lower jaw like an insect's mandible and pushed it to each side of his face. His lips twisted and he grimaced with the effort. Finally a word came: 'Pass!'*

Attila's eyes were on the boy's face but he paid him no attention, did not hear him speak, or notice the contortions of his face. On the periphery of his vision he could see the commander starting to walk towards them, weapon in hand. Ibrahim pressed on the accelerator and the vehicle moved away. In the rear-view mirror Attila watched the commander reach the checkpoint and stop. He watched until the checkpoint was lost from view.

Chapter 10

Kitchens of the Savoy Hotel. The boy perched on a high stool, watchful, unsmiling, had not uttered a word. Attila let him be, but urged him to eat. In the bar of the hotel at the Aldwych Attila had read from the all-night menu: deep-fried crispy wontons, *charcuterie* platter, griddled wild vegetables. The boy gazed at him.

'I know what this boy wants,' said James. 'He wants pepper soup.'

The boy looked at James like a dog recognising a word.

So they had walked round to the Savoy where the kitchens never closed and where Osman was on duty, washed of silver paint. Attila didn't recognise him until he spoke. He had a gentle face and soft, spiky brown hair. James had brought with him the bag of groceries he'd bought on the Old Kent Road. Attila, Jean and Osman watched while he fried chicken and meat on one ring of the massive industrial cooker. In a blender James whisked tomatoes, onions and not one but two Scotch bonnet peppers. You could tell he was a man used to taking care of himself, could starch a collar and mend his own clothes, the sort of person who knew just what to do if a woman went into labour or a dog fell sick. As he worked he talked: he told a story about a young executive staying at the hotel who had returned at 5 a.m. so inebriated he could barely stand. James offered him a cup of pepper soup from the flask he sometimes brought with him from home for the night shift. One hour later, showered, dressed and stone cold sober, the young executive was back downstairs and James called him a cab to his breakfast meeting. 'If you are drunk pepper soup will make you sober. If you are sick it will make you well. It can cure malaria.'

'Like Jewish chicken soup,' said Jean.

'Exactly so,' said James. He held out a spoon for Jean, who took a sip, coughed and wiped her eyes. James fetched a glass of water.

'Good, yes?'

'Good,' she whispered hoarsely.

James smiled. He ladled the soup into bowls and pushed one to the boy. They all watched as the boy took a sip. 'Tell me if this is as good as your mother's.' The boy didn't answer, but he looked up at James and, though he still didn't smile, he bent his head and began to eat.

Attila put the boy to bed in his room. He had called Ama and let the boy speak to his mother. Attila could hear Ama's voice at the end of the line, uneven with emotion. Tano said very little and so quietly Attila could not make out the words. Afterwards the boy handed him the phone. 'When can I go home?' he said.

He had taken a bath, declined Attila's offer of assistance and disappeared into the bathroom, which Attila, when he went in to perform his own ablutions, found steamy but spotless. Now, in a pair of pyjamas supplied by James from the store of items left behind by hotel guests and which fitted tolerably well, he lay asleep on the other side of the queen-sized bed. The sound of his breathing, a childish snuffling, brought to Attila's mind the thought that he had become unused to the company of children.

Over the years he had watched his friends' children grow up. Now those children had children of their own and Attila knew them only at one remove. He was the kindly uncle passing through, they greeted him at the door and craned to see whether or not he held a present behind his back. They were attracted to his size and liked to try on his hats and his shoes. He performed his disappearing-coin trick, one he often found useful in refugee camps, for the popularity it won him among children. For years he travelled with a holdall of deflated footballs and a pump. He would arrive in a village to begin an investigation and immediately pump up a football, throw it into the crowd of children and young men who surrounded his vehicle. Somebody would head it, a game began.

Friendship followed the game and with luck trust might follow friendship.

Yes, if you asked Attila he would say he enjoyed children, their candour most of all. He and Maryse would have liked their own, but the desire had always remained just that, and eventually they adjusted their minds to the knowledge that the desire would never be met. There had been disappointment, but never despair. There had always been other children.

In Attila's view there were many things worse than not having children. He loved, for instance, the fact he knew, every morning when he woke up, what he had been put on this earth to do. Or he had anyway, the knowledge had nourished him for decades. He could not imagine what it was like not to wake with that sense of purpose. Lately he had felt it less. Perhaps Quell was right, it was time to quit. Maryse had always seemed to feel the same way Attila did, and if she ever felt otherwise she had given no indication of it, but then Maryse was not a child, Maryse was capable of dissembling.

Tano's hair was close-cropped, his head dark against the pillow, the back of his skull curved in the shape of the map of Africa. The boy was deep in sleep. Attila reached out and stroked his head.

At seven o'clock in the morning, lumbering back from the toilet, Attila saw that Tano was awake and looking out of the window. He urged the boy back to bed, and waited while he fell asleep again, then he turned on his bedside light and reviewed some papers. After an hour he rose and raised himself on his toes, stretched his arms and turned his neck from side to side, tilting his head one way and then the other, then he performed some more stretches at the window. He moved the curtain. On the window ledge a grey pigeon roosted, wings folded, contemplating the street below with the solemnity of a Wall Street stockbroker in 1929.

On the television Attila watched the news with the sound turned down. War in Syria. The government bombing its citizens in Damascus. Some countries calling on the UN Security Council to charge the Syrian government with war crimes. In Iraq Sunni protesters demanded the resignation of the Prime Minister. The French chasing Tuareg and Islamist rebels out of Timbuktu. Attila had been to Timbuktu, the food was terrible. Images of men in Toyota Hiluxes waving machine guns. In Nigeria another gun-waving gang in a pick-up had killed nine young women administering polio vaccinations to children. Attila wondered where the next telephone call would take him, to whose victims would he administer, which men subscribing to what ideological cover story.

The screen showed a black-and-white image over which hovered a pair of pale cross hairs. On the bottom right of the screen a scale. A line of numbers or letters moved erratically across the top of the screen, dissolved and was replaced by more figures. People moving around far down below, getting in and out of vehicles. From their mode of dress they looked like men, impossible to be sure. The landscape around them filled with nothing but rocks. A moment later a cloud of dust occluded the view of the people on the ground and rose, a darkening tower, until it nearly filled the screen.

Attila removed the glasses he wore to read and watch television and rubbed some sleep from the corners of his eyes. Now the television showed what looked like a poultry farm, a vast space, a coop containing a thousand chickens, the birds were all white, the coop was filling with white foam from an overhead hose. As the birds were covered they began to flap and die in the whiteness, nothing visible except the movement of their wings. Attila could not tell what was happening or where it was taking place. The workers in the images wore blue overalls but their faces were out of shot. The submerged birds looked like angels drowning in snow. Attila could make no sense of it. He reached for his glasses to read the subtitles, but by the time he had put them on the item was over.

Around nine o'clock the boy woke again. Outside the door Attila found the day's newspaper and Tano's clothes laundered and wrapped in paper. They dressed and went downstairs to the restaurant, where the boy stood agog before the breakfast buffet. Attila piled a plate with eggs, bacon, pancakes, whipped cream and maple syrup. He set it down in front of the youngster. For himself he selected an austere breakfast of cold meats, black bread, olives and cucumber, such as a Prussian army officer might eat on the eve of battle. Attila wanted his wits about him and so he ate accordingly.

On the walk to the hospital Tano ran across the bridge ahead of Attila. At the nurses' station he hopped on his toes. When they reached Ama's room to find it empty he became immediately crestfallen. A moment later Ama came through the door and the boy raced over and wrapped his arms around her waist. On the bed he curled up and tucked himself under her arm. He did not seem to be able to get close enough to her.

To his mother he told his story. At the foster home he shared a room with an older boy who scratched himself so much he tore his arms until they bled and he cried in his sleep. The boy told Tano that they would be sent back to the countries their parents had come from. Tano did not know whether to believe him. He only knew he did not want to be there with the boy who scratched himself and the woman and the man, though they gave the boys tinned peaches for supper and that was okay. In the morning, while the other boy watched, Tano took his Nintendo, some juice and cheese from the fridge. The boy asked him if he was running away and Tano asked if he wanted to come too, because he felt sorry for him now. The boy shook his head. So Tano told the couple he was going to the playground opposite the house and didn't come back. He thought the woman would be too fat to chase him. He went back to the flat but his key didn't work. By then it was nearly dark. He didn't want to get into trouble with the woman and the man or the social workers, who would be angry with him, so he never went back. He went to the river because he and Ama had been there once at Christmas. He knew there were big buildings where anybody could just walk in and sit. At night when the buildings emptied he would hide in the underground car park and slip back inside when everyone had gone. He slept in one of the theatres between the rows of seats because the security men patrolled the building.

'What if something had happened to you?' Ama straightened up suddenly, pushing Tano away from her. She took him by the shoulders. 'Do you have any idea how many people there are who might hurt you?' Ama substituted anger for fear.

Tano blinked.

Attila said: 'He used his wits. For everything else we can be grateful.'

Ama was silent, then she bent and kissed the top of Tano's head. 'Can we go home?' asked Tano.

They re-crossed the water by way of Southwark Bridge. Attila had a briefing with the lawyers to discuss the case for which he had agreed to act as a professional witness. Their offices were in a road off Fleet Street. The boy, by his side, had reverted to silence, walked trailing his fingertips along the bridge's balustrade. When they reached the offices Attila settled the boy in reception and told him to wait. The lawyer was about one third the age of Attila, a young man with blond hair stiffened into spikelets. He pushed a file of documents across the empty desk towards Attila. That moment the telephone rang and Attila waited while the lawyer took the call. 'Right,' said the young man after he had hung up. 'Where were we? Okay, so we argued the defendant was unfit to stand trial, but the judge didn't buy that, so now we're going for diminished responsibility. That's where you come in. If that doesn't work we hit them with *mens rea*, argue she didn't possess the mental capacity to form a motive. The report is in the file, along with pretty much everything else. Let my clerk know if anything is missing.' The lawyer pushed a business card across the table in pursuit of the file.

'On what grounds,' said Attila, 'are you going to argue diminished responsibility?'

The lawyer glanced up at him: 'PTSD, of course.'

'The basis?'

The lawyer frowned, reached across and picked up the file, opened it and removed a sheet of paper which he proffered to Attila. 'Her husband was killed,' he said. 'Here's the report from the first psychiatrist.'

Attila kept his hands in his lap. 'How was he killed?'

'Car hit him.'

'Was the defendant a witness to this?'

'Uh-uh. No. But she's his wife.' The lawyer replaced the sheet of paper in the file and slid it back across the desk.

Attila said: 'I was told the charge was arson.'

'That's right. She set fire to the apartment.'

'Her own apartment?'

'No, it was rented, hence the charge. The property didn't belong to her.'

'What kind of sentence is she faced with, may I ask?'

'Arson sentences can be lengthy. That's not likely in this case as nobody was hurt and she didn't intend to hurt anybody, at least so we'll argue. But the flat adjoined other properties next door and downstairs, that's the prosecution's point. And there's something else. She never naturalised. If she's convicted the court can recommend her deportation.'

Now Attila understood how this case had found him. He said: 'When may I examine her?'

'She's already been examined. The report's in the file, like I said. But if you want to do it yourself my clerk can arrange it. She's on bail.'

In the reception area he found the boy just as he had left him and together they stepped back into the street. It was only midday, they had the day to themselves. They walked on and sat on a bench in St Paul's Square. If he had been alone Attila might have gone to a lunchtime recital in the cathedral. 'What would you like to do?' he said to the child, who shrugged and made no reply. There were no children in the square, not a single one except the boy. There were no children at the hotel either. There had been children in the hospital, but since then Attila had not laid eyes on another child. He turned to the boy. 'Shall we go to the zoo?' he said.

At the zoo the animals were all inside their shelters. The pens purporting to hold the brown bears, the lynx, the leopard, the tigers and the hyenas were empty: scattered straw and the occasional turd the only evidence of life. Even the Antarctic penguins seemed to be in hiding. Only the most sizeable mammals remained at large in their pens. Attila and Tano watched a camel: its swaying, soft-footed gait and indifferent gaze. Attila read aloud: '"The large, wide foot of the camel is adapted to walking on desert sand. When there is plenty of food to eat, camels build up fat in their humps. They originated in the hot, dry Sahara Desert in North Africa and the rough, rugged Gobi Desert located in parts of eastern and central Asia. Able to withstand incredible temperatures ranging from forty degrees centigrade to minus thirty degrees centigrade, they grow a dense shaggy coat that they shed in the spring."'

They finally fled the chill for the sanctuary of the small-mammal house. Inside the hot air was thick with the scent of musk and urine, the lights dim. When Attila's eyes had adjusted to the darkness he saw Tano peering through the thickened glass at a variety of rodents as they burrowed, slept and scratched. Attila looked into the terrarium nearest him. He saw nothing. He reached for his glasses and pushed his nose close to the glass where he found himself face to face with perhaps the ugliest living thing he had ever seen. Tiny blind eyes like two weevils, curved yellow incisors, a pair of unadorned holes in place of ears, skin that was pink and wrinkled. Attila noticed the animal also had a pair of upwards-curving incisors growing out of its lower jaw. The whole creature would have fitted in his top pocket. Attila jerked his head backwards and stood up, as shocked as if he had opened the bathroom door on an old man taking a shower. *Heterocephalus glaber.* Naked mole rat.

The animal in the next cage he recognised from his trips to New York City. *Rattus norvegicus.* The brown rat. This lot were awake and looking lively. One of the rats held its paws up in front of its chest and looked at him, or so it seemed. Attila waited to see what it would do next, but the rat appeared to see nothing of interest and turned away, busying itself moving pieces of feed from one location to another. In the next cage came the black rat. "'*Rattus rattus,*'" read Attila out loud. At the back of the cage sat a creature with lustrous dark hair, gleaming elliptical eyes and rounded ears. *Rattus norvegicus* and *Rattus rattus* seemed the most contented of all the animals in the zoo. *Rattus rattus* owned an information board dense with writing compared to the other species in the small-mammal house. From the board he discovered that black ship rats were commonly thought to have brought plague-carrying fleas to London, but recent scientific inquiry now suggested otherwise. The plague had been carried not by rats, but by gerbils. It occurred to Attila that he had never seen a wild gerbil. The text was accompanied by a line drawing of a man wearing a long coat and a tall hat holding a cage full of rats and accompanied by a terrier.

They remained at the zoo another two hours. Attila found a place for lunch and ordered burgers and milkshakes and an ice-cream sundae boat with scoops the size of tennis balls for the boy and a coffee for himself. Tano ate and Attila opened the file the solicitor had given him. He flicked through until he found the case report.

INTRODUCTION
Post-traumatic stress disorder is defined as a mental disorder that arises from the experience of traumatic life events, which cause pervasive distress. Typical symptoms include reliving the trauma, intrusive memories or dreams, emotional numbness, detachment from other people, avoidance of activities and situations reminiscent of trauma. PTSD arising from wartime combat has now been established as grounds for successful legal defence. Acknowledgement of PTSD in civilian populations has been mainly confined to civil law.

That was for the judge's sake. He glanced over at Tano. The boy was spooning ice cream into his mouth in rotation from each of his three differently flavoured tennis balls in turn. Chocolate. Pistachio. Vanilla.

The defendant, Mrs S., moved to this country nearly three years ago to join her husband of six years. Prior to that she had been living in Sierra Leone, West Africa. In July last year the defendant suffered the death of her husband who was hit by a car on his way to work and died in hospital some hours later. DSM 5 recognises the violent death of a loved one as a potential stressor for PTSD. In addition the defendant suffered an earlier traumatic episode when her husband was kidnapped and held for a period in Iraq while working for a civilian contractor providing support services to the British Armed Forces. This event may have acted as an additional early stressor, later compounded by the death of the husband in a traffic accident, leading to a diagnosis of comorbid mental disorders of complicated grief disorder and PTSD.

Attila reread the second paragraph twice. As he sipped his coffee he thought about how Kathleen Branagan had tried to interest him in the case the day after he arrived. Well, he was interested now. He

157

was about to reach for the file to review the other papers when he realised the boy was sitting quietly before both Attila and his empty ice-cream dish.

In the early evening Attila attended one of the receptions for the conference, having failed thus far to make an appearance at any of the events. The party was held in a hotel not far from the Aldwych and Attila, having few other options, took Tano with him. On their way back to the hotel earlier in the afternoon he had stopped at the Gap store in Covent Garden and bought Tano a set of new clothes and, at another shop on the Strand, a small holdall to put them in. Now at the reception he planted Tano on a chair near the food and told him to wait, then he went through the crowd in search of Kathleen Branagan. He found her at the centre of a small group in the middle of the room, and she, as soon as she saw him, smiled and withdrew. She kissed him on both cheeks, deftly stole a glass of champagne from a passing waiter and handed it to him, clinked her glass against his. She tilted her head to one side and raised her eyebrows: 'So?'

'So, indeed,' replied Attila. 'Very interesting.'

'It has your name written all over it.'

'It does.'

'And you'll get her off. Of course you will.'

'The file doesn't give a name,' said Attila.

'That's more or less standard practice. In fact, it *is* standard practice. New rules around confidentiality. You'll find out soon enough.' She looked at him over the rim of her glass.

Attila shook his head. 'Some details sound like another case I knew about.'

'A case concerning a female arsonist?'

'No, a case about a kidnapping.' Over Kathleen's shoulder he could see Tano, who had stopped playing with his game console and begun to look around. Attila raised a hand and beckoned the boy over.

'Is this the boy you told me about?' asked Kathleen.

'Yes.' They watched Tano make his way across the room. Amid so many adults absorbed in their conversations he looked out of place, improbably small and vulnerable.

'How is he doing?'

'Okay, I think,' said Attila. 'It has only been a day.' When Tano reached them he introduced the boy to Kathleen.

'Hello,' she said. 'And do you like long, boring speeches?'

Tano shook his head.

'Then skedaddle!' said Kathleen. She patted him on the head and said to Attila: 'Go on, get out of here! Before we get started.'

Chapter 11

At the police station Jean waited to report last night's events. In a room devoid of natural light and smelling of coffee and morning breath, a duty officer took her statement, exactingly and in long-hand, pressing his pencil into the pages of his pad to inscribe each sentence as if on a tablet of stone. Jean delivered her story one sentence at a time and waited while the sentence was committed to the pad before she delivered another. When she reached the end, the part when Attila and the team had shown up, she stopped. The officer looked up at her. 'What happened then?'

'Nothing,' said Jean. 'The men left as far as I know. The rest of us went home.'

'When was it you were assaulted?'

'I wasn't,' said Jean.

'You said you were here to report an assault.'

'No,' said Jean. 'I'm here to report an illegal fox hunt.' The officer had blue eyes with dark eyelashes, pale skin flowered with pink. To Jean he seemed undersized, not just for a police officer, for anyone, really. 'It's illegal to hunt foxes with dogs and it's illegal to hunt foxes on public property.'

'One moment.' He stood up and walked away from his desk. Jean saw him approach another officer. After a few minutes he came back and sat down. 'Somebody will be in touch with you. In the meantime you might like to read these.' He handed Jean a pair of leaflets from his desk. 'If You Have Been a Victim of a Crime', read Jean.

'I haven't been a victim of a crime,' said Jean trying to hand the leaflet back to him. When he refused to take it she laid it on the desk.

'It's not just for victims of crimes, it's for people who have been affected by crimes as well.' He pushed it back towards her. 'There are numbers for support groups, places to get help.' It was evident to Jean her complaint had just been shelved. She reached for the leaflet and stood up.

At home she climbed the stairs to the roof garden. She was tired, out of sorts. Carrying her coffee with her she began to inspect the vegetable beds. Gardening had always smoothed out her irritations, she did most of her thinking with her fingers in the soil. She reached down and pulled at a few weeds. Now was the time to start preparing the beds, the grasses in the 'meadow' needed cutting back too. The highs and lows of the night before, starting with the search for the boy, the encounter in the park and the threat of violence which left her sweating and sharply alert for much of the rest of the evening, finding Tano in the theatre car park, the hour of calm which the meal in the Savoy kitchens represented – by the time she had arrived back home it was past four in the morning. Then the morning trip to the police station. No word from Attila. She hoped the boy was okay. After all the drama she felt suddenly cut loose. She fetched a pair of shears and a rake and for the next hour went to work on the meadow, pulling at the tangled mat of dead grass.

At midday she called Luke, whose voice sounded muffled and indistinct. 'Flu,' he said.

'Go back to sleep,' urged Jean. 'I'll call you later.'

'No worries. I have to get up anyway.'

'You're not thinking of going to work like that?'

'I'll work from home. I have a report to finish. It has to be in by tomorrow.'

'Tell them you can't.'

Luke sighed: 'You know it doesn't work like that.'

Jean wished she was there but she wasn't even in the same time zone. 'How much do you have done?'

'I've got a draft. I just need to go through it.'

'Mail it to me. I'll do that for you.'

'It's okay, Jean. It's nothing I can't handle.'

'I write reports all the time, it will be easy for me.'

'I've got it.'

'I have time right now.'

But Luke sneezed and didn't hear her, and even to her own ears she was beginning to sound insistent, so instead of repeating herself she said: 'Take paracetamol. And drink plenty of fluids.'

After she had hung up she tried calling Ray at home and eventually got him on his cell.

'Want me to drive down? I can. It's only two hours thirty.'

'He sounded awful.'

'Let me call Luke and get back to you, okay, honey?'

When he called back he said: 'Doesn't sound too good at all. No bad idea to head down there. Give a bit of moral support. Bring him food and stuff, fix us some dinner. I won't stay over.'

'He said yes?'

'Oh he said yes all right.' Ray paused and she could see him, he was smiling, maybe a little sadly: 'It's amazing how it all comes right back. Even when they've left college and gotten a job, they're sick and they just want you. I was the same, just the same.' He laughed softly. 'After I left home I thought I knew it all, but as soon as I got the slightest bit sick l hauled my sorry ass home.'

Jean gave a small laugh but said nothing. Eventually she heard Ray say: 'Jeannie, are you there?'

'Sure,' she said.

She heard him take a breath. She knew that breath. The pause, the breath, the momentary hesitation: he was preparing to give her some news and it wasn't good news. Ray said: 'I've been seeing somebody. We're thinking of moving in ... I'd like her to move in. Jeannie?' The second time he had called her Jeannie in less than a minute.

'That's great, Ray, that's really great. I'm happy for you.' Because that's what people said.

'Thank you.'

'Does Luke know?'

A fractional hesitation, another. I see, thought Jean.

'He met her. At Christmas.'

162

'Wow! You all spent Christmas together?'

'No, no,' said Ray. 'Jodie has her own kids and they stayed over Christmas, they're a bit younger. We just stopped by. I'm sorry, I didn't mean … I should have told you …'

'It's okay. Really. I'm happy for you, I mean that. And thanks for going to take care of Luke.'

Said Ray: 'I'll call you when I get there.'

'It'll be the middle of the night.'

'Then in the morning.'

Jean picked up the binoculars and scanned the locale but found no sign of Light Bright. Rather her gaze rested on a dead tree which stood in the derelict plot just beyond the boundary of the rental van parking lot. She lowered the binoculars and looked at it, the dark wood of its trunk and limbs, the unforgiving silhouette, the tree was dead and yet in death had conceded nothing. Photographers and artists were attracted to dead trees and Jean could understand why: a thing fixed in time, they looked like pieces of missing sky, still standing but no longer living, holding on to the secrets of one hundred or more years. There was something comforting about a dead tree, children were attracted to climb in their branches, bees to hive in their hollows and animals dug through the soft wood at their base to make burrows. After death the tree continued to preserve life.

In the afternoon Jean worked on the plans for the roof garden in City Road. She shifted plants around, added new ones, she went online and placed orders for the bulk of the building materials and pre-ordered a good many of the shrubs and plants, she chose some bulbs even though she had missed the optimal time to plant them, still worth taking the chance and burying a few in containers. In between calls and searching the Net, she checked her cell, she was waiting to hear from Attila.

She stood and stretched and went to the window overlooking the street. Friday evening. Young men in white cotton tunics and skull-caps clutched holy books. They walked to mosque with the same head-down gait, like the clergymen in Victorian paintings. Africans mainly, Jean knew this now. By the time they came out of prayers the street would have begun to fill with weekend revellers, up from the southern suburbs and from Kent, girls with bare legs tottering in high heels, by the end of the evening they would be walking barefoot and carrying their shoes, their boyfriends walked on the balls of their feet, key chains dangling from their middle finger, young Chinese men in sports cars, stretch limousines making their way to central London. Already police vehicles were lined up in the southern reaches of the Old Kent Road. Jean would fall asleep bathed in the blue flash of lights and wake to the sounds of the street-sweepers. By ten o'clock the housewives would be out and waiting in line at the halal butcher and by Sunday morning the evangelical Christians would be on their way to church.

At eight o'clock her cell rang. 'Where are you?' she said.

'Back at the hotel,' said Attila. 'Tano is watching a movie. I'm doing paperwork. Digital paperwork.' He laughed. She listened and realised what it was she had encountered the night before, the thing that had been present throughout the evening, as they searched for the missing boy, as they gathered to review the search, down in the freezing depths of the car park. There had been laughter. Among Americans, among the British, what she knew of them, she could not imagine there being laughter. Nobody would have dared. She had been shocked by it at first. The sound of the laughter had seemed disrespectful to the endeavour, to the plight of the child, the mother. And then in those final minutes in the park, the laughter had dispelled the fear and proved its own worth.

Attila was still talking. He was telling her how they couldn't get into the flat and the mother was likely to be under observation in hospital a day or so more. 'My plan was to keep him with me, to be sure he's all right, but there are just a few things I need to do.'

'Bring him here,' said Jean. 'I can watch him tomorrow.'

But Attila carried on as if he had not heard her: 'I should call his mother and make arrangements, see if she has a childminder or some such.'

She had spoken almost on a whim, but now she grew more certain of the idea. 'I really don't mind. Call her and see if she's okay with it. I've raised a son myself not all that long ago. Plus it's just for tomorrow, right?'

A momentary pause. 'Yes. And I'd join you as soon as I'm free. Would that really be acceptable to you? I'll tell Ama that Tano will be fine with you.'

'It's the weekend. I'm fine with it, really I am.' In fact, she had surprised herself with the offer, but the child had seemed like a good enough kid. As much, more, she wanted to be back in Attila's company.

She wrote an email to the producer of the radio show describing the incident she had witnessed in the park and asking if she might come back on air to talk about cruelty to foxes, who as wild animals required protection. She wrote that it was not just a question of the fox but also of the dogs who were being bred and used for that and other purposes, dog fights for example. Did anyone wonder, Jean continued, why the pounds were now full of a single breed of dog?

A few months ago, in an idle moment, Jean had clicked on a link to Battersea Dogs & Cats Home. Image after image of dogs, almost all of them Staffordshire bull terriers, the home was a dumping ground for unwanted pets. The streets of London, like the streets of Boston or New York, were clear of stray animals. Only once in all Jean's night-time outings had she seen what she took to be a stray dog, a poodle with a terrible case of mange. Jean had tried to encourage it to come to her, but at the sound of her voice the dog fled. She had seen it once or twice again near the gasworks, more spirit than animal. In Mexico on holiday, there had been stray dogs lying under the sun umbrellas on the beach until they were shooed away by the hotel staff. The locals ignored them, a few of the tourists gave them food. A woman holding a bulging paper napkin threw bread rolls at a bitch with elongated teats. As Jean passed the woman gave her a small smile: 'I'm a dog lover,' she said in a confessional tone. 'Can't bear to see an animal treated this way. Tender-hearted, my husband says.' The woman searched her handbag for her wallet and extracted photographs of three Pomeranians. In each photograph the animals, tiny faces alert and intent, stared fractionally off-camera at what Jean supposed was a piece of meat being held by the photographer.

The email was now longer than Jean had intended, but she sent it off. Just a second later a reply arrived: 'Automatic Response: Out of Office'.

She found a rerun of *The Way We Were* on television, fetched a half-tub of ice cream from the freezer and settled on the sofa for the kind of evening she used to enjoy. First time around watching the movie the teenage Jean had been exasperated by Katie, played by Barbra Streisand. Robert Redford as Hubbell she thought most attractive, but now as the film wore on, it was Hubbell who irritated. She wondered what his societal value was supposed to be. The nonchalance she had found attractive as a teen she saw now was fecklessness.

Katie was so brim-full of in-your-face earnestness. All that caring was exhausting, for Hubbell who didn't have a rebellious bone in his body, who had been born wealthy and was already sated. Compassion was tiring for the Katies of the world too, thought Jean. Sometimes Jean envied the heartless, not the cruel, just the casually heartless, untroubled by everything that was wrong in the world, for the quality of sleep they must surely enjoy.

Jean peered at the television and noticed that Redford had had his teeth fixed since the film was made, and Katie's hair was a barometer of her conformity or waywardness. Good Katie wore her hair on her shoulders like spaniel ears. Troublesome Katie's hair sprang from her head in curls. There was a little girl and she had a little curl right in the middle of her forehead, when she was good she was very, very good. And when she was bad she was horrid.

In the final scene of *The Way We Were* Hubbell spots Katie outside a hotel in New York, *Ban the Bomb* flyers in hand. He asks after their daughter who, the dialogue implies, he hasn't seen since the divorce some years before. Katie smiles and tells him their daughter is doing well.

You could never end a film like that these days, thought Jean. Cinema audiences would not stand for it. Even if one kind of love was allowed to fail, the other kind had to be kept safe. Hubbell might be allowed to abandon his wife, but never his daughter.

Lexington Street in Greenhampton runs parallel to South Street where, opposite the now closed gas station, Ray's Classic Car Showroom can be found. South Street is itself an extension of Main Street (J&T Nail Salon, Pam's Family Cuts, Hometown Realtor, Lucky Lanes, the Jolly Tavern, no less than three consignment stores) and it in turn runs parallel to the railway line, along which once ran locomotives loaded with pulp from the sawmills of Greenhampton, carrying passengers to and from Boston and North Adams. Now the red-brick building bears the sign: No Passenger Trains, *and houses a skeleton staff merely to man the lines and signals. Twice a day comes the jangling of bells and the whistle of an Amtrak freight train like an air-raid siren above Greenhampton. Those visitors to the town (passing through on their way to the more picturesque delights of Shelburne Falls, the Mohawk Trail and state parks and who are filling up with gas and/or supplies) stop to wonder and to gaze at the sky. Meanwhile the residents of Greenhampton waiting to take their money or bag their groceries or cross South Street continue unconcerned by the terrifying noise, so that it seems to the visitors that they have wandered accidentally into a colony of the deaf.*

To Lexington Street, where few visitors have any reason to go. In between two of the clapboard houses (the one with the tag sale on the lawn every Saturday and the one converted ten years ago into a local history centre), there stands a carved wooden statue of a man wearing a buffalo calfskin coat. In one hand he holds a long gun by the barrel. Slung across his shoulders, as a shepherd carries a lost lamb, he bears the carcass of a wolf. Above the statue hangs a wooden sign on a chain, and on the sign is carved: The Wolfer, 1834.

The last years of the nineteenth century brought recession to large parts of New England. Around Greenhampton the rock-strewn soil was exhausted and those sheep farmers who had not already sold the last of their animals and headed west were now departed. For the first time in two hundred years the forests grew back, only to be hacked down a second time early in the next century for soft pine to feed the new mills that brought prosperity briefly back to Greenhampton. When the mills died the trees grew up again. In all the years since the wolfer's last visit the wolves never returned to New England.

Instead into this newly emptied territory stole the coyote. Silent, unseen, loping thousands of miles from the scorching prairies of the western states, spreading north-west through Oregon and Washington State, east through the sub-zero snowbound winters of the Midwest to New England. There the coyote found a world well suited to its needs: forest cut through with highways which joined settlements to small towns and small towns to larger towns all the way to the Eastern Seaboard. Like a vagabond, the coyote travelled these new corridors, flitting beyond the boundaries of towns, feeding on whatever they could find: mice, woodchuck, roadkill, apples from the farmers' orchards. At night they howled high in the hills beyond earshot of the humans below.

With the wolves gone, the coyotes became king. The wolves had chased them down, now their pups survived and fattened. Over time they started to cross into the farmers' fields, skirt the suburbs in shallower arcs, trail the boundary fence of a back yard in the dead of night and set the dogs barking, shift from dark into daylight. People began to report sightings of the predators. Some thought they were wild dogs. Others rightly said they were coyotes, but deduced they must have been brought to Massachusetts as pets and abandoned. Others still called them coy dogs, whelped by coyote bitches who had mated with domestic dogs. A last group insisted they were wolves, not the great, grey wolf, but a smaller, fleeter wolf. They called them brush wolves, timber wolves, prairie wolves.

In 1972 one of the beasts was shot and carted into town on the bed of a pick-up. Crowds gathered. Too small for a wolf, too large for a coyote. A team from Hampshire College conducted a study of the carcasses of other animals hit by cars and concluded this was neither wolf nor dog nor coyote, but an entirely new animal. They called it the New Hampshire Canid. The biologists squabbled. The animals were captured and studied. Their paws did not sweat like those of coyotes, their snouts were longer and thinner, they stood taller at the shoulder, they did not form packs in the same way as wolves or hunt as wolves, yet their coats were more wolf grey than red, they seemed less afraid of humans than either coyotes or wolves. But the howl, the howl was the howl of a coyote. Who could explain that?

A conference of experts sifted and scrutinised the evidence, a conclusion was reached. The animals were coyotes. Somehow the species had fast-tracked evolution, in the migration north had mated with the last of the grey wolves and then, in a multitude of ways, had adapted its diet, behaviour and physique to the new habitat not in millennia but in decades. Whether the animal possessed any wolf DNA would be disputed for decades, but the rest of the theory as it stood was accepted. They called it the Eastern Coyote.

Most days Jean could be sure to pass the statue of the wolfer only a few streets away from her house and on the way to Ray's showroom, to Main Street, to the school and Stop n' Shop. She had paused once or twice to read the inscription and learned that the wolfer was credited, if that was the word (the language on the plaque itself was replete with praise) with killing the last mating pair of wolves in the hills around Greenhampton. There were other memorials and monuments in small towns here and there in New England, commemorating the sites of battles against Native Americans, the heroic pioneers and their famous Indian killers, who carried around the scalps of their victims and were paid bounties for each one. This was the only monument Jean had ever seen to a wolfer. Men like him had hunted wolves to near extinction and now wolves were a protected species in many parts, which could hardly have been what the wolfer envisioned. The new battle was with the coyote. But it seemed the coyotes had learned from the fate of the wolves: they did not come out into the open but fought a guerrilla war for survival. Between man and the coyotes, the coyotes were winning.

Had she been headed home now and turned right at Pine Street, passing the fire station, and followed the curve of the road to the left Jean would have passed the wolfer statue in about three minutes and been home in six. But she didn't. Instead she drove past the Pine Street turn-off, past Ray's Classic Car Showroom where the shutters were down and on along the highway to the outskirts of town. It was 2 a.m. One more loop and home. She reached over and played with the dial of the receiver on the Tacoma's dash, adjusting it by increments, listening for patterns of sound through the hiss and crackle. For a moment she thought she caught something only to lose it again. She slowed down. A pair of headlights rushed up out of the darkness behind her, swung out as the driver overtook. Jean looked for a place to pull over and stopped, she played with the receiver until she found the electronic note. Dip-dip, dip-dip. Faintly at first, then it faded out altogether. She searched for another minute then drove on for a mile or so at a crawl, this time ignoring the angry flash of headlights behind her. Perhaps half a mile further on she picked up the sound again. Dip-dip, dip-dip. She kept moving. The sound grew stronger. By now she had reached the golf course. On a hunch she pulled into the parking lot and cut the engine. She parked next to the mini-golf circuit, could just make out the clown that stood on top of the hill the train tunnel ran through. Greenhampton Golf Course and Mini Golf. Daily green fees. All Welcome!

Jean switched off the headlights, picked up the binoculars and scanned the darkness – the signal was still good. A sighting would cap her night, but even without it she was satisfied. Weeks could go by without picking up the signal of any one of the animals in her study group. This week alone she had located three. By the standards of the last five months that was pretty remarkable. Each animal had its own frequency. This coyote, the sixth of six to be trapped and tagged, was a female of about five years. The team had named her Dinger, because Victor, the other full-time member of the team, was a Red Sox fan. There was Yakker, Whiff, Uncle Charlie, Moon Catch and Ace. Months of work, an average ten traps in different locations, a month per animal. Each coyote had been caught, sedated, tagged and released.

Jean opened the door and swung down from the Tacoma. She closed the door behind her before the alarm, which sounded as soon as the door was left open for more than ten seconds, could start up. She had been meaning to ask Ray to disable it. Even though the night was reasonably warm she zipped her jacket as she made her way across the gravel, stepped over the railway sleepers that marked the boundary between the parking lot and the mini-golf course and made her way to the first tee. She raised the binoculars and scanned the edges of the course. On the second pass she caught a movement between the trees. A large animal, it could as easily be a deer. She waited. A short while later the animal broke cover into the open, moving with the rocking canter of the coyote.

Back in the car Jean logged the activity. Time in. Time out. Route. Sightings. On the way home she started to call Victor then realised the time and depressed the red button on her cellphone. Instead she pushed a tape into the old tape deck, wound down the window and began to sing along to Roxette, 'It Must Have Been Love'.

The first coyote study Jean had taken part in five years previously had been terminated after just four months, or more accurately had never received the second portion of funding from the state wildlife authority. Jean, a volunteer on the project, had been disappointed but unsurprised. Nobody then had thought the Ecology and Behaviour of the Eastern Coyote a priority, though that had changed in the five years since. When the programme wound up Jean had been left with the receiving equipment installed in her vehicle, which nobody had bothered to requisition. Jean herself forgot it was there, the equipment lay unused for months. One April day she picked Luke up from the train station in Springfield at the start of Easter break. Sitting in the passenger seat in an idle moment he had turned on the receiver and begun to play with the settings. Distinctly, for just a few seconds, the radio had picked up a signal, it was there and gone. Jean thought it was probably just a fault with the equipment, or an overlapping signal from somewhere else, after all the collars would be right on the end of their battery life, if not dead. All the same in the coming weeks, whenever she neared the place where they'd caught the signal, she turned on the receiver and tuned in. Six weeks later she picked up the signal about half a mile from the old tool factory. This time there was no mistake. For the four months of the study she'd had each animal's frequency locked into her brain. This one belonged to Archie (Veronica, Betty, Reggie and Jughead came later). Jean had trapped Archie alone with a dart gun, in a stroke of beginner's luck never to be repeated, thirty miles west of Greenhampton. A lone male, probably transient. Jean had tracked Archie's signal over the next six months. She located him at different sites, near the reservoir, up at the town dump, and several times right here in town, in the centre of Greenhampton. She had caught glimpses of him, but the first proper sighting of him came when she least expected it. She had been out running. Alone. Bess their dog who used to run with her had died the year before. The day had got off to a sticky start and it was nearly eleven by the time she headed out.

Late summer and hot. At the back of the house a track led down the side of the houses and into a patch of woodland. Some way beyond the last of the houses was a piece of uncultivated land where the grass was tall and wild flowers grew. Forty minutes after she left the house, defeated by the heat and humidity and the blister forming on her heel caused by her new running shoes, Jean stopped to pull them off and walk home barefoot. When she straightened up she saw, just above the height of the grass, a small face, pointed ears, black eyes. A coyote pup. Jean did not move. Neither did the pup, uncertain what to do next. A moment later it turned and bounded in the direction, Jean now saw, of an adult coyote sitting in the grass beyond. There was movement in the grass. A family group. The adult had been wearing a radio collar, and though the whole encounter was over in a matter of seconds Jean had recognised Archie.

It had taken a year to raise the funding for this new study of which Jean was leader, the Urban and Suburban Distribution of the Eastern Coyote, and it had begun with Archie.

Though the next day was Saturday, Jean headed into the office. On the way she remembered to stop at Ray's showroom to see if he had a few moments to disconnect the door alarm. She found Ray talking to a customer. He waved her over. As the customer turned Jean recognised Arthur Wood. Arthur Wood, known as the Woodsman, was a forest manager who took care of a tract of land held by a company which in turn was owned by a family out in Providence. The land straddled the main highway. Jean had had dealings with Arthur Wood some time ago over several miles of Jersey barrier erected along a stretch of the road, part of which lay in the belt he managed. The barrier, essentially a solid wall of concrete down the middle of the highway, replaced the median strip. It prevented lane crossovers and acted as a crash barrier but also caused the death of thousands of animals a year. Where once an animal took their chances crossing the highway, with the introduction of Jersey barriers they became trapped halfway across between an impassable wall and rushing traffic. Either they were hit by a car or died of terror. Every stretch of road where a Jersey barrier stood was littered with the carcasses of racoons, foxes, porcupines, skunks and possums. Wildlife biologists and environmentalists petitioned for the removal of the barriers in many places, and when that failed, for animal crossings, underpasses to be included in the plans for every new highway. The road builders resented the extra cost, the engineers argued underpasses compromised the strength of the road structure. To this day the true nature of Arthur Wood's objection to the crossings was something Jean never understood. Sure he managed the land on either side of the highway, but Jean couldn't see what difference it made where the porcupine or the skunk ended up. He argued the expense was wasted money, but what struck Jean was his vigilance. Arthur Wood never missed a meeting at the town hall. Jean couldn't figure out whether the Woodsman had something against her, or simply held firm to the belief that animals had no right of way.

'Hello, Arthur,' said Jean.

Arthur Wood smiled and tipped an imaginary hat: 'Hello there, Jean.'

'Hey!' Ray put an arm around Jean's shoulders. If he sensed anything of the undercurrents between Jean and Wood, he planned to ignore them. 'What's up?'

'Only if you have a moment. Do you?' She glanced at Arthur Wood.

'You go ahead and talk to your husband, ma'am,' said the Woodsman. 'I'm in no hurry here.' He turned and ran his hand over a Pontiac Firebird on sale at $32,000. Ray said he could as easily take a look at the alarm at home, on the other hand if she wanted it done in a hurry she could swing by later in the afternoon and he'd take care of it.

'Are you home this evening?'

'Maybe later,' Jean said, knowing this was not the answer he was hoping for.

Ray shrugged, he didn't smile. 'Okay, bring her by here this afternoon. Steak all right with you?'

'You want me to pick a couple up?'

'I got it.'

Jean turned to go. She was aware of the Woodsman listening to their conversation, she nodded to him. He said: 'You're busy with the coyotes now.' He turned his question into a statement so that it sounded like a charge.

Jean told him she was.

'I hear they're causing problems for the sheep farmers.'

There had been reports of coyotes packing up and going after sheep, but you'd have to go all the way to Iowa for that. 'There haven't been any reports of trouble in this area.' Apart from the very occasional family petting farm nobody raised sheep around Greenhampton any longer and hadn't for a century.

'If you say so,' replied the Woodsman.

Jean said nothing. She left the showroom and swung herself back behind the wheel of the Tacoma. The afternoon she spent logging data and typing up her notes. She had begun a draft report of initial findings and was working on the introduction. Now she typed:

Increasing urbanisation is characterised by displacement of native vegetation with man-made structures and increased disturbance and hazards to wildlife because of higher densities of people, roads. Construction of houses, commercial buildings, parking lots, and roads alters and fragments habitat. These changes in environmental structure and function may lead to changes in species distribution (Koenen and DeStefano). Many species cannot cope with the changes brought on by urbanisation and become extirpated locally. Other species, like Cooper's hawks (Accipiter cooperii), are attracted to particular features of urban environments.

She enjoyed this part of her job least, but she enjoyed it nonetheless. The setting down of facts, the extrapolation of meaning from those same facts, making sense of the world you could say. Everything happens for a reason, that was Jean's view, and part of her job was tracing those chains of cause and effect, mapping the interconnectedness of things.

Since their work began the team had been getting more and more calls from the public who they encouraged to report coyote sightings. Once or twice they had been called out to deal with a problem. A coyote trapped in a barbed-wire fence. Victor held the animal's neck in a catch pole while Jean cut the wire. A coyote cornered by a pair of mastiffs, the animal was just about dead with terror. Jean didn't understand why the mastiff owner had needed her help, when all he had to do was call off his dogs. He seemed to think that she worked for a pest control agency and would remove the coyote. Jean told him there was nothing to do but let the animal go. 'Just like that?' he said.

'Just like that.'

The occasional call came in to tell them about a coyote killed by a car and one of the team, usually Jean or Victor, went out to check, to see whether the dead animal was wearing a radio collar. So far they'd been lucky and not lost a single member of the study cohort.

A Tuesday some eight months ago Jean had been home with Ray in the kitchen debating whether it was true Sidney Poitier had been considered for the role of Josiah Bartlet in The West Wing when the telephone rang. It was Victor calling from the golf course.

'Can you come down?'

The golf course and mini golf abutted a small lake and by the lake was a barbecue and picnic area and several mobile homes that were rented out in the summer. Together they accounted for the entirety of Greenhampton's tourist industry. At this time of year about half were occupied. When Jean arrived she found Victor and a few of the residents gathered together on the edge of the mobile home park, where it was separated from the golf course by a line of trees. Victor was carrying a dart rifle. At her approach he stepped away from the group and walked the twenty or so yards to meet her. Victor was raised in Hawaii but preferred snow to surf, so he said.

'A couple of coyote took down a fawn,' he said.

'Ah!' said Jean. That didn't happen often, in fact Jean had never known it happen at all for the reason that coyote would eat most anything so long as it was easy to find. Hunting, except for rodents, generally required altogether too much effort. If they were hungry enough, or if an animal was old or injured, then yes. Jean's best guess was they were probably a pair of adolescents, ganging up to see what they were capable of, teen bullies.

'And now?' said Jean.

'No sign of the coyotes,' said Victor. 'The fawn is still out there on the grass.' He sounded like an actor in a TV detective programme. The victim was taking a walk when she was assaulted. No sign of the perp.

'They'll come back for it later tonight.' Jean calculated the possibilities of setting up a watch. See who else was out there.

'You should know,' said Victor lowering his voice. 'There's a little upset around here. Some of the children saw the fawn go down.'

There was a smell of barbecue smoke and grilled meat. Some of the families had been about to sit down to eat when the coyotes made an appearance.

Jean went over. A skinny girl in a Simpsons T-shirt came up to her: 'Were they wolves?'

Jean smiled and shook her head. 'Coyotes.'

'Are they coming back?'

'Maybe. They'll be wanting to finish their supper, just like you. That's like a half-rack of baby back ribs lying out there on the grass,' said Jean. 'All we need is some barbecue sauce.'

'I'm going to get some pictures.' The kid grinned and showed Jean her camera. Jean patted her on the shoulder. The girl reminded Jean of herself when she had been a kid, before anyone started telling her what she could and couldn't be.

'You'll do no such thing!' said a woman. Ah, thought Jean, the kid's mother; Jean was wrong, it had already started. The woman marched up and inserted herself between the girl and Jean. In her hand she carried a plastic spoon and a jar of Gerber baby food. She glared at Jean: 'Are you serious?'

Jean backtracked: 'We can move the carcass if it's a problem for you.'

'Of course it's a goddamn problem.' The woman blinked and looked at Jean as though Jean was a madwoman. 'Those are wild animals and I've got my kids here.'

'A dingo stole my baby,' Jean whispered to Victor in an Australian accent, as they walked towards the deer carcass.

Nobody heard, of that she was sure.

Jean and Victor had loaded the deer carcass into the back of Jean's pick-up and heaved it into the woods a few miles south. A day or so later an item aired on the local radio weekend magazine show and an article appeared in the Greenhampton Gazette. Twice Jean was stopped in the street and once at the store and asked about the incident.

Not everyone was hostile to the coyotes: there are those who call the coyote God's dogs and they praised the work she was doing. Jean began to recognise the voices of one or two of them on the radio whenever an item ran and so did the radio host who would say: 'Welcome to the show again, Paula.' It was around that time Jean began to be called Coyote Jean.

In the months of unfolding Jean refused to believe that people were truly afraid of coyotes, regardless of what they said during the phone-ins, or in the calls and emails she received at the office or the unsigned letters that were sent to the offices of the Gazette. She didn't believe they were afraid that their cats and small dogs would be snatched, not in any real sense. In her view they were even less afraid that their children would be harmed, though you could never say that. The mention of children ended all possibility of rational discussion, an invocation to the god of the moral high ground. If you were not with them, you were against them and against their children.

No, the real driving emotion was something more base, less worthy by far than fear. It was hate. Some people hated coyotes for being what they were, and what they were was beyond the control of humans. Next to the right of humans to do exactly as they pleased, next to the outrage of the woman with the Gerber jar, a coyote had no rights. Not even the right to its own existence.

On Monday Jean and Victor attended a meeting at the town hall, an open forum to discuss the coyote problem, as certain locals insisted on calling it. In the pick-up on the way to the meeting she and Victor discussed strategy and likely outcomes, they expected the business interests and hunters to ask for an extension to the hunting season. Hunt season placed the woods effectively out of bounds for most people with small children, the question was whether the mothers' lobby would think a coyote was more of a threat to their children than a bullet.

Jean arrived confident of her argument. She'd had no part in calling the meeting, she and Victor had been invited because of their work. The hearing was to be chaired by a representative from the state wildlife agency and hunting licences brought in a lot of their annual income. On the other hand whoever the representative was should be sympathetic to the logic of her arguments.

Jean was called to speak after the introductions. She gave her name and occupation and outlined her project. The chairman was *a man of middle age with a beard and a baseball cap. A good choice, thought Jean, he looked like most of the other men in the room.*

'Maybe you can just explain to the room your views, based on your research, of hunting as a form of coyote control.'

'Hunting coyote is different from hunting, say, deer,' said Jean. 'If you remove a coyote from a territory, by whatever means, say even if one dies of natural causes a space opens up. Another will move in.'

'What if you were to kill a number of them, ten per cent of the total population, say?'

'They'd reproduce at a faster rate. We call it hyper-reproduction. Have larger litters of cubs. Begin to mate younger, at a year instead of at two years. All animals do it, not just coyote,' said Jean. 'Humans do it after a war. The last time it happened we called it the "baby boom".' There was a flutter of laughter. Jean went on. 'It's the way a species survives. Some species are better at it than others and coyote are just about the best of all.'

As Jean took her seat Victor gave her a nod.

Other members of the meeting were invited to speak. People had been asked to submit their names in advance and of those a selection had been made. A good few were the kind who liked the sound of their own voices or had a particular enthusiasm for procedural matters. For the next ten minutes not much of any substance was added to the sum total of knowledge in the room.

Then the Woodsman rose. He asked the panel if he could show a short video clip. 'I'm not too much of a speaker,' he said. 'And I'm no coyote expert. But I think the people here in this room would be interested to see this.'

People shifted in their seats and leaned forward, Jean could feel them beginning to wake up and focus once more. The video was a montage of documentary footage. Clips of coyotes, captured and cornered, looking somewhat less than playful. Talk of wolf DNA. Jean heard a woman behind her draw a breath. One interviewee kept referring to coyotes as coy wolves. Jean tapped Victor's ankle with her toe. On camera a scientist conducted a scat analysis: the camera zoomed in on his tweezers as he disentangled the mess of faeces, hair and berry stones. The scientist held something up for the camera to peruse. Jean knew what was coming. A cat's paw, or what remained of one after it had passed through the digestive tract: claws curled pale and tight as a clover flower. The video lasted seven or eight minutes, the final shots were of coyote pulling at the body of a newborn lamb while the birthing ewe struggled to stand. For the benefit of the mothers in the room. The Woodsman pointed the remote at the screen and stopped the video before the grisly conclusion. He addressed the chairman: 'I'm just saying,' he said in a reasonable tone as though concluding an argument, 'that it does none of us any good to let this thing get out of hand. There is no "wait and see" when it comes to these kinds of animals. Thank you.'

'I'm sure most people will be very concerned by that film,' said the chairman. 'I would stress that these sorts of occurrences are very rare in this area and nobody should worry unduly.' The chairman looked out over the crowd. A dozen hands were in the air. 'If we take a short break we can all gather our thoughts and I'll be pleased to take your questions.' He turned to the Woodsman and asked if he was done.

'I have a suggestion, I'd like to put it to the room,' said the Woodsman. 'Some of us would like an extension to the hunting laws. We're not asking here for what they have in Maine.' In Maine the hunt was open year round. 'The woods belong to everyone,' he added smoothly. 'We're just asking for a two-month extension at the back end of the season.' He paused. 'And we want the coyote officially reclassified as a nuisance animal.' There was a murmur around the room.

During the recess Jean went straight over to the Woodsman. 'You know none of those things are happening here.'

'Do I?'

'If they're happening where are the complaints?'

'It's a question of understanding what's happening and what's going to happen,' he said. 'Your pet cat disappears, who's to say it wasn't taken by a coyote? Maybe it's happening, only people don't know it.'

Jean took a breath: 'In my line of work we look for evidence before we make an assertion.'

'Well, goody for you.'

She was unprepared for the hostility, was about to move on when he held up both his hands and said: 'I apologise, Jean. You seem to be taking this personally and none of this is personal, believe me. Coyote don't belong here. You said so yourself when you spoke earlier. This is a prairie animal and it belongs on the prairie, not here in the streets of Greenhampton. You have to agree with me, you know that.'

'I deal with what is, not a hypothetical notion of what should be. I don't know what God's design was when he made coyote, when he gave them the ability to adapt. Maybe you do. I only know that they're here now, so evidently, quite evidently, at some level they do belong. Better than you or me, you could say. They have adapted to what was already here, while we had to change what we found to suit us. I could as easily argue that coyote belong everywhere they live.'

It was evident as soon as the meeting reconvened that the mood was altered. Jean and Victor were cast in the role of appeasers. Jean, when she got the chance to speak, took the film apart as best she could. The wolf DNA connection was pure speculation, had never been proven. Even if it was true, what were the people in this room supposed to draw from it? But she knew. Wolf terror was of a different order. The forefathers of the people in this room had driven wolves to the top of the hills around Greenhampton and then set fire to the hillsides, immolating the wolves and every other living being besides.

As for pet cats, to her this was nature's way. Cats killed songbirds. Everybody loved songbirds. Coyote killed cats. Some people loved cats. To the gathering she explained how rare it was for a coyote to take a cat, unless it was very old. Or very young, but she didn't say that, she stopped talking. Before she sat down she said: 'Can we just remember we're talking about animals here? These creatures don't own property, they don't have the vote, they're not subject to our laws. They deserve our protection.' There was clapping from three, maybe four people.

One by one others rose, less to ask genuine questions than to issue warnings and lay the ground for future blame. They began with phrases such as: 'What I want to know …' 'Who's going to …?' And: 'Can someone tell us …?' One speaker, an elderly man, pointedly ignored her when she raised her hand in order to respond to him. Jean jiggled her leg and Victor placed a staying hand on her knee. Forty minutes later the meeting broke up.

'A two-month extension on the hunting season means they'll still be hunting when the cubs are born,' she said on the drive home.

'They can't make a decision like that on the basis of one meeting,' said Victor.

Victor was right. The hunting season was not extended. Neither Jean nor Victor was prepared for what did happen, which was the reclassification of the coyote as a nuisance animal. Five months later, when the coyote hunting season resumed, a consortium of private landowners (of which the Woodsman was one) posted an advertisement in the Greenhampton Gazette *and in several of the local newspapers in the larger neighbouring towns. The advertisement offered free hunting rights over the Labor Day weekend and $50 for the scalp of each coyote killed.*

The evening of their wedding day Ray and Jean had driven west in a 1958 Corvette convertible headed for a lakeside cabin in Vermont. Ray had spent months restoring the car in secret, it was his wedding gift to Jean. The dashboard of the car held the original eight-track deck and Ray had been scouting the tag sales for cassettes. Jean found Goodbye Yellow Brick Road *and Ray drove while Jean sang along wildly to 'Bennie and the Jets'.*

The lake the next morning was lost behind a nimbus of mist. Jean, a naked bride, carried coffee out to the deck and took photographs of the emerging lake. A great blue heron rose noiselessly up from the mist and flew over the house. From the bedroom she heard Ray say her name but she did not answer until the heron had gone. 'Where are you?' he called, in a voice that betrayed a note of alarm. Jean turned away from the lake and walked back into the house, her feet noiseless on the wooden floor.

'Let's never leave here,' she said. 'Like that movie with Jane Fonda and Redford, after they get married they're in the hotel room, or maybe it's their apartment, after the wedding. They're there so long the newspapers pile up outside the door.'

'Barefoot in the Park,' said Ray.

Over the years Jean forgot the heron in the mist, the way the voice of her husband of a single day had sounded that morning and the feel of that kind of happiness. She and Ray found contentment in the everyday, in Luke and in their respective occupations. Jean believed she knew Ray's opinions on everything. Thus to Jean it seemed inexplicable that Ray did not view the outcome of the meeting, either the reclassification of the coyote as a nuisance animal, or the announcement of the shoot, as nothing short of disaster.

'Coyote aren't easy to hunt,' he said to Jean. 'Wait and see, bet they don't get hardly a one.' Of the other matter he merely said: 'Look at it this way, honey, to some people no doubt they are something of a nuisance.'

Jean saw herself standing on the edge of a precipice facing a terrible danger, while Ray, standing in the same place, was merely looking at a view. His bland optimism, which had carried them through the years of their marriage, suddenly spoke of a profound indifference. To Ray nothing was more important than a quiet life. In the pursuit of that quiet life forbearance soon began to look like inaction, moderation like appeasement, Ray's equable cheerfulness took on the taint of weakness. The greatest betrayal came some weeks before the Labor Day coyote shoot. Jean happened upon Ray and the Woodsman sharing a beer in the Jolly Tavern. The way Ray saw it, he was having a drink with a friend he had known since high school. Simple. To Jean, it was simpler still. Ray should have been defending her, instead he was doing the opposite, by drinking with Arthur Wood he was undermining her, her work and her views.

Thus began the war that would end their marriage. There was no front line, no real battleground, rather this was a war of salvos and skirmishes fought over absences, missed meals, lost weekends. The sex stopped. A trip to Boston to see Luke and then to London where Ray had always said he wanted to go, they would walk the streets, strangers in the city and to each other, they would eat in the Indian restaurants Ray found in his guide, they would witness the death of a whale, they would make love twice and they would return home. The fights stopped, instead they withdrew from each other and the place they had shared for so long lay empty, like the abandoned city Jean had once described. Water entered the fissures in the structure of the buildings, turned to ice and prised the concrete apart, dust covered the roads, the rivers silted up and weeds grew over the playgrounds and the parks.

For years the Corvette had sat in the garage under a plastic cover. When Jean left Ray and their home, the Corvette was still there. Jean drove away in her pick-up. Out of habit she turned on her radio receiver and began to scan. Nothing, no radio-transmitted farewell from the collar of a coyote. As she left the town limits she switched off the radio and did not think about what she was leaving or where she was going. Instead she thought about Archie, the last she had seen of him alive.

Early dawn, maybe three years earlier. She had picked up his signal just north of Greenhampton and was driving the roads back and forth in answer to the strength of the electronic call. It had been one fall. The leaves had begun to redden and swirl. Mornings the woodchuck appeared in the yard to root for windfall apples. Unable to sleep she had left her bed, stepped into the cool morning and slipped behind the wheel of her truck.

At the bottom of a nearby hill she parked and walked up the mud track. In two places the water-soaked path had been dammed and flooded by beaver. Here the land was private, at one point a padlock chain extended across the width of the track. Jean lifted the chain and passed underneath it. Men had been logging, tyre-churned mud sucked at her boots, the air carried the smell of resin and cut wood. Twenty minutes to the brow of the hill, to the right the woods opened out onto a hillside meadow, which would have given out onto a view of Greenhampton had not the town been hidden by a stand of trees further down the valley. In the sky towering cumulus told of a coming change in the weather. The grass was still high, sun-scorched and threaded with goldenrod, meadowsweet and asters. A stream flowed beneath the surface of the incline and broke ground in certain places and there loosestrife ran wild. In the middle of the meadow was a huge dead tree, the ground around it scattered with boulders. When Jean had first come here, brought by Ray, the thought that had come to her, came to her every time she looked over the view of the hidden town, was how much this meadow must have resembled New England as seen by the first arrivals. She had no idea whether she was right or not, probably the hillside would have been covered in trees and such a meadow could never have existed, but Jean had a memory of paintings she had seen as a girl, of settlers and horses in a land much like this, and so she held on to the thought.

The coyote was looking right at her. She almost hadn't seen him, his coat blended so precisely with the grass. Coat of many colours. Only the silvery shimmering of the outer hairs gave form to his being. Where the wind ended and the animal began it was impossible to say. She stood as still as she was able and held his gaze. For several moments she was aware only of her breath, of air entering and leaving her body, and of the orange-gold eyes of the coyote. A memory returned, visceral enough to be real: she remembered the smell of this animal's coat the day she felled him and collared him, the warmth of his body, the blood beat of his life.

Chapter 12

A lone street-cleaning vehicle travelled the arc of the Aldwych, one of those fitted with brushes at the front and at the back a large plastic hose. It nosed along close to the kerb, like a small animal rooting for scraps. After a while it lifted its brushes and sped off towards the river upon which a barge loaded with spoil made its way towards the sea, the boats moored along the banks of the river bobbed in its wake. A cormorant perched on the top of a water-blackened wooden post dropped onto the waves. A moment later the bird ducked its head and disappeared to reappear thirty yards further away. In the days when the power station on the south side of the Thames was being converted into a gallery for modern art, an installation artist accompanied by a team of volunteers headed down to the riverside at low tide and removed and recorded the debris they found in the mud of the foreshore. The findings were displayed in a cabinet of curiosities inside the new gallery. Plastic toys, oyster shells, clay pipes, buttons, rusted chains, more than one letter in a bottle, false teeth, bricks, hobnail boots, bottles and fragments of glass, and the bones of horses. Rib bones, femur, scapula, fragments of the skull, whole jawbones. The fractured skeletons of animals that had once worked the city, pulling carts, carriages and barges, consigned to the waters of the river.

While Tano took his turn in the bathroom Attila listened to a little flamenco. He snapped his heels and fingers experimentally, he had no practice with this kind of dance. It occurred to him this was something he might like to try. He had been to a performance of flamenco only once in his life, not in Spain but in Cuba. Attila had been impressed by the unashamed drama and the willingness of the performers, both musicians and dancers, to share their *dolor*. They stamped feet and snapped castanets, their features contorted with the explosive force of emotion. The singer sang with closed eyes and clenched fists in a kind of anguished scream. A power cut halfway through the second act had not stopped them or deterred the audience, who remained in their seats in the hall listening to the sound of the guitars, of leather on wood and seeing the occasional flash or glint reach out from the darkness. In time candles were lit and placed at the back and to the sides of the stage, it grew hotter, windows were opened but the wind blew out the candles and so the choice became fresh air or light. The audience chose the darkness, the candles remained doused and the dancers performed in the occasional moonlight.

Attila had been in Cuba attending a world meeting of psychiatrists to address the question of the rise in young male suicides in industrialising nations. The Sunday after the conference Attila hired a car and drove across the country, as he was not supposed to do according to government restrictions. The same restrictions denied him the opportunity of changing money and obliged travellers like Attila to use hard currency. He stopped in a small town in the centre of the country to find something to eat but he found his dollars quite useless, for as it turned out no street vendor wished to accept them. He wandered the cobbled streets of the town, it was siesta time and all was quiet. There were barely any shops and no restaurants. Most notable of all there was no advertising, no billboards or posters or flyers or flags. The town felt timeless. In a square he found an arrangement of benches and lights strung up on a frame of poles ready for some sort of event and, having nowhere to go, he sat down and waited. An hour later people began to arrive, men and women of all ages. A dance began. Attila watched, enjoying the fact that among these people, aside from his height and bearing, he did not stand out and nor did he attract stares. At home he was considered a good dancer, at least Maryse told him so, but he did not know the steps to these dances though he knew that they were centuries old. He observed that the women indicated their willingness to accept a dance partner by the way they held their fan. A fan spread meant the bearer was catching her breath, a fan closed and laid to rest on a collarbone meant she was ready to return to the floor. A woman in her late sixties with heavy ankles accepted the hand of a young man in jeans and football shirt. Intently Attila watched how they performed the steps. Later he would learn the dance was a slow rumba. Under the bench he moved his feet fractionally in time to the music. He waited through another four dances until finally the beat of the music announced another rumba. He stood and approached the same woman who had danced with the young man.

Among the dancers nobody spoke and among the onlookers nobody drank or ate. The only purpose for any of them to be present in this square one Sunday evening in the summer was to dance. Attila danced with them. At a false step his partner slowed down to give him time to regain his rhythm. At the end of the dance she smiled, it seemed to him with approval, inclined her head once and walked away to rejoin her companions. In Accra Attila found a dance class held once a week in an empty room on the upper floors of the building that housed the Alliance Française and he persuaded Maryse to join him in exchange for his promise to attend her film nights downstairs in the same building.

In the years to come Attila thought from time to time about the Cuban town. It seemed to him like a place where happiness might exist.

To Jean the child seemed possessed of an unusual stillness. She had watched him enter the apartment behind Attila and go to sit on the sofa. Apart from a shy greeting he had not spoken. Jean realised she was unprepared for his arrival, she had nothing for a child. The books, the pencils, the piles of recycled office paper, board games and toys with which she had lived for years were packed in boxes in the basement of another house on another continent. Tano played for a few minutes on his Nintendo and then he went to the window and looked out. He seemed absorbed by whatever it was he found there. The light arrived so late in the day at this time of year it had still been nearly dark when they arrived. Outside in the street people walked through the grey with curved backs, faces tilted towards the sidewalk, trudging forward, as if at the end of a long march, concentrating on the sight of their own moving feet.

'What does he like?' Jean asked Attila who stood with his hands in his pockets in the middle of the room. She did not know whether he planned to stay or to go so she moved to the kitchen and began to make coffee, in the hope of persuading him to stay a short while at least. He stood rooted to the centre of the sitting room, half turned between her and the boy, and Jean was able to examine his face through the open door. He was impeccable, formal even on a Saturday morning, shaved and collared, his face seemed suddenly both familiar and unfamiliar. The night before, after they had spoken on the telephone, Jean had closed her eyes and tried to summon his face but had been unable. Now she looked at the downward arch of his nose, the definition of the outline of his lips, the grey of his hairline. How had she forgotten? He had kissed her on arrival, in the European way, on each cheek. She had felt his hand at her waist, her breasts had briefly touched his chest.

He turned his head back to her and Jean looked away. Her question about the child remained unanswered, possibly unheard. There was, she thought, a moment between men and women in which a woman can no longer meet a certain man's gaze. Men held the power of the gaze, the freedom to look upon women as they pleased. In public a woman looked freely only upon men with whom there was no possibility of sex or the mistaken presumption of desire, in other words the very (very) old and the very young. In company women looked at men who might be colleagues or neighbours or married to women they knew, but even then their gaze was guarded. The moment friendship transformed into something else the woman looked away.

For the first time since she met Attila, Jean found she couldn't look at him as easily as she once surely had, when she had sat with him on the bench overlooking the Thames, walking the streets of the capital, in the café. There was a shyness within her now, a new awkwardness and urgency. She felt that if their eyes were to meet he would see what was inside. She could feel him looking at her as she poured the coffee, though he said nothing as he accepted the cup she passed. Tano stood with his palms pressed against the window. Jean thought that the only person who seemed uncomfortable in the silence was her. Attila took a single sip of his coffee and set the cup down on the table. 'I'm sorry,' he said. 'I have something to which I must attend.'

'We'll be here,' said Jean as she showed him to the door. She thought he might kiss her goodbye, but he didn't. When he was halfway down the first flight of stairs he turned and waved. In the short time they had known each other they had spent many hours together, more than most people did over a period of months, sometimes it felt as though she knew him well, at other times she felt as if she hardly knew him at all.

At Three Valleys Attila, after a search of the common rooms, found Rosie still in her bedroom, not yet dressed, hair matted, the room foul with the smell of stale breath. Attila marched into the corridor in search of a care worker. The day room was empty of residents though it was nearly ten o'clock, the curtains were still drawn. Outside a bedroom a trolley waited, the door of the room stood ajar, sounds of movement, instructions given in a low, detached voice. Attila headed back to Rosie's room where he opened a window and arranged her pillows behind her, found a soft hair-brush. Rosie said nothing but tugged at the sleeve of her cardigan and at her nightdress.

'Shall we go to the bathroom?' Attila asked and was grateful when Rosie allowed herself to be raised up. While she was sitting on the toilet he went again into the corridor and attempted to summon help. The sound of Rosie moving around in the bathroom sent him hurrying back. She was running the taps, scalding water tumbled into the basin. The back of her nightgown was soiled and so was the floor. Attila shut off the tap. He sat Rosie on the toilet while he cleaned the mess on the floor with toilet paper, then he ran a shower and led Rosie, still in her nightgown, into the cubicle.

In the water she seemed at peace, she held out her arms and turned her face into the flow from the shower, submitting to his ministrations. He pulled her nightgown over her head and discarded the sodden item on the bathroom floor, was shocked by how thin she had become. Her breasts flat, her stomach concave, the bones of her hips jutted. Apart from the silver hair below her belly button, hers could have been the body of a barely pubescent girl. On her stomach, to the right of her indented belly button, a pair of moles. Attila and Rosie had been lovers for three years, he had made love to this body so many times, he had forgotten the moles. Behind her knee she had a small birthmark. The bony bump on her collarbone, broken when she was thrown from her mare as a fourteen-year-old girl. At that moment she reached out and lightly touched his arm. She looked at him and seemed about to speak. When Attila said: 'Go on, Rosie,' she farted sonorously in the tiled cubicle.

On a chair he found a set of clothing and when he bent to help Rosie into the underwear, she leaned heavily on his shoulder while he raised each of her feet. In the same way he persuaded her into her skirt and slipped a sweater over her head, under the bed he found her corduroy men's slippers and he eased them onto her feet.

He knelt in front of her. 'Rosie,' he said. Again: 'Rosie?' He took her hand in his and massaged the fingers. He tried to remember the last time Rosie had recognised him. Soon after she came to live at Three Valleys he had arrived straight from the airport to see her. Exhausted, he had fallen asleep as they sat side by side on one of the sofas in the day room. When he woke up she was curled against his chest, her hand lay on his shoulder. Outside it was nearly dark and the day room was empty, the residents had been taken to lunch. Attila shifted, not wanting to disturb her though he was stiff after the flight, he also needed the toilet. He lifted her hand from his shoulder and she came awake. In that moment of wakefulness before she was sucked back into the quagmire, she was suddenly lucid. She said: 'Good morning, Talker.' A pet name she used for him, during the days of Haywards Heath, for his habit of speaking his thoughts aloud. After he was married and when they reunited as colleagues, she never called him Talker again.

Rosie stared at her hand in Attila's, as though she had never seen such a sight, was making of it what she could. She didn't look up at the sound of her name and when he withdrew his hands she remained as she had been. When he put a hand under her chin, lifted her head and smiled at her, she did not smile back. And when he let go of her head, she let it sink back to her chest.

In the dining room the server told him Rosie had stopped eating: 'These days she don't want to so much as smell the food,' the woman said. She shook her head and put her hands on her hips, lips pursed. Attila felt this was the way she had settled upon to talk to the residents and their families, as though they were all Jamaican schoolchildren. The kitchen was closed until lunchtime but she agreed to fix something for them. 'Someone die today,' she said. 'On a Saturday when they already short-staffed.' She went into the kitchen and soon bustled out with a bowl of creamed cereal. 'A lot of them like it. Put plenty sugar.' She set the bowl on the table and as she stood up shook her hair away from her face, her hair was lustrous with a deep, synthetic glow. Attila realised, belatedly, that the woman was flirting with him. He smiled and assured her of his gratitude. 'Any time, any time,' she murmured. She brought him a spouted plastic beaker of apple juice. Whereas in the past Rosie had opened her mouth obediently, now she refused to part her lips as though she had no idea what was expected of her, as though some new part of her brain had gone still. The server watched a while. 'Here.' She dampened a paper napkin with apple juice and moistened Rosie's lips and Rosie reflexively stuck out her tongue and licked them. The server straightened up and sighed. 'Since he gone, she gone.'

'What can you tell me about the case, the client specifically?' Attila was talking on the phone to the young solicitor who he had found at his desk on a Saturday.

'I'm sorry, I took it on from one of our partners who went on maternity leave. I've never met the client. I know as much as you do, just what's in the file.'

'Then arrange for me to see her as soon as possible. In fact, as a matter of urgency. We are in court in a few days.'

'I'm on it.'

'One more thing.'

'Yes?'

'A name. The file refers to her only as Mrs S.'

'I may be able to get that for you straight away. Hold on.' A few seconds later he was back. 'Her name is Sherriff. Adama Sherriff. Born 1985. Arrived in the UK in 2011.'

In an internet cafe on the Old Kent Road Attila sat on a plastic chair under bright lights and typed the name Adama Sherriff into the search engine. Facebook accounts of people with the same name, the web page of Adams County Sheriff in Pennsylvania, a brief news report of an arrest in connection with a fire in the town of Cuckfield in Sussex. Several other reports, evidently drawn from the same account. No photographs. Next he typed the name Ibrahim Sherriff and Iraq and pressed Search. He hit the tab for Images. He found a Reuters report and another on AP, an image of a young, bearded black man, dressed in a djellaba, features obscured by a bright sun. His hands were held before him, palms upwards, in the penitent prayer of the handcuffed, next to him stood Attila. Another photograph showed Attila and the handcuffed man embracing.

Attila sat in reflection for a few minutes and then heaved himself to his feet and went to the till to pay. 'You got twenty minutes left, mate,' said the young man who took his money. Attila ordered a Turkish coffee and a pastry and regained his place in front of the computer and switched to Maps, looked up the town of Cuckfield. When he found it he said aloud: 'Haywards Heath,' for the two towns were virtually adjacent. Now at the limit of his familiarity with the internet, Attila called the young man over and asked him how to find the most direct route to both towns.

Attila stooped to pick up a scattering of envelopes and placed them on the hall radiator. The south-east London flat had been advertised as a two-bedroom first-floor apartment. He waited for the agent to unlock the second door to the flat. As soon as he saw the vertiginous flight of stairs Attila said: 'This won't do.'

'It opens out considerably.'

'What else do you have?' asked Attila.

With some difficulty Attila levered himself back into the front seat of the estate agent's car, surely the smallest car he had ever seen. Attila hunched forward like a quarterback, his head practically touching the windscreen. Meanwhile Emmanuel had somehow folded himself efficiently into the back seat. Attila was beginning to feel irritable, he was confused by the geography of the streets and felt there was no need for the agent to drive so fast. To take his mind off the speed of the vehicle and the proximity of the windscreen he said to Emmanuel: 'Why did you come here?'

'Everyone, my schoolmates, my friends, all wanted to leave Ghana. When the recruitment agency came looking for nurses I was quick to sign up. Before I knew it—' He whistled. 'We all talked about going to Britain or America all the time, we didn't even know what those places were like. You know how it is. Sometimes everybody heads one way and sometimes they head another way, and you yourself, you get caught in the crowd, like when you see a pack of dogs, they all bark and race each other round the streets, thinking they are chasing something, even the ones in the front don't know there is nothing there.' He laughed.

Attila admired Emmanuel for owning up to not thinking for himself, which was an achievement few could manage, Attila knew this human trait in all its forms. An idea started, grew and became entrenched, only a very few people remained immune. What Attila would give to possess the power to work out where these things began. Was it with a dedicated cast of actors who knew the script? Or by some process altogether more alchemic. Human beings were above all else herd animals. People were scared to be on the outside, would accede to the most terrible things as the price of inclusion. It all came down to whether or not you believed in free will, Attila often thought. His colleagues held firm to the notion of free will, hence the lengthy explanations to account for certain human behaviours. In Attila's view free will was a circus horse you had to stay astride, it took every muscle in your body and every moment of your concentration.

Emmanuel said: 'And now this is where we are.'

'And where would that be?' asked Attila, thinking they were still speaking metaphorically.

'At the next flat. You know, I think this will be the one.'

The building was a house in a residential street, narrow and tree-less. The paint job on the façade of the house spoke of a desire to save money. Attila followed the estate agent down an outside staircase. The ceiling of the flat was about two inches lower than he stood high.

'Is it for you?' said the estate agent looking concerned.

'No,' said Attila. He felt like a trapped beast.

The estate agent's face brightened: 'Oh well then!'

In the farthest reaches of the Old Kent Road, where the road sweeps around the only bend in its course, where the pavements are silted with small, independently owned shops, which change hands frequently, here the new arrival with dreams of a small business can sometimes find an establishment to rent at a price which is within reach only if the most optimistic forecasts for the business come true.

Emmanuel took Attila to a new restaurant. Inside an overlit room: rows of tables covered in plastic tablecloths, on each was placed a large water jug and a plastic mug of splayed spoons and forks, like a vase of metal flowers. The clientele were men mostly. Some looked North African, others from the Horn of Africa, a couple of well-dressed Malians in suits and slim loafers, a Nigerian fellow with tribal marks. A young woman in business clothes sat alone and read a newspaper. Four televisions in the four corners of the room, like winged angels in a church. Crumpled napkins lay like discarded blooms on the brown-tiled floor. A buffet of dishes was kept warm under hot lights. Four kinds of rice: broken, basmati, beans and rice, country. Couscous, too. Chickpea porridge, fufu, cassava boiled and pounded, yams, plantain, steamed and fried. Mealie meal. There was a stew of eggs and coriander Attila had once tasted in Eritrea. Different kinds of *plasas*, okra, potato leaves and cassava leaves. Emmanuel grinned. 'Nigerians,' he said. 'But they bring in cooks from all over.' He was filling his box like he hadn't eaten for a week. At the till, which operated as a weigh station, their plates were placed on a set of butcher's scales and the woman handed Attila the receipt and a pair of empty paper cups.

'I would like to work for myself one day,' said Emmanuel.

'What would you do?'

Emmanuel shrugged. 'Some people have hair salons, grocery stores, taxi firms. A lot of the men you see here are drivers, but now they're leaving the minicab firms and they're going to drive for these companies where you come with your own car and people call you with a special app on their phones. No more shift work, you make your own hours. My boss at the agency is worried, but there's no app to let you call someone to feed you or wipe your bottom.'

'Give it time,' said Attila, who had a faint notion of what an app was.

'Maybe that's the idea I should go with. What would I call it?'

'Wash and Go?' offered Attila.

'So when an old person needs to go to the toilet they use the app and the one who is nearest goes and handles it. So much for a bath, so much to change your clothes, so much to put you to bed or get you out.'

'You'd better believe it,' said Attila.

On the TV a politician Attila recognised was speaking. He was a heavyweight man wearing a suit that looked like a huge black bag. His hair was parted low on one side from where the mass of it surged forward like an ocean breaker onto the beach of his forehead where it was cast backwards onto the crown of his head, finally spilling over the back of his collar. That he was vexed was evidenced by the way he held up his hand, thumb and forefinger formed into the shape of an O which almost exactly mirrored the shape of his mouth; his face seemed to pulsate with fury. Then came a picture of a fox running down a darkened road. Cut to two people standing outside their house. Cut back to the man with the suit and the hair. Attila strained to listen. He had seen the politician on television before, had been compelled by his speech patterns, marked by half-sentences, the man left one thought unfinished as he rushed on to the next, he talked about himself in the third person. He raged, he shouted. All that, plus the lacquered hair. Many politicians were narcissists, it came with the territory, the self-belief required. Narcissists weren't so bad, most great artists were narcissists too. This man though, in Attila's professional opinion, displayed many of the traits of hypomania.

Emmanuel was saying: 'Maybe it's time I went home.'

Attila turned away from the television: 'Are you serious?' he said.

Emmanuel looked up. 'Yes. Ghana is doing great. Many of my friends are going back, starting businesses. The economy is good. Here everyone is getting poorer, except for the people who were rich already.'

He wasn't wrong, thought Attila. The morning's search for a flat for Emmanuel and Rosie had left him dispirited. He said: 'How are you fixed for this afternoon?'

Emmanuel looked at him. 'You want to see more flats?'

'No,' said Attila. 'I need to get out of London. I thought we could take Rosie.'

In Jean's apartment on the Old Kent Road, after Attila had gone, Tano stayed at the window, watching Attila (Jean assumed) as he joined the flow of pedestrians and disappeared. When he turned around Jean said: 'Follow me, I have something you might like.' At the top of the spiral stairs she opened the hatch and she and Tano climbed out onto the roof. The sun was out, a herd of cumulus bumped along a sky cut through with contrails. Tano looked around and Jean saw awe register on his face. He turned his head this way and that as though he expected an even greater surprise to appear.

Finally he said: 'You have a garden on top of your house.'

'Yes,' said Jean. 'Do you have a garden?'

Tano shook his head. 'Just the park.'

The sun had not yet burned off the frost of the previous night, the garden glowed pale. Like most gardeners Jean saw a garden's beauty not just in the late spring or early summer when it was most vividly alive, but now in the winter too, in the morning sun, the nacre-edged leaves of the ferns touched by hoar frost, each filigree and spore outlined in crystals of ice. She had planted winter vegetables – broccoli, kale and leeks and under a row of glass cloches, cabbages. A winter-flowering clematis grew along one wall, clusters of hellebore in the beds. Flames of Midwinter Fire rocketed skyward.

Thirty minutes later they sat together on the bench, cold drifting through the layers of clothing. Tano wore a sweater of Jean's. He had pulled the sleeves down over his hands. A small group of blue tits arrived, they came at the same time every morning to feed from the table where together Jean and Tano had laid slices of apple and raw potato. They perched in a loose circle, tails out, beaks down, the tails dipped and rose, like the petals of a flower opening and closing. Once in a while a bird rose from its place, flew above the heads of the others and landed elsewhere in the ring. Jean had given Tano the binoculars and they watched for fifteen minutes or so during which the number of birds thickened and then thinned and then, all of a sudden, like children at a birthday party called to the cutting of the cake, the entire flock flew away.

A parakeet appeared on the branch of the dead tree. Tano fixed the binoculars on the bird and the sunlight flashed from the lens of the binoculars. The parakeet shifted up and down the branch, gripping with its claws as it craned its neck forward. It seemed interested in the play of light on the binocular lens. Jean remembered the woman who had come to the cemetery with a mirror to try to find her father's parakeet among the dozens that nested in the huge tree. The parakeet bobbed its head, hopped from one branch to another, closing the gap between them by a yard or two. A moment later it alighted on the top of the fencing.

Jean left Tano while she went downstairs to fix them both something to eat. Minutes later she carried a tray of toast and jam and juice up the stairs. The parakeet was gone. There was Tano, still holding the binoculars, though now he had them trained on the yard. Jean followed his eye line and there was Light Bright, negotiating the top of the boundary wall, the ivy and the broken bottles, sure of foot as a ballet dancer.

Chapter 13

A20. M25. M23. A23. Three lanes, two lanes, one lane. They headed south like they were disappearing down a funnel. Redhill, Copthorne, Crawley. It rained and the windscreen wipers of the Jaguar struck a 2/2 beat. The hire company had given Attila a discount on the car, having no mid-range vehicles available. On the A23 they stopped at a garage and Attila ran into the small shop where Christmas lived on in the limp décor. There he asked directions of a young man with pellucid eyes, moonscape skin and an Adam's apple that threatened to break through the surface of his neck like a shark's fin through still water. 'What, no satnav?' said the young man looking out of the window at the Jaguar. He led the way to the car, nodded to the others sitting inside, and ran through a series of the car's features as though he had spent his life selling Jaguars. He set the navigation route for Cuckfield High Street. The young man's last touch was to tune the car's stereo. When he was done Attila drew a £5 note from his wallet but the young man said simply: 'No worries, mate.'

They pressed on to sounds of Vivaldi. They passed through the rain and drove on under a sunlight-splintered sky, a wall of blue-black cloud behind them. Steam rose from the tarmac ahead. High hedgerows bordered the track, it was like they were driving through a maze. Every now and again an oncoming vehicle forced Attila to back up. To Attila the Jaguar handled like a speedboat, gliding in and out of the curves of the road. In the back Rosie sat silently and looked out of the window, the reflected scenery passing like the projection of a film over her unmoving eyes. She must have, Attila thought, driven through these roads and lanes hundreds of times. So far she had showed no particular signs of anything, but she seemed contented. The decision to bring Rosie of course necessitated that Emmanuel came too. Then there was the question of the child. Having made the suggestion to Jean he was warmed when she agreed to come along as well. So now there they all were, out beyond the enclosing circle of the M25 and into the wilderness of the commuter belt. While the light was with them they would go first to Cuckfield and then on to Haywards Heath, where Lady Quell had invited them for drinks and an early supper.

Rain-rinsed Cuckfield was as pretty as could be. The same wind that had ushered out the clouds now shook the trees and the wrought-iron signs that hung from the front of some of the buildings. At a zebra crossing they stopped for an elderly woman in a green mackintosh and plastic rain hood leading a small terrier. Attila leaned forward and peered out and from the back seat, Emmanuel did the same. Jean's only trip beyond London had been west to Bristol to visit a group of researchers who'd carried out the only longitudinal study of a city fox population. During the same trip she had visited Bath, wandered through the town centre around the station which consisted of narrow, cobbled streets and buildings with façades of yellow stone. As for Emmanuel, he hadn't left London since the day he had flown into Gatwick, the turn-off to which they passed an hour earlier. He had received several times an invitation urging him to visit some of his mother's relatives in Glasgow, but the cost of the train fare had shocked him. To Rosie Emmanuel said: 'This is a town called Cookfield, Rosie. It is in Sussex. You may have been here once. You might remember, but it doesn't matter if you don't.'

'Cuckfield,' said Attila. 'Cuckfield.'

'Yes, Cuckfield. Sorry.'

Rosie's eyes moved fractionally. She said quite clearly: 'Cuckfield.' Though she could have been just as easily echoing him as agreeing. They drove on past a church, parted unwittingly from the A272 and soon after passed another church. 'Turn round where possible,' implored the satnav. The road was too narrow to attempt to turn and after a while, goaded by the satnav, Attila pulled into the drive-way of a large house. A man wearing the clothes of the Englishman at leisure: corduroy trousers and a yellow V-neck sweater, was stand-ing on the gravel driveway. At the sight of the car he frowned and became instantly angry. Attila lowered the window and called out an apology. The man strode over waving his arms as if he had just spotted a goat eating his plants. Attila explained they were trying to get back to the High Street. The man's frown deepened. 'This is private property, not a highway.'

'That guy's going to give himself a heart attack,' said Jean. Emmanuel gave an explosive laugh which caused Rosie to start. Back in the High Street Attila parked and they all got out. Tano jumped out first. Emmanuel tucked Rosie's arm in his. Jean shook out her coat and put it on. Attila stood and perused the street, he spotted a noticeboard, strode over to it and began reading. Baby yoga. Casting call for *The Importance of Being Earnest* on behalf of the local dramatic society. Sunday lunch for £7.50 on offer to non-members at the golf club. An out-of-date church newsletter announced a carol service. Another church newsletter advertised a rival event. An aged photograph of what appeared to be the popula-tion of the entire town eating at trestle tables in the street. Protests against the Gatwick Airport expansion.

In a tea room with steamed windows they ordered sandwiches and tea. The waitress, bare-legged in an unseasonably short black skirt, took the order as if she were hearing the words for the first time and seemed to know little regarding the contents of the menu. 'I check,' she said, in an accent Attila placed in Warsaw. Attila's plan to ask about Adama Sherriff and the arson case seemed less viable in the face of the Polish waitress. He remembered the lawyer in London who had seemed to possess a particular aptitude for acquiring information. He stepped back into the High Street and made a call and, by the time he had gone back in and eaten his way through an egg and cress sandwich, there came, accompanied by a vibration against his thigh and a muffled ting, a message containing the information he needed.

A red-brick two up, two down in a row of identical houses, the lower floor of which housed a florist. Attila parked up on the pavement of the narrow street, exited the car and took a look. The windows of the upper floors were boarded. 'Flowers,' he said aloud. It occurred to him it would not be a bad idea to bring flowers to Vivien Quell. A bell chimed as he stepped into the shop and again a moment later as Jean came in, and again when Emmanuel and Rosie entered. Only Tano remained outside, peering in at them from the other side of the glass. The florist scurried out to greet the deluge of customers, smothered her curiosity with a placidly professional smile as her eyes roamed over the group. Attila took a call on his phone. Emmanuel followed Rosie who was headed towards a display of Michaelmas daisies. On the other side of the glass Tano began to make faces. In the void Jean spoke up: 'We're looking for flowers to take to a friend's house for dinner.'

'What kind of flowers does your friend like?'

'I'm not sure.' Jean glanced at Attila who was on his cellphone. 'Give me a moment.'

'Of course. Are you thinking of a bouquet? If you're taking it for a dinner, perhaps something that could work as a centrepiece?'

'Good idea,' said Jean. Roses, freesias, carnations, lilies, throatwort, eryngium, agapanthus, veronica, daffodils, tulips by the score, single-stem orchids, small pots of violets. A lily plant offered an elegant and simple solution.

'These?'

Jean was on the point of saying yes when she realised it was not she who was being addressed but Rosie who had just handed the florist three oriental lilies, followed a moment later by some large white daisies. The florist fashioned the stems into a basic arrangement. 'Let me show you what I think,' she said. She plucked four or five roses, added stems of green bell and two of hypericum berries and showed them to Rosie. The composition in the florist's hand was one of luminous pale shades. Rosie moved towards the display of roses, picked a large apricot-coloured tea rose and thrust it at the florist. 'Very nice.' The woman placed the rose at the centre of the arrangement. The colour clash threw the whole thing off kilter. 'I'll just finish this up for you.' She tied the stems with twine and wrapped them in paper and cellophane, handed them to Rosie. To Jean she said: 'It doesn't matter the least bit, does it? You can take it out before you get to your friends' house, she won't remember. I didn't charge you.'

Attila came over, he frowned briefly at the sight of the bouquet with the orange rose in its midst, reached for his wallet and paid. To the florist he said: 'Have you been here long?'

'Just coming up to the shop's first anniversary.' She was a small woman and had to extend her neck considerably to look up at him.

'Did you know the woman upstairs, Adama Sherriff?'

'I did, yes.'

'What can you tell me?'

'That depends who I am talking to,' said the woman.

'I'm a medical professional involved in her case.'

The florist nodded, she paused as if gathering her thoughts: 'Well the thing is this, I wasn't here when her husband died but I heard about it. I only knew her afterwards. It had only just happened and she was still getting over it. I'd see her on her way in and out. We said hello. She'd pop in, we had tea a few times but I never asked about the husband.'

'Why not?' said Attila.

The woman blinked. 'Well it's awkward, isn't it?'

'Is it?' asked Attila, then: 'It was a car accident.'

'Yes, it happened a little out of town on one of the B roads. I read about it in the paper. I already owned the lease by then, I opened up just a couple of weeks later. That was after the funeral and then there was some kind of memorial a month or so later.'

'The Forty Days.'

'I see.'

'It takes place forty days after the death. There's one at seven days, one at forty days and one a year on. The Forty Days marks the end of the official mourning period.'

'The end of mourning? She didn't seem to be at the end of it, poor thing.'

'It is the end of the formal mourning, not the end of sorrow. Did you go? To the Forty Days?'

'Well, I never knew him, you see. She had something going on upstairs, some of her people arrived. But no, I didn't go. It wouldn't have been my place. I knew her in a manner of speaking, as a friendly neighbour, that's it. She more or less stopped coming in. The weekend of the fire I'd shut the shop and I went to visit my father. He's in a home in Hastings, dementia, like …' She nodded in Rosie's direction. 'By the time I got back it was all over. The shop was fine, thank goodness. Most of the damage was confined to the flat. We all thought it must have been an accident. A candle perhaps.' The woman gave a little shrug.

Scurrying clouds blew them to Haywards Heath, the wind never stopped. Attila had forgotten Rosie's old address and so, employing memories forty years old, he navigated his way to her childhood home. Her parents had lived in a 1930s house with a steep drive fronted by rhododendrons. At the back was a garden with a sloping striped lawn enclosed by ornate borders and overlooked by next door's leylandii which dropped needles onto the lawn and about which Rosie's mother liked to complain. Attila remembered drinking tea on the lawn even on days when the sun blazed and they huddled together under the sun umbrella, unconvinced by the father's insistence that hot tea on a warm day cooled a person, but drinking it out of politeness anyway. Rosie's father had been a ship's engineer in the Merchant Navy, away for long spells. His hobby of macramé was evidenced all over the house, in plant holders, wall hangings, macramé-covered table lamps, the handles of outsize wooden spoons, door knobs, even the pull rope of the brass ship's bell that hung by the front door and whose thunderous peals announced the start of supper. Rosie's mother wore her hair back-combed into a sort of a beehive with a chignon on top and owned an array of macramé necklaces, one of which she sported gamely each day.

Fewer shops now than there had been. The red postbox. Rosie's mother would often ask if he or Rosie could post a letter for her. Rosie and Attila would walk down together, in the shade of the high hedges that fronted each house. In his memory it was always summer in Oakfield Road. Attila's recollections came with the flavours of meringues and Victoria sponge, shepherd's pie, salmon and peas.

The rhododendrons were gone, in their place a low brick wall. The driveway had been concreted over. A tree with copper-coloured leaves whose existence he had forgotten stood like a palm tree on a desert island. A brass plaque next to the front door read: *Samir Singh BDS*. Attila, Emmanuel, Rosie, Tano and Jean stood in silence. Attila looked at Rosie searching for a reaction of any kind, knowing her mind could play only with the deck of memories that remained to her. But her face was empty as she looked at the house without seeing it. The memories now belonged to Attila alone.

After he had left to go back to Ghana but before he took the position as chief psychiatrist at the mental hospital in Sierra Leone, Attila had received a letter from Rosie. Her parents had separated quite suddenly. Her father had gone overseas. When next Attila was in Britain during the time he and Rosie were collaborating on research, he had gone with Rosie to visit her mother. The house was as neat as ever and to Attila's eye unchanged, the brass bell, the plant holders, notable was an absence of cooking smells, instead the house reeked of cleaning agents. At lunchtime Rosie's mother opened a tin of soup which she served with bread and butter. Of Rosie's father no mention was ever made. In the afternoon Rosie put on a pair of leather gloves and they set to work in the garden, Rosie weeding and pruning while Attila was given the task of mowing the lawn, which he discovered to be more challenging than it appeared when he had watched Rosie's father. He failed to reproduce the father's neat stripes, his efforts looked like the handiwork of a drunk.

'Lime. Splash of Angostura.'

'Well remembered,' said Attila.

He and Quell were standing in Quell's office. He took the gin and tonic Quell passed him.

'*Gajan!*' Quell raised his glass.

'*Gajan!*' Attila nodded and took a sip. For a few moments both men gazed deeply into their glasses. 'It's curious,' Attila said presently, 'that the Sherriffs ended up living down here, just a few minutes away from you.'

'Not really,' said Quell. 'I was the one in charge of his debriefing. We carried out a lot of that here. In fact, he stayed here for a couple of weeks over the period, made a lot more sense than putting him in a hotel in London, that was how he got to know the area. He liked to go for walks. I let him borrow one of the cars so he could clear off from time to time. Those debriefs can be exhausting, we were asking him to reconstruct every day of a period of his life he would do anything to forget. Well, you know all about it. You knew him from your time in Sierra Leone, didn't you? It's coming back to me now.'

'He was my driver there.'

'Right, right ... I remember. We brought in your colleague Kathleen Branagan. Competent sort.'

Kathleen had made no mention of her involvement in the case, but now it made sense. Perhaps the defence had even asked her to act, though she would have been obliged to recuse herself.

'He survived the whole experience remarkably well. I don't know if I would have. Thank God I've never had to find out. He'd go for these long drives, for a while we worried he'd bugger off some-where, but she wasn't concerned – Branagan, I mean.' Quell was silent, reflecting. 'Where were you? Had you gone back to Iraq?' Then: 'Ah yes, Maryse. What a fool I am. Forgive me.'

There followed a silence eventually broken by Quell. 'We got decent information from him. We sent it straight to headquarters. When he applied for the right to remain it wasn't denied, it came through and I was able to help him with a job. He started driving for an airport limousine service. He found a flat in Cuckfield.'

'Did you see much of him and his wife?'

'From time to time,' said Quell. He settled himself on the edge of a chair, hitched up a trouser leg and crossed his legs. 'At the beginning, when Ibrahim was alone, more so. He'd come round a fair bit at that time. Vivien had a soft spot for him.'

'What was the wife like?'

Quell chuckled. 'Spirited. Some might call it attitude, I can imag-ine. Ballsy. I liked her, so did Vivien. She'd turn up with dishes of whatever she'd just cooked for us. A sauce with peanuts I remember ...'

'Groundnut stew,' said Attila and smiled.

'Yes, that was good. I wasn't so keen on some of the other stuff. Something made with a lot of okra.'

'It's an acquired taste,' said Attila.

'Is that what you call it?'

At that moment came a knock on the door. Lady Quell to tell them dinner was being served in fifteen minutes. 'Jean is keen to see the grounds though there is barely a sliver of light.' She shrugged. 'We'll all get a breath of air before dinner if nothing else.'

'We'll be down,' said Quell. He turned to Attila: 'I'm sorry to hear she's in trouble. Do what you can, won't you? Another?' He put out his hand to receive Attila's glass.

Attila shook his head. 'Driving.'

Quell went back to the table by the window that served as a bar and mixed himself a second drink. Attila looked around the room, ascertaining the features of it that contributed to its precise ambience. Every surface was covered with objects. Framed photographs by the score. A lacquered box. A pen on a display stand. China figurines. The cut-glass decanter Quell was at that moment holding. Medals and trophies awarded by the governments of various nations. A snow globe, a cheap souvenir, struck a discordant note among so much good taste. Inside the glass dome a model of the London skyline, not London as it was now, a London of twenty or thirty years ago before the Shard and the Eye. Attila picked it up and shook it and petals of snow swirled around the magical city. Quell was standing looking out of the window and, still holding the globe, Attila went to join him. Down below he could see the others moving about on the terrace, except Rosie who Emmanuel was at that moment helping to sit on a bench.

'Ah,' said Quell turning to see the globe in Attila's hand. 'My daughter when she was a child collected those, this is one she gave me. I keep it because she gave it to me and because it reminds me of what I do.'

'How so?'

'This is how most people want to live.' He put his hand out for the globe and Attila handed it to him. Quell held it up to the light. 'They want to be safe, they want to be comfortable. They want to believe that they are in control of their lives, and they want that thing we call freedom. It all comes at a price, but don't you dare mention that. People want choices without consequences. And we give it to them, fools that we are. We are the "somebody" people who have no bloody intention of doing anything themselves mean when they say somebody must do something. I blame books, films, all that nonsense.'

Attila chuckled.

'There's always a bloody hero who makes it all good. At least in Shakespeare the whole lot die in the end. *Lear* is wonderful for that. It's the reward you get for suffering through it. That's why there's always so much applause.'

'In the Comedies everything works out.'

'See what I mean,' said Quell. He put the globe down on his desk and returned to the view of the garden: 'And what about your new friend?'

'What would you like to know?'

'We, Vivien and I, we'd …' Quell turned and shuffled the globe around on his desk like an outsize chess piece. 'We'd like to think, well, that you'd found somebody.'

Attila looked down at the figures below, silhouetted in the arc of the patio light, as though they were on a stage, the garden in darkness behind them. Tano was playing hopscotch on the paving stones. Jean was talking to Vivien Quell, using her hands to describe something in the air. At one point they both looked up at the sky. Attila tried to guess what the story was. He saw Tano stop hopping and look up, a moment later Emmanuel too. Only Rosie, watching Emmanuel, did not look up. Attila saw her smile without understanding the meaning of anything that was being said, but because she loved Emmanuel.

'It's time, I think,' said Quell. He seemed to regard Attila thoughtfully for a few moments and then he said: 'Shall we?' And he moved towards the door.

'Bonan vesperon,' *said a voice on the phone.*

'Bonan vesperon, Quell,' *said Attila and then in English:* 'How are you?'

'Mi fartas bone,' *said Quell.* 'Kiel estas la varmego?'

'Hot as hell,' *replied Attila. His collar stuck to his neck, sweat trickled from the small of his back down between his buttocks, air conditioning was a faraway dream.*

'I need a favour,' *said Quell.*

'I know your kind of favours.'

Quell said: 'Hmmm!' *but carried on.* 'So, one of the contractors out there had a man go missing a year ago. They suspected a kidnapping, and they were right. The kidnappers were in touch but when the negotiations went nowhere they went silent, for nine months.'

'Who handled the kidnapping?'

'The contractors brought in professionals from London. They wanted to be discreet about it, not exactly a great recruitment advert. When it went quiet everybody assumed they'd killed him or sold him on to another group who they duped.'

'Duped?'

'Politely put, he was a worthless asset. He didn't know anything, and on the question of ransom money – his family have no money, his government has nothing but debt. The contractors are under strict orders not to pay out and I don't believe would have been inclined to. He was, let's put it this way, entirely replaceable. Cheaper to compensate the family. Perhaps I'm being too harsh.'

Attila asked what the kidnap victim had been doing in Iraq.

'Working as a driver for a security firm. This is the bit that will interest you. They recruited a good many from Sierra Leone, as it happens. Used to war conditions, hardship and jolly happy to be earning $750 a month. At least that's how the contractors saw it. They brought in several hundred. The men were contracted to work as low-level support staff, cleaners, janitors, drivers, basic security. They had all their expenses covered, food, accommodation, uniforms, the money went straight into

their bank accounts, in some cases the first bank accounts the men had
ever had. Half of them have gone on to do the same jobs in Afghanistan.
You can't fault the efficiency, even if it's brutal.'

'What do you need me to do?'

'The group holding him have been back in touch. We're at the last
stage of the negotiations.'

The package delivered to Attila two hours later contained the personnel
file of the captured driver. Attila spread the paperwork out on the desk
before him. A passport-size photograph of a young man with a small
beard, an open gaze and hopeful smile. The picture was of the kind
taken by a street photographer to whom the sitter paid a small sum, was
placed on a stool in front of a dirty white wall, the photographs delivered
minutes later. The image quality was poor. Attila held it up in front of
his face in order to inspect it more closely, then he checked the envelope
to see if there were others. He made a call and waited. The name was
the same, but it was a common enough name, he needed to be sure. On
the way to his next meeting he asked his interpreter to ask their driver
if anyone knew the kidnapped man. The driver nodded vigorously. He
pulled out his mobile phone, pressed buttons and, continuing to drive
with one hand on the wheel, he passed the phone over his shoulder to
the interpreter who glanced at the image and handed it to Attila. The
photograph showed a line of men, facing the camera, arms around each
other. Behind them were chairs, a whiteboard. The driver was not in
the frame, presumably he was the one who had taken the picture. The
men looked mainly Iraqi, except two who were dark-skinned, typically
West African-looking. One of them was Ibrahim, Attila's former driver
in Sierra Leone. Attila was sure now. The interpreter was talking to
Attila, phrase by phrase as he relayed the words of the driver: 'They
were hired at the same time. This picture was taken at the end of the
induction course. The men became friends. The blacks' – the interpreter
inclined his head and corrected it to – 'the Africans, they were good
drivers but they didn't know the streets.'

The handover was delayed. 'Tactics,' said Quell.

Attila settled down to wait and as he waited he listened to music
or read. There were a number of paperbacks to be found in the mess,

their pages yellowing and crisp. In among the thrillers he found a copy of Goodbye to All That, *he had last read it during his university days. Quell called: 'They're insisting on a face-to-face handover. God knows why, they've dropped all attempts at ransom money. Why the hell they can't just leave him in a marketplace somewhere.' This was Quell as irritated as he ever became. 'Hold still,' he said to Attila, who wasn't doing anything else. 'I'll level with you. The reason we don't want to agree to a face-to-face handover is because there's always the possibility that they'll try to switch their valueless asset for a valuable one.'*

'And that would be me,' said Attila.

'And that would be you.'

An hour later Quell called back. 'They've made contact again. It's happening. The idea is that you show yourself there, they'll bring him to you.'

'Okay.'

'I'll be on the phone. It will be you and your driver and interpreter. It's the only way I can see to handle this without escalating matters. It's a risk. You can weigh it as much as I can once you're there. If you don't like the look of it, you should leave.'

'You've talked to them. What's your sense of it?'

'I'm prepared to go with it. It's clear there's one person in charge now, that wasn't so much the case before, the previous lot of negotiators said it was like pass the parcel, whichever kidnapper had the phone that day took over as chief negotiator. They wouldn't cooperate with the proof of life stuff. Amateurs. Thought they could get in on the kidnapping business. Now they seem to have decided that holding on to Ibrahim isn't to their advantage. I've told them you're keeping your phone on you so that we can keep in communication.'

The meeting point was a café at the end of a small row of shops in a quiet neighbourhood. Attila decided to travel by taxi alone with the interpreter who was a man of calm disposition and modest bearing born of a career spent listening to and repeating other people's words, sidelined yet indispensable. They opened the door to the café and were almost knocked back by the smoke and the sight of thirty or forty men. Attila placed his phone on the table. He had an open line to Quell.

'Kion vi vidas?'

The men and young boys watched Attila with open interest, the young ones in particular, though none spoke. One of the younger men grinned at him.

'I'll tell you in a minute.' He was watching the interpreter, prepared to take his cues from him. The man seemed formal, but relaxed. The owner came with two glasses of water followed by two glasses of a red juice. He smiled as he placed a glass in front of each of them.

'Pomegranate,' said the interpreter and picked up his glass. 'It's very good. Especially in the hot season.'

Attila drained the glass. There was nothing especially threatening in the mood of the room, nothing he could discern either in the men or the patron.

'Well?' said Quell, again in Esperanto.

'Have you ever bought a carpet?' Attila asked, also in Esperanto.

'That's Vivien's department.'

'I mean on holiday in Morocco or Egypt.'

'No.'

'I haven't either,' said Attila. 'But I know a lot of people who have.' And they told a similar story, of the hospitality, the endless cups of coffee, the talk. More of the same once the sale was concluded. Right now, his best guess, and it was only a guess, was that this was what was happening here. Most of the factions were small and operated in local neighbourhoods. If he was right this performance was meant to signify the closing of a deal. Nobody in the room knew that no money had been paid. It was a face saver.

Attila told this to Quell and stopped talking. Three men entered the coffee shop. One was Ibrahim. Attila stood up and immediately offered his hand. He declined to meet Ibrahim's gaze, merely said as though they were strangers: 'So you are from West Africa too,' was pleased when Ibrahim caught on immediately, nodded and said yes. One of the men, not the oldest but evidently the one who was in charge, looked from Attila to Ibrahim and back as though this coincidence was something he himself had masterminded. Attila said: 'Will you be my guest?' and recommended the pomegranate juice, which gave the man the opportunity to insist otherwise. Ten, fifteen minutes passed. They talked about football scores and Berlin, where the main man had family but had yet to visit, they talked about the coming down of the Wall. More minutes passed. In time the two Iraqis stood up. Ibrahim remained seated, but he looked nervous, as though he expected at any moment to be told that he was returning with them.

After the men had gone Attila called for the bill to be told he owed nothing. To Quell, the telephone on the table, he said: 'We're leaving now.' And he put the phone in his pocket.

Outside men lay in wait for them. One of them seized Ibrahim and forced handcuffs onto his wrists. Attila felt himself pushed forward, he collided with Ibrahim. He was aware of the interpreter being dragged aside. There was shouting. Were they being traded? Then, as suddenly as the fray began, it ended. They were not going to be bundled into vehicles, but were surrounded by a crowd of men holding up mobile phones. They were being photographed. Ibrahim was urged to hold up his cuffed hands, a middle-aged man mimed for them to embrace. When they did he smiled, took several pictures and afterwards shook them both vigorously by the hand. Two days later a photograph appeared on an Iraqi news site on the internet, the last part of what Attila had rightly supposed was an exercise in public relations on the part of the new leader of the faction who had been holding Ibrahim.

In the taxi, jammed together on the back seat, the three men, Ibrahim, Attila and the interpreter, laughed with the laughter of those who have survived a close call. Ibrahim and Attila embraced, properly this time. 'It's good to see you, Doctor,' Ibrahim said.

It wasn't until a few minutes later that Attila remembered Quell. He drew his phone from his pocket. 'Sukceso!' he said.

Chapter 14

Jean gave Tano her bedroom and made up the sofa in the front room for herself. It made more sense, she had told Attila, to let him stay with her rather than in the hotel. She would take him to the hospital to visit his mother and introduce herself at the same time. They had breakfasted on yoghurt and cereal, now she had left Tano in the apartment watching Sunday morning cartoons. Thoughts of Attila formed and dissipated before she had a chance to feel what their shape was made of. The day before, in Sussex, dinner with the Quells, she had felt his gaze on her more than once during supper, glances fleeting as moth wings. There were moments when she felt Quell watching them both, Attila and her, and both Quells took such care to include her in the conversation, to ask her careful, tactful questions that did not seem formed entirely out of random curiosity. Tano had sat next to her watching and listening to the adults, until Lady Quell addressed a question to him: she possessed a professional's skill at putting people at their ease. Emmanuel was occupied with the act of feeding Rosie, gently foisting on her forkfuls of fish pie which she chewed for minutes at a time. It was a task that required infinite patience, all the time Emmanuel laid out the facts before Rosie: 'Look, Rosie, peas.' 'Here's a glass of water, Rosie.' Reminding her of that which now could no longer be taken for granted.

In the car on the drive home when Jean turned around to check on the others in the back seat she found Rosie asleep with her head on Emmanuel's shoulder and Tano gazing back at her. He returned the smile she gave him. 'Okay?' she mouthed. And he nodded. 'Do you want to go to sleep?' He nodded again, so she shrugged off her sweater and gave it to him to use as a pillow. Next to her Attila drove with concentration, overtaking each car he came up behind so rhythmically the Jaguar barely changed speed. Jean felt acutely aware of Attila's presence, the movement of his hand on the steering wheel, the occasional flash of his watch as the car passed beneath the lights strung out along the motorway.

Jean had an early sense that Attila's practicality in the matter of Tano was right. As in her world, sometimes there was no fix, sometimes it was better just to let a thing find its own equilibrium. The more you interfered, the more you risked upsetting the infinite variables. Jean's right foot hit a puddle and she ran on, gradually feeling the cold water seep through her trainer and into her sock. Tano's brain was an ecosystem, it would reconfigure itself to survive. The night before, in the eternal twilight that was darkness in the city, when she had gone through the apartment turning out the lights and found him already asleep in her bed, she could hear it in the rhythm of his breathing.

Tano. Attila. Thoughts of Luke and Ray, too – the casts of an old life and a new life. She thought about Attila's wife, whose name she did not know. She remembered a verse of a poem she had learned for a Spanish class presentation in high school, the only poem she had ever memorised. Death slipped into a room where a man's love lay on her sickbed:

> *Silenciosa y sin mirarme,*
> *la muerte otra vez pasó delante de mi.*
> Silent and without looking at me,
>   death again passed before me.
> *¿Qué has hecho?*
> What have you done?

Could she now remember the last lines?

> *¡Ay, lo que la muerte ha roto*
> *era un hilo entre los dos!*

Jean had not thought about the poem for maybe forty years and she was surprised to remember it so well. The poet described the intangible nature of loss: 'Oh, what death has broken was a thread between the two of us.' Had death broken the thread between Attila and his wife? Jean did not know.

The name of the poet she could no longer remember. On the top of the hill in the cemetery with the view of St Paul's, the furthest point of her run, she stopped, she had brought her phone in case Tano needed to reach her. There was a pair of earphones in one of the pockets of her running jacket. She found them, plugged them into her phone, chose some music and turned the volume up. 'Wouldn't It Be Nice?'. 'Good Vibrations'. 'Kokomo'. Songs from many years, many miles and many moods away. The cold spreading across the toes of her right foot, the unremembered name of the poet, the boy at home to whom she would return, the Beach Boys singing about a girl with sun in her hair, the man with the name of a warrior, these things filled her mind. She ran down the hill toward the tree where the parakeets nested. There at the crossroads, no protesters drew her attention, no man with a limp and a small mongrel or woman in a cattleman's hat, no egg addler. Nothing called to Jean to look over in the direction of the great dead tree, even the birds themselves were quiet that day. She did not notice the mark on the trunk where someone had taken a can of red paint and sprayed a rough cross on the bark. It appeared on several of the trees in the cemetery, the largest of which was the big sycamore where the parakeets nested, like someone's lazy tag, just an idle, random work of graffiti.

'Bloody woodpecker,' said Kathleen Branagan. 'I've been trying to figure out what the noise was for weeks.' Attila stood and went to look out of the window in the kitchen door. The rat-a-tat had been going on for several minutes. Outside in the garden on the trunk of a heavy oak sat a bird, black and white with a red crest. 'Greater-spotted, lesser-spotted, I've never known enough to tell the difference,' said Kathleen. Attila returned to his chair and continued to follow the mechanical motions of the bird's head while Kathleen Branagan read through Adama Sherriff's notes, obtained from the solicitor and waiting in his hotel room when he arrived back the previous night. It was Sunday and he was grateful to Kathleen for her time. Upstairs the sounds of her teenage children: feet on stairs, creaking floorboards, muffled calls and rejoinders. Kathleen finished reading the notes, removed her glasses and laid them on the kitchen table.

'The last psychiatrist thought there was an indication of racism. The solicitors seemed very quick to agree, apparently she was shunned by some of her neighbours. One woman crossed the street, that sort of thing. She wasn't invited to events when others were,' said Attila.

'What does that have to do with PTSD?'

'Nothing really, except if the patient is already in an unstable state of mind, certain behaviours could be open to misinterpretation. Exacerbate matters. Did you ever meet her?'

'No, I didn't. I only dealt with the husband after his release. I was there to help with the debrief, keep him on track. It was all very standard. People weren't worried about *radicalisation*.' She gave the word inverted commas in the air. 'In those days they hadn't even invented the word. All they wanted, Quell and that lot, was to find out what he knew. He was cooperative and useful as far as I understand it. He had a good memory.'

'The kidnappers had made a mistake in taking him, they soon realised they'd never get any money, so they agreed a handover. If they'd killed him, well, that would have raised the stakes differently.' Attila tapped his fingers on the table in unconscious echo of the bird outside. 'They soon realised he had little value in terms of leverage. He was a poor man from a poor country and that's what saved him.' And then: 'That's a lesson the kidnappers learned from. How was his mental state?'

'He was functioning well, and those symptoms that he did have were dissipating. He was mentally strong. He seemed to take it with great stoicism. He was naturally resilient. He never asked why me.'

'I've never known an African who did.' Attila smiled. 'Our expectations of life … are more modest than the European's. What I mean to say is that the script of life for most of us is, dare I say, a great deal more fluid.' He paused. 'In other words we know shit happens.'

'Point taken. Anyway, we talked about his resettlement. He never mentioned any problems with locals.'

'They were different kinds of people, he and his wife. He'd never get into a confrontation. Also, in his circumstances, probably he wouldn't have made an issue of it, I shouldn't imagine. Just happy to be here.'

'Yes.'

'And she'd been here since 2011,' Attila said, he was thinking aloud.

'So her PTSD,' said Kathleen, 'according to the first expert witness, was caused not by the kidnapping, she was living with her parents when that happened, it was more or less ancient history. No, hers was believed to be caused by the accident. He survives all of that, basically two wars, and then he gets hit by a car on his way to work. Then you might start asking why me.'

An accumulation of traumas, one upon the other, multiple blows, the last landing on the punch-drunk fighter like a knock-out blow. The news of a death sudden and unexpected could act as a stressor for PTSD, so claimed Attila's fellow professionals. The witnessing of the death itself was considered immaterial, so was whether it took place in a neighbouring room or street or on another continent. 'What are you thinking?'

Kathleen twirled a pen and gazed through the glass of the window to where the bird tapped furiously on. 'I'm thinking it would do *something* to you,' she said.

Tano picked up the muffin and bit into it and chewed mournfully.

'What's the matter?'

'Nothing,' said Tano.

'You don't like it?'

'It's okay.'

'No, tell me.'

'It doesn't taste the way it looks.'

Jean bit into her own muffin. It squeaked faintly against her front teeth and broke up into floury pieces in her mouth. The kid wasn't wrong.

'What would you like instead?'

Tano shrugged. Jean said: 'Have you ever had a peanut butter and banana sandwich?'

Tano shook his head. Jean went into the kitchen and fixed sandwiches for them both, carried the plates back to the sitting room where she watched Tano take a bite before she began on hers. She had forgotten how good they tasted, remembered being fourteen and home alone with her father who regarded the peanut butter and banana sandwich as an advance on the peanut butter and jelly sandwich, its creation a fine art: the banana, overripe by a day, smooth peanut butter, Wonder Bread. Once he told her that a diet of sardines, spinach and something else, she forgot what, contained every nutrient the human body required. 'You could live on just that,' he said, pushing a sandwich across the Formica table at her. 'I mean, if anyone wanted to.' Living alone again, Jean realised, she had begun to exist on almost as pared-down a diet.

'What do you think?' she said to Tano, who nodded at her, his mouth full.

On the Old Kent Road on their way to the hospital they met Abdul. He was not wearing his uniform but dressed in a flowing outfit of peach lace, trousers and a long tunic, and accompanied by a woman and two children dressed in clothes made of identical cloth. The family were on their way to a wedding celebration. He invited Jean to join them and meet his relations, but she shook her head and told them they were going to visit Tano's mother.

'So this is the boy, the runaway boy!?'

Jean nodded. Abdul high-fived Tano. Abdul's wife said something in their own language. Abdul nodded. The woman looked at Tano, she stepped forward and touched a hand to his cheek. The gesture, so small, was replete with kindness. Jean told Abdul about the police, their refusal to investigate the illegal fox hunt. Abdul acted simultaneously outraged and unsurprised. 'Oh wait one minute, Jean. Let me see if I have my notebook with me.' He searched in his pockets and produced it, tore out a sheet and handed it to Jean. Three sightings in two days, the foxes were abroad. Rocky, Redbone and a fox that fitted none of the descriptions of the others. A newcomer. Abdul was easily the most assiduous of her informants, he approached his task with the methodology of a forensic expert, second only to Jean herself. She could trust him if he said he had never seen this fox before. She thanked him and pushed the paper deep into the pocket of her jacket.

Churchgoers dressed in their best, men and women in colours and fabrics created for a faraway sun, floating like mid-winter butterflies to the Global Holy Mission, the Church of Jesus the Redeemer, the True Assemblies of God, the Holy Fire Ministry. Churches carved not of stone but from spaces inside community centres, offices, empty stores and Portakabins. Churches without spires, mosques without minarets. Next to Jean the child was alive, walking with elongated strides, his hands in his pockets. Jean could feel the change in him, from the tightly bound boy of a day or two ago. Through the rotating hospital door they passed into a sudden blast of heat, the wide-open noises of the street replaced by the susurrations of machines, slippers, whispered voices, wheels across linoleum, the static of the PA system. Ama urged upon Jean fruit from a basket next to her bed and warm orange juice from a carton, before she turned her attention to her son. Jean watched, she felt a sudden stab of loneliness. She said: 'I'll let you two catch up. I'll be back soon.'

Outside she headed towards the river. A woman wrapped in a huge, belted overcoat, a scarf around her head and a shopping trolley loaded with plastic bags, sat on a bench and fed pieces of bread to a gathering of pigeons. A pinstriped passer-by frowned and checked his cellphone. A couple in camel coats and polished shoes stopped. The man took a photograph of the woman on the bench and the pigeons. The woman clucked and cooed. Jean walked against the flow of the river, following the same route she had with Attila. Ten minutes later Jean stood in front of Osman who, in turn, stood perfectly still, head cocked, a hand to his ear, fingers spread as if listening for the sound of distant birdsong. A cluster of young people stood in front him, eating bratwurst whilst perusing his body for signs of movement. Jean stepped forward and put a coin in the hat at the base of his plinth. Osman's head swung around and his eyes switched suddenly so that his gaze was upon Jean. Jean smiled at Osman who stuck out his tongue. Jean waited. Osman performed, the pound coins gathering in his hat. A memory came to her. Sitting, sun-warmed, on the edge of a raised bed in some open space, noticing a bag hidden in the bushes. Clothes, a pair of worn sneakers and an exercise book covered in the lettering of an unknown language. She looked around and saw a group of jugglers, slender and dark-skinned, barefoot and dressed in matching outfits, loose red pants and singlets. The bag must have belonged to one of them. Something about it, this pitiful collection of belongings, the ambitions encompassed by the study notes in the exercise book, the men performing for an uninterested public; watching them brought Jean a feeling of pity and a strange protectiveness as she tried to guess to which one of the jugglers the bag belonged.

'Where do you keep your clothes?' Jean said when at last Osman stepped off the plinth.

'I used to change in the toilet at the hotel, which caused some problems with the management, but now Ayo and Olu let me get ready in the back of the theatre. Much better. How is the kid?'

Jean told him Tano was doing just fine.

'Good.'

'And how's your fox?'

Osman shrugged. 'Has not been for three nights now. Last time was the night they kill the other fox.' Osman stared at the tips of his silver hobo's boots, frowned and shook his head. 'Strange.'

The young woman walked into the café where Attila waited. He had never seen her before but he recognised her at once. He stood up and, though she did not acknowledge him, she steered herself in his direction. She was late and offered no apology. Attila drew out a chair and resumed his seat opposite. He introduced himself and the young woman raised and lowered her chin, as if to say she believed him if he said so. She was neatly coiffed and made-up, her lips glossy and everted. She did not look Attila in the eye, but chose generously from the menu. Attila went to the counter to place her order, then returned to the table and waited with patience. He stretched out his legs and drained the remainder of his tea. He had brought neither pen nor notebook, he folded his hands on the table in front of him. After a minute he sat up and pulled in his chair as if to mark the start of business. 'There are a few things it would be helpful to talk about before I give evidence,' he said. She looked at him then and looked away, the shadow of a sneer on her face, let out a sound, a slow, sliding hiss, a sucking of the teeth whose meaning, out of all the nuances of meaning of which that sound was capable, was unmistakable. She despised him. Attila regarded her with interest. He had met angry people before and this woman, Adama Sherriff, was furious.

'Who was it,' he said getting to the point of most interest to him, 'who crossed the road?'

She looked at him then. 'Who told you?'

'It's in your notes.'

She took a sugar packet from the metal container on the table, tore it open and tipped sugar onto a wetted finger and put it in her mouth. 'She thinks she's so fine,' she said in a voice, now he was hearing it for the first time, which was well-modulated, unhesitant. Attila transformed an urge to smile into a welcome for the waitress who arrived with Adama's plentiful order and he watched as Adama arranged her food, more than she was ever likely to consume, and now gave it all her attention. A waltz was taking place, a waltz of manner, speech and thought. Attila looked out of the window and into the street. At moments like this Attila didn't feel as if he were with a patient or a client, rather he felt as though he were with somebody it might be interesting to know. A kind of asexual seduction which would have been impossible if he did not find the person, people, all of them, absorbing. They told him things, not because he was a professional full of a professional's intrigues or dispassion, but because he wanted to know. Somehow, in some alchemic way, he willed their confidence. Everything he had heard about Adama Sherriff told him she possessed strength, was a survivor if you liked. Attila had known people who could walk through fire. He'd seen them in all the places he had been, they withstood what destroyed others, even rose to it. 'Whatever doesn't kill me makes me stronger.' Isn't that what they used to say? And yet even such a person might yet be undone by the breaking of an egg. Attila was following a hunch and so he had come here not to talk about her husband's kidnapping or his death, but with a sense that the truth of Adama's case lay not in the obvious drama of her story, but in the breaking of an egg.

He was in no hurry. In the street a man was walking his dog. The dog was walking directly behind its owner and at very close quarters so its head butted the back of the man's knees. The man made several efforts to drag the dog forward by its lead and for a few paces would succeed, but then the animal would slip behind again. There was something immensely comical about the frustrations of the owner, the indifference of the dog, which seemed to Attila to verge on some sort of obstinacy. At the sound of Attila's laugh Adama Sherriff looked up, she followed his gaze and for several seconds watched the man and his dog, she sucked her teeth, but this time to different effect.

'How's the food?'

She shrugged.

'May I?' Attila helped himself to a chip, dipped it in ketchup and ate it. A moment later he did the same again.

'Maybe you want to order some food for yourself?'

'No, no.' Attila smiled. 'Not if you don't mind.'

Attila took one last chip and then helped himself to a paper napkin from the dispenser. While he was wiping his fingers he said: 'You were telling me about the woman who thought so much of herself.'

Defiance battled compliance in her expression. Eventually she said: 'At first, you know, you think no, what I think I'm seeing is not what I'm seeing.' She pushed the plate away.

'Tell me.'

'There was a woman in the village. She started to cross the road and walk on the other side whenever she saw me. One time I waved at her and I know that she saw me, but she pretended she didn't.'

'You knew her?'

'I was a seamstress.' She used the old-fashioned word. 'I used to make clothes for that woman and her friends. I had been into her house. I have seen her in her underwear.' She gave a dry laugh.

'So what was going on?'

Adama raised her shoulders and let them drop.

'But you had lived in the village for a while and this hadn't happened before. Whoever compiled the report thought it had something to do with race.'

'The solicitor,' she said. 'Or maybe the other one who came to do your job. You know how it is with white people. You say it's race, they tell you you are mistaken. Then they say it's because of your race when you say it is not. They always have to say the opposite.'

'So help me here.'

She let out a long breath. 'I don't know what was wrong with them. Maybe somebody lied about me. My bookings went down, several of my regular clients stopped using me. Nobody told me what it was. It only takes one person to say one thing. Not so?'

A customer tried to squeeze behind Adama's chair and she turned to give him a furious look before shuffling her chair forward a single inch. The man pressed on, forcing his belly through the narrow gap.

'What were you thinking about the evening of the fire? Were you thinking about those women?'

'Yes.'

'You'd had something to drink?'

'Did it say so in my notes?' She tilted her head to one side as she regarded him. 'Some brandy a friend brought. It was left behind in the house. I wasn't drunk, only I hadn't eaten so . . .'

'What was your mood?'

'I was tired.'

'Would you say angry, maybe?'

'Maybe.'

'Were you generally angry in those days?'

'It's you who is saying that, not me.' She turned her head away from him.

The police report said the fire had started in the front room, where Adama did her work. The room was full of cloth, paper patterns. She had used half a bottle of white spirits that had been stored under the sink since Adama and Ibrahim had painted their bathroom. She'd walked out of the apartment and left it to burn.

'Would you like anything else? Something sweet? Some coffee?'

'Are we finished yet? Only I have to pick up some things.'

'Oh,' said Attila. 'Sorry. Yes. Finished. Let me get one thing straight. This all happened, the women, it all happened after your husband was killed?'

Jean headed back to the hospital to collect Tano. Today was Sunday, tomorrow she would visit her client, she wanted sight of the roof terrace one more time and to discuss access so she could arrange deliveries. For now she had the rest of the day free. Someone blocked her path, she heard her name. She looked up and saw her former lover, the Romanian émigré. Jean said hello. He told her how well she looked, he spoke softly, he stood before her, blocking her path, without aggression, instead with the presumption that accompanied a shared intimacy. Everything was well with her, yes? And him? Good. She apologised and said she had to get going, she did not suggest he call her or that they meet again. He reached out a hand and Jean controlled the urge to flinch. She liked him, had liked him, but now all she felt was the faint but real distaste a woman feels for the lover she no longer desires.

Through the cross-hatched window of Ama's room Jean saw Tano lying across the bottom of the bed playing on his games console. Jean knocked softly on the door and heard Ama's voice. When Jean entered Ama, who was lying with her arms folded behind her head, smiled. Tano though did not look up.

'Tano!' said Ama.

'Don't worry,' said Jean. 'I wish I had that ability to concentrate. When my son reached this stage we thought he had a hearing problem, we nearly took him to the doctor to have his ears syringed. My husband came up with the cure though.'

'What was it?' said Ama. 'You must tell me.'

'I'll do better. I'll show you.' Jean crept up behind Tano and bent down so that her lips were a few inches from the back of Tano's head. She whispered: 'Chocolate cheesecake.' Tano's head shot up, he looked around the room then from his mother to Jean.

'You'll have to get him some now.'

'Of course,' said Jean. Just then her cellphone rang and she stepped outside to take the call.

'Jean Turane?'

'Yes?'

'I'm calling from *The Big Show*. London City Radio. I wonder if you'd be free to come into the studio today, we're doing a live special.'

'To talk about what?'

'The fox attack. Eddie wants your view on it.'

'Eddie?'

'Eddie Hopper.'

Jean said: 'Does it have to be today? I'm tied up right now. I emailed your producer ...' She searched for the name of the person. 'Was it you? On Friday. Can it wait until tomorrow? Nothing's changed.'

'You emailed on Friday? This has just happened yesterday.'

'There's been another attack?'

'I don't know, this is the first one I've heard about. The toddler.' The producer had started to sound impatient. 'We're doing a segment on it. We have a one-hour show on Sundays.'

Jean measured her words: 'I haven't seen the news or a paper. What exactly happened?'

'A fox attacked a little girl. Or a boy. Anyway, the kid was in his cot. Are you free? We can send a car to pick you up? We'd need you in forty-five minutes. You'd be clear by 2.30.'

Jean hesitated, then she said: 'No. Sorry.' And she pressed the button to end the call.

When Maryse died, when Maryse had been dead for a week and the funeral was over, Attila had received a letter from Vivien Quell. Written in ink on a black-edged cream-coloured card and in Vivien's fluid cursive script, the letter elegantly summarised Maryse's qualities, the history of her relationship with the Quells, the fondness they had felt for her and the sympathies they now extended to Attila. At that time Attila had met Vivien Quell on perhaps half a dozen occasions, three of which had been in the company of Maryse. He put the card on the desk in his study upstairs and walked through to the bedroom. On the back of the chair that stood before Maryse's dressing table hung the jacket she had worn to a meeting at work the day before he left for Iraq. He crossed the room and rubbed the cloth of the collar between his thumb and forefinger. On the dressing table was the evening bag she had carried with her to a reception at the Austrian Embassy held for a visiting artist. Neither Maryse nor Attila had cared for the paintings. Maryse preferred sculpture, while Attila had no particular feelings, nor was he in the mood to be there. His mind was on the mission ahead, which was not the kind for which he cared, a seminar on frontline trauma for the military. Young men giving their bodies and their minds in battle, sent by middle-aged men who only ever handled a gun on their weekend duck shoots, and men like Attila tasked with the job of trying to keep the young men sane while what they were being asked to do was an insanity itself.

He stopped to peer at the title of a forest scene in which naked people dashed between trees. Burgenland, 1995. He'd been in Bosnia that year. He looked for Maryse and found her in conversation with the Ambassador who had a fondness for her because she spoke German to him. Somewhere past ten o'clock they arrived home. Maryse put her bag down on the dressing table, removed her evening gown and hung it in the next room where she kept the overflow of her wardrobe; she returned wearing her house dress, removed her bracelet and put it in the vanity's top drawer. Attila sat on the bed, took off his shoes and socks and watched her in silence. When she went into the bathroom he stood up and took off his own clothes and when she came back he was wandering the room naked looking for his reading glasses. After a few moments watching him she handed him a pair of her own glasses from the nightstand and Attila, unclothed, wearing a pair of gold half-moon ladies' spectacles, resumed his search with Maryse on the edge of laughter. Afterwards they had worked on their respective papers for half an hour, he in the sitting room and she in the downstairs study with the cot bed where he knew she would spend the nights once he had caught his flight the next evening. He woke up twice in the night and reached out for her. The first time she was there, the second time, in the early morning, she was gone, the sheet cool to the touch.

Three weeks later the letter of condolence arrived from Vivien Quell. A month on came a telephone call from Quell asking him to head up a mission. Quell made no mention of Maryse's death except once at the end of the conversation when he had said: 'Ah, Maryse.' A pause. 'What a business! What a business!'

Attila left Accra ten days before the forty-day mourning period was over, leaving the house open for the last of the mourners.

Responses to Adverse Life Events read the poster on the board outside the conference hall. Attila shouldered open the tall oak doors, stepped inside and took a seat in the back row. Kathleen Branagan in the same row leaned forward until she was in his eyeline. Attila touched his fingers to his forehead. He raised his right buttock and pulled free the flyer beneath, which gave the order of papers to be presented for the day. *Additions to the Diagnostic Criteria of PTSD. Children and Disaster: The Social and Emotional Effects of PTSD Ten Years On. PTSD Symptoms Following Surgery. The Impact of Images: Witnessing Trauma through Social Media.* He slipped the paper into his coat pocket and turned his attention to the speaker on the stage behind whom illuminated images slid into view one after the other. 'Victims of trauma are less trusting, they feel less in control of their lives, hold a greater belief that the world is a place where random acts of violence can occur than those who have not been victims of trauma.' Behind him appeared the words: 'LESS TRUSTING. LESS IN CONTROL. UNCERTAIN WORLD.' 'In other words they view their lives more negatively than those who have not experienced trauma.' Attila consulted the paper in his hand which gave an abstract of the lecture as well as the speaker's credentials. Columbia. Stanford. 'The core assumptions about the world we hold true, in the psyche of the victim of trauma become corrupted, they cannot view the world with the same confidence as before.' Who did he mean by 'we'? wondered Attila. 'We' in this hall or 'we' in Stanford? Or 'we' wearing $600 suits? Tonto and the Lone Ranger caught in an ambush of thousands of Red Indians with no way out. The Lone Ranger turns to Tonto: 'We're trapped. We'll have to shoot our way out.' Tonto to the Lone Ranger: 'Who's "we", white man?'

Kathleen Branagan caught up with him thirty minutes later in the crowds easing themselves out through the narrow gap in the doors. She slipped an arm through his. 'Are you joining us for lunch?'

Attila said he was.

'Excellent.' She patted his arm and disappeared.

Attila helped himself to a plate of food and found a place at one of the ten or twelve large round tables. A conversation was already underway. Attila shook the hand of the woman next to him, the other chair was empty. No gap in the conversation opened up which might have allowed Attila to introduce himself to the others and so he applied himself to his plate. They were discussing a case.

'How did the damage present itself?' said a woman with short blonde hair and a voice which possessed no lower register.

'We've yet to discover it.'

'It'll be there. I'd be interested to know how it manifests.'

'Maybe it won't,' said Attila.

The woman swung her head round at the interruption, her hair following fractionally behind. 'A person doesn't go through a trauma of that kind without damage. There's got to be damage.'

'Suffering, yes,' said Attila. 'There will be suffering, but suffering and damage are not the same. In other words, suffering does not equal damage.' In the air he drew an equals sign and crossed it through with a diagonal stroke.

The other people at the table, sensing the onset of battle and perhaps recognising the keynote speaker, looked from Attila to the woman with silent interest to see what she would say next. The woman did not disappoint: 'So you would have us believe that people just walk away from a house fire or a car accident without any kind of effect?'

'The effect may not necessarily be what we have chosen to assume, what we've chosen to treat as fact, what we spend our time unearthing more and more evidence to bolster. The effect may even be positive.'

The woman laughed incredulously. 'Are you serious? '

She was looking at him with a half-smile of condescension, she thought he was an African hick, someone to invite to international conferences and then treat less as a trained scientist and more as some sort of native informant. He returned her smile. 'There is nothing inevitable about the impact of trauma, except perhaps the way the victim is going to be treated by professionals like us, who will then ascribe every subsequent difficulty in their lives to what has happened to them in the past. We don't blame victims any longer, instead we condemn them. We treat them like damaged goods and in so doing we compound the pain of whatever wound has been inflicted and we encourage everyone around them to do the same. The fact of the matter is that most people who have endured trauma do so without lasting negative effects, but we over-look the ones who cope because we never see them. It's a simple logical fallacy. You already have the answer, so you construct the supporting argument. Trauma causes suffering, suffering causes damage. But what we don't know is whether the absence of adverse life events creates the ideal conditions for human development. We just assume it does. And if damage does somehow occur in a life lived behind the white picket fence, we must find something, anything, the behaviour of a parent, the death of a pet, and we call it the inciting incident. You're saying that if there was an incident, ergo there must be damage. Equally if there is damage ergo there must be an incident. Both logical fallacies. And what is life without incident? Is such a life even possible?' He took a sip of his water: 'How do we become human except in the face of adversity?'

In Attila's second year of medical school the psychiatric establish-ment was rocked by an incendiary laid, treacherously, by one of their own, a psychologist called David Rosenhan. Rosenhan had attended a lecture by the Scottish psychiatrist Ronald Laing, a hard-drinking radical who liked to irritate his peers by challenging psychiatric shibboleths, among them the notion that psychiatric diagnoses were objective and could be compared with medical ones. Rosenhan wondered if there were any empirical way to test this assertion and decided to conduct his own experiment. He recruited a group of six volunteers including (alongside several medical professionals) a painter and a housewife and himself as the seventh. Each volunteer was detailed to ring one of several psychiatric hospitals and to request an appointment, to which they presented themselves unwashed and unshaved. They were to describe hearing voices. Nothing too dramatic and always the same words. 'Empty'. 'Hollow'. 'Thud'. All but one of the volunteers was admitted, after which the six, in accordance with their instructions, behaved perfectly normally and told staff the voices had gone away. Nevertheless the participants were held for an average of nineteen days, and one poor soul was kept inside for fifty-two. When eventually they were discharged each of the patients was described not as sane or cured but 'in remission'. In every case the only people who suspected the volunteers of being perfectly sane frauds were other patients.

Attila's professor had his own variation of the Rosenhan experiment with which he entertained himself at the expense of his new students. After they had all known each other a few weeks he would take each of his students aside and ask, in confidence, about the behaviour of one member of their group. He expressed concern about the individual's mental health and asked the other students to help by keeping an eye on him. In Attila's year the victim was a large-boned chap with red hair and a persistent sniff. After a week the other students handed their findings to his professor, the next day in class the professor revealed the trick and its results. Five students described the subject as displaying levels of anxiety, paranoia (looking up at the door each time somebody passes), motor tension (sniffing), one suggested a possible dissociative disorder after discovering the subject stumbling home after a night in the Student Union bar. An anxiety disorder was the most frequent diagnosis, with psychotic features (the fugue type wandering). Between the seventeen members of the class they recommended a light cocktail of antidepressant and antipsychotic drugs.

The victim, under the circumstances, took it all in good spirit.

Following the class the professor asked Attila to accompany him back to his office. 'Take a seat,' he said once they were inside. The professor searched in his coat pockets and handed Attila a clean handkerchief and a small packet of antihistamine pills, as well as the note containing Attila's diagnosis: 'Hay fever.' He shook Attila's hand.

Attila had come of age as a psychiatrist at a time when the profession seemed to be under attack from every quarter: it was the era of the asylum, of electroshock therapy, the prefrontal leucotomy, insu-lin-coma therapy, the revelations of the Soviet writers, Alexander Solzhenitsyn among them, of the use of psychiatric methods to control the political dissidents of the USSR. In Attila's final year the film *One Flew Over the Cuckoo's Nest* was released and his professor paid for the entire class to see it.

Attila learned to interrogate his own motives and assumptions and those of his profession. Toure, who would later become his mentor, was a philosopher-psychiatrist who argued psychiatry was more art than science. A Senegalese who had studied in France and had known Frantz Fanon, he possessed a passion for war films and Eartha Kitt. Attila adored him, his ability to sift through intellectual junk. Toure loathed orthodoxy and was suspicious of consensus. When Attila graduated Toure gave him a bound copy of Fanon's collected works. Inside he had inscribed the words: 'If everyone thinks alike then someone isn't thinking', a quote from General Patton.

It was paradoxical, but nevertheless true that in his life and in his career Attila had often observed joy amongst those who had suffered most: it was what life gave in exchange for the pain. The speaker at the conference had described the reframing of the trauma victim's mind into one which saw the world as an uncertain and dangerous place. But what if you already saw the world as an uncer-tain and dangerous place, what difference did it make? Perhaps you would consider yourself lucky to be alive. He had told the woman at the conference that suffering did not necessarily produce damage. Change, yes. And change was not always a bad thing. His old mentor now spent his retirement days in his Gorée Island home contemplating the colours of the bougainvillea that surrounded his terrace and reading books on subjects that interested him, forestry one year, the history of masquerade the next. Once he had given Attila a lengthy explanation of the effects of forest fire, how the incredible speed and heat of the fires razes the forest. Afterwards it seems as though nothing is left, then gradually the scorched and burned trees grow back just as lushly, more so even, the process is called succession, and as the forest rises again its ecology may be altered, different from before. He had taught Attila the need to consider the simultaneity of ideas, that their field of study was not one of either/or, rather it was one of and/but. That the path to reason was not always a straight line.

On the way back to the hotel Attila remembered a poster he had once seen in a spinal injuries unit intended to demonstrate the damage done by certain kinds of poorly designed chairs. It showed a seated crash dummy, the caption read: 'Major trauma at 0 mph.' What if damage was not contingent on suffering? What then? He walked down the Strand, past the Savoy. On the other side of the river the lights of the South Bank theatre and concert halls were up. The actors would be preparing to perform emotions for those who had never felt those kinds of emotions in their lives and perhaps never would. Suffering had become a spectacle that served not to warn of the vagaries of misfortune but to remind the audience, sitting in warmth and comfort, of their own good fortune.

A society went numb, Attila thought as he waited for the lights to change, as often from being battered by fate as from never being touched. The untouched, who were raised under glass, who had never felt the rain or the wind, had never been caught in a storm, or run from the thunder and lightning, could not bear to be reminded of their own mortality. They lived in terror of what they could not control and in their terror they tried to control everything, to harness the wind. The women for whom Adama sewed clothes, upon whose bodies she fitted dresses, so afraid of their own mortality they would cross the road rather than confront a reminder of it. No shadow could be allowed to darken their lives as they imagined them. They were terrified of the slightest hurt, afraid of fear itself.

The glass dwellers were terrified of the cloche being lifted. They treated the suffering of others as something exceptional, something that required treatment, when what was exceptional was all this.

'All this!' he said aloud. In the cold and dark nobody turned to look at him.

All of this.

Chapter 15

A sound, a punctuation point hitting the air. A ladybug landed on the glass of the window. In the corner of the sill lay several dead ladybugs and when Jean pulled up the sash she had been met with a small cascade of desiccated corpses. They died escaping the cold, she had seen the same in Massachusetts, harlequin ladybugs, brought in to control aphids and now the dominant species here and in many places.

On the other side of the room Tano played on Jean's computer. They had returned from the visit to Ama, stopping in shops along the way to buy groceries, and arrived at the apartment where Jean cooked and Tano helped her. He had washed the vegetables and peeled the onion, sniffing, eyes streaming but continuing nonetheless. They baked a chicken (free range) casserole and sang along to the songs on the radio. Now Jean went into the kitchen to check on the dish and as she did so turned to gaze out of the window and there was Light Bright. The vixen looked in good health, her coat had thickened. Jean had heard her the last three nights calling for a mate, she suspected Light Bright had moved into Black Aggie's old den underneath the shipping container. By the time Jean and Tano had arrived home Jean had missed hearing *The Big Show* go out live, had meant to tune in to the evening rerun and forgotten. Now she leaned over, switched the station and turned up the volume. She heard the tones of Eddie Hopper, that blend of sanctimony and sarcasm, which passed, the first for caring and the second for cleverness, on the media.

'. . . could have been much worse. It was bad enough. The child is recovering in hospital, six stitches to the wound. We have Andrew on the line from north London. Andrew.'

Andrew had called in to say he was worried about letting his children play in the garden. He wanted to be told what to do.

'Ah well, one of our guests here is clear about what needs to be done,' said Eddie Hopper. 'You've taken matters into your own hands, haven't you, Bruce Townsly?'

'Well,' the guest laughed. 'Not strictly speaking I haven't, no. Everything we do is within the law.'

'Tell us what you do.'

'I run a specialist firm. We're stepping in where local councils have failed to deal with nuisance foxes. Even if they don't attack, as in this shocking instance, foxes can cause damage and carry diseases.'

'When you say remove, what you mean is exterminate, don't you? You kill them.'

'Yes.'

'And how do you do that?'

'I'm a licensed marksman.' This impressed Andrew who was still on the line and let out an awed murmur. In the UK where gun laws were tight very few people were allowed to own guns, let alone wield them in public.

'And would you mind telling us your personal record?' asked Eddie Hopper in a voice that suggested he already knew the answer.

'I've taken down seventeen in a night.'

'Seventeen, you say?'

'It just shows how many there are out there. What we see is only the tip of the iceberg.'

Eddie Hopper invited a representative from the council where the attack on the child had taken place to explain their inaction. The man did his best and said all the things Jean would have said, but his voice lacked conviction. Hopper was like a matador, the council man the exhausted bull lumbering around the ring after him, each question a spear to the neck until Hopper went in for the kill.

'Is the council prepared to cull the foxes?'

'We are looking at all solutions but—'
'Yes or no?'
'It's that—'
'Yes or no?'
Yes or no. Yes or no. Yes or no.

Attila walked across Waterloo Bridge. Since the conference he had remained deep in thought, automatically stepping around the oncoming pedestrians, for once he ignored the view of the river from the bridge. On the far side of the bridge, out of nowhere, he tripped and fell. One moment he was upright, the next he was on his hands and knees. A bolt of pain shot through his body as his knee hit the pavement. He remained on all fours in the moments it took his brain to reconfigure what had happened to his body, aware of the grit of the pavement beneath the palms of his hands, the feet of passers-by, entering the grip of the heat and nausea caused by shock.

'D-D-D-D-D-Doctor!' It was Komba, the traffic warden who had helped in the search for Tano. Within a moment Attila felt hands gripping his upper arms, the rustle of waterproof jackets as he was raised to his feet, people were patting him down. Komba insisted on calling a cab. 'Let me call my cousin, he drives for a minicab firm right here.' A few minutes later Attila was in a cab headed south, at quarter past five he rang Jean's doorbell and soon afterwards was sitting on the sofa with his trouser leg pulled up over his knee while Jean dabbed at the bruise with a cotton-wool ball soaked in witch hazel and Tano looked on with the kind of awed concern children demonstrate when an adult is hurt. 'I'm fine, I'm fine,' said Attila. His knee hurt badly, he did not admit it. When Jean handed him a Jack Daniel's he took half the glass in a single swallow. Gradually the leg felt better. He let his eyes rest on Tano, to whom he was grateful for allowing him to be in this flat at this exact time, but he was in reality studying Jean where she stood across the room. For once she was not wearing black, but barefoot in a pale, high-necked sweater and cream-coloured trousers. She seemed entirely at ease and later, much later in his life, this image of Jean would rise up, the many expressions on her face, all of which seemed to coalesce at that exact moment.

The reckless open their arms and topple into love, as do dreamers, who fly in their dreams without fear or danger. Those who know that all love must end in loss do not fall but rather cross slowly from the not knowing into the knowing. Attila watched Jean from where he stood on the dark side of the doorway.

He remembered something he had meant to ask. 'What was the story you were telling? On the terrace.'

She frowned, drew in her chin.

'At the Quells',' he said. 'I saw you outside on the terrace, you were telling the others a story.'

She could not remember. 'No.' She shook her head.

'You were telling us about the stars,' said Tano.

'Oh that's right. It was an impromptu lesson in navigating by the stars.'

'You can do that?' asked Attila.

'Yes,' replied Tano firmly. 'She can.'

After they had eaten the three climbed the spiral stairs to the roof. Jean found the North Star and gave Tano the binoculars, guiding his gaze by cupping her hands around his head. In the steel February air, she traced the patterns of the stars upon the sky. It had been easier to see them in Sussex, without the lights of the city. Perseus. Andromeda. Gemini. Taurus. Cetus. Cassiopeia. Ursa Major. Canis Major. 'If you remember any of them remember the North Star and Ursa Major, the Big Dipper we call it, here you call it the Plough, and Cassiopeia.' Jean told the story of Cassiopeia, the queen who boasted of her daughter Andromeda's beauty and was banished by the gods to the skies of the North Pole. Andromeda was tied to a rock as punishment to be rescued by Perseus. When Perseus and Andromeda died, the gods placed them both among the stars.

Much later, Jean had taken Tano down to bed. She had persuaded Attila to let Tano stay on with her another night, and the boy had clearly taken to her. It would only be for another day and it made more practical sense than his having Tano at the hotel. Attila could go back and forth. Now Attila sat alone on the roof and waited for Jean's return. What kind of woman creates such a place? he thought. The outlines of plants hovered in the darkness. There was a smell of rain and the perfume of a flower, faint like scent on bedsheets. In the middle of the city he sat surrounded by stillness, so still he felt he had interrupted something by coming up here, as though around him everything in the garden was holding its breath and waiting for him to disappear.

Somewhere nearby a firework went off, a rocket shuddered through the blackness, traced an uneven arc through the sky and flared before it fell back to earth. Afterwards nothing of it lingered. Attila could not be sure he had seen it at all. A moment later came more fireworks seemingly from every direction. They were detonating sometimes singly, at other times in sequences, nearby and far away. A pause, the air would subside into stillness, and then another firework would go off. Jean came up the stairs and stood beside him. On the other side of the river extravagant sprays of colour bloomed and died. 'Chinese New Year,' said Jean.

She stood next to him without moving, not even to pass him the wine she had brought up. They both stood in silence, feeling the finite nature of the moment, understanding that one of them would have to be first to speak or to move. It was Attila, he eased off his gloves and, raising Jean's hands one by one, he slipped them on her. He placed his bare hand on the side of her neck and Jean tilted her head and lightly trapped his fingers. Then she lifted her chin, took his hand and placed it upon her cheek. With this touch Attila passed through the door and into the knowing.

Men began to arrive in Greenhampton, pick-up trucks in camouflage colours, gun racks and roll bars. At the Jolly Tavern and Lucky Lanes business was good, the motels were pleased with the upturn in profit at the season's end. Inasmuch as the plan was designed to bring a last-minute flush of visitors and money to Greenhampton it succeeded. Saturday morning, a stall was set up on South Street where the hunters were to register. The rules. Allowed: Guns. Bows. Bait. Predator calling equipment. Disallowed: Traps. Lights. Compulsory: Hunter orange. The town's firefighters stood next to their parked fire truck and pressed plastic helmets, pens and buttons on passers-by. By mid-morning the hunters were gone. They stayed out until an hour after sunset when they returned to the Jolly Tavern to order steak tips and onion rings. Spirits were high though not a single coyote had been taken between them. Sunday a good few started out before daylight. Still the first group came back empty-handed and the next and the one after that. They drank to their bad luck. Those with furthest to go packed their gear and headed home in the dark. The others crawled to their beds in the early hours to rise and drive home in time for the family Labor Day barbecue.

Ray said: 'A stunt, didn't I tell you?' He cooked a chicken jalfrezi with fresh Mexican chillies. The heat stung the tip of Jean's tongue and she blew the air in and out of her mouth. Ray poured a glass of water and handed it to her. There'd be no coyote killing any time soon. Ray opened a bottle of wine and without any more being said a truce was called in the marriage.

Two months later when some folk had already fixed snow ploughs to the front of their utility vehicles, Victor and Jean listened to the weather report on the truck radio. A light snowfall was predicted. They were in the closing stages of the coyote study and knew certain things about the habits of urban and suburban coyotes. They knew that at night coyote walked the streets of Greenhampton. They knew that the animals crossed lawns, circled darkened houses. They knew that some coyote returned to the hills while others slid from view when the first house lights went on. By the time people were running their car engines the coyotes had slipped beneath the surface of the day, below the floorboards of abandoned buildings, in garden sheds, to their dens in empty plots and the edges of parking lots. In towns and cities across the country, coyotes lived side by side with men, though only the coyotes knew it.

Snowflakes drifted across the windshield, began to settle on the road. Thanksgiving was days away. Victor was going to Hawaii. He and Jean discussed those things that needed doing and those things that could wait. Victor complained of the restrictions placed upon him by a recent diagnosis of hypertension, of his wife's diligence in replacing the contents of the fridge with prescribed foodstuffs, a diligence he felt came laced with glee. 'She's enjoying it, I'm telling you. You don't believe me?'

'I believe you,' said Jean who knew that what Victor was really doing was offering evidence of his wife's love.

The first buzz of the receiver went unheard beneath the sound of the windshield wipers, Victor's stories of cupboards swept of mayonnaise and cookies, beef patties and sausages vanished from the freezer. Jean leaned and turned up the volume, Victor stopped talking and they listened. They were moving towards the source of the signal which grew steadily and consistently stronger. Normally there were breaks in reception, the animal had the advantage of being able to move across the landscape in any direction it pleased, those in pursuit were confined to the roads and the rules of the highway. Later Jean considered how this single fact should have served as a warning, but it did not. It felt like a Thanksgiving gift.

Beyond the boundaries of Greenhampton and on they drove, down the highway carved in two by Jersey barriers, the land on either side owned by absentee landlords and managed by the Woodsman. The signal grew stronger and then began to fade. Jean doubled back. A track led directly from the highway into the woods and from there, Jean knew, to an open space used as a parking spot by dog walkers and sometimes necking couples. Four pick-ups were parked there, they included the Woodsman's blue Dodge. Now using the hand-held receiver Jean and Victor followed the signal for which the coordinates had not changed in all this time. One hundred yards ahead was a bridge and then a small clearing in the trees, in the summer a patch of scorched grass showed the remains of recent bonfires. That winter day too there was a bonfire. Jean saw the smoke from it first. Heard men's voices. The smell of burned fat and singed hair. The collar lay on the ground between the bridge and the bonfire, some twenty yards off and already becoming lost in the settling snow. A collar she had fitted herself in the early morning five years ago, three nights of waiting and a lucky shot with the dart gun. She was aware of Victor's hand on her arm, she shrugged herself away. No sound except the voices of the men, the hiss and spit of the flames. She moved further into the clearing. The hunters were gathered around the fire, their backs to her. Nearby stood an open beer cooler. Above the flames on a spit, the skinned and gutted carcass of a coyote. And on a stick, pushed into the earth close to the fire, as though it were a guest at the barbecue of its own flesh, was the head of the animal.

Chapter 16

Jean came back from her run to find the Mayor on the morning news. He was standing on the steps of a building, his hair rising and falling in the wind, a large man with a small mouth, which he opened wide when he spoke (shouted) in a way which emphasised its proportions. 'To me it's really very simple. People in the countryside hunted foxes because foxes were a pest. Right? They did it for centuries and nobody ever said hey, don't bother, that doesn't work!' Jean went to the fridge, opened the vegetable drawer and pulled out a zucchini that was past its best, from the fruit basket she took an apple. As she cut them up she tried to remember when she had last been out on a night-time study trip and had to check her notebook. Wednesday. Not since the business with Tano came up. Today was the first day of his spring break, Jean had persuaded Ama she was fine to hold on to him until Ama was discharged. A tapping caught her attention, a ladybug at the window, fluttering against the glass. First you want in, then you want out, she thought. Tano came in, spotted the plate of fruit and vegetables and said: 'Can I take it up?'

'Put something warm on,' and the words came automatically even though she hadn't used them for fifteen or more years.

The blue tits appeared first, punctual as factory workers, then the flock of sparrows. Jean counted them not for any particular reason but the habit of a professional data collector. There were eleven, always. She thought of Attila and the thought gave her a small jolt, an involuntary tightening of the muscles. She wondered what he

241

might be doing at that moment. To her left she saw a fox enter the yard, a male with a white blaze that travelled his entire underside. The fox jumped onto the wall, remained poised for a moment on the top and then dropped down. Light Bright appeared at the same spot and she too jumped down. The male sat and scratched in a patch of sunlight while Light Bright stood and waited next to him. Once she reached out and sniffed his ear. A moment later they were gone.

'Did you see?' Jean said to Tano.

Tano nodded.

'That's our fox and she's chosen her mate. She's invited him to share her territory and from now on he'll make sure no other males come anywhere near. We'll see the cubs probably.' She did a rough calculation in her head. It was February now. Fifty-two days. 'Probably the beginning of April.'

'My birthday's April the 5th.'

'Well, come back and we'll see if you've got some canine siblings.'

'When am I going to go home?'

'Very soon, I think,' said Jean. He'd been with her only two days but the thought brought a weight to her chest. She had always loved being alone, suddenly she had ceased to crave it. 'Soon,' she said.

At that moment in his hotel at the Aldwych Attila had just taken a call.

'Yes!' The lawyer's first word. Then: 'I told you I was not a miracle worker, not so?'

'That's right,' said Attila.

'Well, my wife says I'm too modest for my own good.' He laughed. 'The apartment,' he continued. He had it back along with the keys. The new owner lived overseas, the culprits had been the managing agency. The owner, once the wrongful-eviction notice had been served, elected to avoid trouble.

When the call was ended Attila went to the window and looked out over the Aldwych, at the pigeons on the windowsills of the shrouded windows opposite, the crescent of road, the street-sweeping vehicle skirting the kerb. In West Africa he awoke to the sound of cockerels and of his steward and the stewards of all the houses sweeping the yards and the road in front of the houses, bent over brooms made of a bundle of bound, dried stems. They moved, one arm held behind their back, with the appearance and rhythm of speed skaters. He lifted the receiver of the hotel telephone and, taking out his notebook, pressed a long sequence of numbers. A voice answered. Attila asked for Dr Toure. The sound of the receiver at the other end being placed on the table: 'Sir, Doctor? Long distance!'

It had been three years since Attila's last visit to Senegal. These days the two men spoke but rarely, only for the reason that it seemed superfluous to their friendship. Every now and again Attila received in the mail an academic journal in which the title of one article had been ringed or given a hasty star or sometimes a trio of question marks. On the occasions they did talk it was as though they were resuming a conversation that had been briefly interrupted. Attila got straight to the point and his mentor listened. He explained Adama's case, sketched some of his own thoughts. When he had finished the man on the end of the telephone broke into laughter. 'What's that joke?' said Toure.

'I don't know,' said Attila. 'How does it start?'

'I can't remember. I can only remember the, what do you call it, the punchline!'

'Give me the punchline, then.'

'The person says, "It's not me, it's you."'

'Shouldn't that be the other way round?'

Toure chuckled. 'That's the point. "It's not me, it's you." Remember that book?'

Attila replied patiently: 'What book is that?'

'I lent it to you to read.'

'You lent me a lot of books.'

'*Goodbye* ...'

'*Goodbye to All That*, Robert Graves.'

'Exactly. See, I knew you'd remember. What was it he said?'

This time Attila waited in silence. Toure continued, his voice completely serious now: 'He goes back to the trenches of the First World War when he doesn't have to. He re-enlists, I think I am right. He goes back. He preferred the suffering of war to the insufferableness of civilisation. He yearns only to be back among people who recognise the sound of shellfire.'

'You look familiar,' said Eddie Hopper to Jean as she took the seat opposite him.

On the other side of the studio glass Jean saw the producer lean into the mike. 'Jean Turane was on the show last week. We wanted her for the special yesterday, but she couldn't make it. Since the story's hotted up we thought we'd include an update on today's show. The Mayor's calling for a cull on foxes.'

'Cool,' said Eddie Hopper.

'Fifteen seconds left on the audio,' said the producer, pushing back from the mike. The sound in the room lifted, the Mayor's voice: 'And what about the children? And what about our pets? Our health? I'll tell you what, we've done some telephone polling on this and the polls say people agree with me. They actually agree with me. The point is there's a lot to be done and somebody needs to start doing it. You know, we've listened long enough. First they banned fox hunting, now the cities are full of foxes. Someone has to stand up to this kind of political correctness.'

'And that was Don Cob talking about a possible fox cull. In the studio we have' – he glanced at his notes – 'Jean Turane, who is a fox specialist.' He looked up at Jean. 'Who says culling foxes is plain wrong, am I right, Jean?'

That annoyed her. 'It isn't a matter of right and wrong,' she said. 'This isn't a question of morality but of what works and doesn't work. Culling foxes simply won't work.'

'You kill them, they're dead. That seems pretty effective to me.'

'There's the question of what you would use. Poison is far too dangerous in an urban setting, especially if you're worried about children and household pets. So is shooting large numbers of foxes. How many marksmen would you need, at what rate of hourly pay? And think of all those bullets flying around in a densely populated area. Somebody would be bound to get hurt. That leaves ...'

Eddie Hopper held up a hand to silence her. Surprised, Jean went quiet. 'What do you say to that, Mr Cob? We have an expert here who says your idea won't work.'

Jean hadn't realised the Mayor was on the line.

'Oh for heaven's sake, listen, if I had a penny for every expert who told me I was wrong I'd be a rich man. That's what they're paid to do, forgive me, Miss ... I've said it before and I'll say it again – we haven't even tried this and already we've got some sympathiser objecting.'

'I'm a scientist,' said Jean.

The Mayor continued as though she had not spoken. 'What I'm interested in here is solutions, not more problems.'

Eddie Hopper nodded at Jean and she picked up where she'd left off. 'Trapping is inefficient. You'd need thousands of traps. And even then you're right back where you started, the trapped foxes would have to be taken somewhere else to be disposed of.' Better to have said killed, or exterminated.

'It's been done before. There's nothing that complicated in getting rid of a pest,' said the Mayor.

'Yes, what do you say to that?' said Eddie Hopper. 'There were once bears and wolves in the hills. Of course, you'd probably like them back.'

'The situation today is different, the environment, the risk to life ... listen, the fox is an animal completely adapted to urban living.' She didn't want to say what she said next, for how it might play, but it needed saying. What was true of the coyotes in New England was true of urban foxes: 'These are animals, they're conditioned to survive. Start to kill them and they'll hyper-breed, bigger litters year on year, sometimes two. You'll have more than the number you started with.'

'From the mouth of an expert no less,' said Eddie Hopper with a note of triumph.

'You see what I'm saying,' said the Mayor. 'Even the so-called experts admit we have a problem.'

'It's not a problem unless you call it one.'

'You're saying children being attacked by foxes isn't a problem?'

'Of course not—'

'The safety of our children is my foremost priority. I'm not kowtowing to a load of PC nonsense. I'm a man who gets things done. Whatever it takes. Any fool knows the answer.'

'Well then you're a fool,' said Jean.

Behind the glass she caught the exaggerated expression of the producer, her silent mouthing to the sound engineer: 'Did she just say that?'

Attila's formal interview with Adama Sherriff took place in a room Kathleen Branagan had organised at the hospital. Time being so short it was scheduled for early afternoon Monday. Her hearing was due to take place on the Tuesday. Attila would have to draft and submit his report later the same day. Attila sat with one buttock hitched onto the edge of the table, he said: 'Tell me three things you remember about your husband.'

'He got up that morning. He had a motorbike he went to work on, he would ride in and pick up whatever car he was driving that day. He used to go very early in the morning because, you know, the time the flights arrive, he had to be at the airport to meet the clients. I was asleep when he left, I was still in bed when the hospital called. By the time I reached there they had already removed his body. But I told the last doctor this and the lawyer, it's all in my files. You read them yourself.'

'Yes,' said Attila. 'I didn't mean tell me about the day of his death, I meant, just tell me about your husband, that's all. Three things. Any three things? Like, what kind of pizza did he like best?'

Adama Sherriff looked at him. Attila said: 'I knew him, did you know?'

She narrowed her eyes, she said nothing, considering his statement for its veracity.

'He was my driver for a short while, during the war.'

'You're the Doctor? He told me!' She clapped her hands together, then she pointed at him. 'It's you! Oh my God! He told me about you, about that time you went to collect the crazy man John Bull. So that was the two of you, eh? The checkpoint and the peacekeeper and all that. He told me that story so many times.'

Attila smiled and looked down at his hands as he too remembered the incident. 'He was a very good driver. You'd think he was born with a steering wheel in his hand.'

'He tried to teach me to drive,' said Adama. 'He said I had, what do you say? No aptitude. He wanted to tease me, to provoke me, but it didn't bother me. He said he was going to buy me an automatic car when he had enough money.'

'What else?' said Attila.

'You know, he snored and then denied it, I never told anybody that. How would you even know, I asked him, when you're asleep? You know what he would say? That the snoring would wake him up if it was as loud as I said. One day I took his phone and I recorded the noise he was making.' Her words splintered into laughter.

'What did he want in life?'

She paused. 'Well, one thing he always said was that we would build a house back home and go and live there. He drew plans for it all the time. He would sit with them in the evenings, sometimes he made adjustments, or drew the plans again on a fresh piece of paper.' She pressed a finger into the corner of her eye and inhaled.

'Go on,' said Attila.

'Where are we going?' asked Tano. They had left the studios of the radio station in central London. Jean walked with purpose but no destination in mind, all she wanted to do was put some distance between her and the studio. She had planned to take Tano to spend the afternoon with Ama. At Tano's question she stopped and looked around, squinting in each direction while she tried for her bearings. 'Your phone,' said Tano.

Jean reached into her pocket. 'Here, why don't you figure it out for us?' She tapped in her access code and passed him the phone. No sooner had she done so than it rang. Luke.

'Hey,' he said.

'Hey,' said Jean. 'How are you? Better?'

'I'm good. Pops came down. He's like the cavalry. They stayed until Saturday evening and then headed back to Mass. I mean ... he stayed ...'

'It's okay, he told me.'

'About ...?' Luke said cautiously.

'Jody. Yes.'

'Are you okay with it, Mom?' At least he was calling her Mom again.

'I am,' she said. 'I really am.'

'Okay.' A short silence. 'Actually I was just talking to him. Um, have you seen Twitter?'

'No,' said Jean. She had a Twitter account which she had set up in the name of public engagement for her project and then barely ever used.

'You might want to take a look. Just, you know ... well, there are always a few idiots. I don't want you to get upset, but I wanted to tell you first.'

'About what?' said Jean, not connecting any of this.

'You were just on a radio show over there, right?'

'But how?' Jean wasn't sure exactly what she was asking.

'Probably the radio station began tweeting. Listen, Pops and I don't want you to worry about it. This stuff happens all the time. We just thought you should know.'

'Thanks,' said Jean.

'Just one thing, Mom, my advice? Don't answer. You know what they say?'

'What do they say?'

'Don't feed the trolls.'

They said goodbye and Jean asked Tano if he knew how to get Twitter on her cellphone. Tano downloaded the Twitter app and asked for Jean's login and password, which she remembered only because she used the same password for everything. She watched as he typed '@JeanLondonFox' into Search.

'There.' He handed the phone to Jean. She scrolled down the screen, dozens of tweets. She began to read at random, and scrolled backwards:

Wiz@WizBazz 19 mins
@EddieHopperShow @JeanLondonFox Here comes that stupid howl for the next 3 minutes! Grab da shotgun!! #foxcull #madfoxwoman

Bee Wilson@BLiever 19 mins
Who is #madfoxwoman??? Cob only one talking sense on #foxcull
@doncobmayor@EddieHopperShow @JeanLondonFox

Brian@2brawny 20 mins
Foxes should be relocated in country. Send them back.
#Madfoxwoman @doncobmayor @JeanLondonFox

Melodie@PurringPlace 22mins
@EddieHopperShow. No problem with foxes. Just don't want
their diseases and stuff. No to foxes in the city. #madfoxwoman @
WordsOnLife @JeanLondonFox

Wiz@WizzBazz 24 mins
Cull dumb PC experts. Loves animals over kidz.#madfoxwoman@
EddieHopperShow @JeanLondonFox

WordsOnLife @wordsonlife 25 mins
Save The Fox, Cull The Slobs @doncobmayor@JeanLondonFox

Tom@Tomgraham221 25 mins
Can I help? *cocks shotgun* @BLiever #madfoxwoman@
JeanLondonFox

Bee Wilson@BLiever 26mins
First #foxhuntban. Now way too many foxes. Time to cull the population. @doncobmayor@EddieHopperShow@JeanLondonFox

Rachellous @Rachellous 28 mins
For fox sake! Howls of anger over fox cull. @EddieHopperShow @
JeanLondonFox

That one had five retweets and seventeen likes. She typed in '@
EddieHopperShow'. There were dozens more tweets:

Johnny@PapaBear33 28 mins
Foxes belong in country not city. Can @EddieHopperShow tell at
#madfoxwoman??? @doncobmayor

James@JJhackney 33 mins
#madfoxwoman haha! Who just heard fox expert call Mayor a moron on @EddieHopperShow

Radio London@RadioLondon 30 mins
Should we cull London's foxes? Have your say. Mayor calls for fox cull. @EddieHopperShow

@EddieHopperShow 35 mins
Tune in to hear Mayor Don Cob discuss possible fox cull with @EddieHopperShow and fox expert Jean Turane @ JeanLondonFox.

Jean scrolled forward, typed in '#madfoxwoman'

Jenny@JennySW11 30 secs
#madfoxwoman I live in Clapham. Foxes are ridiculous there. Can't say I oppose a cull. @doncobmayor @EddieHopperShow

Tom@tomgraham221 2 mins
@JammingSaturday @EddieHopperShow. No one's making a living off the fox cull, you're really reaching now, kinda sad. You and #madfoxwoman

JoJo@JammingSaturday 3 mins
@EddieHopperShow #madfoxwoman What's the motive for #foxcull. Who's making money?

Tom@tomgraham221 4 mins
@JammingSaturday Who's paying for neutering??? You?? Not London taxpayer! @Doncob @RadioLondon @EddieHopperShow #madfoxwoman

JoJo@JammingSaturday 5 mins
If foxes are a problem then cull them humanely. If not then don't. Better spay/neuter to stop breeding. @Doncobmayor @ EddieHopperShow #madfoxwoman

Giovanni@Giovanni996 5 mins
#Madfoxwoman Haha! Next up 'hyper-fucking foxes'.
@EddieHopperShow

The number on the tracker at the top of the page rose as more and more tweets arrived. Jean turned the phone off and shoved it into her pocket. She walked on quickly, as if to outpace the source of her irritation, and in so doing she forgot about Tano who she remembered only when she became aware of him trotting to keep up. She slowed. 'Come on,' she said and she put her arm around his shoulders.

Kathleen had offered Attila the use of her room for the rest of the afternoon so that he might type up his report without going back to the hotel. He walked down the corridor, past half-open doors, the occupants of which looked at him with haunted eyes. For ten or more minutes he sat with his laptop open in front of him, thinking about his conversation with Toure in the early part of the day, his later conversation with Adama which had gone on for well over an hour. He removed his glasses and rubbed his eyes, passed his hand over his head. In Kathleen's study all was quiet. Five chairs arranged in a semicircle. The corridors were silent. Even in the institution where he had spent most of his working life, you passed through the gates and you left all the sounds of the street behind, the revving motorcycles, the squawk of chickens, the cry of the sellers who once sold roasted peanuts and fried dough balls, and these days sold packets of gum and plastic bags of cold water. In the old days people called this bedlam. Bedlam was noisy. Bedlam was shrieks and screams, tin bowls banged against walls. Bedlam meant pandemonium. Bedlam had come to mean uproar, anarchy. Yet modern bedlam had been drugged into silence. The compliant mad shuffled and drooled, keened and slept and when they spoke they spoke in whispers.

Adama Sherriff refused to go quietly. Throughout the duration of the interview her voice rose and fell. Her laugh, when it finally came, was as loud as her anger. Attila began to type. He was a fast four-fingered typist who made many mistakes. His thoughts outpaced his hands. He pressed on, drafting one paragraph after another, errors compounded by spell check into new and more imaginative mistakes.

Two hours earlier:

'What do you want, Adama?'

'I want to be in a place where people don't treat you like there's something wrong with you.'

'Did they treat you like there was something wrong with you?'

'Yes.'

'Because you were a widow?'

'Yes.'

'You were a widow and you were barely thirty.'

'Yes.'

'What do you want, Adama?'

Chapter 17

ON WATERLOO BRIDGE

There is a time one sees a new love, a person who might perhaps become a new love, when the possibility of love has been spoken for the first time, but the possibility of retreat still exists, when one or other might still step away from the abyss. In the hours apart a space opens up between the could-be lovers. A false word or misstep and all might yet be undone. Beneath the possibility of joy lies the fear of shame. Jean saw Attila the moment he stepped onto Waterloo Bridge. She saw him walk towards her. And she saw him stop.

Attila walked onto the bridge and saw Jean standing at the brow, where the plaque is with the etching of the view of the river. He thought, if he could he would use his mind as a camera bringing the shutter down on that moment, committing the frame to his visual memory. He stopped to look at her. She had a way of stand-ing, her hip at an angle, the ghost of the teenage girl self-conscious about her height. She leant against the balustrade, the wind was behind her and blowing her hair over her shoulders so that it flew around her face. She reached up a hand and caught it, pulling it back and tying it with the band she kept around one wrist. Those gestures, already Attila knew them all. He saw her straighten and look up, seemingly in his direction, but she must not have seen him, for she returned again to her view of the river.

Jean saw Attila standing without moving at the mouth of the bridge. She turned away and turned back and he was still there. She did not wave or begin to walk towards him, she turned away so that she would not see him change his mind. When he laid his hand on the middle of her back, her surprise was not entirely feigned. A smile of pleasure and relief that the fear that he might have changed his mind, the fear was gone.

At the hotel James stepped forward and opened the door, nodded just once at Attila. They did not stop at the bar for a drink. What Jean wanted right now was the most sober of love-making, she wanted to remember everything that passed between them. She walked beside him in silence. Together they rode the elevator and Attila led the way. Inside the room he drew the curtain and when he turned he found her waiting for him, he walked to her and laid a hand on her shoulder. He felt her stretch her neck, her face came close to his, but she did not kiss him, instead she pressed her nose into the skin of his neck and inhaled. As he moved into her she regarded him with a gaze that was steady and devoid of self-consciousness, her body had been waiting for him. Then she closed her eyes and kept them closed, until, following the long seconds of her climax, she opened them and the blackness of the pupils gave Attila, who had watched her face throughout, the momentary impression that her eyes had changed colour. He felt a drop of sweat fall from his forehead and saw it land upon hers like a drop of silver.

'This?' she pointed to a light mark on his skin.
'I don't know. I was born with it. These too. At least I suppose I was, I didn't notice them until I was ten or eleven.'
She ran her fingertips along his appendix scar. 'Age?'
'Twenty-one. I had just arrived in this country. The first thing I did was avail myself of the health services.'
'A toast to the British health care system,' she said. 'Here?'
'I fell on some rocks when I was a child. And this was from a pot of boiling water.' He raised his elbow to show her the underside of his forearm. 'Carrying it from the fire into the house for my grandmother.'
She ran her fingertips along a scar on his shoulder, back and over the wax-smooth ridge.

'A spear tip,' he said. 'A raid by a rival tribe. My grandmother saved me.'

'Bullshit,' she said.

He agreed. 'It was an infected tropical boil. The doctor visited and lanced it.'

'Gross!' Jean pulled a face. She traced the pattern between a sequence of small moles on his chest, as if mapping their exact location in order to find her way there again. She described her own scars, beginning with her shin. 'Helter-skelter burn. Strange, it never went away. Here.' She searched her forehead with a fingertip. 'Chicken pox. And this,' scars the size and shape of puncture marks on her lower thigh. 'Four doors down, the Pattersons' ridgeback.' And to her stomach, 'Luke.'

They found and compared smallpox vaccination scars, obsolete in a new generation.

Later he stood up and walked to the other side of the room, needing to put distance between them. From the safety of the opposite wall he regarded her, flexed a calf and then another and found himself returning to her a moment later. She was without physical modesty in a way he had not encountered in a woman, strolled across the room to fetch a glass of water, to shift the curtain and check the arrival of darkness, walked to the mirror to consider her appearance. She carried in her long, muscular body and long silver hair a touch of the Northern outdoors. He could imagine her in a bearskin.

She found his comb and began to rake it through her hair. She walked back to the bed, not with the gingerly tread of the naked but swung her legs and hips with the same long stride she used when she was fully dressed. She sat on the bed, twisted herself round and rolled onto her belly, pulled herself up onto her forearms, took hold of his cock and circled the head with her tongue. He watched her shadow on the wall behind, took her hair in his hand and wound it around his knuckles. He flexed his arm to slowly raise her head and then gently let it down again, feeling her closed lips move slowly down the length of the shaft, her tongue inside trailed the journey of her lips. She could smell and taste herself on him. On the return she kissed the crown of his cock and sat up. She swung a leg over his chest and sat astride him, laid her head and breasts against his chest. For a few minutes she listened carefully to the beat and echo of his heart. With an effort of will, she thought, she might match her own to his. She closed her eyes, he had a good chest, broad enough to curl up on and go to sleep. For a few moments she relaxed and let her weight rest on him.

'I'm hungry,' she said.

She didn't shower, she dressed and left with the scent of him caught beneath her clothes like a second skin.

When she had gone Attila lay on the bed with his hands folded behind his head. He sat up, swung round and put his feet on the floor and he sat with his head in his hands for a long minute. He stood and collected the dishes and glasses and replaced them on the room service tray. He selected some music and thought that he would dance, but he failed. Instead he turned up the music until it smothered the sound of the dead woman weeping in his heart.

Chapter 18

'We all know the facts of the case here, so I don't plan to rehearse them,' said the lawyer for Adama Sherriff. 'The hearing is tomorrow and time is extremely short so I thought it might be best to bring us all together and try to work this out. In Dr Greyforth's opinion, as outlined in his initial report for the judge, Adama Sherriff is suffering from PTSD, post-traumatic—'

'We know what it stands for,' said Attila.

'PTSD. I thought we were agreed on that.'

Greyforth nodded. Attila remained still.

'But your report' – the lawyer looked at Attila – 'disputes Dr Greyforth's finding.'

Attila nodded.

'Would you mind telling us why?'

'The death of a spouse is a natural life event and Adama, the patient's, response to it is wholly proportionate, requiring neither diagnosis nor treatment.'

'And yet Dr Greyforth disagrees.'

'The manner of the death,' said Greyforth obligingly, 'was sudden and unexpected. DSM 5 states that learning of the death of a loved one—'

'Yes, we know what the literature says,' Attila interrupted. Already he could hardly contain his annoyance. 'We can all find a justification for any diagnosis, but you saw Adama Sherriff yourself. What did you see?'

'I saw signs of emotional blunting, detachment, a person who was unresponsive. In my view there was evidence of depression too. All of this arose within six months of a traumatic event.'

'All right,' said Attila. 'If we're going to play it that way then for a diagnosis of PTSD to hold there needs to be evidence of intrusive recollections.'

'I asked her and there was. She talked of dreams, memories, of hearing her husband's voice.'

'A woman whose young husband died in a road accident might be expected to think about him a good deal. I spent some time with Adama Sherriff and do you know what I saw?'

'Go ahead.' Greyforth waved his hand as though to say be my guest. Attila leaned forward, he rested his forearms on his thighs. Greyforth's face was without expression. The solicitor was watching, arms crossed.

'I saw a young woman who was sad and angry, and who probably didn't like you very much. She didn't like me that much either to tell the truth.'

'That's not a diagnosis though, is it? The defendant was sad and angry at the time of the arson,' said the solicitor.

Greyforth did not appear perturbed, the word urbane might have been invented for him. Attila could see why the law firm had chosen him as their expert witness in the first place: he would be excellent under cross-examination. His patients must trust him, Attila thought.

'I'd accept what you're saying …' Greyforth settled his gaze on Attila. 'But for the exceptional circumstances of this case. Her husband was young. His death was caused in a violent accident. I would not say that was normal.'

'By what measure do we define normality? Where do we draw the line? Do we take the life experiences of the people of Cuckfield as the measure and decide all else is deviant? Statistically that might just about hold up around the British Isles, but even then … Adama Sherriff lost a husband at a young age, a very common occurrence in many, if not most, countries in the world.' How to construe normality was not a new argument, but it remained the fact that preventing practitioners in places like this from defaulting to the values of the West was to wage an unending campaign. Attila suspected that Greyforth was the kind of person who when he said 'people' meant 'white people'.

Greyforth, who had listened without interrupting, leaned back in his chair. 'Complicated grief,' he said. He nodded in the direction of the solicitor, though he remained facing Attila.

'I'm listening,' said the solicitor.

Attila said nothing.

Greyforth continued: 'Intense sadness and anger, bitterness even, are symptomatic of complicated grief. I will accept your rejection of PTSD. I'd expect to see fear as the predominant response if we were talking about PTSD, therefore I stand corrected in my initial diagnosis. In Adama Sherriff's case the predominant response is sadness and anger, symptoms of complicated or pathological grief.'

'Emotions,' said Attila.

'I beg your pardon?'

'You call them symptoms, I call them emotions.' He felt tired. He wondered if one day every feeling in the world would be identified, catalogued and marked for eradication. Was there no human experience that did not merit treatment now? He thought of Jean, just a few hours and yet the memory of the feel of her was fragmenting, like those mornings when he woke to the sharp colours of a recent dream, only to lose all sight of it a moment later. He had watched her dress, covering her breasts, her pubic hair, her skin, one by one removing them from his gaze. She had stepped back into the room from the corridor to kiss him.

Greyforth was frowning at him. 'They become symptoms when they are intruding on a patient's quality of life and therefore deserving of both recognition and treatment.'

'Whose quality of life were Adama Sherriff's emotions intruding upon?' said Attila.

'I don't know what you mean.'

'Her own clients crossed the road to avoid Adama Sherriff.' Attila spoke in the voice of one musing aloud. 'She told me they would not look her in the eye, could not meet her gaze. She thought she was being victimised but she didn't know for what. Your report considered the possibility of racism. No. They were avoiding her because she was bereaved. So instead of being comforted, Adama Sherriff finds herself ignored and isolated. She thinks people are avoiding her and she is right, but not for the reasons she supposes. She sees a doctor and is offered antidepressants. All along she is treated like there is something wrong with *her*. Should we be surprised if her grief transposes into anger? She sets fire to a pile of sewing belonging to those people who had shunned her. And now here we all are, us, the law, the courts, treating Adama Sherriff as though she *is* abnormal and not those who showed nothing but a cold disregard for her suffering. In the circumstances I don't find Adama Sherriff's reaction especially hard to understand. I expect I might feel the same way.'

Greyforth gave a small smile. 'But you wouldn't burn a house down, I hope?'

'The only thing she did which landed her in a courtroom was to externalise her despair instead of internalising it. If she'd taken an overdose or slit her wrists, the law wouldn't be bothering with her.' Let bedlam be silent. Attila considered the monstrous absence of empathy it required to cross a road in avoidance of another person's anguish. They weren't afraid of death, these people, they were afraid of life. Now, that should be classified a clinical disorder. 'Are we forgetting what it is to be human?'

Greyforth said nothing. He made a gesture, opening and closing his clasped hands, a gesture of release. 'We're just trying to do our best by her, that's all.'

'We really need something conclusive.' The solicitor spoke. 'Something the judge will accept.'

'Complicated grief,' repeated Greyforth.

'What if,' said Attila, 'what if we presented a third option, a plea bargain?'

'What would that look like?' asked the solicitor.

'Adama Sherriff will accept voluntary repatriation in exchange for charges being dropped.'

That, he thought, was what doing best by her would mean.

Jean collected Tano from the hospital where he had spent the afternoon with his mother and where Ama told her she would be discharged the next day. Fingers crossed. Jean smiled and held up her crossed fingers. How strange was the thought that in a single week Jean had returned to having a child and a man in her life. Stranger still was the thought that in another week they might both be out of it. With Tano she could stay in touch, but what of Attila? Was it possible to love somebody but not be near them? It happened in novels but in real life love fed on sex and breath and flesh.

At the apartment Jean washed Tano's clothes and put them through the dryer. She remembered nights when Luke was going away or had just returned from some place. When he was nine and had been away on a camping trip during which the weather had turned unseasonably cool, Jean had given Luke a hero's welcome and a condemned man's supper. Later it became a small tradition between them, if he was going for a sleepover, or a camping trip, right up until he went away to college. Then Jean had gone to the kitchen to cook pasta and meatballs. Right now she had ground beef in the fridge as well as last summer's bottled tomatoes.

Tano was standing in his favourite place at the window gazing at the street. 'What do you say we watch a movie?' said Jean. 'And make popcorn. Have you ever made popcorn?' Tano turned to look at her, his downward-sloping eyebrows made his face so sweet and serious. He shook his head.

'Ah, well, that's something you need to learn. You have no idea what you're missing.'

Jean heated oil in a pan while Tano took the remote control and found a film streaming service she didn't know she had, which apparently came as part of her subscription. In the kitchen she checked her messages to see if Attila had called. When the corn began to pop she called Tano and they stood and listened to the soft thud of the corn as it hit the lid of the pan. Jean gave the pan a shake and then lifted the lid to let Tano see the cumuli of popcorn. She tipped it out into a bowl, threw in a slab of butter, sprinkled the contents with salt and carried it through to the sitting room to find Tano had chosen *I Am Legend*.

'That is a very scary movie,' said Jean. 'You're a little young. Are you sure you really want to watch it?'

'I know,' said Tano. From where he sat with the remote control in his hand he looked over his shoulder at her and said quite simply: 'But you're here, aren't you?'

Attila left the solicitor's office and caught a bus on Fleet Street in the direction of his hotel and took a seat next to a man holding a dog on his lap. The dog reached across the space between them to sniff Attila's coat and then, apparently satisfied, reclined in its owner's arms from where it watched him with polite inquisitiveness. Attila, who did not know the etiquette of petting other people's dogs, looked back at the dog and wiggled his fingers. The dog wagged its tail and reached out to him with its nose. Attila liked the look of the dog: its expression seemed sympathetic and encouraging of friendship. He might have reached out to pet it had not the sight of the dog's owner reading his texts made Attila reach for his own phone. He needed to check in with Kathleen, and he would call Jean and make an arrangement for later in the evening. For a few moments he rested in the thought of her. The feeling it gave him was articulated through the physical senses, a pressure within his chest, the tightening of the belly and guts, for fear and love produced similar physical responses. Attila looked at the dog, he let go of his phone, withdrew his hand from his pocket, reached out and patted the silky crown of the dog's head.

At the Aldwych he dropped off the bus and headed to the hotel. In his room he showered and as he shaved he listened to music and for a moment or two he danced a bossa nova with his reflection in the mirror. The irritation of the afternoon had dissipated. He had been pleased with the outcome of the meeting with Greyforth and the lawyer, things were being resolved one by one. He wiped his chin dry and dressed to the rhythms of a cha-cha-cha.

Early yet and so he headed to the bar where the Brazilian barman served him a gin and tonic. Attila contemplated the evening ahead. The hours until midnight that he would spend in Jean's company lay half in and half outside the reach of his imagination. Belatedly he realised he had omitted to call. He reached to check his phone.

Seven missed calls. Five from a London number he recognised as the Three Valleys' switchboard. Two from a mobile number he did not recognise. Attila had put his phone on silent during the meeting with Greyforth and the solicitor and he had forgotten to switch it back on. Since he had never set up the answering service the caller or callers had been unable to leave a message. A single text from the centre director asked Attila to call the mobile number or Three Valleys' switchboard as soon as possible.

The receptionist looked up to see Attila and lifted the phone as he passed. He did not break his stride the entire length of the corridor with its sweet, stale air and nickel taint of medicine, not until he was intercepted by the centre director. She did not smile, she asked him to accompany her to the office and spoke to him in the kindly, carefully coded script of the professional care worker. Off her legs. Not eating. Possible kidney infection. Common. Her age. Condition. Unnoticed. Possible complications. Antibiotics. Very weak. Hospital. Hospital. Hospital. Her voice was smooth but her face bore the gravity of what she was not saying.

Rosie had been saying his name. She had been asking for him again.

Once, years before she entered Three Valleys, but after her diagnosis, Rosie had called him. It was late in the evening, she was living in her former home with her mother by that time and she had taken up drinking whisky again – she could do what she wanted now, she said, in a way it was a liberation. That night she was a little drunk. Attila, dead tired, had just flown in and was staying at an airport hotel for the night. The next morning he hired a car and drove down to Haywards Heath. In the freckled light of a September morning they had talked, soberly, through every implication. A lawyer had already done the necessary work. Attila made no effort to dissuade Rosie, or to challenge her. She had chosen him for this task for being the one person who could look at her and believe she still knew her own mind.

On the director's desk was the paperwork drawn up by Rosie's lawyer, typewritten and bearing his signature on the final pages. Rosie's requests were specific and detailed, ever the unsentimental scientist.

In her room Rosie lay propped up on some pillows, her head lolled to one side. The director moved ahead of Attila to straighten the pillows and shift Rosie into an upright position. She wiped the corner of Rosie's mouth with a tissue and then withdrew. A chair had been placed next to the bed and Attila sat down.

The sound of breathing, a hollow churn which nevertheless barely disturbed the stillness of the room. Beneath the bedclothes Rosie's chest moved with a trembling judder. Her eyes remained closed. For a minute, maybe two, he watched. Many years ago he had thought he could see her dreams sketched upon her sleeping face, the movement of her lips, electric pulses that traversed her face and disappeared.

Once, as he lay in bed facing her, her eyes had flown open quite suddenly and for two seconds she had stared right into his soul. That all-knowing, furious and lustrous glare had unsettled Attila. He had lain there with his heart pounding. A moment or two later Rosie had raised a hand and placed it upon his chest, as if to feel the disturbance of his heart. Her eyes had opened a second time. Drawing herself slowly out of sleep, she saw him and smiled. Attila smiled back. He said nothing of what had happened, of that other being who had hunted him from some unreachable beyond.

Now he raised a hand and put it to her cheek just as she had put her hand on his chest once before, and with his thumb he stroked the sharp ridge of her cheekbone, the escarpment in the landscape of her face.

On the dresser next to the bed lay the book of poems Attila had bought for Rosie just the week before. *A Child's Garden of Verses.* He opened the book and began to read. "'When I am grown to a man's estate, / I shall be very proud and great. / And tell the other girls and boys / Not to meddle with my toys.'" Poems for children. He wondered if Rosie, in some part of her brain that remained critical and alert, was thinking, Attila you ass. He put the book down and began to talk instead. He reminded her of the robins they had seen in the garden from the window of the residents' day room, of their freezing walk together in the same garden, he moved back to a time forty years before, to begin with a young woman who met a man and challenged him to pronounce the name of her home town. It made him smile to remember, he stood up and went to the window where he felt less self-conscious in his soliloquy.

Many minutes passed, he did not know how many, he had entered the world of which he spoke so fully. An instant later something smashed against the glass of the window. A bird, at least he thought it was a bird for what else could it be? The jolt it gave him was tremendous. He looked at the windowsill and peered down at the garden, but he saw nothing. He turned to look at Rosie. She lay untroubled, eyes open now, averted. It was impossible to tell if she was aware of his presence. He turned and stepped back from the window into her line of sight. Her lips moved, he thought perhaps she wanted something. He looked around the room to see what it might be, but apart from a plastic jug of water and a cup, nothing else lent itself. He poured water into the cup but her lips remained closed. A few drops spilled on the bedspread and Attila brushed them off. He replaced the cup and jug where he found them.

Now Rosie was making sounds for which there was no name, sounds like the echoes of lost words. Attila sat on the edge of the bed. 'Rosie,' he said. Her gaze shifted again and settled on his face, he thought. He smiled but she didn't smile back. He put out his hand and placed it on her shoulder. A mistake, for she shrank from it. Attila had been thrown off balance by the bird, coming suddenly out of nowhere. To put some space between her and him would have been the thing to do, but he failed. Instead he tried to soothe her, to reach her. 'I am here,' he told her. 'I am here.' She began a terrible mewling and to throw her head from side to side. He was aware, suddenly, of an ammoniac odour. He stood up and tried to adjust the pillows behind her, to stop her hurting herself. He turned to see if there was someone who might help him. Moments later, a blunt pain to his forearm. He pulled his arm away. On his sleeve: saliva, the faint indentations of tooth marks.

She had bitten him. Rosie had bitten him.

At the far end of the compound, where two tall fan palms stood, was a grove of dwarf bananas. The old gardener stopped and pointed out the bird to the young boy. The bird was fast, the man was slow, old but full of ordinary cunning. This evening he'd gone next door to ask his friend the steward for the loan of the steward's grandson. Madam had ordered chicken yassa *for Thursday, that meant the Doctor was coming home. It was the gardener's job to catch the chickens and these days though he was slow he was still prideful. He would keep the cockerel penned until Thursday. Early Thursday morning Efua the cook would set the water on the fire and when it was boiled the gardener would wring the bird's neck. By mid-morning she would have it plucked, gutted and cleaned. The gizzards would go to one or other of them, whatever was left to the dogs.*

He advanced upon the bird, moving from side to side, arms outstretched. The cockerel moved its head sharply this way and that, eyeing him twitchily. It had stopped hunting the ground for rice grains and insects, and as the gardener moved forward the cockerel stepped away with jerky, mechanical strides to restore the distance between them. On the other side of the cockerel, hidden in between the bank of shade and pooling sun, stood the boy. The cockerel had nowhere to go, not the branches of a tree, the palms were too high, the banana trees had not the limbs to hold the bird's weight. The man swept the bird closer and closer to the boy, and by the time the cockerel sensed the trap, the boy was upon him. The gardener dropped a coin into the boy's hand. The boy looked at the coin and closed his fingers tight around it. Nestled in the crook of the gardener's arm the bird was still, but the gardener could feel the pumping of its heart.

The Peugeot was parked in the drive, as it had been since Madam arrived home in the late afternoon; the gardener had opened the gate for her. Bending to pull up the catch he had caught sight of his own swollen knee. He would go now to the house to ask Madam whether she planned to be in or out for the evening. And then there was the matter of the beds on the far wall and what vegetables he should plant there this year. Madam liked spinach and eggplant. He thought, too, that he might consult her about the arthritis in his knee. His blood pressure was up again. Madam was a doctor, and so of course was the Doctor, but he only tended to the mad.

At the back door of the main house the gardener slipped off his plastic shoes and opened the fly screen, moved across the cool tiles of the kitchen onto the wood floor of the hall. Ordinarily at this time of day Efua would be here. He would wait in the kitchen until she was ready to carry a dish through to the dining room and at the same time deliver the information that he was waiting to be seen. But Efua was away at a family burial. Conscious of the dirt on the soles of his feet he skirted the wool rugs on the hall floor. In the centre of the hall he stood and cleared his throat. The cream woollen rugs, their black and red geometric shapes, the wooden chest, the pictures in their frames were all familiar to him. He stared up at the ceiling. Ten minutes passed.

The gardener walked across to the front door and knocked on the inside of it. Usually he could hear Madam and the Doctor wherever they were in the house. How was it a person could tell when there was another living soul nearby? In the years of his marriage, before the death of both his first son from polio and his wife years later, he could always tell if his wife was home, even if she was in a deep sleep on the bed. If Madam was sleeping he might go away and come back. He knew she was not on the verandah or he would have seen her as he passed, but from the verandah he would be able to see through the study window. The verandah could be reached by way of the sitting room. Had the Doctor not said many times he should just go through?

'Madam,' he called softly in the direction of the sitting room. He cleared his throat: 'Madam.'

On the polished wood floor the gardener's feet made vanishing footprints. He passed through the sitting room, its hushed and shadowed interior. The doors to the verandah were closed and locked, the cushions used for the outdoor furniture stacked by the wall. The gardener recrossed the sitting room and hall and left by way of the kitchen.

After the gardener had eaten his supper, as he left his house, two of the compound dogs slipped in behind him and trailed him on his short journey. One paused to investigate the hollow of a tree, the other meandered on in his wake. When the gardener reached the chicken cages the dog slumped down to its hindquarters to watch. The gardener went to the cage into which he had put the cockerel after the boy had caught it for him. He refilled the bowl of water from the trough and threw down some rice. He scattered ant powder onto the beaten-earth floor of the yard around the cage – he did not want the bird bothered by the red ants that swarmed around the dogs' bowls. In his village he had seen roosting chickens eaten alive by soldier ants, feathers falling like orchid petals to the ground.

He looked over at the big house where no windows were lit and no curtains drawn.

The gardener thought of his sleeping wife. That night when he lay down on his bed a cold unease spread on the inside of his chest. He left his house and, shadowed by a single dog now, he walked to where he could see the big house, the silhouetted lines of the walls, the angle of the roof broken by the branches of a flamboyant tree. He wished for Efua, for somebody, to help him decide. In the morning he would go to see his friend the steward, the steward had a wife, a woman was useful in these matters.

The gardener slept and rose and returned to the big house where he performed the same act of the evening before, slipped off his shoes and stepped into the kitchen, made his way to the hall where he knocked on the inside of the front door and called out. Back outside he climbed the three steps to the verandah. He knew from Efua that when the Doctor was away Madam sometimes slept in the study. Shading his eyes against the growing sunlight he peered in through the window to the sight of an empty chair and empty cot. He went to the gate and let himself out with the dogs behind him. Halfway down the lane the dogs left him in order to approach, with raised hackles and low heads, an unknown dog. The gardener slipped in the side gate of the next house, past the pens where the animals were kept, and knocked on the steward's door. A few minutes later the three hurried down the lane, the steward's wife hastily knotting a cloth around her head. It was she who would knock on the door of Madam's bedroom while the two men waited at the bottom of the stairs, would come out and wordlessly beckon to them, would open the door to the bedroom and point at the woman lying beneath the arch of the bathroom door.

A tacky wind blew into the face of the steward's grandson as he turned out of the lane and onto the main road. He had a coin in his *pocket, two coins now, the one given him yesterday by the gardener and the one given him a few moments before by his grandfather so that he could catch transport to the hospital. But the boy knew he could run the distance faster. There in the traffic waited the* tro tro *he might otherwise have been sitting in. The boy overtook the minibus three times, dodging and weaving like Didier Drogba whose image he bore on his T-shirt. Through the pedestrians, past the stalls selling cones of shaved ice coated in sweet syrup, leaving the* tro tro *behind at a gridlocked junction. At the hospital gate the guard pointed the way to the director's office, because a breathless errand boy can carry more weight than a man with a briefcase. Some minutes later, sitting in the passenger seat of the director's car, the boy turned to look at the stall selling shaved ice and rubbed together the two coins in his pocket.*

Quell was standing in the garden when the call came through from Accra. He didn't hear the phone ring, he was outside pretending to take the air, though in reality he was waiting for Vivian to call him in for lunch. He had gained weight in retirement, a little. It made no sense as he no longer ate lunch in restaurants. The thought of his girth failed to deflect the feeling of well-being in whose embrace he stood as he watched a bumblebee lurch through the air like a drunk driver – Quell was obliged to raise an arm in self-defence. As hostage releases went the negotiations for the Iraq case were not unduly difficult and yet also held their own challenges. That this hostage possessed little value to his captors carried a risk of its own. They might grow bored, belligerent or weary or paranoid and skittish and then before you knew it some idiot had put a bullet through the captive's head. What the world needed wasn't people like Quell and their teams of negotiators, they just had to put bromide in the drinking water, saltpetre in the coffee or whatever the modern equivalent was.

Attila had been a godsend. 'Gratulo!' Quell had said on the phone to Attila when it was all over. He could hear a modest celebration in the background, somebody had found their way to a few cold beers. A small victory, yes, and all victories mattered. The month before an American soldier in Camp Liberty had opened fire on the team of 'combat stress' counsellors. The soldier was awaiting court martial.

Quell was relieved to be out of it all, true, but there was no beating the exhilaration of a success, it broke up the tedium of retirement.

A knock on the window. Quell looked up to see Vivien gesture to him from the kitchen window. Excellent, he thought. Lunch.

The temperature had passed a hundred degrees by late morning and was still climbing. In the camp people moved as little as possible, a flurry whenever a vehicle arrived or left, otherwise stillness. Lunch was eaten early and Attila, who had survived three days on a diet of army rations, was already hungry. He had endured a long explanation of the nutritional content of ration supplies, MREs as they called them now, Meals Ready to Eat. A single MRE provided an average of 1,250 calories, a precise balance of protein, fat and carbohydrates, and one third of the Military Recommended Daily Allowance of vitamins and minerals. MREs were designed for young men on active duty who required close on 4,000 calories a day. In theory, Attila, who would be persuaded to break into a run only in the face of a clear and present danger, would grow fat on a diet of rations.

Ibrahim, thought Attila, looked good for a man who had undergone three hundred and seventy-five days in captivity. Thinner now than when Attila had known him, certainly, but in reasonable physical health according to the army physician. Ibrahim had eaten every scrap of his MRE. Later in the day Attila would give Ibrahim a psychological assessment and from there he would be debriefed, for that they would take him out of Iraq.

He found Ibrahim walking on the track which ran around the inner rim of the camp perimeter and which the men used to train in the early morning. He was wearing the sunglasses given him by the army doctor to protect his eyes against the sunlight. 'Hey, boss.' Ibrahim held up his hand to high-five Attila. Attila slapped Ibrahim's palm awkwardly with his own and walked in step with him. In a few minutes Attila's forehead, underarms, his crotch, the backs of his knees, were running with sweat. He said: 'What did you spend most of your time thinking about?'

'Whether they wanted to kill me or would let me live.'

Attila nodded. 'I mean after that.'

'I thought about my family, my god.' Ibrahim smiled. 'But you are asking me what I thought about most? To tell you the truth what I thought about was food. Food, boss. Everything I wanted to eat. I made meals in my head and I even cooked them, groundnut stew, Jollof rice, fried plantain, snapper, spinach.'

Attila looked up. A soldier was running towards them in the heat, one who could only be coming for them, his boots kicking up the dust in such quantities that he took on the appearance of an approaching sandstorm. Phone call for Attila. So Attila left Ibrahim while he followed the soldier. In an empty office he took the call. It was Quell.

'Bonan matenon. Kiel vi fartas?' said Attila smiling.

'Are you alone?' said Quell in English.

'Jes,' said Attila. Usually it was Quell who persisted in speaking Esperanto.

Quell said: 'It's Maryse, I'm afraid.'

The gardener had risen from his bed late at night to the sound of a car horn, had hastened to open the gate. A car he did not recognise drove in, the Doctor in the back. The gardener dipped his head to look in the window and raised a hand. The Doctor raised a hand in reply. 'Welcome back, sir,' said the gardener. Then the car came to a halt and the unknown driver stepped out to open the back door and the Doctor was gone. The gardener would have helped to carry the luggage inside, but the driver did that too. All that was left to him was to open the tall iron gates and let the car out.

The next morning the gardener went up to the house, slipped off his shoes and entered the kitchen where Efua was preparing breakfast. Efua had been crying. At the sight of him she shook her head. The gardener waited. Like Efua he felt sorry. He thought of the evening Madam died, the house in the shadow of the bone-bright moon. The steward's wife, the steward and he had carried Madam to the bed, he had seen the dead before, the sight did not frighten him. The steward's wife had made Madam decent before she had allowed the men inside the bedroom. He had been right to fetch her. They placed Madam's head on the pillow and laid her arms at her side. Life was random, wildfire or locusts could take away all you had planted. Children died, his own son had died of polio. Madam died.

Now he could hear Efua tell the Doctor he was waiting. He had made sure to be here early. When Efua returned to the kitchen she

271

inclined her head to let him know he might go through. The gardener brushed the soles of each foot against the opposing trouser leg. He wiped his face on the face cloth he carried in his pocket. At the door of the dining room he placed his right hand on his heart and stepped through to offer his condolences to the Doctor.

In the yard, watched by the silent dogs, the gardener bent to untie the knot of the wire on the chicken cage. With two hands he lifted out the bird. By now Efua must have the water on to boil, he thought. Today she was to cook chicken yassa. *He grasped hold of the chicken's legs in his left hand and let the bird's body fall, with his right hand he wrung its neck and for a half-minute more he held firm his grasp of the bird's legs while its dead body continued to flap and writhe in his hand.*

Chapter 19

In the year that followed the death of Maryse Attila gave himself over to the industry of war, its aftermath. The clean-up crew, his colleagues liked to call themselves, in the banter of the hard-nosed and ideologically driven. They arrived after the emergency medics, before the road builders and bridge engineers. Once the teams had done their work the visitor to the country would be hard-pressed to discern any sign of the violence, for what was left lived in the souls of the people. Attila was older than most of his colleagues, who were mainly in their late twenties and thirties. Those who were his age were beginning to see the job not as a progression, but a series of loops that often journeyed past familiar places. Once in the space of weeks Attila found himself travelling to Darfur, Gaza, Congo, Afghanistan and to Sri Lanka twice. In the years since Maryse's death he had never returned to Iraq.

Among those things lost with Maryse was the desire for the company of more than one or two people, also the desire to read. He could not concentrate on a book. In Afghanistan a young driver introduced him to the MP3 player and taught him how to use it. In an airport duty-free shop Attila bought the two best MP3 players he could find, one of which he sent with a returning colleague for the Afghani driver, the other he filled with the music of his choice. Like a child learning his letters he applied himself to the task of buying, downloading and transferring music. At some point he bought a pair of noise-cancelling headphones and most evenings, wherever he was, he would lie on his hotel bed or on the cot in his tent, converted container or Unaccompanied Personnel Housing unit, and close his eyes. At first he listened to things that were familiar, Handel's *Messiah*, *Carmina Burana*, Bach's Air Suite and *Madame Butterfly*. He especially liked Wagner, Tchaikovsky and Rachmaninov for the scale of sound which came with the power to obliterate all conscious thought. He listened to the recommendations of others and grew to admire Debussy and Sibelius. He found himself the delighted possessor of catholic tastes. Somewhere along the line he was introduced to Spanish guitar music, flamenco, Argentinian tango, which music made him feel capable of dancing and weeping at the same time.

He wished Maryse back into life, in the dreams which he could not control. He imagined, what if, what if, what if he had never gone to Iraq? Or if Ibrahim had not been kidnapped? Or someone else instead of Ibrahim? Magical thinking – he recognised it in himself as he recognised it in his clients. One day he sat down and considered all Maryse's faults, the times they had argued, those aspects of their marriage that dissatisfied him, trying to force himself back into reality. All of this passed with the years, though the dreams continued. Attila was not unhappy, he was simply living with a grief that had become his quiet companion.

Attila did not care to swim, but loved the feel of the water's edge, the comfort and the threat of the sea. Once in Sri Lanka, and after a spell in countries where the freedom of the sea was thousands of miles away, Attila allowed himself to be persuaded to accompany his colleagues to the beach. Once there they drank beers and soon afterwards undressed and ran into the water. Attila said he would stay and watch their belongings, but when the barman offered to hold them behind the bar, Attila left his beer, rose and walked along the shore. He followed the footprints of a man and a dog, the dog's prints looping and circling those of the man. He passed bare-chested men who stared at him and offered no greeting. The sky was full of frigate birds: huge, dark, pterodactyl. Attila had read somewhere that the birds did not have waterproof feathers and so could not land on water. Out at sea they could stay aloft for months at a time: riding the air currents they soared from cumulus to cumulus. He listened through his headphones to a piece by the

Argentine-born composer Astor Piazzolla, a *nuevo tango,* of which Piazzolla was the exponent. Piazzolla was raised in New York and Mar del Plata, classically trained, his tangos came flavoured with jazz and baroque. Attila liked the way the music went straight to his heels. He removed his shoes and carried them in one hand as he walked away from his colleagues. He did not see the frigate bird dive for the scrap of fish thrown by the fisherman, nor did he see his colleagues cease their horseplay, treading water the better to watch him as he danced alone on the wet sand.

In Three Valleys Rest Home, Attila, watched by the centre director, pulled at the plastic covering of a sterilised dressing with his teeth. 'Let me,' she said, but already he had succeeded in ripping the covering apart. She watched him dress the bite wound on his wrist without any further offer of help. 'You should see a doctor,' she said.

'I am a doctor,' replied Attila.

As Attila rolled down his sleeve, the director said: 'She's a great deal younger than any resident we have ever had in this situation. I wonder if you would use your power of attorney to reconsider and have her removed to a hospital. I'm aware of the instructions in the paperwork but as I say, once an infection like this takes hold, and it has ...' She stopped and began again in a different place. 'We don't know exactly what kills a patient with Rosie's condition. The brain forgets functions one after the other, starting with memory, speech, continence, some patients forget how to swallow, to breathe. Long before that the immune system becomes compromised and an intercurrent infection like this one can—'

'She was a psychiatrist. She knew exactly what she was asking.'

'Of course.' She had said what needed to be said. 'We'll make her comfortable. Meanwhile ...' She pushed several leaflets across the desk towards him. 'Depending on her progress from this point on you might need to make other choices.'

TUESDAY

Red sky at night, sailor's delight. Red sky in the morning, sailor's warning. Jean had never known the maxim to fail. It had to do with high and low pressure. A red evening sky meant high pressure, in the morning it told of low pressure.

'What's that got to do with red sky?' asked Tano.

Jean paused and tried to figure out how to explain to him about light refraction, dust and moisture, easterly and westerly winds. She had woken in the early morning to a bloodied sky, had climbed the spiral staircase to sit alone and watch the dawn. An hour later Tano had appeared looking for her. She liked the way he asked her questions, his good faith in her answers, the sense of usefulness which came from sharing her knowledge. Today the parakeets had arrived before the other birds. They were rambunctious feeders, squabbling and pecking each other as they fought over the food. A bird ousted from the table flew up into the branch of the dead tree. Tano held a piece of apple on the palm of his hand and whistled, a series of short pips, enough to make the lone parakeet turn its head. He stuck his hand out further and cooed. The bird turned away. Tano whistled again. The bird shifted on its perch. Tano carried on whistling. The bird turned its head ninety degrees to look over its shoulder and then swung it back in the boy's direction. Tano tipped his palm in the bird's direction.

'Try putting it on the table,' said Jean.

Tano tossed the piece of apple onto the table in front of them, where it rolled to the edge. A few seconds later the bird launched itself from the tree, snatched the piece of apple from the table, and returned to the branch. Balanced on one leg and grasping the piece of apple in the claws of its other foot, it began to tear off pieces of the fruit. Tano turned to Jean with a big grin and Jean smiled back. She remembered she had once walked almost all the way home with a swallow-tailed luna moth, pearl green and the size of a sunbird, on her forearm. She had been a kid, in tennis shoes and shorts. When she left the shade of the wood she felt the moth begin to move until it finally lifted off from her arm and flew back towards the haven of the trees.

Once Jean became a biologist she joined in the professional disapproval of human/animal interaction, with the exception of bird feeders, and yet you had to wonder what was it in humans that made them crave contact with wild animals, when the animals steadfastly resisted the same. People paid money to swim with dolphins, they went on safari, took their children to petting zoos, some, the deranged ones, climbed into the enclosures at zoos, tried to join packs of wolves or live with grizzly bears. Where did it come from, the yearning? Something missing in human society or some other more basic drive towards the remnant of what was once wild, not in the animal, but in us.

An hour later, after breakfast, she and Tano caught the 21 bus north and walked the short distance to the hospital. Jean carried Tano's overnight bag, absurdly light in her hand. In a store she bought him snacks and drinks and from a stand selling souvenirs she found a T-shirt which said: *Keep Calm and Carry On*, which she liked, and she bought that too because she suddenly very much wanted to give him something to remember her by. She found herself touching him constantly, his hair, his shoulder, the back of his neck.

'We travelled once to the east coast. It was the only time we went anywhere alone together, apart from conferences, but that was later. At the time we were still students. The erosion over the years is so dreadful, villages have fallen into the sea. All that appealed to Rosie. We ate at a fish restaurant and the owner told her that on certain nights you could hear the bells of the underwater churches toll. He told us of a place called Shingle Street he thought Rosie would like. So the next day we went there, we had hired a car, Rosie liked to drive. It was an extravagance because we had hardly any money. I had my scholarship and I suppose she had her grant money. The roads were very narrow, but Rosie was used to that sort of thing; being brought up in the Sussex countryside, she never could see the point of slowing down around a bend. Shingle Street, when we got there, was a godforsaken place. A spit of land and a line of houses that faced the sea, no café, not even a shop. Just a strip of beach and these houses. Something called a Martello tower. Rosie loved it, as only an Englishwoman would, she wanted to buy a house there, she imagined it in winter. I thought it was bad enough in the summer.' Attila laughed briefly at the memory. He could picture it, the line of houses marching out to sea, the waves throwing themselves on the shore like shipwrecked sailors. 'The beach was made of stones, the water was freezing. You call that a beach, I said. I'll show you a beach when you come to Ghana. I shouldn't have said that. We'd never talked about her coming or me going. Especially not me going.' Attila paused. 'We pretended it was never going to happen.' And then: 'Of course there was some great mystery to the place. It had been entirely evacuated during the Second World War, the locals were given three days to pack up and leave. There was talk it had been used for weapons testing, Germans had landed there and so on. Rosie looked it all up in the local library after lunch.' He stopped there and looked at Emmanuel. 'Tell her that story, she'll like it.'

'Shall I go in now?' asked Emmanuel.

All night Attila had sat outside Rosie's room. Now it was 7 a.m. He walked to the kitchens where the woman who had briefly flirted with him was making breakfast for the residents. In the early morning the dining hall was empty, the residents were on the whole late risers. She gave Attila a plate of scrambled eggs, which he discovered to be made from powdered eggs, and a cup of the weakest coffee he had ever tasted.

He had not been there for Maryse, he had been stranded in a desert thousands of miles away. Thirty-six hours to get back to her: by then she was lying in the funeral home mortuary. Attila railed silently at the circumstances, the conflation of events that had allowed her to die alone. Efua gone from the house. The old and inept gardener. The aneurysm that could have taken hold of her when she was at the hospital, but waited instead for when she was alone. Nobody knew how long she might have lain there, whether she was conscious or not, and if she was conscious, at what point she had imagined her death. Thought Attila, if ever Adam and Eve existed, this was the punishment meted out to them by their creator for eating the forbidden fruit. It was not to be cast out of Eden, nor the knowledge of their own nakedness, but the gift of an intelligence great enough to be able to imagine their own deaths, the awful foreknowledge all humans possessed, not only in the moment of it happening but for every day of their lives.

Rosie's condition at least spared her that. And if a coincidence of circumstances had brought him here now, just as it had taken him away from Maryse, he would do the best he could do.

He was grateful for the cluck of sympathy that accompanied the kitchen worker's practical efficiency. She gave him a tray and a sandwich for Emmanuel and a bowl of ice cubes. 'You rub the lips with them,' she said. 'To stop them feeling the thirst.' He passed the care workers arriving for the early shift, heard the sound of the residents of Three Valleys beginning to rouse themselves: slow shuffle of footsteps, sighs and small cries.

The door to the room was ajar. Attila placed the tray on the chair outside. Through the gap he could see Emmanuel, sitting next to Rosie and holding her hand in both of his. Attila shifted to bring Rosie into view. She lay without moving, her face was pale, darkened in places, as though shadows were blooming from within. Her breathing, the sound of which carried to where he stood, sometimes stopped for several seconds. Above the sound of her breaths, every now and again Emmanuel's murmured voice as he told her the story of a trip once taken to a place named Shingle Street.

Chapter 20

The woman opened the door of the City Road apartment as though Jean was the very last person she expected, although they had spoken by phone just the day before. She lowered her head and shuffled backward to allow Jean to pass, spoke with her hair over her face and persisted, as she had the first time, in the painful habit of worrying at her inflamed cuticles. Biting at the edge of her thumb, she appeared to be working at a tear in the skin, preparing to rip it off. On the sideboard stood the same photograph of the woman and her husband, the one in which the woman, whose skin was now translucent, wore a tan and freckles.

Jean had decided to use containers for the planting, better suited to the weight capacity of the roof than layers of drainage mats and soil. It made the job more manageable, the effect would be almost instant. The woman stood hunched at one end of the sideboard as two deliverymen hefted in troughs and planters, sacks of soil and compost. When they had gone Jean went out to the terrace and set to work. It was an easy enough job, the raised beds had been designed with dovetail joints, it was only a matter of sliding them into place. Next she positioned the containers where she wanted them. She drew the planting plans out of her back pocket and showed them to the woman.

'We'll plant the garrya in those two containers over there. That will give you a little more privacy and act as a windbreak. They're evergreen. That long planter will be all rosemary and that one's for the lavender. In this big square one over here will be a mix. I've ordered up some salvia, euphorbia, Little Spire, alchemilla … I'll put some bulbs in there too, tulips and alliums to give you some spring colour. We'll have a magnolia over there.'

The woman blinked as though she were memorising the words. Jean said: 'I just need to …' She indicated the bags of soil. 'Maybe you could give me a hand,' though the woman looked weaker than a newborn calf. The woman looked surprised but nodded. Together they hefted the sacks one by one, cut them open and upended the soil into the planters. Jean handed her companion a short rake and showed her how to spread the earth. A short time later the delivery arrived from the nursery.

It took the two women thirty minutes to arrange the plants the way Jean had in mind, putting each one in its designated spot so Jean could check whether there were gaps. She gave all the plants a dousing of water and instructed the woman to keep the soil damp. Let them sit for twenty-four hours, Jean told her, she'd come back and do the planting tomorrow. Jean wondered if this garden had been the husband's idea, hoping to lure his wife outside or perhaps simply trying to replace something of the world she was missing.

When it came time to say goodbye Jean stepped into the hall. She did not extend her hand but waved from a distance. Some of the woman's awkwardness had returned but her cheeks still held two small spots of colour.

Jean walked south through the streets of the city beneath a light drizzle. It took her forty minutes to reach Attila's hotel and a further four minutes to establish that he was not there. It seemed that their relationship might end where it had begun. There should, thought Jean, be a special place in hell reserved for men who didn't call after sex. It wasn't the calling itself that mattered, it was the not calling. She was angry at herself, at the possibility of a misjudgement or misstep, but obstinately refused to replay how she had arrived at it, if indeed that were the case. To do so served no purpose. Those girlish discussions about what men did and why, they had never provided answers and Jean had drawn no pleasure from them back in the days when her girlfriends tried to draw her into them and she would not stoop to them now, even to herself. Readied for disappointment she averted her mind from all thought of Attila, of the afternoon the day before.

There were perhaps two hours of daytime left, but the sky seemed weighted and close. On the opposite bank Jean saw the figure of Osman. From a distance, moving through the crowd in his silver suit and bowler hat, he looked like the spectre of a long-dead stockbroker from another time, one who had thrown himself off Waterloo Bridge and whose ghost, every weekday of every year, boarded a train in Surrey to disembark at Waterloo Station. Jean caught up with Osman and clamped a hand on his shoulder.

'Hey!'

'Jean, ciao!'

'Can I walk with you?'

'Sure.' Osman said he was on his way to pick up his things from Ayo and Olu. They walked to the back of the theatre where they found the two security men who were pleased to see Jean and insisted on making coffee for them both. They asked after Tano and were assured he was well and had gone back to his mother. Osman excused himself to go and change. Olu said: 'So, Jean, we all heard you on the radio, you called the Mayor a fool.' He laughed loudly and Ayo gave a rumbling chuckle.

'Don't remind me,' said Jean. She told them about the Twitter row.

'Never worry,' said Ayo. He spooned Nescafé into four mugs and poured in the boiling water and added a large splash of evaporated milk to each mug. 'Sugar?' Jean shook her head. He began to ladle heaped spoons into two of the mugs and, after giving Jean hers, he handed Olu the other. 'These kinds of people, they get all fired up and then they forget. Bap!' He touched his hand to the crown of his head and let it fall to his side, a thought tumbling out of a brain.

Osman rejoined them. He had changed and washed the paint from his face, dispelling the spirit of the dead stockbroker. He had heard of the broadcast from Ayo and Olu who he now told Jean listened to their radio all day: 'You won't find many people better informed than these two.'

'Jean is a very strong woman,' said Ayo. 'Remember her and those men in the park? Even without us she would have dealt with them.'

'With one hand in her pocket,' agreed Olu.

Jean smiled and then said: 'The Mayor is talking about culling foxes.'

'That *fool* Mayor,' Olu said. He seemed very taken by the fact of Jean's temerity.

'They won't do it.' Ayo shook his head. 'How long have you lived here, Jean? I have lived in this city for twenty years, I've seen a lot of things. This is what this man does. Maybe once a year he jumps up and says, Oh, there are too many foxes, what are all these foxes doing in London? He turns people against the foxes. He says he wants a cull, but he has no plans to do that, because he knows he cannot. He makes out it's people like you who are stopping him, but it's all just talk to make people think he's tough. That way he makes himself popular.'

'Anything they cannot use or control, they want to kill,' Olu said.

'Or make money from,' said Ayo. They both laughed. Ayo continued: 'Cannot become rich from them, cannot control them, not even kill them. That's why the foxes make some people angry. The problem with those people is that they themselves have forgotten they are alive.'

Ayo and Olu were right, almost. Sure enough when Jean checked her Twitter account she saw the number of tweets had dwindled to almost nothing. But later at home she found in her post a brown envelope containing a photograph of a pair of foxes in the act of coitus and a pink ribbon carefully knotted into a noose.

In the last hour of light Jean set out on her run in the direction of Nunhead Cemetery. The two iron gates of the graveyard were locked at nightfall. Near the entrance stood the man with the little brown mongrel and limp leaning on his cane; he tipped an imaginary hat at her and gestured to an imaginary wristwatch. Jean waved at him. It took her less than six minutes to reach the opposite gate. Past the monument to the Scottish Martyrs the path followed in a straight line and then veered left and began to climb until it plateaued out to where the bench sat with the view of St Paul's. At the top of the hill Jean jogged in place for a few seconds to steady her breathing – the older she got the more running felt like a zero-sum game. She bent to touch her toes and then raised each arm over her head and leaned her body to one side and then the other.

A movement in the air drew her eye: a dark shape, silent glide, unhurried wingbeat. An owl was flying between the trees. The great round head and torpedo body – the owl was the B52 of the night skies. At that moment a pair of birds appeared, heading straight for the owl, like kamikaze pilots, only to veer away at the last moment. The owl flew on. More birds appeared, three or four, they were parakeets mobbing the owl. Jean was close to the tree where the parakeets nested, they were driving the predator away. The owl seemed unfazed, it flew in a wide arc as if coming around for a second pass, but instead it dipped a wing, changed course and headed out towards clearer skies. The parakeets went at it from all sides until the owl was out of sight. All the dignity belonged to the owl, who never changed the pace of its wingbeat. But all the courage belonged to the little birds.

At some minutes past four Jean reached the big double gate to find it chained and padlocked. She tried the side gate. Locked. She ran the most direct route to the opposite gate, the one by which she had entered, straight down the central avenue, up and over the hill and past the chapel. She was not afraid, she was used to being outside alone in the night and this was no different really from being in the woods.

That gate was locked too. Jean had imagined she would scale the fence, but now she had a closer look at the fifteen-foot pointed stakes she saw the foolishness of the idea. She'd left her cell at home, but there was a phone and an emergency number attached to the warden's office. That meant running back the way she had come, and a wait while somebody was sent out to unlock the gates. She had just begun back up the hill when she heard an engine and all around her was illuminated by a pair of headlights. A van had drawn up right in front of the gate. Jean stepped sideways out of the glare and shielded her eyes. The doors opened and two men stepped out; they slid open the side door of the van and began to haul out equipment. One of the men approached the gate. Silhouetted against the headlights he was wearing a beanie hat and a big jacket, like a pea jacket. She remained standing still.

The man looked up: 'Christ!' he said.

Jean took a breath and stepped forward: 'I was locked in.'

'Christ, love, you just scared the bejesus out of me, I thought you was an apparition.'

'The gates were locked. I was too late. It was dumb.'

'Happens all the time, my love,' said the man. 'Don't you worry. We'll have you out in a jiffy.' He took a set of keys from his pocket.

'You're not the wardens.'

'Sent by the council, love. Here to do some work. There's a couple of them trees that's unsafe.' The storm a few years ago, he explained, the clear-up was still going on.

'You're going to cut down trees in the dark?'

He laughed: 'We're just dropping off the equipment. We'll get started in the morning. That way we can be out of your hair by the time you come for your morning run.' After some searching for the right key, he opened the padlock and drew the chain through the bars. Jean thanked him, she slipped out of the gate, bounced twice on her toes and ran home.

In Attila's younger days, once, when he had drunk too much and lay on his back while the room revolved around him, he felt the cool of Rosie's hand on his cheek, the strength and comfort in that hand enough to stop the room from spinning. He had opened his eyes. Attila paused in the memory. The face he saw was Maryse, not Rosie. How could that be? His university days had been his drinking days. The spinning room, where had that been? The room changed and changed again. The house he and Maryse had first rented in Freetown in the year he was assigned there. Rosie's parents' house in Sussex. White-painted walls, spotted with dead mosquitoes, a sixty-watt lamp. Wallpaper of green abstract shapes. He no longer knew.

Attila was standing at the window of the empty residents' day room. It was dark again and raining. In a room, in Emmanuel's arms, Rosie lay dying. Attila had been witness to many deaths, that moment when a still and silent presence entered the room, revealed only by a change in the air, a knowledge never to be unknown.

Would he know, he wondered, standing here, the moment at which Rosie died? Would he feel it? When Maryse died he had been drinking cold beer in the night heat, he had been celebrating, laughing. He did not awake into a changed world. He had woken early and written on a sheet of notepaper the words, 'Dear Maryse'. His plan had been to give her the letter himself, knowing he would make it out of Iraq before the army mailbag. 'Dear Maryse'. A few lines and then he stopped because he heard the sound of Ibrahim rising and listened to the voice of the young man reciting his prayers. He had never returned to the letter.

Attila walked back down the corridor and stood at the door of Rosie's room. A single lamp shone in the corner, Emmanuel sat on the chair, his forehead resting on the bed. He held one of Rosie's hands in both of his. Rosie's eyes were slightly open, her breathing a muted roar. Attila waited until Emmanuel, seemingly sensing his presence, turned to face him. He gave a barely perceptible nod and Attila entered the room. He took a chair from the corner and sat next to Emmanuel. He reached out and touched Rosie's feet. He spoke her name. 'Rosie.' She had only ever loved one man, she had told him. She had only ever loved one man knowingly. Innocently she had loved two.

Attila had been there all day, crossing from darkness to darkness. It is a curious vigil, the wait to death. Every society has searched for a way to ease the lonely crossing of the Styx. Ancient Egyptians sacrificed a king's retainers and servants to wait on him in the after-life. Six people were poisoned to accompany King Aha, including a child of five, a beloved son or daughter, archaeologists believe. The Sumerians of Mesopotamia demanded as duty the death of the queen. In China during the Han dynasty *mingqi*, terracotta figur-ines of all things from dancing girls to dogs, were buried alongside the dead. In a refugee camp in Sudan, a mother tucks a doll made of two crossed sticks into the arms of her dead child.

Attila was woken by Emmanuel's touch on his shoulder. In the now silent room the knowledge formed itself into a fourth presence.

Chapter 21

Attila walked with the dawn behind him. He had slept for only two hours yet he had no want of sleep. He passed through quiet streets, enclosed by buildings in which the dreamers lay, murmuring in their dreams, asleep in the crystal citadel. Under street lights his shadow formed, shrank, lengthened and was left behind. He did not hear the bird call, muted under the sound of early morning traffic. A small flock of pigeons scattered in his path, hobbling sideways on crabbed feet. At first there had been nobody, suddenly he was a man in a crowd. He saw through them and walked through them. At the sight of him a white beggar with a dog pushed off a wall and approached him with upturned hand, but then fell away and let him pass.

By the river on a bench he sat with his back to an inscription to three drowned boys. He stared at the view on the other side of the churning water, seagulls like vultures encircling the dome of St Paul's.

Soon he would be gone. This was the final day of the conference. He had barely attended an hour of it. This morning he would give his speech, the same speech he had given many times before, all that was needed was to stand before the room and form the words. In five hours.

He had closed her eyelids, had bent and kissed them, her cheek, her hair. He had picked up her hand, turned it over and pressed his lips to the palm. Her warmth lingered. He unfolded her fingers and folded them back towards the palm one by one. He wanted to lie down and put his head on her chest, not of the woman of the same name who had just died, but the Rosie who had lived in this body once, who was now allowed the possibility of return.

Few of the people who passed Attila on that morning turned to look at him, a black man sitting on a bench facing the river. He closed his eyes. Someone sat down next to him. Attila was far, far away. The man who had sat down looked at the big man on the bench, the elbows resting on thighs, the hands that hung between his knees, the sag of his back, the bristle of silver rising on the man's face, for several minutes, until finally Attila opened his eyes and became aware of a person next to him.

'Doctor,' the man said without raising his voice, the familiar thrust and swing of a jaw.

'Komba,' replied Attila. 'How are you?'

'Surviving,' said Komba. 'And you?'

'Surviving too.'

'But what are you doing here at this time?'

Attila told him. Komba laid a hand on his shoulder, he said: 'You will miss her.'

'She was already gone,' said Attila.

'Still you will miss her,' Komba said. 'Take time.' He said it the way people said it back home. 'Take tem.' You said it to a child running downstairs, a person crossing a busy street, or one who had tripped on a kerb stone. Take it slow. Komba went on: 'Let me sit with you a while. There's a story I must tell you. You know, there was one time we met, but you don't remember.'

'I meet a lot of people,' said Attila.

'Of course, of course,' said Komba. 'Anyway in those days I was a small boy. Nobody would have noticed me except that I carried a big gun.'

Attila smiled. 'You were with the rebel fighters.' He liked Komba.

'I saw you at the checkpoint. It was my job to guard the checkpoint to check each car that passed. You had two madmen with you. One was naked. The other one was dressed like an Englishman from a long time ago.'

'John Bull,' said Attila. 'He thought he was John Bull.'

'The commander was very suspicious of the naked one, he said he looked like a foreigner. He smoked so much ganja, that commander, he had started to become suspicious of everybody. I could see how he was changing his mind, he wanted to stop you again and maybe keep you there, maybe he was even going to shoot you all. But I let you through the checkpoint. He was too slow. Later he punished me, he said I was not checking the cars thoroughly. But then there was nothing he could do but curse.'

'I remember that. I don't remember you.'

'As I told you,' said Komba. 'I was just a small boy.'

'You think about those times?'

Komba tapped his heart. 'My grandfather was once a signalman on the railway. That was the reason I asked the commander to give me the job at the checkpoint, I wanted to be like my grandfather. Sometimes in the days when he lived with us he would show me the grey uniform he used to wear. He could recite the train timetables. My grandfather would be pleased to see me in this uniform, I believe so, yes. And I have a wife now, I have children, two daughters, I have this job. So I am hopeful.'

For some minutes they were silent, somewhere the sound of a church clock striking the hour. 'Look,' said Komba. He pointed to the river. At first Attila didn't see it, then he thought it was a swimmer, wondered what a person was doing in the water on such a day. And then he saw a slim snout, a hint of whiskers, and realised it wasn't a person but a seal. A grey seal swimming in the waters of the Thames.

After Komba had gone Attila remained sitting on the bench and watched the water. He was looking for the seal and now and then he thought he saw it, but they were just pieces of flotsam. He imagined the seal swimming upriver, through the dark, dense water. He thought of Jean, whom he had failed to call these past two difficult days. He took out his phone, tapped out a message to Jean and he hit Send, returned the phone to his pocket. He looked again at the river. He should return to his hotel, shower and change, arrangements needed to be made in regard to Rosie. Kathleen and Quell must be told. An announcement of some sort perhaps, at the conference: Rosie had been at the forefront of so much of the study of trauma. The idea diverted him for a moment. What, he wondered, would she make of it, the conference? He imagined Rosie coming back with all the intellectual alertness of old, but with the space of twenty years between herself and her subject. What *would* she think? He stared at the water, no longer waiting for the seal to resurface. He knew what Rosie would think. He knew. He stood up and walked to the Aldwych.

I am hopeful, Komba had said. I am hopeful. He did not say, I am happy. That was his outlook on life. Another person might have talked about happiness, but Komba did not. Hope was of a different order from happiness. People owned the narrative of their own lives, it did not belong to the professionals. Komba was not a fighter, he was a signalman's grandson.

The trouble with happiness, thought Attila, was that, perhaps because infants seemed such happy creatures, people were led to believe that happiness came with a mother's milk, happiness was man's state of nature, of which all else was a warping. The search to return to that state became unending. But they were mistaken, for what they desired so badly wasn't happiness but a state of pre-lapsarian innocence, the thing that babies possessed. They wanted desperately not to know the truth. They thought that, if they knew, if they knew what Komba knew, there would be no return.

Attila drew out a legal pad and a pen, paused, put the pen down and called Kathleen Branagan. He told her about Rosie.

'Are you up to doing the keynote today?' she asked.

Attila replied that he was. 'I need a favour.'

'Go ahead.'

Attila named a couple of reference books and asked her to send them over to his hotel. 'And one more thing. I need a book called *Goodbye to All That*. It's a memoir about the First World War.'

'Robert Graves. I can do that. May I ask what all this is about?'

Attila told her he had decided he wanted to change the subject of his talk.

'Okay,' said Kathleen carefully, 'I might just mention that the posters are printed and up. Flyers too. And eight hundred copies of 'The Management of PTSD in Populations Affected by Violent Conflict' rolling off the copiers as we speak. I just thought you might like to know.' A short silence, then: 'But it's up to you. If you have something you want to say I won't stop you, in fact I'd like to hear it.'

'Thank you.'

He showered and by the time he had shaved the package had arrived and was delivered by James who also brought a break-fast tray, fruit, coffee, eggs. He already knew about Rosie's death, Komba had let them all know. 'You must have cared for her very much to look after her for so long.' He wanted to know Attila's movements for the day and said he would arrange the car to take Attila to the conference hall for 10.30. Until then Attila had three hours.

Attila opened the envelope which contained the book. Attila had read it years ago, had come across a copy during those days in Iraq. Graves had survived the trenches of the First World War, suffered shell shock, returned to England. Wandering London he had found another kind of insanity, the insanity of the insulated, the sated emotions of sufficiency, the coldness that comfort creates, people who had little knowledge and even less interest in what the uniformed men who walked among them had endured. And so he had returned himself to the trenches, to be once again among his peers. Of a conversation with his friend Siegfried Sassoon shortly before his fourth and final return to France, Graves wrote: 'I took the line that everyone was mad except ourselves and one or two others, and that no good could come of offering common sense to the insane. Our only possible course would be to keep on going out until we got killed.' Sassoon, on the other hand, had written a letter of protest about the war to the War Office, refusing to fight on, for which he would have been court-martialled but for Graves who intervened, arguing that Sassoon was shell-shocked. 'The irony of having to argue to these mad old men that Siegfried was not sane!'

Attila picked up the pen again and traced his thoughts on paper. He wrote: 'Resilience: Ability to maintain a state of equilibrium in face of adversity.' He wrote the words: 'Hope. Humour. Survival. Adaptability. Expectations. Impermanence (acceptance of).' These he wrote on one side of the paper. On the other side he wrote: 'Denial. Protectiveness. Control. Environment (creation of the perfect).' After a moment he drew an arrow across the page from 'Expectations' and repeated the word in the second list. 'Trauma = suffering = damage.' This he wrote in the middle of the paper and underneath: 'Trauma = suffering ≠ damage.' And then: 'Trauma = suffering = change.

He sat back and reread the words. At the top of the paper he wrote: 'HAPPINESS' and underlined it with two dark strokes, and underneath he wrote the words: 'THE PARADOX'.

Chapter 22

WEDNESDAY

Wednesday, an hour before dawn, two men sat in a van outside the gates of Nunhead Cemetery. They drank coffee out of polystyrene cups. One had a Cornish pasty in a paper bag which would be his lunch. Neither man lived in the city. The older of the two lived in Kent and liked to get on the job early. Beat the traffic in, beat the traffic out. He had risen sometime after 4 a.m., eaten a bowl of cereal standing at the kitchen counter, had donned his work boots at the door and thrown the ropes and harness into the back of the van. He wouldn't be the one to wear the harness – the job of going up the tree belonged now to the younger man. Forty minutes later he was outside his workmate's flat, listening to the radio announcement for *The Big Show*, with Eddie Hopper and the show's forthcoming discussions on football violence and drugs.

Now he downed the remainder of the coffee, dropped the cup onto the floor of the van, climbed out and slid open the back door. Together they unloaded the bag of ropes, the harness and the two chainsaws. He slung several yards of line over his shoulder. The evening before, when they had found the woman runner locked in behind the gates, they had dropped off the wood chipper and winches and left them in a Portakabin on the cemetery grounds. Now he brought out a torch and the plan of the graveyard. By his estimation once started the job would take several hours.

The two men trudged up the main path, past the ruined chapel, past the burial place for Muslims and other non-Christians, and turned right at the fork just before the consecrated ground where the newer graves lay. The sound of their boots on the gravel, small rustlings among the fallen leaves, the first plane of the morning travelling overhead, its engines howling as it made the turn towards Heathrow: these were the only sounds. The first man consulted the plan in his hand and cast the torchlight from tree trunk to tree trunk until he found the red markings. He placed the bag he was carrying on the polished granite of a tomb, shirked off the loop of lines from his shoulder. For the next ten minutes the two men hauled the larger equipment up from the Portakabin to the site. The older man consulted his watch.

The younger man put on his heavy overalls and stepped into the harness, he sat on the steps of a mausoleum, his spiked boots in his hand. The older man shone the torch up the length of the tree, a huge-limbed giant wearing a crown of thorns.

He said: 'Sycamore. Big one.'

The young man followed the torch's light. There was more than a morning's work there and he was going to have to do it all himself, climb up there with a chainsaw and bring the branches down one by one, while his mate fed them into the chipper. As he made a rapid assessment of the branch sizes, to decide which ones to take down first, a movement caught his attention. 'Give me that,' he said to his companion and held out his hand for the torch. Hollows in the trunk of the tree, he counted three of them and then three more. He held the torch still, let the outer edges of the oval of light rest on one of the hollows. Less than a minute later, a head popped out. He passed the torch back to his companion. 'Birds,' he said. 'There are birds' nests up there. Has anyone checked the permissions?' He meant had the older man checked.

'There'll be an exemption permit somewhere.' The first man held the torch between his teeth and leafed through a folder of papers. Whoever ordered the job would have had to think to get an exemption, if they knew there were birds with nests in the tree. The man was a private contractor and the job had come to him through an agency. He preferred to avoid ringing the council if he could, it all depended who you got on the line, some jobsworth with a different view of the matter could hold up the whole process. 'Here,' he said. He found the paper, held it up near his nose and shone the light directly upon it. 'Dead tree.' He scanned and found the words he was looking for. 'Safety hazard, it says right here. It could come down, hurt someone.'

The young man looked up at the tree. He knew trees, this tree was solid, would stand another ten years. But it wasn't his job to argue. That the paperwork was in order was all he needed to know. He checked his watch and then went to fetch the big flood-light from one of the bags, this he balanced on the ledge of a monument. He hauled the tarp off the wood chipper and heaved it into place, he laid the two chainsaws on the ground and began to check them over. Ten minutes later he looked up and saw light breaking in the sky. Time to get the first lines up. The bare winter branches made life easier – no leaves to snag the throw rope, a clear line of vision. The first throw was clean and looped the throw-line over one of the bigger branches, he pulled the climbing rope into place, set the knot, circled the tree and put another line up on a branch on the opposite side. He would take down a couple of the lower branches first and then the two big ones. He pushed his feet into his spiked boots and zipped them up, he put on his helmet, pulled on the thick rubber gloves, tightened the harness, attached himself to the first rope and gave it a tug. He lowered the visor and took hold of the chainsaw held out to him by the older man. Moments later he began his ascent into the upper reaches of the huge sycamore.

The young man loved his job, loved the view of the world he had from above, the way it made him feel somehow apart from human life, he loved the sheltered world he found in the branches of a tree. As a child, whenever his parents argued or were angry with him, he climbed into the arms of the oak on the recreation ground half a mile from home. He liked the feel of the bark, the cradle of the branches. Later, he took to sleeping in trees. Sometimes at night when sleep didn't find him in his own bed, he would carry a sleeping bag down to the tree by the stream in the garden of the house to which he moved with his mother and new stepfather. Once or twice, in his college years, after a party he had slept in a tree when it was too late to find his way home. He wasn't a tree hugger. He loved trees, but he was a practical-minded sort. He didn't like people who wrecked ancient woodlands, but he'd pollard the big trees in the city and would bring them down when it was required.

This job though looked like crap. They could have done with two climbers, though he had no particular doubt he was up to the challenge, it would just take that much longer. The problem was the birds. He reached the big branch, secured his lines and eased himself into position. The birds' nesting holes, just a few feet away from him, were in the trunk of the tree, which would be brought down in sections at the end. There was one of them now, a dipping head, a flash of an eye, a parakeet popped its head out of the hole and disappeared again. Cute little buggers, thought the young man. He stood up and walked the length of the bough. When he reached a point about one third from where it branched out, he sat down with his legs astride the limb. He nodded to the older man who watched him from the ground.

At the sound of the chainsaw the first of the birds began to flee the tree. Out of the hollows, in twos and threes and fours, they fluttered upwards. First those in the nests closest to the sound, which was monstrous, they rose almost vertically into the air. Those birds went in silence. The cries of panic came from the birds in holes further up the tree as the vibrations caused by the chainsaw travelled down the branch, entered the trunk of the tree and reached their nests. Fear swept the colony, one hundred birds took to the air, green-winged angels, screaming banshees. The air roiled with wingbeats. Then nothing. Not even the sound of the chainsaw as the young man silenced the machine to look up at the sky. Only falling feathers.

Jean had been awake since sometime after five. How quickly she had grown accustomed to the company of the last few days. For the first time, perhaps in her entire life, she found herself not especially happy to be alone. Somewhere around six her phone had flashed. She picked it up from the side table. A message from Attila, but her smile disappeared when she read the text: 'Forgive me.' She fell back on the bed, lay there for several minutes and then sat up, reread the text and deleted it. She dressed quickly, grabbed her bag of gear, her notebook and binoculars and headed out. At seven she came back, drank a coffee and ate some bread. She took food up for the birds, but she didn't wait to see which ones came first. She considered a run, but lacked the will. She dithered and by the time she decided to change into her running gear it was close on 8.30. A series of messages on her phone delivered a small jolt to the heart, but they were not from Attila, rather a name she didn't recognise and it took her several seconds to fathom their meaning.

Jean ran. She ran faster than her usual pace. Faster than she had run in years. The cold air stung her face and made her eyes water. She arrived out of breath, her lungs and side aching. There was the man with the collarless mongrel dog and the walking stick, he stood with his head bowed as if in prayer, the woman dog walker in the Australian cattleman's hat, the young man with long brown hair to whom Jean had given her cell number less than a week before. There were just six or seven people, a few had joined hands, whether in mutual comfort or in the start of an attempt to surround the tree, it was hard to tell. The man with long brown hair was on the phone rallying people to the cause.

How had they missed it? How in the hell had she missed it?

Now it was too late, all too late. That much was obvious to Jean from the moment she arrived on the scene, for even if they succeeded in stopping the final felling of the tree, the desecration of the nests was complete. The birds would never return.

When Jean reached her apartment, when she was alone, she cried. She sat down and wept, because it felt like there was nothing else to do: she would not call the radio station or send out messages of outrage on the internet. When she had finished she washed and dried her face. On her schedule for the day was the planting at the City Road site, she should get going. On the table in the main room her computer rang. Disorientated, she reached first for her phone. An incoming call from Luke.

'What time is it?' said Jean.

'Um, I don't know. Middle of the night. I haven't gone to bed. I've been out. I was waiting until you were up. I've got news.' He was excited and then, characteristically, switched to modesty. 'It's not that big a deal really.' He had a new job, not a huge shift, but the pay, the position, were better.

'That's great,' said Jean. 'Really great. I'm proud of you.'

'You okay, Mom? You sound weird.'

'It's nothing,' said Jean automatically, and then changed her mind. She told Luke about the destruction of the tree, the birds. She was more in control of herself now.

'That really sucks. But, Mom, you lost the battle, not the war. Maybe that's the way to look at it.'

'Maybe.'

'Oh come on, you would have said the same to me. You're the thin blue line, or whatever it's called. Is that what I mean? Maybe in your case it should be the thin green line. You can't catch them all, but you're there and that's what counts. Imagine if you weren't.' He was quiet for a moment. 'I seem to remember you used to say to me, whatever doesn't kill you makes you stronger. That made me so pissed sometimes.'

'Oh God,' Jean groaned. 'That was my father speaking.' She laughed: 'Nobody says *that* any more. Thanks for the reminder.'

'My pleasure. That's what you have a son for, to remind you of all these things. So what's up with the fox-cull talk, anything new?'

'It seems to have died down.'

'Until the next time, eh?'

'Yes.' A moment's silence. Jean said: 'Have you told your father about the job?'

'Not yet, I'll call him in a minute.'

'You called me first?'

'Sure. Why not?'

'No reason. I suppose I just kind of imagine you always tell your father these things first.'

'Well, this time I called you. I don't always tell Pops everything first.'

'Don't you?'

Luke laughed. 'Only some of the time. I guess I got used to not being able to reach you because you were fifty miles from the nearest cellphone tower, or imagining your phone ringing while you were out stalking a moose. Anyway there's something else.'

'Go ahead.'

'Air fares are super low right now, it's off, off season. I have a few days' vacation left over. Use it or lose it. I thought I might come over.'

'I would love that,' said Jean. 'I would really really love that.'

'Great.' Luke paused. 'I've missed you, Mom.'

'I've missed you too, you don't know how much.'

Jean worked hard throughout the morning and the early afternoon, digging the holes for the plants and covering their roots with soil. She stopped only to eat the sandwich she had brought. Everything came down to this: earth, water, the creation of a splendour that would arrive with spring. She did not think of Attila, at least to the extent that was humanly possible. She distracted herself with the work. This time her client did not join her on the roof or offer to help, but watched Jean from behind the glass door, tugging at strands of her hair. Whenever Jean paused in her work she was aware of the woman standing there, inspecting the hairs that she had pulled free, casting them aside as if they could contaminate her fingers. Whenever the woman in turn looked up, Jean averted her gaze. She worked, she forgot the city around her, the smell of diesel fumes was replaced by the smell of earth. She worked without gloves, as she always did, crumbling the earth between her fingers. Once she broke off a leaf and rubbed it between her fingers, lifted it to her lips and tasted the bitterness, another time she discovered an earthworm and carefully lifted it up in her hand and placed it on a bed she had already planted. She stood up and stretched her back and gazed at the sky, the clouds as they moved like migrating beasts. There was just the wind about her, faint but insistent. She lifted her arms, closed her eyes and let her skull rock back in the cradle of her vertebrae. When she opened her eyes and turned around she saw the woman had taken a step outside. 'Come on,' Jean beckoned her. The woman didn't move, she gazed at Jean out of extinguished eyes. Jean walked over and reached for the woman's hand. It lay limp, cool and dry in hers. The woman let Jean lead her outside into the air. Once she flinched at the approach of a flying insect but otherwise she allowed Jean draw her on. They went slowly and stood in the middle of the space. Jean said nothing, she let the woman look around at the garden, took the fingers of her hand and laid them against the bark of a small cherry tree.

Chapter 23

The car to take Attila to the conference hall waited outside the hotel. James took Attila's briefcase, opening the door for Attila to climb inside before he handed it back to him. He treated Attila as if he were his child being prepared for school. Attila leaned back in his seat, let his head fall on the headrest. He had barely slept in close to thirty-six hours. When he arrived the hall was almost full. There was Kathleen coming down the aisle, smiling at him. Attila smiled back. Her voice, when she said hello, seemed to come from somewhere else. There was a room set aside for him to wait in at the back of the hall and he followed her. The sounds of the room were muted and heavy, his footsteps like muffled thunderclaps. He became intensely aware of their rhythm as he concentrated on putting one foot before the other. He passed a table loaded with copies of his speech. On the front of each one was printed the words: 'The Paradox'. In the room he sat on a chair, and drank a glass of water. When Kathleen offered him something to eat he shook his head. To compose his thoughts was all he needed.

Several miles away Jean was walking home and as she walked she thought about the day. The awful silence when the chainsaw stopped. The birds had taken to the air and fled. In time they would come back, once they thought it was safe. By then the tree, the colony, the nests that contained their addled eggs, would have been destroyed. The council had decided on an early strike to terminate the protests before they could gather momentum, that was the most likely explanation for the felling of the tree. They had sent in the tanks. She thought about her client in the City Road apartment, stroking the bark of a tree, who knows how long since she last touched another living thing. She thought of Attila, from whom she still had not heard. She took out her phone to reread the single text though she knew very well what it said and anyway had deleted it. Forgive me. It sounded like the end of something yet to begin. He would leave soon and then what? Would she think of him, sometime in the future, remember him as a lover whose life had collided briefly with her own? She had refused, in the two days since their lovemaking, to allow her thoughts space to grow, had forced them down. Now something Luke had said stayed with Jean. He had said he wanted to tell her first.

Love is a gamble, the stake is the human heart. The lover holds his or her cards close, lays them out one at a time and watches each move of the other player. To whom do you go first? This is the 'tell' of love. When a thing happens, be it good or bad, when you pick up the telephone or push through a crowd, who is it you most want to reach? More than anybody else Jean wanted Attila.

Kathleen Branagan pushed the doors of the conference hall closed and instructed the staff member at reception desk to direct late-comers to the small door at the back. She walked down the length of the aisle to the green room and told Attila they were ready to begin. She settled him on one of the chairs reserved for them both in the front row. She smiled and gave him the thumbs-up. He smiled back and returned the gesture, and she climbed the stairs to the podium to begin her introductory remarks.

A child with a grazed knee zigzags through a gathering to find a parent, a grandparent. We go first to those we love. Attila was lost in love. Since the death of Maryse he had lived and breathed, he had travelled, attended conferences like this one, he was comfortable in this world, but he had not yet found his way back to his former self. At times, when his work went well, he felt a great contentment. Now, standing up, taking to the stage in the hush of the hall, he felt the tension in the air. The audience knew about the last-minute change to the programme, that the speech he was to give was not the one originally planned. He had worked on it in all the time he had that morning. The copy of the final speech had been sent to Kathleen Branagan. Four assistants had been dispatched to print shops in different parts of the city, eight hundred copies had been made in an hour, rushed back to the conference hall, to be placed, still warm, in piles upon the trestle table at the back, the contents yet unknown even to Kathleen Branagan.

Attila climbed the stage, shook Kathleen's hand and crossed to the podium.

James saw Jean arrive. Before she could reach the revolving door he stepped forward, he told her Attila was not there. Jean thanked James, she turned and began to walk away. James watched her, he ran after Jean, he told her of Rosie's death, where Attila could be found, he raised his hand and stopped a taxi, directed the driver to the conference hall.

Attila let the hall settle into silence. He neither sipped the glass of water, nor arranged his papers. He waited. When the hall was still he began: 'We, the professionals in this hall, have come to the belief arrived at over years, which we now hold as an article of faith, and the belief is this, that trauma causes suffering and that suffering causes damage.' There was a murmur at that, followed by a deepening of the silence. Attila stared out over the field of heads, the tiredness he had felt was gone, replaced by a surge of energy he knew to be partly adrenalin and partly the conviction of what needed to be said. 'Once,' he continued, 'men returning from war were left by a wider society to suffer in silence, or in hell. Then over time came a greater awareness, the members of our profession were the first to realise that what these men needed was help. And willingly we gave it to them. In time, too, we realised that combatants were not the only victims of war. Those of you in this room are here because of the tireless efforts of those men and women who dedicated their professional lives to understanding the effects of trauma. The world owes them a debt of gratitude.' There was a hum of assent. Attila continued: 'Over the decades since, however, and out of that desire to help, a determinism has taken root, one which says that those who have seen the darkness of the human soul are irrevocably damaged by so doing, and are as a result less than the person they once were. I am here to challenge the orthodoxy that has crystallised and to say what I now believe needs to be said.' Here Attila raised his voice: 'Trauma does not equal destiny.' He paused. There were a few murmurs, a scattering of nods, for everyone here could handle a gentle critique of their profession.

Kathleen Branagan leaned forward in her chair, elbows on her knees, chin cupped in her hand. She was waiting. Eight hundred faces were turned towards him. Attila had a sudden memory of Rosie, looking up at him from the typewriter, trying out a phrase as they worked to refine their paper. How differently they had seen their mission then. He imagined her sitting in the audience, in her tweed trousers and tasselled shoes. He thought of Maryse, who rarely attended his talks, but afterwards would listen intently to his breakdown and analysis of the way in which each one had been received. He saw his mentor and friend on the island off the coast of Dakar, leaning back in his wooden planter's chair, smiling his secretive smile. Attila resumed speaking: 'What if, by labelling our patients damaged from the outset, we not only condemn them to a self-fulfilling prophecy, but have overlooked a potential finding of equal importance? That the emotional vulnerability of trauma is oftentimes transformed into emotional strength. What if we were to have revealed to us that misfortune can lend life quality? Whatever does not kill me makes me stronger, yes. What if I told you that there are times when whatever does not kill me can make me more, not less, than the person I was before?'

Now there was a distinct shifting in the room. At the back of the hall a door opened and closed.

'I want to talk to you now about a realisation that my decades of work in trauma and trauma-related fields have given me.' Attila began to tell a story related to him by a man he had met once, who, learning of Attila's work, had told him about an experience of his own as people often did. Sensing he was about to hear something of importance, Attila had listened carefully. The man had survived internment in a jungle camp in Asia during the Second World War. The first to die, he had told Attila, were the college sportsmen, the fittest, the most muscular. You would be hard-pressed to believe it, but Attila had believed it. He could see that this man, who was born and grew up in rural Italy before his family emigrated to Brooklyn, who went on to become an artist in New York after the war, had what it took to survive, which in him was a curiosity about the nature of existence, in all its shades. That curiosity provided the elemental defence against despair. In others it might be humour, stoicism, adaptability, or a sense of something greater, something that goes beyond themselves. 'The sportsmen,' he told the audience, 'coddled by their coaches, fed special diets, protected from anything that might cause upset and affect their performance, taught to think of nothing but their sporting future, when they found themselves in the heat and humidity, among rats and mosquitoes, hungry and sleepless, had nothing to fall back on, they had muscular strength, but no inner resources, that thing we call resilience.'

Some members of the audience were frowning but they were listening. People were leaning forward, it was as though the whole room was holding its breath. Attila was about to resume speaking when he caught sight of the only movement in the hall – at the very back a woman raised her arms and retied her hair in a gesture he had come to know. Jean, dressed in work boots and a heavy shirt, was leaning against the wall and listening. He smiled at her and saw her smile back. She gave a small wave. In that moment, in that very moment, Attila felt a sense of ease, of arriving at a destination he had not realised he was travelling towards.

'The realisation,' he said. He spoke no more loudly than before, but the words seemed to rise from his core. 'That I have come to is this, that in our well-intentioned desire to describe and label the psychological wounds of the survivors of war and conflict and terror, we have failed to examine the psychological wounds of those who face the void without ever knowing the reality of life, of the creeping numbness that the fear of suffering, the terror of pain has created. We, professionals and lay folk alike, have used the suffering of others to reinforce the myth of ourselves: their unhappiness becomes the bolster to our happiness. We are terrified of their pain, simultaneously attracted to it and repelled by it. We want to be assured that all pain is treatable, while we comfort ourselves with the belief in the superior quality of our existence for never having encountered trauma, for this to continue we must build psychological fortresses to protect ourselves against the possibility of pain. Now you see that all of the weakness is not in them, those who live through the agony, who survive and transform into something else, but in others too. Here ...' He swept out an arm, to take in the room, the building, the city, and what lay beyond. The whole of it.

Chapter 24

March the 1st comes and goes, the crows begin to nest in the upper reaches of the trees in Burgess Park. The air remains glassy and cold, but more often now the cloud lifts and the sun touches the city. The buds of flowers in Jean's roof garden are beginning to emerge. Each morning she climbs barefoot up the spiral staircase to the roof garden, wondering what new showing the day will bring.

There had been a memorial for Rosie, not at forty days, which had been Attila's first instinct. The centre director, whose name he had discovered to be Mrs White, had told him that none of them could rely on the residents' ability to remember Rosie, or even to still be alive. He laughed at himself, the absurdity of imagining otherwise. Attila had started the dancing. At first alone in the middle of the dining room, then with Emmanuel and then with Jean, who was shy of dancing, but did so feeling few in this room would judge her, not the residents for being incapable, nor the staff because they had seen more and worse, nor the other visitors whose attention had shifted to the plates of rice and lamb being served in generous portions by the woman in charge of the dining room. They had come: Maurice and Vivien Quell, James and Komba, Abdul, Osman, Ayo, Olu, the traffic warden with the bright weave and her companion, Tano and Ama, everyone who knew Attila and Emmanuel, even if they had never known Rosie, they came as much for the living as the dead.

This is the time of day she tries to imagine him, wherever he is and whatever surrounds him. She finds she listens to the news more, repeats the names, Raqqa, Fallujah, Mosul, imagines his tall figure moving through a landscape of rock and dust. Still, however hard she tries, it feels like he has left the city for a place where time and space are held to a different order. She is unable to contact him. If she could what might she tell him? She would describe how the boy comes to visit her with or without his mother, of the rising humour she observes in him and his comfortable way around her, she would tell him about the disappearance of Light Bright and her mate, whom Jean hopes have moved to a new territory and are raising a litter of cubs, and she would tell him of the dead tree she could see from her garden, how it now houses a small colony of parakeets, which Jean feels certain must have come from the old colony in the cemetery. She can watch it for many minutes at a time, and often does. She is considering a study of some sort, the form of which is yet to come to her, maybe some record just for herself. She is aware that everything she sees or does or hears that is worth repeating, she wishes to tell him first, so she talks to him in her mind, rehearsing the form of words as if to an unseen audience of one.

From the dead tree at the end of the parking lot a parakeet glides from one branch to the next where a second parakeet perches. They rest there for a moment, then take off in unison, joined by six or seven others, to fly across the city, who knows to which parks, gardens and squares. The only thing she knows is this: come dusk, they will return.

Every living creature reminds him of her. The gecko that rolls an obsidian eye from its perch on the wall. The ant bearing a sugar crystal away from the saucer that holds his coffee glass, in which now only the grounds remain. He admires its tenacity, its superior strength. On the table before him lies a near completed letter. Attila adds a few lines and his name and seals the envelope. A knock at his door, the driver with details of his journey which will begin in the morning. As he talks the young man looks past Attila into the room with an impertinent curiosity, to take in the furnishings, the bed, chair, table and the letter. Attila watches the young man in silence and then clears his throat. The driver covers his embarrassment with an offer of helpfulness, to post the letter. Attila shakes his head. He closes the door, puts the letter in his briefcase and presses down the latches. He goes to the window and stares out over the flat roofs of the city.

In two days, less, he will deliver the letter to her himself.

Acknowledgements

My thanks go to the Donald Windham-Sandy M. Campbell Literature Prizes at Yale University for their generosity to writers, poets and dramatists. Without their support *Happiness* might not have been written.

To Stephen DeStefano and Kaina Koenen I owe a debt of gratitude for the generous gift of their time and expertise, for teaching me about the ways of coyotes and the work of the urban wildlife biologist, as well as sharing with me the warmth of their hospitality. I am hugely grateful to those people who read the first finished draft of *Happiness* and shared their observations: Stephen DeStefano, Louise Lyon, Sam Kiley, Michael May, Ellah Wakatama Allfrey and Simon Westcott. Thanks also to Helen Shields for having kindly answered my questions about care of the elderly.

Hedgebrook gave me space and time early in the writing process and a sighting of a coyote family on the lawn. I thank them and the Lannan Foundation for a month in Marfa where the writing of *Happiness* was completed.

Many years ago somebody I didn't know sent me Boris Cyrulnik's *Resilience*, a book the reading of which crystallised thoughts into meaning. Attila Asare's theories of resilience in *Happiness* are based on the work of Boris Cyrulnik, and also drawn from conversations which took place during the writing of *The Memory of Love* with Dr Edward Nahim. I thank Boris Cyrulnik for his research into the human mind, Edward Nahim for his wisdom and forthrightness, and I thank the unknown sender of *Resilience*.

The poem which appears on page 214 is called 'Una Noche de Verano', by Antonio Machado.

At Grove Press, I am forever indebted to Morgan Entrekin for his early confidence in *Happiness* and for his foresight and faith over many years, and to Amy Hundley for her clarity, intelligence and precision. I am grateful to Alexa von Hirschberg my editor at Bloomsbury for her thoughtfulness and care.

David Godwin, my agent and good friend, is my first sounding board and reader. Thank you.

And to Simon and Mo, for love and good times.

A Note on the Author

Aminatta Forna won the Windham Campbell Literature Prize and has been a judge for the Bailey's Women's Prize for Fiction, the Samuel Johnson Prize, the Caine Prize and the International Man Booker. Forna's last book, *The Hired Man*, was selected for several best of the year lists: NPR, San Francisco Chronicle and Boston Globe.

Forna's *The Memory of Love* won the Commonwealth Writers' Prize for Best Book; was shortlisted for the Orange Prize for Fiction, the International Dublin IMPAC Award, and the Warwick Prize for Writing; and was selected as an Indie Next List Notable selection and an Essence Book Club Pick.

aminattaforna.com / @aminattaforna